Maid of DECEPTION

Also by
Jennifer McGowan

Maid of Secrets

Maid of Wonder

A Thief Before Christmas

JENNIFER McGOWAN

SIMON & SCHUSTER BFYR

New York London Toronto Sydney New Delhi

For Ann.

I'm blessed you are my sister. And proud you are my friend.

SIMON & SCHUSTER BFYR

An imprint of Simon & Schuster Children's Publishing Division

1230 Avenue of the Americas, New York, New York 10020

For information about special discounts for bulk purchases, please contact Simon & Schuster Special Sales at 1-866-506-1949 or business@simonandschuster.com.

The Simon & Schuster Speakers Bureau can bring authors to your live event. For more information or to book an event, contact the Simon & Schuster Speakers Bureau at 1-866-248-3049 or visit our website at www.simonspeakers.com.

Also available in a SIMON & SCHUSTER BFYR hardcover edition

Book design by Lucy Ruth Cummins

The text for this book is set in ArrusBT Std.

Manufactured in the United States of America

First SIMON & SCHUSTER BFYR paperback edition August 2015

2 4 6 8 10 9 7 5 3 1

The Library of Congress has cataloged the hardcover edition as follows:

McGowan, Jennifer.

Maid of deception / Jennifer McGowan.

pages cm. — (Maids of Honor)

Summary: In 1559 England, Beatrice and her fellow Maids of Honor, Queen Elizabeth I's secret all-female guard, must rely on their charm and deadly spying skills to investigate a brewing Scottish rebellion.

ISBN 978-1-4424-4141-5 (hardcover : alk. paper) — ISBN 978-1-4424-4143-9 (eBook)

[1. Courts and courtiers—Fiction. 2. Spies—Fiction. 3. Elizabeth I, Queen of England, 1533–1603—Fiction. 4. Insurgency—Fiction. 5. Sex role—Fiction. 6. Love—Fiction. 7. Scotland—History—16th century—Fiction. 8. Great Britain—History—Elizabeth, 1558–1603—Fiction.] I. Title.

PZ7.M4784867Maf 2014

[Fic]—dc23

2013033412

ISBN 978-1-4424-4142-2 (paperback)

Acknowledgments

Maid of Deception is the result of many people who helped bring Beatrice's story to life. In particular, I remain gratefully indebted to Alexandra Machinist, who has made this entire journey so worthwhile. The entire team at Simon & Schuster Books for Young Readers also deserves my sincere and profound thanks, not only for making my first year as an author such a tremendous experience, but for devoting themselves to the reimagination of the look and feel of the Maids of Honor series. Bara MacNeill, the copyeditor who worked on this book, was tireless in her efforts as well. She labored long and hard to ensure that my words and details were accurate—any mistakes are, of course, my own. Last but without question most important, I would like to thank my editor, Christian Trimmer. Without his grace, discernment, and insight, *Maid of Deception* would never have found its light. Thank you, forever and always.

CHAPTER ONE

SEPTEMBER 1559
WINDSOR CASTLE, ENGLAND

There would be no tears on my wedding day. I would not allow it.

As the music from the Queen's own orchestra filled Saint George's Chapel, a perfect blend of viol and harpsichord to complement my perfect union with Lord Percival Andrew William Cavanaugh, I clasped the clammy hands of my fellow Maid of Honor Sophia Dee and smiled into her large, worried eyes.

"Hush, Sophia. All is well," I said, giving her fine-boned fingers a light squeeze. She shivered despite the stifling heat of the chamber. "If you keep crying, you'll draw attention to yourself."

That caught the girl up short. The youngest of our group of royal spies, and the most uncertain, Sophia hated attention. Her eyes, if possible, got even bigger.

"But, Beatrice—you should b-be *happy*—"

"I *am* happy, Sophia," I assured her. And, strangely enough, I was. For all my well-rehearsed sophistication, Lord Cavanaugh represented more than just my crowning achievement at court. Yes, of course, he was one of the richest men in the kingdom. And he was from a respected family whose reputation was not at daily risk from either a drunken father or a muddle-minded mother. And his ancestral home was not overrun by brawling foundling children.

And, perhaps most important, he had no idea whatsoever how desperately I needed this marriage.

But there was more to it than that. Lord Cavanaugh was gentle, fine, and soft-spoken, with a rich, drawling voice that I thrilled to hear. He was gracious and educated, in a court filled with rakes and curs more intent on the hunt than on conversation. He was devout, respectful at service and in court. He was polite to women of every station; he appeared to genuinely care for his mother.

And he loved me.

I saw it in his eyes, in his smile. In the way he nodded his approval as he took in my gowns and hair. I saw it as he watched others watching me. Though I'd worked very hard to ensure that I was perfect for him in every possible way, I still could not believe I had succeeded so well. . . . Lord Cavanaugh *loved* me. The rest meant nothing beside that truth.

"Babies with my husband will come in time, I am sure," I said now, addressing Sophia's current cause for distress. She'd seen—somehow—that my groom and I would have no children, and the shock of her vision was quite undoing her. Sophia, it should be said, had a gift of intuition that might well become the full-fledged Sight at any moment. But Sophia's predictions were not always clear, and she was definitely wrong on this score. My marriage to Cavanaugh would be perfect. It had to be. "Today I am the most joyful woman alive." Still, the tiniest thread of fear skated along my nerves.

Sophia raised a trembling chin and gave me a smile, looking like a frail raven haired ghost in her gorgeous white silk gown. That gown had cost five pounds if it had cost a shilling, and it was embroidered with Italian lace. It would have taken a farmer a *year* just to earn enough to pay for a dress like that, but it was only one of a dozen gowns Sophia's betrothed had gifted to her. I pondered that a moment. Had Cavanaugh given me any gifts of late? I'd been so busy with my duties to the Queen, I hadn't much noticed.

"It's almost time, Beatrice," Anna Burgher chirped from the doorway.

We'd participated in the loud and boisterous procession from the Upper Ward of Windsor Castle down to Saint George's Chapel, and then—just as I'd orchestrated it—my bridesmaids and I had slipped in here while Lord Cavanaugh had moved toward the front of the chapel, to give me a last opportunity to make sure I was completely prepared.

Now Anna was up on her toes, bouncing in her yellow satin skirts, her ginger mass of hair brutalized into a tight coil of braids. I smiled at the back of Anna's head, imagining her eyes darting this way and that. She'd record every person in attendance of this, my most triumphant public appearance yet. We would spend hours poring over the lists she made, analyzing who was most appropriate to approach, to flatter, and to watch in the weeks following the wedding. The Queen's birthday was coming up, and there would be time to cement alliances there.

Speaking of. "And Elizabeth? Has she arrived yet?"

"No! She must wish to do you proud, Beatrice," Anna said staunchly, still scanning the chapel floor. "She will grace you like the Queen of the Fairies at exactly the perfect moment."

I pursed my lips, the thread of doubt within me thickening to a coarser yarn. Elizabeth was many things, I knew. "Fairy Queen" was not among them. But she had blessed this union, taken pride in it as if it were her own. That was what mattered.

The music shifted in subtle counterpoint just then, and I straightened, casting a glance over my soft pink gown. Unlike the rumored splendor of the recent bridal ensemble worn by Mary, Queen of Scots—all white, if you can believe it—my gown's skirts flowed down in rich, pale pink panels, parted at the front to reveal a luxurious swath of cream-colored satin, delicately picked out with golden thread. The skirts were attached above to a stiffly embroidered V-pointed bodice that featured a virtual garden of pink, gold, and brilliantly red roses, all of them swirling, twirling, and fanning out along a neckline cut to showcase my blushing porcelain skin—still modest enough, but an effective display of maidenly beauty. My lace sleeves were so fine as to be nearly sheer, ending in delicate cuffs edged, once more, in pink and gold. I was a vision of English sensibilities, from head to toe.

Everything was perfect.

"God's bones, half of England is out there," Meg Fellowes observed as she ducked into the doorway, tall and straight in her simple gown of dove-grey satin. I smiled, feeling uncharacteristically charitable toward our resident thief, which I never would have believed possible at the start of the summer. I'd even loaned her the dress she was now wearing. Of course, it was two seasons out of date, but Meg didn't seem to mind. Probably didn't know, either.

And she was no rival, that much was certain. Somewhere out in that audience was Meg's special Spanish spy, Rafe de Martine. I'd watched her sneak glances at the boy since he'd entered the chapel, and now I felt something curiously empty in my chest, as though I'd gone too long since breaking my fast.

Anna, usually the smartest of our select company, was convinced that Meg was truly in love, though I couldn't quite see the point of that. Rafe de Martine was a courtier, but he was Spanish. He was fine for a turn on the dance floor, or even a stolen kiss—or a dozen—behind a darkened tapestry, but nothing more. Rafe had wanted me first, of course, but I could never have given him what he wanted. So he'd turned to Meg.

It wasn't as if he were going to tuck himself into a corner with Jane Morgan, after all. Her unkind cuts would have left him bleeding.

Still and all, the Queen would never approve a match between Meg and the Spaniard. And Meg, for her part, insisted she had no interest in marriage. This of course was utter folly, but the girl was still new to court. She would learn, I thought as I returned my attention to my gown. Marriage was not about love. I knew that, no matter how desperately glad I was that Cavanaugh loved me.

Marriage was about power.

"So who created this guest list, exactly?" Jane was the last to enter the chapel, and her flat voice interrupted my reverie. Our troupe's official ruffian generally kept her mouth shut, which is how I preferred it. Still, my attention sharpened not at Jane's wry words so much as Anna's reaction to them. Even Sophia lifted a hand to her mouth, her eyes darting first to Anna and then to Jane, and then, resolutely, not to me.

I frowned at Jane's profile as she turned to stare back out the doorway, but the girl's grin wasn't cruel or dark. Just amused. Irritation kindled along my nerves, and I steeled myself against it. I was the future Marchioness of Westmoreland, a future that would be arriving in a few short moments. I would be kind and patient. Even if it killed me.

"*I* created the guest list," I said, then offered a careless wave of my hand. "And Cecil and Walsingham reviewed and approved it, of course." As if there'd be any chance those two wouldn't want to control every aspect of such a grand court event.

Sir William Cecil and Sir Francis Walsingham were not just the Queen's most powerful advisors, after all. They were instructors to a very special group of spies within the Queen's court. The Maids of Honor comprised five young women from all stations of life. Anna and Jane, Sophia and now Meg—and, of course, me. Each of us with unique skills, selected by Queen Elizabeth herself to serve her in a very specific capacity. To be her eyes and ears—and sometimes mouth—and to ferret out secrets that no mere man could hope to uncover. I had been the first young woman chosen to head up this secret sect, a favor that had, I daresay, shocked Cecil and Walsingham. I had not been surprised, however.

The Queen and I had more history between us than Cecil and Walsingham could ever guess.

None of the other girls spoke, and I frowned into the silence. "And probably the Queen stuck her nose into the guest list, as she is ever wont to do. What of it? Who do you see?"

"The Queen?" Meg's voice had a peculiar tone to it, but I never could tell what the Rat was thinking. "Well, that would do it."

Irritation crested with a snap. "Who do you—"

"Oh, Beatrice, darling! You look lovely!" I glanced up, startled, then moved forward three quick paces to catch my mother as she stumbled into our little chamber, her breath smelling of honeyed mead and, more faintly, a light, sweet tang; a scent I'd come to know too well.

"Lady Knowles," Jane said stoutly, and suddenly she was at my side, her strong arms around my mother as if she knew exactly what to do with a woman too muddled to stand upright. My cheeks burned with mortification. Today of all days!

"Beatrice, your father is coming!" Anna squeaked. I whipped my gaze back around toward the door. No! Not now, not with my mother in one of her states.

"He can't see—he can't see her like—" I swallowed the words, remembering discretion too late. I turned to the only maid who could possibly understand. "Oh, Anna!"

"Relax. We'll take care of her," Meg cut in smoothly. "You just smile like it's your wedding day, and keep moving. Don't let him stop to look and see anything." She sounded like she was directing a play—or a battle. I'm not sure which comparison was more apt. In any event, she took up her place on the other side of my mother and nodded to Jane, two serious maids escorting the mother of the bride. "We'll be back in a moment."

"Or two," Jane muttered, eyeing the woman now listing between them.

Then the pair of them was through the door as they clutched my mother, who'd begun to burble something about "beautiful." She was the beautiful one, not me. Even with her eyes going glassy and her expression a little lost. My father had done this to her, I knew. Had killed her with a thousand cuts.

If only . . .

My jaw set. I had no time for "if only." I just needed the woman to keep herself together for another quarter hour. I boosted myself up on my toes, using Anna's shoulder as a brace, and watched Jane and Meg smoothly steer Mother into her place, even as their attention was captured by someone in the crowd. All three of them were staring, actually. Including my mother.

What in the world could have penetrated her fog?

"Beatrice! Now!" Anna breathed. I dashed back to the table to catch up my bouquet, and turned to receive Lord Bartholomew Edward Matthew Knowles with my face set into an expression of perfectly practiced ethereal joy.

My reward was swift and complete. "Beatrice, you are the most entrancing of women, and the grandest lady in all of England," my father said, bowing with a flourish.

"And you, my father, are the most depraved lord in all of Christendom."

"I own it." He grinned at me with a smile that I knew—from long and occasionally bitter experience—had made women's hearts melt for the past thirty years. "But say, Lord Cavanaugh is standing up like a strawman at the tilt. Think he'll have the stamina to make it through the ceremony?"

Anger flashed through me even as my father turned my hand into the crook of his arm. "Lord Cavanaugh is a good man, Father, and will do far more for our fortunes than—" I hastily swallowed my ill-advised words. *Control!* "Than we have any right to ask."

Father snorted, seeming not at all convinced, for someone who had heartily approved of this match. "Lord Cavanaugh will have a care around you, anyway, you can be sure of that," he said, patting my hand as we moved back through the doorway.

His fingers grazed the ring I'd decided to wear next to my betrothal ring, and he glanced down at it now. I felt his fingers tighten as he recognized the bauble I'd recently received from Rafe and Meg. Oh, he recognized the ring all right, more the shame to him.

When Rafe had first arrived on our shores these several weeks past, the Spanish spy had carried with him a ring that his mother had retained as a "souvenir" of her own visit to the English court during the reign of old King Henry. Of course, the King hadn't been old then, and neither had Rafe's mother . . . nor my father. The nature of the "friendship" between Rafe's mother and my father was not something I wanted to dwell upon, but thank heavens both Rafe and I had already been born by then. I could barely tolerate the arrogant young man as Meg's suitor; I could not have stomached him as a half brother. Still, now I had another family heirloom back, a precious treasure reclaimed. And from the guilt-ridden look on his face, Father clearly knew I had discerned yet one more of his secrets.

Vindication swept through me like a cleansing fire. *Look hard and long, you skirt-chasing ballywag.* I was the one taking care of the family.

Father blinked and stared, like a bear stumbling out of his winter slumber. "But where . . . How . . ." He bristled at me. "Where in the bloody hell did you get—"

"The music is beginning!" Anna's quick cry mobilized us, and she rushed into position behind Sophia, even as Jane and Meg hurried into place as well, both of them favoring me with knowing glances. What was going on with them? What had they seen?

There was no time, however, and we moved forward into the multicolored radiance of Saint George's Chapel, the entire hall lit up with light pouring through the stained-glass windows, as if God himself were adding his illumination to my day.

I stepped into the long aisle and held my head high. It was total perfection, and all according to a plan I'd labored to bring to light for the past ten years. Finally I would be married. Finally I would be respected. Finally I would be . . .

Safe.

We moved forward with the elegance due our rank and

station in the Queen's court, and I craned my neck this way and that, taking in the congregation that had filled Saint George's to bursting. My gaze moved along one thick knot of admirers and over to another—many of them relatives of mine or my lord's, but some who were nobles, even courtiers from other lands. There were Cecil and Walsingham, stiff in their proper garments. There was Rafe de Martine and the grinning band of Spaniards. There was even Lord Brighton, Sophia's intended, who stood a bit nervously next to a serenely lovely woman.

And all of them were looking at me.

I nodded graciously in the midst of their open stares and bright eyes. I felt beautiful, suddenly, with my pink-gold dress, my blond hair piled up in an impossibly ornate coiffure pinned with pink roses and bits of white lace, my eyes and mouth touched delicately with careful paints. Within my chest my heart swelled until it seemed almost twice its proper size, the smile on my face now completely unabashed. *I was getting married!*

The whole of the court seemed to beam back at me, sharing in my joy. I glanced past a particularly gorgeous nobleman I didn't recognize, in a blue silk doublet and a short cape. Despite myself I hesitated, favoring him with a nod even as my heart fluttered a bit in my breast at the roguish glint in his eye.

That glint seemed vaguely familiar, but surely I would have remembered *this* young man. He was tall and fierce, with the kind of arrogance that would make him a liability in any court, particularly ours. Had the Queen invited him?

Elizabeth was always looking for ways to surround herself with new men. I shook myself, realizing I was staring, but I couldn't quite tear my eyes away. Nerves, I decided.

Then the young man grinned back at me, his gaze dropping quite obviously to fix on the moderately deep V of my wedding gown as it plunged between my breasts. I knew that look. I knew that leer.

And I almost stumbled in my stride.

I wrenched my gaze away, grateful now for the near murderous grip my father had on my arm as I strode ahead, poleaxed.

This was what Meg and Jane had been grinning about, and why they'd been so eager to escort my mother into the chapel. *This* was what Anna and Sophia had known but had dared not tell me. *This!*

Alasdair MacLeod was at my wedding!

The boorish Scot had trampled into the refined English court not four weeks past, part of a grand onslaught of foreigners who'd come to pay court to the Queen. He'd seemed instantly out of place to me, for all his apparent high standing within the Scottish delegation, a bull among chickens—all brawny shoulders and roguish leers and rough manners and knowing grins. The Queen, with her usual perverse pettiness, had assigned *me* to fawn over Alasdair, of course, to see what secrets I might find out about his true intentions toward the English. As a result I'd been forced to dance with the hulking brute on far too many occasions, and he'd taken every opportunity to embarrass me, press me, hold me too close. The worst had been during a late summer wedding

I'd been forced to attend with the oaf, wherein the Clod MacLeod had put both hands around my waist and drawn in a breath so deep it seemed as if he'd sought to distill my own essence within himself. Thank God he'd never tried to kiss me.

Still, *had* he tried, it would have been entertaining for me to disable him. I had my choice of methods too, one of a half dozen favorites I'd honed during my schooling as a spy. Each more painful than the previous.

There were some benefits to being a Maid of Honor, after all.

Still, whyever is he here? Weddings of commoners were open to all, true enough. But I was *not* a commoner.

And he had *not* been invited.

I stared ahead stonily, feeling the cur's eyes scorch through my gown as I walked sedately toward my future husband, Lord Cavanaugh. My future respected, respectable, and very *respectful* husband.

The young Scotsman may have been heir to some hulking rock of a castle in the middle of the northern sea, but he was nothing next to Lord Cavanaugh. And he had *no business* being here. Especially . . . especially looking the way he did now.

This Alasdair had been bathed and shaven smooth, his thick beard now gone; his wild, unruly mane now trimmed and luxuriously thick, its dark blond curls draped carelessly over his sun-warmed face and fierce blue eyes. This Alasdair must have stolen his clothes, so fine were they, the blue and gold doublet undone just enough to show a snowy white tunic beneath, and the slightest glimpse of his broad, firm, powerful chest—

"Beatrice, you're wounding me."

I blinked up at my father's words, and saw him now looking at me with genuine concern, all the anger that had lit his aristocratic features gone. We were at the front of the chapel. The minister was there and Lord Cavanaugh was there, looking handsome and perfect and holding my entire future in his hands. He was everything I wanted and needed, and as if in recognition of that fact, the chapel was finally quieting to allow the solemnity of our service to take place.

I smiled, my heart no longer bursting with joy as much as whirling in utter confusion, but I forced my expression into one of absolute bliss that I hoped would carry the day. My father seemed satisfied, and patted my hand before turning me forward.

To my right, Lord Cavanaugh eyed me with approval.

In front of me the minister lifted *The Book of Common Prayer*.

And behind me, somewhere in the knot of courtiers and noblemen, aunts and cousins, and neighbors and enemies and friends—stood Alasdair MacLeod.

I straightened my back and drew a deep breath, gratified at Lord Cavanaugh's soft exhalation. He was staring at me now, taking in every detail of my gown. Good.

Alasdair MacLeod could go hang himself.

The minister began to speak, and I heard his words as if from far away. ". . . for their mutual joy; for the help and comfort given one another in prosperity and adversity; and, when it is God's will, for the procreation of children and their nurture . . ." I frowned, instantly recalling Sophia's concerns. Would Lord Cavanaugh and I not have children? There must be a male heir, eventually. There had to be. I had only to look back at Queen Elizabeth's own long and troubled history to explain why. How many lives had been changed irreparably, in houses grand and small, all for the want of a son?

A bit of murmuring struck up in the back of the chapel, but my eyes were trained on the minister, and on the play of light shining down from the stained-glass windows, rendering him into soft reds and greens and blues. He looked like something out of a dream landscape, holy and inviolate, and I finally began to relax.

"Into this holy union Lady Beatrice Elizabeth Catherine Knowles and Lord Percival Andrew William Cavanaugh now come to be joined. . . ."

Behind me the whispering grew louder, and even the minister looked up, his face flickering with shock. I stared at him as he kept speaking, my stomach slewing sideways as Lord Cavanaugh turned with a gasp that had nothing to do with my neckline and everything to do with what he saw coming up behind us, as relentless as a winter storm.

And still the minister pressed on, as if he could no more stop the sacred words than he could stop his own breath. "If any of you can show just cause why they may not lawfully be married," he cried out, his voice sounding almost desperate to my ears, "speak now; or else for ever hold your peace!"

A moment of deafening silence passed, and then another, and the clutch of terror in my throat was only just coming undone when the sudden sharp, imperious crash of a staff striking the floor nearly turned my knees to water.

"This wedding shall not go forward!" came the voice, as loud, proud, and mighty as the wrath of God, and every bit as damning.

It was the Queen.

CHAPTER TWO

I kept my eyes forward for just a bare moment more. I focused on the minister, whose mouth was still moving, though no words issued forth. The sweat on his balding head was gleaming in the candlelight, and he looked stricken, his anguished eyes going first to the Queen and then to me.

And that was why I needed the moment desperately. I could never show weakness in court, especially not to the Queen. Especially not when she had just stretched out her long, bejeweled fingers and crushed with a sharp, triumphant squeeze the only thing I'd ever wanted in this life. I felt the tears rise up within me, an implacable tide, and I steeled myself against them.

It was my fault for holding on to this hope so tightly, I knew. For thinking I could keep it precious and safe from the one woman who would delight in ruining even the joy that she had so pompously delivered into my hand.

I would not show weakness.

I turned then, finally, my blue eyes still serene, my blond hair still perfect, my skin still porcelain fair, the soft folds of my petal-pink gown showing all the world that I was a true flower of England. I lifted my gaze to meet the Queen's down the long church aisle, not missing the high color that slashed our monarch's cheekbones or the fevered glint in her eye. The expression I'd plastered on my face was cool and beneficent, but Elizabeth was not so cunning. She could not hide the smug twist to her lips.

She was majestic and regal, and she would be obeyed. Even in—especially in—God's own house.

In one small corner of my mind, the only place not suffused with bitterness, I had to grant the woman this: It truly was a grand play she had devised. What faster way to get the whole of the court wagging its tongues on the one subject she favored most—herself? Even now fans and hands were raised in apparent shock to many mouths. The better for the courtiers to speak in low tones among themselves, of course.

I sank into a deep curtsy, remaining just a heartbeat longer than propriety dictated. Whether those who watched raptly read service or defiance into that heartbeat, I did not care. It turned the tide of attention ever so slightly back to me. I might not have ruled the land, but I would rule this mob . . . and unlike with the Queen, it would not be because they *owed* me their fealty.

I rose and spoke over the whispers that slithered through the gathered crowd. "How may I serve you, Your Grace?" I asked, pitching my voice loud enough to be heard at the back of the hall.

The Queen drew herself up sharply, astute enough to

sense the shifting focus of the congregation, though I had done her no overt insult.

"It is unseemly for this wedding to proceed with such haste in the middle of the royal celebrations," she pronounced, her hauteur firmly in place. "I am fatigued by the distraction and require you to attend me during these most auspicious events."

"Of course, Your Grace," I said promptly. My voice was as smooth as the silk with which I wanted to strangle her. She was the one who had given permission for the wedding to move forward, and she was the one who'd set the timing—after her first grand ball but before the revels that followed. The "auspicious events" she referenced were her interminable and ongoing birthday celebrations. The woman was only twenty-five years old! To think the Crown would be financing these celebrations for her entire reign. . . . England would be bankrupt before the harpy showed her first grey hair.

I said none of these things, of course. Instead I turned and curtsied to a shocked and wild-eyed Lord Cavanaugh, inclining my head to him as if we'd just completed a country dance. He barely returned my bow, so suffused with emotion was he, his lips thin, his face white, and his eyes filled with fire. If anything, his outrage made him even more handsome to me. *So he loves me this much, then!* It was a blessing and a marvel.

I turned away and walked down the long aisle, my shoulders straight, my head high. The Queen, well in advance of me, spun officiously and banged her ceremonial staff hard upon the chapel floor again, effectively stifling any further discussion.

But she couldn't stop the shock and dismay that colored the features of the members of court, nor the shrewd-eyed calculation among the most seasoned of them. And she certainly couldn't stop the pity.

I had sworn long ago that I would never be the object of that hateful sentiment, and anger and bile roiled within me. It was all I could do not to scream.

Then we gained the doorway, and someone did catch my eye just as I swept out of the chapel. A young man, broad-shouldered and long-limbed, his face alight with interest, stared at me unabashedly while everyone else in the room had the grace or wits to look away. Alasdair MacLeod would no doubt be laughing deep into his miserable Scottish ale after this debacle.

Well, he could go to the devil. They all could.

I exited the chapel and found myself surrounded by a gaggle of the Queen's ladies-in-waiting. We marched behind Her Royal Insufferableness as if we had been summoned to her presence to discuss the latest dance steps out of France, but I was not fooled by Elizabeth's carefree manner. Not when she started laughing again with her advisors, and not when she consulted with a bevy of servants to bring us refreshments. Instead I nodded serenely at the other ladies' exclamations of how lucky I was to enjoy a precious few more weeks in Elizabeth's court as an unmarried woman. I watched. And I waited.

"Lady Beatrice Knowles!" As if on cue, Gloriana's broad tones rang out over the space. She did so love to hear herself shout.

I turned immediately and curtsied to her, every inch

the dutiful maid. "Your Grace?" I offered, in the excessively respectful tone I'd learned to affect in her presence.

"Attend me." She glided into her Privy Chamber, and I followed, not at all surprised to see Cecil and Walsingham joining us, shutting the doors quietly to cut off the clutch of curious-eyed females we'd left behind.

The moment we were alone in the Privy Chamber, the Queen's manner changed.

We had no need of disguises anymore. To all the court, I was with the Queen and her maids and ladies. To all the maids and ladies, the Queen was calling me in for a conciliatory chat. Elizabeth and I both knew better, however.

The Queen was my enemy.

She would always be my enemy.

I suppose we could be nothing else to each other.

When Elizabeth had come to power last fall upon the death of her sister, Mary Tudor, she had set immediately upon the idea that she would have a group of young women around her—unmarried, of course, that their loyalties be fixed solely on her; and young, that they might be overlooked more easily, or considered stupid.

She'd immediately named two girls to join this special corps of Maids of Honor: Marie Claire and me. Marie Claire had been the darling of court, a laughing, haughty flirt who'd been as adept as Meg at thieving, and far more knowledgeable than Meg about the ways of the nobility. But Marie had grown too careless, and she'd died because of it, in early spring. By then we'd added three other maids to our number—brilliant Anna, moody Sophia, and murderous

Jane. And then there was me, the Maid of hidden truths.

Secrets were my treasure—and had been since I'd been very young, a bright, pretty girl of noble blood shipped off by my father to serve as an elevated companion to young women in other royal houses. Whether he'd done this to protect me from the darkness of my own home or simply because he hadn't been able to stand the sight of me, I never knew. But the result was the same. In my half servant, half elite role, I'd quickly realized that knowledge was power. In no time at all I'd developed a mental ledger of information on every noble I'd met . . . dozens of them; hundreds, even.

I'd learned a great deal in those great houses. And in one of those houses, I'd met Elizabeth.

And oh, to her everlasting horror, what I'd learned about her.

She'd been only fourteen when I had met her at Sudeley Castle, and I a mere seven years of age. Elizabeth had lived with the King's new widow, Katherine Parr, and the woman's even newer husband, Thomas Seymour. Even at that tender age, the princess had been vain and self-serving, prideful and reckless. I'd been assigned as her child-companion, a fetching girl she liked to keep around as a sort of exalted slave.

However, all was not as it should have been in that household. Thomas Seymour had been a scoundrel and a schemer, and he'd liked the young Elizabeth far too much. She'd thought it was her beauty that entranced him; I thought otherwise. But either way, the scandal that erupted in Elizabeth's young world nearly destroyed the princess when the details later came to light.

Who had been there to see it all happen? I had. Who had helped save Elizabeth's misbegotten skin when the questioners had come? I had. She'd defended herself brilliantly . . . and I had defended her as well.

But there was the truth Elizabeth had told her questioners, and then there was the truth we alone both knew. She could never forgive me for knowing her secrets, nor ever overtly destroy me. For I was no fool. Even at a young age, I'd ensured that my secrets were not solely locked in my own head. And Elizabeth had no way of knowing what information might come out, were I to meet a bad end.

But that didn't mean she had to treat me with kindness. She'd raised me to the highest position at her court that I could attain, true. And she made me pay for it daily.

So now we were squaring off yet again under the watchful and almost reproachful eyes of her advisors. The conservative, tight-lipped Sir William Cecil was the titular head of our small select group of spies, but the darker, more audacious Sir Francis Walsingham, the Queen's spymaster, was never far from our midst. I suspected Sir Francis and Sir William rather hated our corps of maids, and we certainly held no affection for them. However, our group had not been assembled by them but by the Queen. And in this (as in many things), she brooked no opposition.

"You may approach!" At the Queen's haughty command, I swept forward and dropped into a low curtsy, straightening only after she bade me rise. I'd learned to time my responses to a fine art, but I didn't play such games when I was alone with the Queen. No need to stoke the fire that was always banked low, waiting to flare to life.

Now Elizabeth looked at me, assessing, clearly trying to decide between the roles of benevolent dictator and horrible shrew. I could almost see when she landed just to the side of benevolence, and I let out the tiniest of sighs. She was still my Queen, and I was her pawn. As much as it grated, I dared not ever forget that.

"We are *most* distressed to command you to put off your wedded state, Beatrice, but the demands of the Crown know no season," she said, her words almost pious. It was all I could do not to throw up.

"Of course, Your Grace," I said, keeping my voice even. "How may I serve you?"

"Your betrothed, Lord Cavanaugh, will doubtless be . . . sorely distressed at the postponement of your wedding night." Elizabeth went on as if I hadn't spoken, and I stifled a groan. Apparently the Queen wasn't quite ready to let my humiliation pass. "True enow, he is a well-regarded courtier, his family without compare. But he is still a man, and as such ever sensitive to the comments and knowing glances of the court around him. You must endeavor to set his mind at ease, to let him know that naught is amiss with your love of him."

I nodded, forcing myself not to furrow a brow at the woman. What did she mean, *my* love? I was not the one who'd delayed the wedding.

"There is also the matter of his manly . . . requirements," Elizabeth went on. And now I did furrow my brow. This area in particular was none of her concern. "You know I absolutely forbid any interaction between my maids and the men of the court," she said sternly. She looked at me as if awaiting a response.

"Of course not, Your Grace. Your court is devoted to reflecting your virtue." I framed my words with a completely guileless tone, not missing her sharp look. Elizabeth's court was a debauch, make no mistake. My fellow Maids of Honor and I were chaste, but that happy state did not fully extend to her entire retinue of maids and ladies-in-waiting. Still, one thing was certain: If Elizabeth caught out an indiscretion among any of her court, her wrath was swift and sure. Ladies were sent packing home, and gentlemen fell out of her favor, or were married off to the first plain-faced, simpering fool the Queen could find.

"Then you will note that I will not make an exception in your case," the Queen continued repressively. "You are not yet married to Lord Cavanaugh, and you will conduct yourself in his presence with the ultimate care of a chaste and godly maiden. Do I make myself clear?"

"Completely," I said, the word just shy of a snap. Beside me Cecil and Walsingham stirred restlessly, but the Queen did not seem to notice.

"Good." She nodded, a small smile playing around her lips. Instantly I tensed. I'd thought with these intrusive comments on my personal life, she'd finished with the worst part of this conversation. But I knew that smile. The Queen was a conniving witch when she wanted to be, and her aspect of delicious anticipation never boded well.

I did not have to wait long to know what amused her so.

"I have a new assignment for you, as it happens. One

which, I'm sure you'll see, requires you to be unmarried, undistracted, and in full command of your . . . charms. In this assignment, should you have a need to appear less than chaste, well—I would be more lenient."

I could not avoid the flaring of my eyes. "An assignment?" I managed. The Queen noted my confusion and took ultimate delight in it, her eyes going even brighter.

"Yes," she said triumphantly. "We are given to understand that the Scottish rebellion continues to gain ground against the hated French, and that outright conflict is not long off. And here, in our very midst, we have more than a dozen Scotsmen milling about. They beg for my intercession, but can I truly trust them? Their country is so steeped in Catholicism, how can I truly know their loyalties to a Protestant Queen?"

I frowned at her. "Forgive me, Your Majesty, but the members of the Scottish delegation have already pledged their allegiance to you in bold and overlong manner." To a man the Scots had been loud in their praise of the new English Queen. "They could hardly do otherwise if they wanted to gain your assistance, and they clearly want the French at their threshold even less than you do. I cannot see how they would be false in this."

"Talk is meaningless with so much at stake. I would know their hearts." The Queen was serious, I realized. She did want to know more about the Scots. I supposed it made sense, though I would rather not have been the one thrown at the delegation to learn their secrets. Still, I could be accommodating.

"Very well, Your Grace," I said. "I am happy to associate more closely with the delegation—"

"No." And now Elizabeth's edge of malice returned, all the more alarming for its swiftness. "It is not the *delegation* as a whole that concerns me but one member in particular of their group. There is just something about him that I find . . . intriguing."

"One member—" I frowned at her, bemused, and then the reality of what she was asking smote me so hard in the face that even I lost my composure. "Oh, Your Grace, you cannot mean it!"

"And yet I do." She trilled off the words, exultant that she had made me flinch. "You will attach yourself quite completely to the young Alasdair MacLeod, draw him out in that way I have seen you draw out men of the court since you were barely seven years old, and gain the secrets of his holding and his people. MacLeod plays to our perceptions that he is an inconsequential part of that rabble, but the others clearly look to him for guidance. We can use that to our advantage. "

"But—" I swallowed my own words. MacLeod did have the ear of his men, but of course he would. He was the biggest. And the loudest. That did not mean he was the smartest.

"I wish to know what confidences his men are sharing with him," Elizabeth continued. "I wish to know how much truth there is in the Scots' assurances of fidelity to the English cause."

I gave a pointed glare at Walsingham, who surely had

better men than me to carry out this simple task of spying. "But why do I—"

"Because he fancies you, you stupid girl!" The Queen's words struck out, as sharp as knives in the quiet room. I took a step back at her sudden, vicious anger. "Do you think me blind? He watches you whenever you enter a room and takes note of when you leave it. If I'm going to have a tool fashioned so prettily for my use, do you not imagine that I would wield it ever and always when I have need? Fie, the work should be easy enough for one such as you. Simper and pout and distract the boy, and learn what there is to be learned." The Queen lifted her chin, curling her lip disdainfully. "This conversation bores me. You may go. But I will expect your report within the fortnight, on the truth of Alasdair MacLeod."

"Your Grace." I sank down into a curtsy, then rose again, backing away as protocol dictated. My face was flaming with outrage and embarrassment.

I was supposed to get married today! Not be set upon a thick-witted boor like some common street trollop, to bat my eyes and coo in his ear, all for secrets he probably didn't even possess. I was a noblewoman; I should be respected! Everything I'd done up till then had been leading to one end, and yet the Queen, with a snap of her fingers, was setting me back days—probably weeks! It was not to be borne!

Fury dogged my heels as I finally turned, gathering my composure before I strolled out into the Presence Chamber once more.

I would spy on the accursed Alasdair MacLeod, and I

would get the Queen the information she was so determined to acquire. But she would not defeat me.

She would never defeat me.

I was still steaming when I cleared the outer chamber, but I'd gone not three steps more when a hand reached out from one of the antechambers—and I was whisked into a completely undesired embrace.

CHAPTER THREE

"F-Father!" I spluttered, peeling away from him. He already smelled like the spiced ale of my wedding banquet, but I supposed he'd paid for it, so he might as well drink it. "What are you—"

"Beatrice, ol' girl, that Queen of yours is a royal bi—"

"Hush!" I said hurriedly. Cecil and Walsingham may not have been hard on my heels, but the very walls had ears in Windsor Castle. "What is it you want? Why are you here?"

"He wants an explanation," came the cultured voice, as sharp as a slap. "As do I."

I felt my heart turn to stone. Now more than ever I had to play Lord Cavanaugh expertly. He was a proud man, as rich men often are. And he remained an exceptional match, despite the ruination of our wedding day—tall and slender and elegantly turned, his coolly patrician features a perfect counterpoint to my own soft beauty and feminine charms.

My feminine charms. My stomach almost turned at the phrase. The one thing that had ever gotten me out of the scrapes of my family had now sorely landed me in the center of a thicket. But there was no time for thinking on that now. Lord Cavanaugh had to be assured of my love, my devotion, my fidelity. Starting immediately.

"Dearest!" I beamed, turning to him with a delight that was no less heartfelt for all that it was feigned. "How kind of you to come to me, when you must be sorely put out at this morning's delay. You handled the Queen's command with such grace and dignity as I have never seen. She commented on it herself."

"Well, I certainly—" Lord Cavanaugh's pompous outrage was effectively blunted with that salvo. "She did?" he asked, after a pause. "What did she say?"

I smiled with genuine affection. I truly appreciated this man, perhaps most of all because he was so easy to redirect. "She said you were gallant and proud, and that I should hasten to assure you to not worry overmuch about the capriciousness of your Queen. She will get you your bride in good order, once our royal birthday revels are at an end." I blushed credibly, even in the low light of that inner room. "She was afraid I would be too blind-eyed with love were we to be married, as to be completely of no use to her."

Cavanaugh's eyes were on me again, but I felt uncomfortable beneath his gaze, as though he were inspecting a prize goat. I pushed the thought from my mind. "Hmmm," he mused. "I suppose the wait could be turned to my advantage. . . ."

"An' how long was she thinking, Beatrice?" my father cut in, ruining—well, ruining nothing at all, in truth. The moment I'd just shared with Cavanaugh had not been precisely the coming together of tearful all-but-wed sweethearts after their most cherished love had been torn asunder. It had been more like—merchants coming to terms. Still, I had to be reasonable about this. Marriage was a contract first. I was blessed that Cavanaugh loved me, but that of course could not be his primary concern at all times. "Will it be a month or a year?"

"Well, surely not a year, Father—"

"A year would entirely be outside of too much!" Lord Cavanaugh blurted, but when I favored him with an appreciative glance, he was not looking at me but at my father. "We had an agreement, Knowles, as well you know. The marriage contract did not assume—"

"The marriage contract didn't have a date attached to it either, *Cavanaugh*," my father snapped back. "You'll get your dowry and to spare when Beatrice is your legal wife, and not before."

Dowry? I barely forestalled a gape at my father. What nonsense was this? My family had barely two shillings to rub together once our court allotment was factored in. Our manor house, Marion Hall, was a falling-down heap in the middle of a vast and unruly estate. Only God knew what was happening there now, with both of my parents here at court and our extended raft of foundlings and foster children left to wander its grounds. "Now, well and truly," I said in my most conciliatory voice. "There is no need to argue. I will be free to wed no later than—"

"Am I supposed to simper and dance attendance, then, a half-married man?" Cavanaugh proclaimed, as if he'd just now thought of this, a new outrage. "She cannot expect me to—"

"You have a problem with paying attention to my daughter?" My father cut him off coldly. "Is it too much to ask you to accept the role of a married man?"

What? No! I put my hands on both their arms, all soothing grace and comfort. "Indeed, I know you both must be sorely disappointed not to complete this, ah, most felicitous of transactions, but I can assure you—"

"What is it you are implying?" growled Cavanaugh to my father. "You cannot tell me that you, of all people, expect me to change my life over the simple eventuality of becoming married."

"We had an agreement, and agreements must be honored," my father said, his voice dripping equal parts syrup and lye.

"Gentlemen!" I cried out, desperate to break through their conversation, even as my head began to whirl. "What is all this talk of contracts and terms? Lord Cavanaugh and I were just interrupted in the most sacred of events, and he is understandably hurt. As am I!"

"Of course you are," Cavanaugh said, as if such hurt were only my due. Just as I felt my own embarrassment prick, however, he turned to me. He lifted my hand, his eyes going soft and gentle as he brushed my knuckles with his thin, aristocratic lips.

"You are a prize of the court, my lady," he murmured. "And I will be delighted to stand up with you in a month's time."

Then he dropped my hand with an almost unseemly haste, and leveled a look at my father. "No longer, I suspect."

"I rather suspect not," my father agreed.

Lord Cavanaugh glanced again to me. "Until such time as that, however, we have no need to consort with each other as betrotheds. You can tell the Queen whatever is the most expedient. That I do not trust myself near you, that I am swept away by your charms. But I shall not be made to dance for Her Majesty in hopes that she may hasten to grant me that which is already mine by contract and decree."

I stood there, stunned, then startled myself back into the moment with all the composure and grace I had left, which was precious little at that point. "I thank you for the compliment, my lord Cavanaugh," I managed. "I am sure I will come up with a suitable explanation for Her Grace. Do not trouble yourself at all on my account."

"It is no trouble at all." He glanced again my way. "You will be mine by month's end, and we can depart this court for my home. You will be comfortable there."

"Of course," I replied, though in truth his words struck fear straight to my core. I had just assumed we would remain near the Queen and the other maids until such time as Her Grace tired of needing spies. I'd imagined I would be put up in some fine apartment, perhaps one of the small homes in Dean's Cloister, but still be close enough to keep my pulse on the court and its ever-changing politics. The idea of immediately going to Cavanaugh's estate at the back edge of beyond had never even occurred to me.

"Just plan on doing your part, and you'll get your just rewards, Cavanaugh," my father said, with his calculated callousness that never failed to grate on my nerves. He exchanged bows with Cavanaugh, but lingered long enough after my good lord left to see the fury seethe unchecked across my face.

"Oh, now that's the Beatrice I've come to know and love—"

"How dare you!" I hissed. My father, to his credit, backed up a hasty step. "How *dare* you take what was already a ruined day and make it even worse!"

"Beatrice!" He seemed genuinely shocked, but I did not have time for his silver-tongued apologies.

"Is that all I am to you, still?" I demanded. "A tool to do your bidding—a negotiating ploy?" I lifted my hand to forestall his denials. "I must report to my quarters, on order of the Queen. Enjoy the rest of the wedding ale, and try to find Mother before she falls off a castle wall."

And with that, I was off.

But as I rushed with officious dignity through the halls of Windsor, the cord of uneasiness that had begun curling within me during my own wedding twisted yet further, until I was choking with doubt and confusion. How would I regain my position with Cavanaugh when I would have to be throwing myself at Alasdair at every turn?

And what did my father mean by Cavanaugh doing his part? In my distraction and dismay, what had I missed?

CHAPTER FOUR

I didn't know whether to rip my hair out or scream with frustration. Of course, I could do neither. The first was unsightly and the second unseemly. And if the walls of Windsor had ears, well, of course they had eyes as well. I would never—ever—allow my composure to be shattered on so public a stage. Deliberately I slowed my steps, smoothed my gown, schooled my expression, and remembered what was important.

Cavanaugh loved me. He'd pledged his hand, his heart, and his future to me. And in hopefully one month's time he would be my husband. Until then I simply . . . needed to pay court to another man under his very nose.

What could be easier?

By the time I rounded the corner into the maids' quarters, I'd almost managed to square myself with the idea. Such were the games at Windsor, and who knows? Perhaps I could even turn—

"Beatrice!" Sophia's lilting cry shocked me out of my reverie, and I was smote with a whirl of flying silks topped by a mop of ink-dark hair. Sophia threw her arms around me like she hadn't seen me in weeks, and there were actual tears staining her face. *What on earth?*

"Beatrice, I'd no idea she would go so far or be so cruel. I'd feared there would be a disruption, verily I did, but I can never know exactly how such things will manifest, and I thought it could just as likely be a spurned suitor or a heartsick—"

"Sophia!" I shouted into the barrage of words, not unkindly, but in truth enough was enough. My tone was sufficient to stem the tide, but Sophia hiccuped, hugging herself.

I took the moment to glance at the other Maids of Honor, ranged as they were around the room. They all looked positively morose, which meant yet more work for me. "I'm well, truly I am," I said, raising a hand as Sophia stumbled back, staring at me like she was the most wretched of souls. "It is not as bad as all that." *It is far worse.* "The Queen has need of me to spy for her, and so spy I will." *On an accursed Scotsman who stinks of sweat and leather and ale.* "She's postponed my marriage, and I have already discussed the matter with both my father and Lord Cavanaugh." *And I* will *turn it to my advantage. Somehow.*

I switched my gaze back to Sophia. "Your visions were not so terribly far off, you see? You worried I would not have children with Lord Cavanaugh, and in point of fact, I cannot help avoiding the state of motherhood while I remain unmarried to him. So all is well." I gave her what I hoped was an encouraging smile. "Your gift is closer than you think."

"I just do everything wrong!" she blurted, so startling me with her anguish that I forgot myself and opened my arms to her as if she were one of the foundling children at Marion Hall. I gathered her slight frame close for a soothing hug.

"Oh, Sophia, not at all," I said, willing her quaking to cease. "You are doing the best that you—"

"No, I'm *not*." Sophia straightened away from me, scrubbing at her face, the action merely serving to brighten her cheeks in lovely counterpart to her huge violet eyes. "I know too much and too little. I hear too clearly and not clearly enough. I see what isn't there, what might be, and what may never be. I'm useless."

I bit my lip and exchanged a long look with Anna, as Jane and Meg suddenly seemed endlessly fascinated with their own hands. Sophia *was* a riddle, there was no denying it. But she was far more powerful than even she realized.

I'd been in my position as a Maid of Honor a scant month when John Dee had come calling to Elizabeth's chambers, with his arms full of charts and his words full of portents. As the new young Queen's official astrologer, Dee had become a constant guest in the waning days of 1558. Together he and Elizabeth had puzzled out when the Queen's coronation should be held, when every important meeting should be scheduled, who should be added to her list of confidantes and who should be turned away.

He'd brought his young ward, Sophia, with him after the third visit, and Elizabeth had quickly become fascinated with the girl. I'd been more wary, not that the Queen paid me any mind. Still, Dee had seemed too careful, too skittish around the quiet girl, too unsure of her even as he'd doted on her, too watchful and eager.

It hadn't taken long for the Queen to realize that Dee thought the girl possessed a budding psychic gift, that he'd waited long years for that gift to manifest, and that—finally!—he thought the time was nearing for it to arrive.

After that the good astrologer hadn't stood a chance.

Dee had found himself being "honored" by having his own niece swept away from him and taken into the Queen's care, with vague assurances of access to her that never quite materialized. Then Lord Brighton had shown up, and all too quickly Sophia's betrothal had been announced—with no apparent word from Dee on the subject. The astrologer barely darkened our doors after that, preferring to stay cooped up in his library at Mortlake, a western district of London that was a good hour's ride from Windsor Castle.

It appeared all the same to Sophia. She swooned at least three times a week to avoid confrontation, she suffered from terrible headaches, and she was as pale and trembling as a newborn lamb. Her greatest fear appeared to be of her own betrothed. And truth be told, for all his generosity, Lord Theoditus Brighton was about two decades too old to be considered a decent choice for the girl. Sophia was only now nearing her sixteenth birthday!

I frowned, a new thought striking me. What would the Queen do with not just one of her Maids of Honor being married (myself) but two? How would she shore up the corps of spies she herself had created? Had she even given the matter thought?

Knowing Elizabeth, she had. Her Maids of Honor were important to her. We were governed by Cecil and Walsingham in our day-to-day spying activities, but in the end we were the Queen's women.

"Sophia," I said gently now, returning to our less than easy conversation. "Have you learned something to make you particularly afraid?"

"Ah. Well, then, yes," Meg interrupted. I shot her an annoyed glare. *I was speaking here!*

But Meg and Jane were looking at each other fiercely, and I straightened to take their measure. "I think," Meg said carefully. "I think it's time that we share some news of our own."

I narrowed my eyes. If one of them had become betrothed without my knowing it, I truly would lose my temper. There were certain things that were not to be borne, and the marriage of a common thief or a deadly assassin before mine was one of them. "What sort of news?"

Sophia had turned as well, her eyes impossibly wide now. Jane just grinned, leaning up against the wall. "One less secret to keep," she acknowledged, and Meg gave a short laugh.

"Should I give them the long version or the shorter one?" Meg asked.

"I think you've already strayed into the long version," I said, folding my arms. "Does this news have a beginning point? Or should we just start guessing?"

"Briefly, then; briefly," Meg mused, looking up at the ceiling. I knew she was doing it just to bait me, and I was all the more irritated that it was working. I seethed quietly, about to burst, when she finally began speaking.

"In the hunt for the killer of Marie Claire last month,

Jane and I stumbled on secret passages cut into the very walls of Windsor," she said. "Quite by chance, I assure you."

"Quite," agreed Jane, with the slightest twist of her lips.

"But something found cannot be unfound, and so of course, we began mapping the passageways below the castle."

"Are we drawing near a point sometime soon?" I asked. "What is this great discovery you are dying to share?"

"I'm getting to it, I'm getting to it!" Meg grinned at me. "In our searching we encountered a section that stretches all the way down to the Lower Ward, into the areas behind the Cloisters."

Beside me Sophia gave a little gasp, and even Anna was leaning forward now. I'd known about the passageways—well, some of them—for many years. But before Jane and Meg had begun their mapping, even I had had no idea of the labyrinth of corridors that had been cut beneath Windsor. You could spend days trying to find their ends, as Jane and Meg certainly had. But this was the first they'd spoken of what they'd found down there.

"Once we'd found our way behind the Cloisters," Meg continued, "the passage allowed us access into the apartments. We were running late, and, again quite by chance, we stumbled into the living quarters of Lord Brighton."

Sophia stood frozen, but it was Anna's turn to gasp. She clapped her hands to her face. "Oh, say that he wasn't there!" she moaned. "That would be a disaster!"

"It would have been at that, but we, um, were lucky. He wasn't in residence. However, his papers were."

I lifted my brows, approval curving my lips. "Do you

mean to tell me that you spied on Lord Brighton? Rifled through his belongings?"

"It wasn't like that!" Meg protested, but Jane just shrugged.

"The papers were there and we were there, and the good lord wasn't," Jane said.

"But it wasn't like we went looking for things," Meg countered quickly. "And we stole naught but information, if you can even call that a theft."

You could, and I certainly did. "So what is it you found?" I prompted, if only to allow Sophia's heart to beat again.

Meg took a deep breath. She walked over to Sophia and took the girl's hand in her own. "We learned why you are so worried about Lord Brighton, Sophia. Do you already know the truth?"

Sophia had begun trembling again, and I looked from one maid to the other. *What is this?* "I . . . I couldn't be certain," Sophia said. "It is all so confused!"

"Of what couldn't you be certain?" Anna demanded, saving me the trouble. "What is it you learned about Lord Brighton?"

"He's been carrying on a gambit of his own, he has," Jane said, gesturing toward Sophia with her knife. I frowned at her. When had she pulled out her blade? And was now truly an appropriate time for her to be cleaning it with the edge of her kirtle?

"He has, yes," Meg said, her eyes still trained on Sophia. "He has masqueraded as a suitor to ensure that Sophia is not married off to anyone while she is still so young."

"But why would he go to the trouble?" I asked, barely repressing my need to stamp my foot. Elegant noblewomen didn't stamp their feet. Even when their need was great. "I mean, if he didn't want to marry her himself, then why would he—"

"Because he is my father," Sophia said, her voice a tortured whisper. She stared from Meg to Jane and back again, as Anna and I both stiffened in shock. "That's it, is it not?" she asked. "That's what I have feared all these months, since he first stepped foot in the Queen's Presence Chamber. That's what I have seen. Lord Brighton is not Lord Brighton at all—but a wraith, a ghost, a—"

Meg closed her fingers over Sophia's hand. "A father, Sophia," she said quietly. "He lost your mother years ago, when you were barely a babe in arms. Then you were taken from him— The papers were not clear on what had happened, but it appeared that from that moment forward your father was determined to find you and ensure your safety. He sold all of his belongings and arranged his own death. He re-created himself as Lord Brighton. He amassed great wealth and security, and then he came looking for you."

"He found me," Sophia said, her words stronger now even though she had begun to tremble again. "He found me and tried to protect me, by offering his hand for mine."

I pursed my lips, trying to make sense of it. A father who'd lost his daughter and then found her again, in service to the Queen. What choice did he have? He could not demand Sophia's return—the Queen had already claimed her, and her trusted astrologer had presented the girl as his own niece. Brighton could not even declare his own existence as a father wronged, for fear those who'd stolen Sophia away from him long years ago would return to repeat the act. And so, he betrothed himself to her, perhaps never seeking to fulfill that contract, just to keep Sophia unwed until he had time to come up with a plan. It made a certain sort of sense, I supposed.

Oddly enough, Sophia did not seem as shocked as she should have been. Relief shone in her eyes; the most important prediction of all had just been verified. Then her expression dimmed and her skin turned noticeably paler.

"My head . . . ," she murmured, lifting a hand to her brow. "Whenever I listen to thoughts such as these, it hurts so bad—"

"I've just the thing for that," Anna said quickly, hopping off her perch and bustling over to Sophia, some random posset in her hand. "I have been wanting to try this. Mix it in with mead, and you'll be right as rain."

Sophia smiled, accepting the posset. "I thank you, Anna," she managed, but Anna was already looking back at me.

"'Tis a dangerous game her father is playing," she said. "No monarch would take kindly to being toyed with, our Queen least of all. If she were to find out—"

"Well, she cannot find out," I said, surprising even myself with the firmness of the statement. "It is not her place to stand between a father and a daughter, no matter who she is." *Or thinks she is.* "However"—and here I slanted a glance at Meg—"Lord Brighton also can't stay betrothed to Sophia. That's just . . . unseemly."

Jane barked a laugh, and even Meg looked at me in amusement. "Unseemly!" Meg repeated. "Yes, yes, it is at that, Beatrice." She grinned. "But how in heaven's name will we unshackle Sophia from her father's well-meaning chains? Do you know how it's done, the unmaking of a betrothal?"

I paused, considering. I knew, certainly. I'd been working so hard to get and stay betrothed, however, that the dissolution of such a happy event seemed foreign even to consider. But there *were* ways, of course . . . ways that could be put into motion . . .

"It can be done," I said. "But it would help if—" I shot a glance toward Sophia and drew in a tight breath. "I don't suppose your, um, father . . . has any affection for a woman in the court?"

"Surely he wouldn't dare!" Anna breathed, outraged at the betrayal of even a sham romance.

"Why wouldn't he?" Jane shrugged. "He was at the wedding this morning with a woman, was he not? Some older woman—but not too old—a widow or some such, I think?"

"Lady Ariane," Anna supplied, as of course she would. "Her husband died this Christmas past, and Lord Brighton has taken to squiring her to official functions when Sophia is not in a mood to endure festivities."

"Which is often," Meg put in with a grin, and Sophia blushed.

"Still, she is the soul of propriety," Anna protested. "There has not been a whisper, nor even a hint—"

"There doesn't have to be." I waved Anna off, my mind churning now. If Sophia's father were to be caught in the arms of another woman—no matter how innocently, no matter how chaste—it would be cause enough for the Queen to withdraw her blessing from the forthcoming union. Elizabeth was ever going on about the virtue of her court and the value of marriage for everyone but herself. Now we would see how much she truly believed her own prattle.

Now I could disrupt the Queen's own plans, as surely as she had disrupted mine.

I allowed the first genuine smile to form on my lips since the moment Elizabeth had arrived in Saint George's Chapel.

"I have an idea," I said.

CHAPTER FIVE

No sooner had the words come out of my mouth than a clatter sounded down the hallway. Moments later the door to our chamber was swept open. Cecil stood there, glowering at us.

"Good," he said sourly. "You're all here, though I refuse to speak with you in your bedchamber. Meet me in my offices at the quarter hour, and for the love of heaven, Jane, sheathe the knife."

Jane started, and as quick as a breath, her knife slid out of view. Cecil continued to stare at us a moment more, nodding. "You're at least dressed presentably. I suppose I have the wedding to thank for that."

He reddened then, and his gaze swept to mine. I met it evenly. I didn't need the man's pity, and he knew it. But Cecil, for all his many flaws, was at least becoming more predictable in his changes in temper. Now I could see that he felt bad for how my day had turned. Still, I tilted up my chin a little higher, silently reassuring him that I was well able to carry out any task he might have in mind. I could not afford to have him thinking of me as weak. If my father had taught me nothing else of value, he had taught me that.

Cecil nodded. "You, if anything, should choose something a bit less dramatic, Beatrice. The task at hand this day requires discretion and humility. Try to remember that, all of you." He swept out of the room with a rustle of his black cape, and the five of us split off—Sophia and Anna to go find some mead to help Sophia choke down whatever refined poison Anna was experimenting with, and Jane and Meg to help me unlash myself from my wedding finery. I would swear the gown was more stitches than fabric, but we still managed to get all of its pieces disassembled without creasing the garment. It would keep until month's end, if I would wear it again at all.

I sighed then, fingering the heavy cloth. Everything I had worked for all these long years, gone just like that. I shook myself. Of course I would wear it again. Of course I would still marry Cavanaugh.

Of course I would.

We gathered in Cecil's office less than a half hour later, as he'd requested. To get to his chambers we had to run the interminable gauntlet of Spaniards who seemed to have made the public antechamber off the main Presence Chamber their personal gathering spot. I saw Meg brush by Rafe with the barest of nods, but I watched closely and was rewarded for my care. He'd given her a letter in that brief moment, and Meg's color was just a tiny bit higher in her cheeks as she strolled into Cecil's office.

I found myself unaccountably annoyed, and stiffened my

spine against it. I should not care about Meg and her grubby Spaniard. I had problems of my own to solve.

But now Cecil was talking. "What do you know about the Scottish rebellion?" he asked, looking pained.

Anna jumped in immediately. "It's been an uneasy thing for the Scots for nearly two decades," she said. "With King James dying seventeen years ago, and his French wife, Mary de Guise, remaining, the Scots have chafed under the threat of French control for longer than they ever expected. Now Mary de Guise serves as regent for her and King James's daughter, Mary, the true Queen of Scots—but young Mary just wed the French dauphin last year. So the French remain a threat, and Mary de Guise is of a mind to make trouble. Especially of late, she seems determined to enforce French will upon the Scots." Anna made a wry grimace. "The trouble is, you can't force a Scotsman to do much of anything unless you've got him at the edge of your sword, and that never works for long. I should think Mary de Guise is making more enemies than friends for her daughter, and that will not serve the young Queen of Scotland in the end."

If anything, Cecil now seemed more irritated. "I did not ask you what you *thought*, Miss Burgher, merely what you *know*." He rubbed a hand over his brow. I wondered if he had a headache like Sophia, who was looking markedly better than she had in weeks. Well, he would spend a cool day in hell before Anna would give him a posset, if he expected her to stop thinking.

"My apologies, Sir William," Anna said smoothly. She then launched into a purely factual accounting of how the devoutly Catholic Mary de Guise, mother and regent of the young Scottish Queen Mary, was advocating for French (and Catholic) rule of Scotland. And, further, that while most of that barbarian land was, in fact, Catholic, they most certainly weren't French. Nor did they like France. Of course, they didn't like England, either, but at least we weren't trying to rule them. Yet.

"Now even more Scotsmen are opposing Mary de Guise, including the clergyman John Knox, who is the loudest of them all. With him having just returned to Scotland after more than a decade in exile, there will be only upheaval to come," Anna said. Then she colored again, immediately recognizing that she had employed her mind once more without express permission. "Forgive me, Sir William. I mean only to say that John Knox has returned, and rumors have started that he also means to incite the Protestants to rebellion against Mary de Guise and her Catholic sympathizers."

"Knox isn't alone," I put in, carelessly. "He's finding able support from the Lords of the Congregation."

Cecil's gaze sharpened on me, and I instantly realized my mistake. Anna was the only one of our number whose brain was supposed to be sharp. I was merely the manipulator, the wide-eyed miss whose cunning was confined to the way I played the people around me. But truly, I wasn't an idiot. Since the Scots had deposited themselves on our threshold in early August, they'd talked—and I'd listened. Even my own father muttered on about the Scots and their rebellion when he was in his cups, which was often. Our estate was well south of the Scottish border but still well north of Windsor.

I suppose I shouldn't have been surprised that he would care about a war that close to his home.

"What do you know about the Lords of the Congregation?" Cecil demanded. I felt even Anna's eyes on me, though Anna, God bless her, wanted only for me to do well. I didn't like the set of Cecil's jaw, however. "Where have you heard them mentioned?"

"Oh, la," I said, airily waving a hand. "You can't expect me to be surrounded by Scotsmen morning, noon, and night without hearing them go on about the most audacious of their countrymen playing 'wreck the church hall,'" I said. "I'm not certain which of them started the conversation, but they seemed all to know the Lords well enough, though none could say for certain who these august lords truly were. It seems to be something of a grand secret, though they've spent endless hours of speculation on it." *When they weren't busily draining the Queen's store of ale, that is.*

"Pay closer attention going forward, then," Cecil said. He didn't snap the words, but they were an order nonetheless. "The Lords of the Congregation are, in fact, a group of staunchly Protestant noblemen who would rather not see France hold sway in their homeland. To that end, they are approaching us for our aid. Secretly, I might add, as far as the bulk of the court is concerned. We expect them to join us within the next few days, and to remain for a week, little more."

"They've called before and met with grief," Sophia said, her voice striking and lyrical in the musty half darkness. "Lord and servant to their belief."

Her words silenced the room.

Cecil turned and narrowed his eyes on the girl, just as she nervously laid one of Cecil's silver pens back upon his desk. "And just what do you mean by that, Sophia?" he asked.

"Oh, God's bones. It's not a secret," Jane said, her loud, plain voice brooking no argument. "There was that boy who came over the Channel from France and remained in London for—what—a week? When the Queen made haste to London last month. He stayed at your own house, Sir William, and took tea with the Queen at Hampton Court. He might not have been one of these Lords, but he was tied to them, 'tis certain."

Cecil turned a steely look upon Jane. "I thought you remained behind at Windsor during that trip."

She shrugged. "Even if your guards do not tell tales to outsiders, they canna always remain silent among themselves. And if I happen to be tucked away when they have a conversation, then I hear it as well, no?"

Cecil exhaled a disgusted breath, and I watched the glance of unspoken satisfaction between Jane and Meg. Though Jane had originally spoken to draw the attention away from Sophia, her words had betrayed more than she realized, at least to me. There could be only one place where Jane could have hidden to overhear the Windsor guards speak of such a tightly held secret that even I had not caught wind of it: the hidden passageways beneath the castle.

Entire new realms of possibility opened up to me in that moment. What secrets could I hear had I access to passages such as those—and with those secrets, what power could I wield? I'd have to ask to tag along on Meg and Jane's next foray beneath the castle.

"Very well," Cecil said at length, as if coming to a grave decision. "If you know the half of it, you should know the whole, so that you have the story correct. The Earl of Arran, the boy Jane just referenced, had been a prisoner of the French Catholics. He was returned to his father from France this summer, with the aid of the Queen." *By that Cecil means with his own aid, his and Walsingham's foreign spies.* "His father, the Duke of Châtellerault, had previously supported the French—and the Catholics. With his son's return, however, he has become one of the most prominent members of the Lords of the Congregation. There is no doubt that the rescue of the duke's son made his conversion to the Lords' cause possible. Which provides additional opportunities for us."

"We return the son, and ensure that powerful men in Scotland are allied with England and not France," I said. "Nicely done." Cecil's glance flitted back to me, but I didn't mind his scowl. This *was* my area of expertise, the give-and-take between friends and enemies, boons granted and debts repaid. "And now is the time when you will discuss the resulting agreement between England and the Lords of the Congregation?" I asked. "Who will be arriving?"

"A half dozen of the Lords, and their guards, of course," Cecil said. "While we meet with them, your roles are to watch everyone else in the court. If you see anyone talking with any Scotsman too closely, I want to know about it. Immediately. I expect the Queen will have her own tasks for you as well." Once again the tiniest thread of irritation underlaced Cecil's words. "But, Beatrice, you must begin at once."

"I must?" I opened my eyes just so, all winsome innocence and frail pain. *I was supposed to get married today, you cur. Do not even begin to tell me that you are attaching me to—*

Cecil finished my thoughts. "Alasdair MacLeod," he said flatly. "The young Scot is clearly some sort of leader of the delegation, and his family is old and well regarded." This meant he had money, in Cecil's manner of speaking. As if a stone fortress on a wind-battered island off the Scottish coast could have cost anything more than a herd of sheep. "There is some rumor he is tied to the Lords of the Congregation, though I cannot believe it. Still, if that is the case, it changes things."

"Such as?" I asked, unable to help myself.

"Such as, if the Highlanders all the way up to Skye are ready to support a cause against the French, then we need only send a token force to Scotland to show our own support," he said. "Or perhaps we need not send any support at all, and instead let the Scots deplete their men rather than risk our own."

I opened my mouth to protest, but at Cecil's black look I thought better of it. "Very well, Sir William," I said sweetly. *You skittering, slithering snake.* "I cannot imagine a better use of my time than to play court to a loutish Scotsman."

That did cause him to smile, though in the gloom of his chamber it looked more like a sneer.

"Funny," he said. "Neither could the Queen."

CHAPTER SIX

We were given the rest of the day to prepare for our various tasks—Anna to learn the histories of the men who would likely be arriving from Scotland; Jane and Meg to see what else might be known from either the Scots' guards or our own. Sophia claimed a headache and so escaped to a quiet room to, as Cecil put it, "do whatever it is you do."

But I was not so lucky.

With the promise of a wedding having fueled the influx of visitors into the Lower Ward, an unofficial Market Day had been assembled, all the more boisterous because the wedding had not, in fact, come off. It was into this rabble I was headed now.

But not before I was stopped a dozen times. First to endure, counter, or spread, as necessary, gossip related to my own interrupted nuptials. Windsor loved a story, especially a story of a noble being rebuked. It was my task and honor to supply enough fat for the court to chew on long after the taste had gone out of the tale. Second, I had to reinforce my own position in the castle. There was no question that I had been delivered a terrible blow, and yet—this was important—here I was looking as fresh and unspoiled as washing-day linen. I parried this query and that, none more frequent than "Had the Queen spoken to my lord Cavanaugh directly? He looked so amazed, so distraught!"

To that I said simply that what my Queen and my future husband discussed was not for me to know. This was the virtuous answer, this was the maidenly and modest response. It made me want to retch, but such was the price of position.

Now I stepped into the bright light of the Upper Ward, the easternmost area of the enclosed walls of Windsor, a quadrangle of manicured lawn and walkways that made any approach instantly known to those watching from the high windows of the most royal section of the castle. Shielding my eyes from the sun, I took a bare moment to grimace in peeved annoyance. The sun *would* choose this day to shine forth in glorious splendor. It was supposed to have been my wedding day. Even the stars in the heavens were doubtlessly planning to shine the brighter for it. *God save me from a meddling Queen.*

"Such a frown as I've never seen upon your face, Beatrice. Would that I could help take it away."

I barely kept myself from stiffening, and instead turned and favored Meg's Spaniard with a smile. "What a charming surprise, Count de Martine. What brings you out into the sunlight?"

Despite my pains to be polite, Rafe grinned at me, then took my hand in his and curled it into his arm. "No need to stare daggers at me, fair maiden, or tire yourself with attempting friendship. I merely wish to serve as an escort to you. A young lady of your soft beauty should not ever have to take her air alone." He paused then, considering. "Unless that was your goal? To flee the confines of the castle and all who rest within it?"

If only that were possible. But Rafe's sudden appearance was something I could use. He was a dashing, handsome Spaniard, for all that he was still a Spaniard. Half the women in court swooned over him, though he only had eyes for Meg. He would do as a young man to squire me into the Lower Ward, I supposed. For as I'd already learned to my chagrin, nothing drew the attention of one Alasdair MacLeod to me as when I was receiving attention from another courtier.

"I think you see the value I may bring you," Rafe observed blandly, and I glanced to him, startled by his laugh. "Worry not, fair maid," he said, patting my hand. "We shall put on a fine show of it until I get you to your destination."

"Perhaps I have underestimated you, my count," I observed archly, and was rewarded again by another of his chuckles.

"You would not be the first." We walked several paces more, down the quadrangle's northern passageways and through the Norman Gate. We crossed into the Middle Ward, shadowed by the enormous Round Tower that marked the highest point of Windsor Castle.

I stopped Rafe there, staring up at the Tower's round bulk as if I hadn't passed by the thing nearly every day for the past several months. But there was something else I wanted to ask of him, before we descended into the chaos of the Lower Ward.

"The jade stone ring you brought to England," I began. "How did . . . how did you come by it?"

Rafe hesitated. Then I felt the warm pressure of his hand over mine. "Meg didn't tell you?"

"She said it came from your mother," I said coolly. "I could only assume that your mother knew my father in an earlier time, and that he gifted it to her. On that topic you need explain no more." *God save me from philandering fathers as well.* "But was there anything else she shared with you about it—or any other of my family's treasure that my father seemed so fond of casting about?"

"Fair questions all," Rafe said. He gave me a little tug, and we moved back into the sunlight, strolling like bosom friends along the flower-edged lane. "She said nothing of your father. I have no idea how she came by the ring, only that it gave her great satisfaction to keep it secret from my own father."

I snorted. "As one might well expect."

"But as to other bits of your family treasure being strewn about the castle, she did say this—''tis but the smallest trifle from a wealth laid in the very earth of his holding.'" He shrugged. "I took it to mean that whatever lord she'd charmed was very rich indeed."

"Rich!" I burst forth with such a grim laugh that even Rafe was forced to check his stride, looking down at me in concern. Too late I realized my mistake, and struggled to amend it. "Rich we would be indeed if my father would forestall his own hand in giving away all our worldly possessions." I glanced up at him with as rueful an expression as I could muster. "I do apologize, Count de Martine. I should not prattle on about something so inconsequential."

"We can only marvel at the actions of our parents," Rafe agreed, turning again to escort me into the Lower Ward. "Their decisions remain a puzzle even to themselves, I suspect."

Or to any rational person alive. The Knowles family may have been rich at one time—our mansion in Northampton was a hulking effigy to that largesse. But the money had long gone from our coffers, which were systematically being emptied even further by my spendthrift father and addled mother. I'd not been back to Marion Hall since the Queen's coronation early this year, and I had no great need to see it again anytime soon.

"Ah, here we are, then. Shall I tarry with you farther, or have I served my purpose?" Rafe's eyes were alight with good humor, and I supposed I could see why Meg fancied him. Even if he was a Spaniard.

"Pray, you may consider yourself released to enjoy the day, good sir." I found myself laughing the words, grateful for the moment's respite from my own twisting thoughts. I curtsied to him with the coy flirtation of a blushing maid. "I do thank you for your gallant rescue to ensure I did not walk alone."

Rafe, for his part, executed a perfect courtly bow. "Your brightness only illuminates me further; I could not stay away," he said, straightening with a flourish. His eyes shifted to something over my shoulder, and he winked at me. "I think we've caught our fish," he said lightly.

"Would that he not stink of one," I returned, but I let

Rafe, now laughing openly, take my hands in his. He brought them to his lips for a final flirtatious coup, and winked at me again. Then he took his leave of me, and I busied myself with my velvet pouch, as if I were searching for shillings to pay for a market day pie.

I had just opened the strings when I felt a strong tug at my right arm, curling my hand over a thick, corded biceps. Even though I'd been expecting something along these lines, I could barely forestall my gasp at the temerity of the young man's touch.

Alasdair MacLeod turned me around smartly and walked with me into the midst of the teeming market, as if proclaiming to all that I was his property. He said not one word, and I strained against his arm. "I do beg your pardon, sir, but—"

"Do not tempt me, m'lady." Alasdair cocked a glance down at me. The faintest of smiles now stretched his lips. "The idea of you begging for anything would be too much for me to bear."

Irritation surged forth, as it always did with the impossible Scotsman. "May you at least lighten your grip? You're hurting my arm."

That did it, as I suspected it would; the oaf loosened his hold at once, contenting himself with maintaining his hand over mine on his arm, as if he were afraid I would collapse if left completely free.

Alasdair was a head and a half taller than I was, though I was certainly of a fine height—nearly as tall as the Queen. But he seemed overmuch concerned for my personal safety when he was around. "Thank you," I managed, though I had done myself no favors. Now the Scot's large hand covered mine, and I had left the castle interior without gloves. The feeling of Alasdair's rough fingers on my skin left me oddly breathless, and I struggled to remember why I needed to speak with him in the first place. Thinking to head off any comments intended to nettle me, I broached the subject of my failed wedding directly. "'Tis a fine day, is it not? For all that it began with a disrupted wedding?"

He grinned fiercely, firming his fingers on mine once again. "The day is all the better for that turn of events, aye." He glanced down at me. "Tell me you were not relieved. I saw you watch me with hope in your eyes even as you strolled down the aisle."

"You saw no such thing!" I snapped. That only seemed to goad him on further.

"You like me shaven clean and fit for your English weddings, eh?" He lifted my hand in his meaty paw and drew it down his cheek, before resettling it on his arm. "Find me much more civilized this way?"

"Never fear that I will ever find you civilized, sir," I said frostily, though my stomach had tightened at the bold caress and how quickly he'd managed it, and my fingers still tingled with the roughness of his face, his beard already returning though he'd likely shaven mere hours before. "In truth you may unhand me completely, if you please. I am well able to walk unassisted."

"'Tis no bother to me," Alasdair said, and he tugged me along, only the crush of the crowd ensuring that I did not stumble over my own skirts in trying to keep up with his long stride. "You belong on my arm."

That drew me up short. "Sir, you must be mistaken. My wedding was postponed, not canceled."

"It looked canceled to me," he countered. "The look on the face of that stick you were tying yourself to was something to behold. He looked like he'd eaten spoiled haggis."

"Lord Cavanaugh had every right to be upset," I reasoned, pricked despite myself. "He was very much looking forward to being my husband."

"More like he was looking forward to having you all to himself. Not that I can blame the man, but I'd not wish marriage to him on my worst enemy."

"And you think what you have to offer would far outweigh one of the most noble houses of England?" I scoffed, at once furious with Alasdair and incensed with myself for being drawn out by him. This was not what I needed to learn from the scoundrel!

"I have more to offer in my little finger than he does with all of his horses and land," Alasdair replied, drawing his fingers over mine to emphasize his point. I felt the color rise in my cheeks, but he just continued talking. "Though your Queen does have an eye for making an entrance in the most dramatic way possible. I'll give her that."

"She does," I said, grateful for the change of subject. "Our Elizabeth is nothing if not dramatic."

Alasdair slanted me a look. "She is jealous of you."

I grimaced as we stopped before a stand that sold savory pies. "I rather doubt that," I said, though with Elizabeth it was well possible. Even though she was the most powerful woman in England, I'd seen her devolve into an apoplectic fit when she felt she was being slighted by one courtier or another. They'd quickly learned to not invite her wrath, but mayhap I should have had more of a care myself. If she felt I was trying to outshine her, then far more than a postponed wedding would be my reward.

I blinked as Alasdair ordered enough food to feed a family of twelve. "I'm so sorry, sir. Did I interrupt your provisioning of your men?"

"You canna interrupt me, m'lady," Alasdair returned, tucking the pies into a sack he'd pulled out of somewhere and catching up a flagon of wine as well. He tossed a pile of coins to the vendor, waving off the man's offer to count it. "I merely thought you must be fatigued at having your future so effectively ruined. I wish to help revive you."

"My future is not ruined." *Other than being dragged around by you.* But I allowed Alasdair to pull me to the edge of the market, where benches had been set up in a loose group. He hooked a bench with one of his long legs and sat down upon it, patting the space beside him.

"Eat something, wench," he said, breaking off a piece of steaming pastry. "You're skinny enough to see through."

"I am not—" I opened my mouth to protest, and he shoved the bit of pie in, as neatly as if I were his truculent niece. "Oof!" I managed, my eyes watering.

He uncorked the wine and handed me the open bottle. "It's hot. Drink this."

And thus was I in the middle of the teeming rabble of the

Lower Ward, drinking wine straight from a bottle like any common Street Sally.

Lo, had my fortunes changed.

Still, I had my part to play, and by God I was going to play it. I handed the bottle back to Alasdair, noting his satisfaction as he stared at my wine-stained lips. Forcing myself to keep from snatching a handkerchief out of my pouch, I licked my lips instead. His eyes darkened, and I plunged forward.

"I will tell you plain, I think the Queen's decision had less to do with me and more with your countrymen." I sighed, canting my head to the right in a way I knew presented the curve of my jaw to best effect.

It served its purpose. Alasdair went very still, watching me. "My countrymen?" he asked. "What role do they play in this?"

"Elizabeth is just so *nervous* about all of you." I fluttered my hand vaguely to the north, as if in one gesture I could encompass the whole of the Scottish kingdom. "She sees the rebellion gathering steam, but also the violent and prolonged opposition from the Catholics. And with more Scots now in Windsor than we've had in an age, she is ill at ease, wondering who is her friend and who her foe."

"The Scots are here for one thing alone, and that is English arms and support," Alasdair said flatly. I almost caught my breath, and it was all I could do to not betray the quickening of my heart. Would it really be so easy as this? I could tell Cecil—Walsingham—the Queen. I could be done with all of this and married within the fortnight. I stared into his eyes, willing him to spill all of his secrets like so much cheap wine. "Our intentions are not so cloaked as those of you Englishers," Alasdair continued. "If you wish to know something for your Queen, m'lady, you have but to ask."

Then his smile turned into more of a leer, and he leaned forward to speak words that only I could hear. "But I'll tell you plain. There will be a price for the information."

Despite myself, I jerked back. "What sort of price?" I asked, trying and failing this time to mask my reaction. "You cannot mean, sir—"

When his grin just deepened, I felt the outrage spill out of me.

"No!" I hissed, forgetting myself entirely and placing my hands squarely on his broad chest, shoving him back. "Sir, you go too far! I refuse to be treated like some wayward tavern girl and have you disrespect me as if I were the rushes beneath your feet. I will not have it!"

Alasdair tilted back his head and howled with laughter, the sound loud enough to draw the eyes of even the most raucous of the market day rabble. I jumped up from the bench, blind with anger, but no sooner had I turned away than he was right there with me, turning me back to him as tears fairly streamed down his face, his body shaking with mirth.

"Well done, well done!" he managed, his voice low and resonant. "You've met my only condition, my lady. I will tell you all you wish."

That caught me up short. "What do you mean?" I demanded. "I will not be trifled with, good sir." *Not this day, and certainly not by you.*

"I do not trifle, my lady," Alasdair said, lifting a thick hand to brush the tears away from my eyes that I hadn't realized I'd allowed to surface. "I sought only to see your first true emotion, one not laced with guile or artifice. You've satisfied my request, and to spare. I now know you can express genuine anger. And never have you been more fine."

"I—" I stopped, mystified. *How can I respond to that?* I hastened on. "I need to know of your loyalties, Alasdair. Do you support the Protestant cause, or are you allied with the Catholics? You are at no risk in either case. The Queen is ever tolerant, especially of those who are not her God-given subjects, but—"

"Shh, m'lady. Doona trouble your heart about me, at least not on this account. The MacLeods and all we tarry with do not want French rule. That is really the issue here, for me and mine. Our God is our master, and we will worship him as we see fit, but the French will never own us, as long as we draw breath. For that reason alone do we support the rebellion, and all the men committed to its cause. And I will tell you this much more, fair Beatrice. A MacLeod will never back down from his word, nor change his heart once it is given. He will never swerve in duty nor steadfastness, and he will *always* protect his own." He eyed me with a piercing gaze, his face suddenly intense with the fire of his fealty. This was a young man who knew what he wanted. Who, once committed, would not stray from the course. This was a young man who lived by his heart.

Where did that thought come from?

"Is that what you wanted to know?" Alasdair recalled

me from my reverie, his words naught more than a whisper now, but as loud as thunder in my ears. I stared back at him, momentarily unable to speak. Then the breath returned to my lungs, and wits to my brain. I favored him with my archest of smiles.

"That's what I wanted to know," I said.

CHAPTER SEVEN

The next several days passed quickly enough, and I was happy to be able to avoid Alasdair as I bent myself to the Queen's service.

Jane reported when the Lords of the Congregation arrived—a string of men and horses approaching the castle under cloak of darkness, who were then hastened off to the heavily guarded Visitors Apartments, none of the hundreds of castle inhabitants the wiser. A few of their number departed just as quickly, then approached with all public fanfare the following day. We assumed the "public" members of their party allowed the closeted Lords access to what was going on in the court proper, and passed information back and forth. There was also the usual collection of guards, thick-necked Scotsmen who kept to themselves, dressed in matching dun-colored tunics, belts, and loose-cut breeches. Really, you would think they'd try a little harder to make a statement if they were here to save all of Scotland.

Even though the Lords had taken pains to hide their faces, with Jane's keen eye and Anna's knowledge of the peers of the Scottish realm, by nightfall we knew which Lords had traveled to Windsor. And it appeared that the one Protestant I was most keen to see had thought the wiser of showing his face in an English court.

John Knox had earned no blessings of our Queen.

A strident and outspoken proponent of Protestantism, the clergyman Knox would ordinarily have cultivated Elizabeth's favor. But while she had still been a princess with Queen Mary upon the throne, the reverend had "anonymously" printed a rather unfortunate booklet detailing his true opinions of ruling Queens, *The First Blast of the Trumpet against the Monstrous Regiment of Women.*

Even though he had not included our Elizabeth in his disdain for female monarchs, since she hadn't been one at the time, he was doomed. The Queen could carry a grudge like no other. Knox would never openly gain her goodwill.

As morning broke, bright and fair, we were gathered off the Queen's Privy Chamber in a room that had until quite recently served as our schoolroom. With the current, endless round of celebrations to mark and honor the Queen's birthday, the room now generally served as one of the few places where we could go and know we would not be overheard. This day, however, we'd been called here specifically by the Queen, and even I was curious to see what the summons might mean.

"Think you that Cecil knows the Queen has called us here?" Anna mused, sitting at the long table in the room's center. "We've already reported to him all that he has asked about the arriving Lords."

Meg glanced up from her small leather-bound book, where she was working through the cipher that Anna had created for her. "Cecil is still in his chambers," she said. "It seems this is a play scripted only by the Queen—even Walsingham has no hand in it. It will be interesting indeed to see what it is we learn this day."

"True enough," grunted Jane, but I was still eyeing Meg and her journal. The book had been a gift to Meg from her long-lost parents, who had apparently been spies in their own right for old King Henry, Elizabeth's father. As Meg finished unraveling each passage, she would share it with us. I envied her being able to learn of her parents this way, only the parts they saw fit to write down in an extended letter to their then-baby daughter. Far worse to see your parents in every moment of their imperfections. By now my mother at least had returned to Marion Hall, while my father remained behind at Windsor, no doubt to drink his way through any open cask of ale that he could find.

"The Queen knows only that there is much she doesn't know, and it is infuriating her," Sophia said, her lyrical voice cutting through the gloom of the chamber like a beacon of light. She held up a thimble to peer at it, one I'd not seen before. "She draws us here to regain the advantage against her foes who are yet her friends." Then she let the thimble fall from her fingers, picking up instead one of my fans; a magpie looking for treasures to line her nest.

Anna's head had come up sharply at Sophia's first words, and now she shot a glance to me. I read its meaning instantly. That was one of Sophia's clearest predictions yet, and not expressed in the dreamy swoon that had so signified her earlier visions. Sophia turned to me as well then, but the beautiful girl's face stopped me cold.

It was . . . *Blank* was the only way to describe it. Like a page of unblemished parchment, open and vulnerable, her eyes large dark violet pools. She looked centuries older, her expression wiser, sager than any I'd ever seen on Sophia's face.

"Sophia?" I asked carefully, and took a step toward her. Jane rustled by my side, having come away from her perch in the shadows at Sophia's first words as well. "Sophia, can you hear me?"

"Deception upon deception covers you over, shadows your heart," she murmured directly to me, "but love so deeply buried can tear your world apart."

What is this? I quickly took the final steps toward Sophia, gathering up her hands in mine as my fan fell away. This wouldn't do at all.

"Sophia!" I said, not sharply but with the tone I used to roust the scrabbling children of Marion Hall from their daily fisticuffs. It served; Sophia's eyes cleared instantly, and color returned to her cheeks.

"Oh!" she exclaimed, the relief evident in her eyes. "Beatrice. I had the most curious thought about—"

"Well, you're back now, and that's what's important," I soothed, talking over her words and keeping her focused. "Now look placid. The Queen is on her way, and she'll want to believe you are fit to serve." As if that were possible. Of all of us, Sophia seemed the least fit to serve, no matter how prescient her ramblings. And what on earth had she meant about a buried love? The only thing buried about me, and not all that deeply, was my eternal disdain for—

"The Queen!" Anna said from the doorway, where she'd drifted.

And it was true. We could hear the long strides of Her Royal Unbearableness sounding down the corridor, and were barely in our places before she swept into the room.

We sank into our dutiful curtsies as she surveyed us all, not speaking. As ever, I found myself counting out the long seconds in my mind until we could rise.

The Queen lasted only five counts. "Up with you. We don't have time for that," she barked, and we popped back up like corks on the open sea. She surveyed us with grim approval.

"You all have conducted yourselves well in my service, and by your troth you are pledged first to me," she said. She gave a glittering wave, flashing the jewels that adorned her sleeve and wrist, and I suddenly felt the weight of the ring on the second finger of my own right hand. The Queen had extended her protection of us, ensuring that Cecil and Walsingham—though they could order us about at will—could not accuse us of any crime or put us to questioning that might result in our own harm, unless the Queen herself was present. It was a neat solution to a problem that had already presented itself. Meg had known a secret of the Queen's, and she hadn't shared it with Cecil and Walsingham. To express their displeasure, they'd imprisoned her.

Given the secrets I myself knew of the Queen, of which Cecil and Walsingham had no idea . . . I could appreciate Elizabeth's decision to ensure that her Maids of Honor need only answer to her, and not to her advisors.

I slanted a glance at Meg without appearing to do so, and saw her straighten ever so slightly under the Queen's regard.

Meg had suffered more than any of the rest of us at the hands of the Queen's advisors. I hadn't liked the girl much when she'd arrived at our door, a dirt-smudged thief of no appreciable merit other than her light fingers and quick mind. But she'd done the best she could, I supposed, and for reasons quite beyond me, she seemed in awe of our Elizabeth. Even now her eyes shone with a curious light, as if the Queen filled her whole world. I didn't know the secret Meg had learned about the Queen, though I could guess. That Meg remained loyal to the woman was the important part, however.

Our resident thief thought Elizabeth would set her free one day, but as God was my witness, if Meg didn't stop adoring the woman, the Queen would never let her go.

"And so now I will give you a commission that is to me alone. You are to tell no one of this, neither guard nor lord nor"—her lips curled slightly—"advisor. Do you understand?"

We murmured our careful assents, and the Queen nodded imperiously. "Good. This night marks the first of a three-day revel culminating my birthday festivities." *And it's about time too. The Queen will be rapidly coming up on her* next *birthday if she doesn't leave off celebrating this one soon.* "As you know, there are several new nobles from Scotland in our midst who do not know the castle and its people well. I need you to circulate among them and learn just what is being discussed when I am not present in the Visitors Apartments."

"The Visitors Apartments?" interjected Anna, perturbed. "You believe you are not being fully briefed on the negotiations with the Lords of the Congregation?"

"It is not a matter of belief; I know I am not," Elizabeth snapped. "I cannot spend the whole of my day closeted with those jabberers. But neither do I imagine that it takes hours upon hours of Cecil's time to result in the scant updates he is providing me. I want to know what they are asking *him* that they are not asking *me*, and what he is granting in return."

Even I was shocked by that. Cecil could not grant the Queen's grace without her knowledge. It was career suicide for him and potentially treasonable as well.

"But he will serve you long and well," said Sophia, in that curiously dead voice of hers. "All your policies his to tell." *Careful, girl.*

"Of course he will," I said quickly to draw Elizabeth's attention away, my tone breathless with ardor. "Cecil would be mad not to do your bidding, Your Grace, or to serve you to the fullest of his ability." The Queen was so startled that her gaze swerved off Sophia and rested upon me, her manner instantly hardening.

"And what of you?" she asked. "I notice you have not been following MacLeod so closely as I would like. What *use* are you to me if you do not obey my command?"

Let me be the first to say it: I really hate the Queen.

"Your Grace," I said, bowing to both compose my face and to curb the sharpness of my tongue. I lifted my head again and spoke with soft assurance. "As I have already shared with you, I learned all that may be useful when the learning was needed—MacLeod and his men have no religious fervor to speak of, but they well and truly despise the French. In that you have their staunch support. If your needs require me to question them further, I will of course begin again at once."

"Hmm," she returned, still scowling at me. "Do that. Find out if the Scottish Highlanders would respond to an English call to arms against the French. Not that I can imagine the French would last long that far north, but they are a tiresome lot."

She turned her gaze to my right. "And you, Meg. I need to verify that what my advisors are telling me is *all* that they are being told and not some abridged account. But I cannot ask such questions myself, precisely. Not with Cecil and Walsingham dogging my heels at every step. You say you are an actress. Could you take on the role of the most important woman in England?"

Beside me Meg gave a quick grin. "I am almost of a height as you, Your Grace, and can make myself seem quite like you indeed. With your meanest castoff costume and a borrowed wig—" Meg tilted her head then and placed her hands upon her hips in a perfect imitation of the Queen, as though she were still a member of the Golden Rose acting troupe that had brought her into our fold—a gaggle of men, women, and children who were all consummate actors . . . and unrepentant thieves. “I cannot spend the whole of my day closeted with those jabberers,” Meg said severely, mimicking the Queen’s tone and cadence precisely. “But neither do I imagine that it takes hours upon hours of Cecil’s time.”

“Ah!” The Queen clapped her hands together, for once looking like the young woman I always forgot she was. I resented Meg for liking Elizabeth so well in that moment, though I knew it was uncharitable of me. Meg did not chafe so much as I under the Queen’s constant demands.

Then again, Meg had never been sent off to giggle over boorish Scotsmen with wandering eyes. And hands.

“I approve,” Elizabeth continued. “The Festival of the Moon will provide us ample opportunity for you. You will dress as me, Meg, and go into the crowd, seeking out any members of the Scottish delegation whom we suspect to be the Lords of the Congregation. Once you gain their ear, ask them plainly what they need of me. I will be curious to know if their requests match those Cecil has shared with me, or if he is hiding something.”

“I understand,” Meg said, and the Queen nodded again.

“There has been a flurry of horsemen arriving today, and I suspect messages will be sent back and forth. I would know them for myself, before Cecil has a chance to refashion their contents to words he considers more palatable to my ear. See that you are ready to act as me, and to report all that you hear.” She paused then, and glanced back to Meg, as if expecting something more than Meg had already given.

“Of course, Your Grace,” Meg said, curtsying for no

apparent reason. She had a habit of that, but it seemed to please Elizabeth.

"Excellent." The Queen crossed her arms and surveyed us again, including even me in her approving gaze. "We'll learn what there is to be learned, and not rely upon the accounts of men who think they know more and better than we do," she said, a thread of defiance in her words. "We begin tonight."

CHAPTER EIGHT

The Festival of the Moon was not an ancient pagan rite, though it was made to look like one. No, it was merely an excuse for another of Elizabeth's balls.

For myself, I ordinarily did not mind the Queen's penchant to spend what money she had in her coffers on revels and routs. I had enough clothing for anything Her Willfulness could foist upon us. But I knew Jane would sooner have her teeth cleaned than stand in the overstuffed Presence Chamber for hours on end, and Sophia was usually a quivering wreck at the idea of a public presentation. At least that had changed. Tonight Sophia would be in attendance, and even hoped to dance with her "betrothed," should Lord Brighton appear as well.

I put my hand to my head just thinking of the complexity of that trial. They should *not* remain betrothed. For all that it was inspired merely by a father's need to protect his daughter, it still was not seemly for this charade to continue.

"Beatrice, can you help with—oof!" Meg was turned around and almost tripping over the enormous court gown the Queen had chosen for this night. We were once more in our schoolroom chamber, and Meg's disguise was masterful: a flame-red wig beset with jewels, the Queen's favorite indigo-blue gown, and Meg's skin powdered to porcelain perfection. As long as the girl could keep from sneezing, she would achieve the impossible. She would be Queen.

The Festival of the Moon would begin in the deepest dark of late evening, with only a scatter of candles lit throughout the Great Hall. Rumors had been put out that Elizabeth would mingle among the guests in a deep blue gown, allowing any and all to bend her ear. Cecil and Walsingham had already made a great noise about how they needed to "protect" Her Majesty, and so they would follow around Elizabeth proper, who would indeed be wearing a dark blue gown.

Except she wouldn't be the only blue-garbed Elizabeth in the room. And in the darkness, no one would know precisely which Elizabeth they'd seen.

After an hour of what would no doubt be a highly raucous interchange between the lords and ladies of the court, the "moon"—a great candelabra of white candles—would be lit by unseen hands and lifted to the sky. Then the real Gloriana, Queen of the Night, would return to the ball with a triumph of music, now miraculously dressed in a gown of pure white to bring the revel to a full burst of celebration. Meg, for her part, would leave the Presence Chamber as well, returning to the festivities as a simple maid once more.

I hurried over to Meg and tossed a cape over her shoulders, but she was still bent over and endeavoring to remove her wig from the bodice's lacings when Anna bit out a command.

"Cecil," she said to us, her voice low and urgent. "Be quick!"

There was nothing for it. Meg stood frozen in the center of the room as Cecil bustled in in a flurry of black robes.

"Sir William!" I protested. "Have a care. The Queen is not—"

"What the deuce are you doing here and not in your chambers, with your own servants to dress you?" Cecil demanded as Meg hunched farther over and bit out a curse that sounded precisely like a peeved Elizabeth. "I cannot talk to you like that!"

"Mayhap I could help you?" I asked as Anna rushed by me to take over my ministrations with the Queen's wig and effectively urge Meg farther into the shadows. "What message can I give the Queen when she is fully dressed?"

"This entire enterprise is folly," gritted out Cecil, in a voice low enough for only me to hear. "Three days of celebrations—" He caught himself, as if remembering to whom he spoke, and he straightened. "Very well," he said, raising his voice loud enough to be heard across the room. "Your Grace, remember that you must remain with me or your guards at all times tonight prior to returning to your chambers to change for your revelation." He said this last word without any sneering inflection at all, and I had to admire the man. I don't think I could have managed it. "Although there will be no opportunity during the ball itself for us to speak, I can join you in your chambers after you have left the event and provide you with the update that you requested."

"Oh, Your Grace," Anna said, a little too loudly. "We'll need to undo the back of your gown to get it straight."

Cecil stiffened. "I will speak with you this evening, Your Grace" he said again. Then he turned on his heel and fled the room.

"Master stroke," I said, turning back to Anna and Meg, the latter of whom was looking a little too red-cheeked for good health. "Are you well, Meg?"

"I was hanging upside down that whole time!" Meg gasped. "You try it, and tell me how it feels!"

We finished our preparations and cloaked Meg in a hooded robe of ermine, then waited for the guards to arrive. I thought about the guards that surrounded Elizabeth at every turn. Were they protecting her—or entrapping her? It was a question I wasn't sure I wanted answered.

I trailed the "Queen's" procession with Anna at my side, and wondered at her stillness. Normally she would be all abuzz with the excitement of another ball, but perhaps she too was tiring of the eternal round of forced merriment.

Anna spoke before I could ask her what was amiss. "I'm going to move off on my own this night," she said. "Will the rest of you be sufficient to make sure Meg comes to no harm?"

"Of course," I said. "Jane is her watch, in any event. That girl can see clearly in the dead of night. I'm just to be on the periphery in case I need to distract anyone."

Anna favored me with a smile. "'Tis a task for which you are well suited."

"I suppose." I smoothed my hand down my own gown of embroidered silk. For all that it was grey and supposedly in keeping with the sumptuary laws that guided our every clothing decision, it still made me feel light, almost ethereal.

Like I could slip away on the mists of dawn, never to return.

Of course, where, then, would I go? I'd been aghast at the idea of being removed to Lord Cavanaugh's estate, far away from Crown and court. Where did I most want to spend the next months and years of my life?

I found I had no answer. So much of my youth had been spent in tireless pursuit of my own wedding, I had no idea what might transpire once I achieved the married state. And now that my wedding had been postponed, I didn't find myself thinking of Cavanaugh as often as I would have expected.

Why was that?

My mood turned unaccountably sad, but entry into the darkened Presence Chamber chased away all other thoughts. The Queen, once again, had outdone herself. The musicians played a haunting melody of lute and harpsichord to evoke an eerie late-summer night, and I found myself drifting along in the sudden darkness in time to the music. I felt Anna leave my side almost immediately, and with a swish of her gown Jane stepped up in her place.

"You look like you've lost all your sunlight," she gibed. "And the night holds naught but shadows for you." She was peering around the darkened room with narrowed eyes, but showed no discomfort.

"It's what I deserve, I daresay," I muttered, hearing too late the sadness still in my voice. Jane glanced sharply at me, and I quickly waved her off. "Pray, don't wait for me. In this darkness I will lose sight of Meg the moment she steps into a knot of three people." I made to move away, but Jane caught my hand.

"He is behind the first banquette and to the left," she said, her voice flat and hard, as if she were giving me the location of a murderer or a madman. "And you do deserve better, Beatrice."

I blinked at her "What?" I asked, completely at sea. "What do you mean?"

At my words, Jane's face took on a cast of bone-deep weariness. She'd thought she was doing me a favor. And instead she'd just realized she was delivering some sort of blow. "I thought you knew," she muttered. She glanced around, but there were no other girls with us. None but myself and Jane, uneasy friends at best—but fellow spies, too. Spies who looked out for each other. *I thought you knew. You deserve better.*

There could be only one person who could betray me, I realized in a flash. "Cavanaugh?" I asked, my words barely audible. The sadness that had been growing within me now made a certain kind of sense.

Jane didn't even bother with a nod. "He—is behind the first banquette and to the left," she said again, the words no longer angry but hollow now. Defeated. "Not alone."

I swallowed, willing myself to speak. "How long?" I asked. "How long have you known? How long has this gone on?"

"Beatrice—"

"Fie, Jane, how long?" *Stupid, stupid, stupid!* I'd been cow-eyed and blind. So wrapped up in my own plans that I'd missed the most obvious of threats to my perfect plan with Lord Cavanaugh.

Another woman.

Jane paused a moment. "I noticed them in each other's

company at odd moments early this summer, but not inappropriately so." She said the words stiffly, as if she were giving a report to the Queen. "It was of no concern to me. You were not betrothed to the man, just dangling him."

I opened my mouth, but swallowed the words just as quickly. Jane wouldn't have known of all my years of planning. She couldn't have known. This wasn't her fault.

"Then you became engaged, and I did not see them together again—until I did. And did again. Last week. This week. The day before your wedding. And then the day after. It seemed I could not look but see them. And when you did not lash out against Elizabeth's cancellation of your wedding, I thought . . . Well, I thought . . ." She shook her head and cursed, looking away.

It was a postponement, I wanted to say. *A postponement, not a cancellation. The wedding would still happen. All my plans would still work out.* But the words would not come.

I reached out and touched Jane's arm. "Thank you," I whispered. And I almost meant it.

Jane stared back at me another moment, hard. Then she melted into the darkness, and I stood there, my mind scrambling. Perhaps Jane was wrong, I thought now, and instantly hope rekindled in my veins. The more I thought on it, the more I knew it to be true. Jane was wrong—had to be wrong. She'd seen a man and a woman together, and had considered it suspicious. I had no doubt her concerns were well intended. For all her strength of sinew, Jane did not have the resolve to lie so easily and well. But what did she know about love? Or of the court, for heaven's sake? Men and women consorted all the time in the halls of Windsor Castle, laughing and flattering and paying undue attention to each other. It was all part of the royal game. But Lord Cavanaugh loved me; I knew he did. He'd promised me his hand in marriage. He'd promised to share his life with me.

And I would prove Jane wrong.

I turned smartly to my right, to where the long tables of refreshments had been placed against the wall, in easy reach of the servants who would be keeping the nobility satisfied with food and drink throughout the long night. My eyes grew accustomed to the murky light, and with a skill born of long practice I shifted through the groping knot of men and women. Court events were always a crush, and darkened revels, well—you knew what to expect going into them.

I'd just come up to the first banquette when I saw them, and I almost shouted with triumph. Ah! So there it was, and I had been vindicated. A man and a woman had paused together, yes, loitering by the refreshment tables. But this was not an issue, given the woman in question. There was no way that Cavanaugh would—that he would choose such a . . . such a—

The scene shifted just a bit, and I stiffened beside a thick stone column, my entire body going cold.

Lord Cavanaugh now stood against the wall, shrouded in what I am sure he thought was total darkness. But the woman gazing up at him seemed lit from within, her beauty plain and without artifice, her eyes wide and clear, her expression luminous. She was a lovely woman, but that was not what made my heart catch in my throat. That was not what had made me assume that this couldn't be a true lovers' interlude. Even until the very end, I had been blinded by my own class prejudices. And who would blame me?

The woman was a *serving maid.*

And she was also, apparently, Lord Cavanaugh's . . . mistress.

I had never seen her before, exactly, but I knew her station by the cant of the head, the cut of the dress. This was a commoner pressed into royal service, whether for the night or for the season, to fetch and carry for the Queen and her court. She likely had rough hands and chapped lips, straw hair beneath her cap and loose teeth, but at this moment, as she stared into Lord Cavanaugh's—my betrothed's—face, all I could see was the ardor of her passion.

And she was Lord Cavanaugh's *mistress*!

Worse—so much worse, so much more impossibly worse—Lord Cavanaugh stared back at her, his face suffused with an adoration so intense, it almost hurt to see. He'd never looked at me like that—never! Even when he held me close, even when he stole kisses from me in a laughing, arrogant seduction, chuckling at my blushes and palming my body as if I were already his own. Never had he once stared at me with eyes full of wonder and a mouth gone slack with desire. Never once!

Fury and humiliation roiled in my gut. I knew it should not matter who it was that Cavanaugh had tumbled. But I had worked so *hard* and so *long* to merit the hand of a true nobleman. The idea that he would cast me aside for anyone burned badly enough. But to know that I was so worthless, that I was so meaningless to him, that my rank and station and education and charm counted for nothing at all, that he would cast me aside for—for—

"My lady." I felt the hand on my shoulder, turning me round even as I felt my vision blur. "It is dangerous for you to move unescorted through such a rough crowd. A pursuer might get quite the wrong idea indeed."

Alasdair MacLeod was there. Of course he was there. Of course he would see this—see me in all my humiliation—and seek only to amuse himself. And I was too numb to deny him.

I could not tell you where we walked, or how, only that an instant later we were swallowed up again in the noise of the ball. Had he seen what I'd seen? Had he seen even worse? I could not speak; I certainly could not stop him. My heart was now hollow, my very face somehow heavy. I felt as if I had tears flowing down the inside of my body, though none would dare escape my eyes. A few steps farther, and I realized we were in the thickest part of the rabble, the laughter and chatter rising above the crash and ramble of music. This was also the darkest part of the room, and a dim part of my mind registered the danger of that. But I couldn't quite bring myself to care.

I could not bring myself to think.

Everything was lost to me, everything was gone. Lord Cavanaugh was in love—and not with me. Never with me.

Everything was lost.

Alasdair tilted my chin up, and I could almost see him now, though my eyes were blanked as if by fog. He shifted closer toward me, and I caught the scent of vanilla and lavender, mixed with the earthier fragrances of leather and open sky. He'd been out riding today, I suspected, no doubt trying to keep pace with the very wind. He shifted again, and I knew he wanted to kiss me. He always wanted to, though I never allowed it. He always looked at me with his dark and intense blue eyes flashing from within the hard, sun-bronzed planes of his face, his powerful hands gentle around me but insistent, so insistent, and his heat so strong, it seemed to light the very air on fire, causing it to flare up around us. He would stare at my eyes, my lips, and his own mouth would open, and it seemed that he could well and truly survive only if he could taste the barest hint of me. And his face would lean toward mine, and his eyes would hold my own gaze—just like now—and he would look at me as if I were his entire world. And I would feel a stirring unlike anything I'd ever felt before, a stirring that I could not control, could not plan for and could no more deny than my own next and ever-more haggard breath, and then—

I blinked.

Alasdair's sigh was ragged. "When you look at me like that, my lady," he breathed, his words low and husky, "you place yourself in greater danger still."

Then suddenly it was all gone—all of it, and I was laid bare before him with only one question that seemed to matter, one question that burned inside me no matter how stupid, how dense, how impossibly pointless but that still I could not keep myself from asking, so desperate was I to know. "Do you—" I swallowed, then blurted my words in a rush, as if I were eight and not eighteen, a stammering girl instead of a full-grown woman. "Do you find me at all a-attractive— Do you, could you— Oh, never *mind*!"

I turned to flee, at once mortified by the words that should have never ever crossed my lips, and certainly not to this oafish Scot who would just as easily laugh at me as speak. But no sooner had I angled away than Alasdair hauled me back again, hard, my back pressed up against his chest as he leaned forward and inhaled deeply, as if he were finding his life's breath anew. His mouth was excruciatingly close to my ear, and when he spoke, his lips brushed against the tender skin, sending a jolt of sensation across the whole of my body.

"Lady Beatrice Elizabeth Catherine Knowles," he murmured, "you've become my very breath, my beating heart. I canna sleep but that I dream of you, I canna wake but that I think of you. You are life and love and magic, in every step you take."

In front of him, my breath hitched, my heart now pounding violently as he moved his left hand down the fitted waist of my gown, firm and powerful and sure.

And then, of course, he kept talking. "But you are as skinny as a chicken, I will give you that."

"Oh!" I thrust myself away from him and propelled myself on sheer anger through the crowd, my cheeks burning as I heard him laugh in a long and knowing roll. So incensed was I that I almost missed Anna entirely, bustling through the crowd on a tear.

"Beatrice!" she squeaked. "There you are. You never will believe— Meg fell into conversation with the young Earl of Southwick, who, due to Meg's magnificent clothing, bearing, mimicry skills—and, no doubt, the darkness of the room—well and truly thought she was the Queen. She picked his pocket before he'd gotten out his tenth word, and passed this along to Jane." She flared a letter in the murk, and I picked up her excitement. "We must read it and quickly, or the Queen's reveal will be here and we'll not have a chance to return it!"

"This way," I said, and hastened to the side of the Presence Chamber, where another table stood with servants at the ready. We circled the table, then plunged into the open doorway, startling a servant whose candle was held high to light the way of the serving staff.

"Your candle, if you please, for just a moment?"

The young man gaped at me, puzzled, but we were beyond him and into the long hallway that led to the kitchens before he could gainsay me. We darted into another room, and I held the flame close as Anna fumbled out the letter, its seal already broken.

"Can't be helped," I said as she mewed her distress. "Look there—it is addressed to Elizabeth herself! What does it say?"

"Reading—reading now," Anna muttered, her finger tracing the page as her eyes memorized everything the letter held. I managed not to scream my frustration as she gasped out her surprise not once but fully three times. Then she was up and assembling the letter again, and we turned at once to go.

"What 'o!" It was the young man from the corridor, come to claim his candle. "A right terrible thing it is, stealing from me when I—"

"Oh, leave off!" I thrust the candle back at the servant as

Anna scooted past, and I frowned as he blustered in confusion. "Do *you* think I'm as skinny as a chicken?"

"What! Well, miss, I surely—"

"Ugh!" I shook my head and hastened after Anna. If we found what we needed to for the Queen, the night would not be a total loss.

But only just.

We burst back out onto the floor, and Anna shoved the letter at me, to complete its return to its rightful owner. I was not as light-fingered as Meg, but I had not lived my life among courtiers for naught. I could slip a letter into a pocket with some credible skill. No sooner had I greeted the young earl with a formal kiss and courtly hug—and replaced the letter just so in the pocket Anna had directed me to—than the melody started to swell to indicate the next stage in the evening's events: the lighting of the "moon" and the revelation of Gloriana.

From all corners of the room, Elizabeth's ladies-in-waiting glided through the crowd with lit tapers, each adding their flame to the enormous candelabra that stood barricaded off in the center of the floor. They accomplished this with impressive speed, returning to gather at the entryway while they awaited the Queen, their tapers still lit. Then, with a surge of music, the chandelier was hoisted up by a half dozen black-clad men in an upper balcony, so that it soared up into the space above the hall.

I had to admit, it was impressive. The Queen might have been many things, but she certainly knew how to make an entrance.

No sooner had the candelabra been secured than another surge of music announced the Queen's entry. The crowd gasped and held its breath, mesmerized the moment she stepped into the light. As if they wouldn't have gasped anyway, even if Elizabeth had shown up as a milkmaid.

But this was no milkmaid.

Gloriana Elizabeth Regnant stood at the front of her Presence Chamber like a goddess in our midst. Her hair was sewn with dozens of diamonds and pearls, and there were more pearls at her neck and wrists. Her gown was a gleaming swath of diaphanous white silk, slashed to reveal panels of shimmering silver satin. Another rope of pearls spanned her waist, veeing down over her skirts as if she'd tethered the very stars of heaven for her gown.

The gathered assembly broke out into wild applause, the noise shocking in the hall but serving to please Elizabeth like no other reaction, especially as it was unforced. These were not commoners stupefied by Her Royal Magnitude. These people in many ways were nearly her equals, yet in this moment she had taken their breath away.

As her gaze swept the room, noting her admirers with shrewd calculation, I clapped mightily along with the rest of them. For despite our obvious adoration, all of us knew how quickly the Queen could decide to take our breath away for good.

CHAPTER NINE

It was midnight before we could meet with the Queen—and even then, not in our own bedchamber. Cecil had taken to posting guards at the door to keep track of us, and though Jane and Meg had tried ceaselessly to find hidden escape routes from the room, they had not been successful. Of course, those corridors had to be there; Windsor could not be so riddled with secret passageways that the *one* place that was purely inaccessible was a room traditionally occupied by unmarried women. It made no sense. And yet, we hadn't found them, so there we were, back in our schoolroom.

A room surrounded by secret passageways that we could easily check.

Since our schoolroom had not been used much of late for its intended purpose, the long study table had been set off to the side, to allow us to gather the chairs around in a tight circle, that we might speak with even less chance of being heard.

In the center of that circle now sat Anna, her hands folded on her lap and her eyes alight with intensity. "I am telling you, I am not mistaken," she said. "The hand was disguised, but the Reverend John Knox wrote that letter, not 'John Sinclair' as the signature claims. I would swear it."

Jane nodded. "If you say it is, then so it is. You'll get no argument from me." She glanced to the door, then stood and drifted away from us.

"But does he think Elizabeth is stupid?" I protested, mainly to legitimately place "stupid" so close to the Queen's name. "Surely he knew he would be caught out. She hates John Knox—he knows that. Why would he send her a letter she would readily recognize as his own?"

"Well, for one, his hand was disguised. Heavily." Anna's tone was just the slightest bit peevish. "I am quite good at what I do, you know." She waved off my apology and continued on. "And two, it's entirely possible that he never intended the letter to actually reach her. If he is aware that Cecil is reading all of the Queen's correspondence and that the letter would never get reviewed by her own eyes, or perhaps in only a cursory fashion, well . . . perhaps he grew more bold."

We sat back and pondered that. The letter begged prettily for the Queen's intercession into the Scottish rebellion, with arms and men and money. But the Queen and Knox were avowed enemies, and she would never openly support him. Cecil no doubt knew this. Was Cecil trying to secure the Queen's aid without fully apprising her of who specifically she would be helping? Was he aware of Knox's duplicity? Or had he even seen this letter yet? The seal had been broken, after all. . . .

"She won't be happy," Meg mused. "She puts too much store in how she is perceived. This is an attempt to dupe her, no matter how benign."

"But it's for the good of England too," Anna pointed out. "Let's say we tell her, 'Och, you're being played the fool here, but go along with it.' Will she believe us, or will her outrage color her perceptions and lead her to a different conclusion from the one that's wise for England?"

I gave a labored sigh. More than any of the other girls, I knew the right answer here, much as it pained me to admit it. "We should do it this way—"

"The Queen." Jane's words were a mere murmur from the door, but we were up and turning sharply, sinking at once into our line of curtsies that the Queen favored so well.

"Up, up. I have little time. Cecil is at my heels like a baying hound." The Queen waved to us impatiently. "What is your report?"

I felt the girls' eyes upon me, and I stepped forward. "Your Grace, Meg was in fact successful in her role as you. Though, only because the darkness cloaked her so well could she carry the day." In truth Meg had played a better Elizabeth than Elizabeth herself, but this was not the time to belabor that point. "She lifted a letter from a young Scottish earl, a letter penned to you from a man who named himself Sinclair."

"Sinclair?" The Queen frowned. "I know no lord named Sinclair in the Scottish ranks."

I bowed to her. "It was a subterfuge, my Queen, from a man desperate for your aid, and knowing that he needed you more than he needed his own pride. He disguised his hand,

and changed his name, but Anna recognized him for who he really is."

That caught her attention, as I knew it would. The Queen's brows lifted. "He lied to me?"

"Only that you might read his words without judging the source, and decide on the merit of his cause and not his person," I said quickly. "He does not know your mind rests ever on the good of the state and not on your personal opinions about its servants."

The Queen was nodding along with me, as if she agreed in my noble assessment of her dispassionate rule. There was no getting around this next part, though, so I plunged directly in. "The letter was written in fact by John Knox."

"Knox!" That drew her up short. "He is an *abomination*."

"And he is groveling at your feet, for he cannot do anything without you." I nodded firmly, trying to ensure that I kept the Queen's head bobbing along. "Knox needs your support to oust the French Regent Mary de Guise and all her men at arms. He knows it plainly. He also knows you detest him, so he is adding his voice to the Protestant cause in the only way he feels you would find palatable. It was a gamble on his part—he must know for certain you would figure out his game. But his need is great enough that he could only try to appeal to your desire for an allied isle, despite your opinions of him."

"Hmmm," Elizabeth mused, tilting her head to the side. "You agree with this assessment, Anna? I assume you were the one to read the letter?"

"Indeed I was, Your Grace," Anna said, her voice uncharacteristically serious, making her seem older than her seventeen years. "The letter is now safely returned to the earl's pocket, but Beatrice is quite right. When you receive the letter in hand, it is up to you whether you will unmask its author to your advisors—but you will know the man straight out, and why he put forth his words in such a way."

"Whether I would have known it or not is not a sure thing," the Queen said, showing a remarkable candor. "But in either event, I know it now. And you say you returned this letter?" This question was put to Meg, who curtsied, as I knew she would.

"Yes, Your Grace. The earl was none the wiser for its temporary misplacement."

"Very well." She nodded. "Tomorrow is the minstrel performance. Nothing much will happen before that happy event, with all of the court sleeping off my wine and good nature. But the final event of my birthday celebrations is the Harvest Festival, two evenings hence. For that you must—"

But her words were cut off as Cecil rounded into the room, the irritation on his face wiped clean away as Elizabeth turned to him and he bowed deeply. "Your Grace," Cecil said after he straightened. "Though the hour is late, I would speak with you. I have summarized correspondence for your review."

She nodded benignly at him, but there was no missing the challenge in her gaze. "Of course," she said. "But the hour is late, as you say. I shall look forward to reading it myself, rather than taxing you with a summary." She strode past him through the open doorway, head high and shoulders straight.

So imperious was her gait that Cecil blinked at her, then glanced back at us.

We all smiled as innocently as possible. He looked pained again, then left the room.

We received no new assignments for the next day's performance, nor for the Harvest Festival, but that was just as well. The court seemed at last to be tiring of the endless roll of entertainment. Instead we were set upon once more by tutors who seemed intent on teaching us a world's worth of knowledge in a few short days—art history and church history in particular. We all remarked upon it. What had Elizabeth learned that had convinced her we should know who the Church's favorite goldworkers had been in the twelfth century? Who could possibly care?

As for me, my own discoveries weighed heavily on my mind. How should I manage the indiscretions of Lord Cavanaugh? And should I—could I—tell the Queen?

The other maids were kind enough not to air the distasteful subject to me, though they had to have discussed it among themselves. In truth a titled lord enjoying the services of a mistress was commonplace in the court. I knew that. Of course I knew that. And for all of my seeming sophistication, I also knew that I was an untutored girl—not trained in the relations between a man and a woman. Who would train me, after all? My mother was all but mad, I refused to speak of it with my father, and my fellow maids were far less facile with men than I was. It's possible that Walsingham could help—I rather thought he would appreciate having a sultry seductress in the group who could put actions behind her words—but the very thought of approaching him made me ill.

So it was perhaps not surprising that Cavanaugh had found solace in the arms of a more experienced woman. But really . . . *a serving wench*?

And what did it say about me that I was mostly offended not by the woman's existence but by her station?

I didn't want to think on that too long. But I also couldn't bring myself to tell the Queen about the situation. The words just wouldn't come.

Further, I had no idea how she would react. Use Cavanaugh's indiscretion to advance her own aims? Laugh in my face and tell me to grow up and accept the fact that my husband would not be solely my own? Unless the Queen was forced into action, she would likely never do anything about Cavanaugh's mistress, I realized. She would merely use it as yet another reason to mock me.

After that, my mind was set. I could not tell the Queen straight out. Instead, for two days, I roamed Windsor Castle as always, smiling, laughing, flirting . . . and dying a little more each moment.

And now we had finally reached the Harvest Festival—the last of Elizabeth's birthday festivities, thank heavens. It was styled as a more traditional festival, not unlike ones held in villages throughout all of England at the close of a successful season. The Presence Hall was lit up like full day, and there were savory pies and sweetmeats of every description for the guests to gorge themselves upon.

I hovered near the tables, too distracted to eat, but I

could not deny that Alasdair's words from two nights before did bait me. I was hardly "skinny." The fact that I was not as round and buxom as a tavern wench notwithstanding, I hardly looked like a sickly waif. Perhaps a little hollow, but who could blame me? My betrothed had found another, and my future was ruined.

And speaking of my betrothed . . . I searched the corners again, the tiny alcoves, as I made my way around the hall, laughing and dancing with this courtier and that, as the Queen had decreed. It was not so difficult to find Lord Cavanaugh, now that I knew he'd be skulking in the shadows.

And the woman he was eyeing so lasciviously mere days past his own postponed wedding, in front of God, the world, and the entire assembled court? Yes, it had to be said. Not only was she pretty, sweet, and apparently biddable, to accept my lord's attentions in such a public place, but she was far more shapely than I.

It all hit me at once then, there in the Queen's Presence Chamber, surrounded by people I'd spent my entire life deceiving. Here, at the very end of my campaign for an inviolate position in the court, for the safe haven of marriage and respectability, when triumph had seemed assured and all that had been left was to bring one benign and apparently respectable man to heel . . . I had failed. I had been tricked, made to look the fool. I had been thrown over like so much linen on washing day, so inconsequential that Cavanaugh had not even thought to keep his dalliance with another woman secret bare days after our own sacred union had nearly been consummated. I could feel the prying eyes of the court upon me now. They knew—not all of them, perhaps. And perhaps not everything. But enough of them nevertheless were chuckling behind their elegant fans and upraised fingers, laughing at poor, stupid Beatrice who thought she knew so much and yet could not even guess at her own betrothed's indiscretion.

I had been cheated.

Betrayed.

Humiliated.

So I perhaps could be forgiven for what happened next.

Cavanaugh and his mistress had drawn themselves neatly behind a temporarily hung curtain of flame orange, a testament to the colors of a very English autumn. The bolt of cloth was close enough to the dance floor to warrant concern for any man with his blood still in his brain, but apparently that requirement did not currently fit Lord Cavanaugh. When I saw him sink into an embrace with the woman, I whirled back to the floor, accepting the first gentleman's arm that was proffered to me. The Queen herself had taken to the floor during this country dance, and we soon were swirling and whirling in the rush of music and laughter.

I was not laughing, however. I was far from laughter, as every wilder turn made the orange curtain flutter just enough for me to see my betrothed in a clinch with his ladylove.

I couldn't bear it anymore. I wouldn't be made the fool.

He needed to pay for this.

And then the Queen moved from the center of the floor to dance along the edges, twisting and turning through the arms of her courtiers. It took a bit of maneuvering, but I finally worked myself into position a few couples ahead of the Queen, madly whipping around courtiers and ladies alike, ducking under arms and smiling broadly, as if I had not a care in the world. Always watching, always judging. If Cavanaugh had chosen any of a dozen moments to step away from the floor, to break off his kiss with the woman in his arms, then I would have abandoned my campaign to unmask him before the Queen. I would instead have sought him out—talked to him—perhaps made him see reason . . .

But no. With every turn as the music built and crashed around us, with every wider arc, he seemed to draw closer to the woman, not farther away, gathering her in his arms as if she truly were the love of his life, the light of his night and day.

And so, in the final twisting, snaking rush of the dance, when I spun out to the farthest outreach of our expanding circle, I caught up the edge of the fluttering curtain and gave it a hard, twisting snap, causing it to flare up. Then I dropped the cloth just as quickly, as I whirled and twirled away. I was fully twenty feet past the curtain when the music abruptly stopped, but my work was done. The curtain had been yanked hopelessly askew, revealing all. The two young lovers looked up, aghast, as all eyes of the court turned to the sudden revelation.

None more so than the Queen's, whose position in the dance had been timed perfectly, as I had known it would be.

She now stood directly in front of them.

The moment stretched out, long and taut. I turned, as if I could not understand the reason for the sudden hush that had come over the room, and saw Lord Cavanaugh set aside his lady fair with a thrusting shove. Dutifully I put my hands up to my cheeks, as if I were shocked—*shocked*—at what my eyes did plainly see. Cavanaugh's mistress, for her part, looked more startled than embarrassed, but she sank down into a curtsy, then slipped nimbly away, disappearing into a side door with the quickness of a cat. She was not to blame, after all. She was not a noble.

Lord Cavanaugh was.

"My good Lord Cavanaugh," the Queen said coolly, her tone brooking no question but that everyone in the room would hear and know her wrath. "While it does our heart good to see you quite recovered from the disappointment of your postponed nuptials, it is perhaps a step too far you have taken? Do you not respect the virtue of this court?"

Cavanaugh died a thousand deaths in that moment. There was really no explaining his actions, and he was a shrewd enough courtier to know it. "Forgive me, Your Grace and one and all," he said instead. How thin his voice sounded, I realized suddenly, even at its loudest pitch. How reedy and slight, like the man's own character. "I was caught up in the joyous celebration, and did not mean to offend."

"Well. Offend you have. You may retire for this evening, as the celebration has quite undone you." The Queen's eyes swept the room, finding me with my hands now clasped tightly at my waist. "'Tis not the only apology that must be made this night, and reparations given."

The tiniest thread of alarm skated through me. To the gathered crowd, the Queen implied that Cavanaugh had *me* to apologize to as well, as indeed he should. If he'd not fallen in love with a woman other than his betrothed, none of this would have happened!

But I knew Elizabeth better than nearly anyone else in the room. The flame-haired shrew laid this disruption at my feet.

And reparations would be given.

CHAPTER TEN

At the Queen's command the music started up again, and I turned away from Cavanaugh's outraged face as Meg rushed up to me, Sophia at her side.

"Well! That was more excitement than I was expecting this night," Meg said, drawing my arm into hers. To my surprise Sophia pulled my left arm into her embrace as well, though she was a good deal shorter than me. The two walked me off the dance floor as if I might be attacked.

"Your heart is so heavy and dark, Beatrice." Sophia sighed, her eyes seeming to search the room without seeing anyone. "Would that I could ease your pain, but I have seen your path. There's no way out but through."

I exchanged a startled glance with Meg. Then by common accord we stopped and gave our attention to Sophia. "Are you feeling well, Sophia?" I asked.

"Is your, ah, betrothed here?" Meg's words trailed mine by only a heartbeat.

Sophia, for her part, merely beamed at us. "I am well, and Lord Brighton is well. We danced the opening set, and then he retired. He thinks I do not know of his plan to protect me. He does not realize I have always known, though even I refused to admit it." She sighed happily. "Now I am only glad that I do not hold this secret alone. It paints it all in a different hue."

That was all well and good, but it wasn't Sophia that I was most concerned about at the moment. "Um, Sophia," I began, leaning in close. "What exactly do you mean about 'There is no way out but—'"

"My lady." The booming voice broke over us, and I was startled as a hand suddenly gripped my arm. I looked up into Alasdair's face, which looked grimmer than I'd ever seen it. "A dance, my lady," he said. It was not a request.

I slanted a glance back to the floor. Another country dance was in the offing, a Trenchmore. And I'd had my fill of dancing. "I must decline, good sir," I said sweetly. "I find I am quite fatigued."

If anything his face grew darker. "Then a walk to revive you," he said firmly, and pulled my hand over his arm as if he possessed me, body and soul. I was about to object, when he looked at me with such intensity that I would have stepped back if I could have reclaimed my own arm. "Don't," he bit out.

"I would be honored," I replied archly, drawing myself up to my haughtiest. He barely nodded to a bemused Meg and a now radiant Sophia before he tugged me off to stalk his way down the long chamber, a crowd of onlookers scattering out of our way.

We'd gone for nearly a hundred paces like that, not

speaking, when finally I'd had enough. "Did you want my time for a purpose, sir, or do you simply wish to ensure I have my exercise?"

"Oh, I think you've done enough *exercising* for one night," Alasdair growled. He'd found the one area of the Presence Chamber that was not choked with people, the open space near the great hall's entrance, where the guards now milled around. He positioned me against the wall, well away from him for propriety's sake, and planted his fists on his hips. "Now explain to me why all of *that* was necessary. The ways of you English make my head hurt."

"Why all of *what* was necessary?" I asked in return. Did the whole of the court know that I'd staged Cavanaugh's downfall?

"Always scheming, aren't you?" Alasdair's words were mocking. He leaned closer to me. "I watch you, my lady. The moment you step into a room and the second you leave it. I watch you laugh and smile, and I watch you frown and calculate. So, aye, I saw you lift that curtain away to expose your betrothed to the Queen. What I want to know is, why did she order you to do it?"

"Wha—what?" I stammered, staring at him, wide-eyed, as a roil of emotions rushed through me. First the idea that he should be watching me, then the realization that he'd caught me out, and then the confusion over why he thought the Queen would ever order a disruption in her own hall. "How can you ask such a thing?"

It was a stall, and he knew it, but even I was surprised at his curse as he looked away. He folded his powerful arms over his chest, and I could not help but think of those same arms around me. "You do everything she says, don't you?" he asked irritably. "Even when it makes no sense."

My cheeks burned, but I could not bring myself to admit the truth—that the Queen had not ordered the public chastisement of Lord Cavanaugh; that in fact she was likely incensed with me more than with any cheating nobleman. It was humiliating enough to know that Cavanaugh preferred to hold someone else in his arms, that he didn't love me—that he had likely never loved me. I'd been fooled—deeply and unutterably tricked. And I should have known better. I was Beatrice Knowles, the darling of the court. The schemer and plotter, the keeper of secrets. I was the one who was supposed to have the upper hand in all things—but mostly, especially, in my own marital negotiations. Cavanaugh was supposed to love me. To be entranced by me. To want nothing more than for me to be his bride. It had all been perfectly planned from the moment I'd met the arrogant nobleman four years earlier, when he'd still been but a boy and I a dutiful member of Queen Mary's court. I'd seen him and I'd chosen him.

And I'd just assumed he'd chosen me, too.

Opposite me, Alasdair sighed. "I should not expect more of you," he said, almost more to himself than to me. That brought me up short—how dare he judge me at all! He was from Scotland, for the love of heaven. "You are in service to your Queen."

I paused with my response, ever careful of my words. "I am in service to her, but she is a monarch who should best be judged by her politics, which are ever for the good," I said, trying to work my way away from my personal issues and back to where our conversation rightly belonged, on the foibles of nations and their royal caretakers. "My Queen wants only what is best for England, and what is good for Scotland, too."

He gazed down at me then, his eyes now taken with a light not unlike the fervency I'd seen in Sophia's stare. "And what about what is good for Beatrice Elizabeth Catherine Knowles?" he asked. "Does the Queen want what's best for her?"

Not until a cold day dawns in hell. "Of course," I said smoothly. "As it serves the good of her people, she is stalwart in her care and protection. Do you not follow the direction of your chieftain, knowing that he wishes most to protect his own?"

That caused Alasdair to laugh roughly. "You've clearly not met my chieftain," he said, but at least he was smiling again. "Still not right, though. The Queen's command has put you at risk, which makes it rash and not terribly smart. Your wispy English lord looked like he did not take well to public attack. I'd stay well clear of him till his temper cools. It's always the little ones you have to watch out for."

"As I suspect he's no longer my betrothed, I doubt I'll be much in his company," I observed coolly, trying not to laugh myself at Alasdair's characterization.

The words caught him up short. "Not your betrothed?" he asked, slanting me a glance. "In truth? *That* bit of non-sense would undo a marriage contract?"

"That bit of nonsense—yes! Yes, it would!" I said fiercely. Or at least it should. I remembered again my father squabbling with Cavanaugh over that very document. Well, they could both sit and stew. I'd find another man to secure my position in court; hopefully one who was not so easily led astray by rounded curves and fluttering lashes.

"Then I take back all my harsh words against your Queen, my lady." Alasdair's lips parted fully into a wolfish leer, and he reached out for my hand, drew it to his lips—effectively pulling me closer to him as he did so. I tried not to hitch my breath as his lips brushed against the sensitive skin of my fingers, my heart positively stopping in surprise. "I rather like this turn of events."

CHAPTER ELEVEN

Dawn had barely broken the next morning when I was summoned into the Queen's Privy Chamber. Seeing the Queen at any hour was never a thrill, but being hastened into her presence early was a particular chore. Worse, I felt a pounding dread with every step I took. None of the other Maids of Honor had been summoned.

Had I really upset her that greatly with my revelation of Cavanaugh's duplicity? Did she truly care that much that I had been driven to lay bare his lies—and that I had chosen not to lie myself, to protect his good name?

My doubts tasted like ash in my mouth.

I passed the stone-faced guards at the doorway, unsurprised to see both Cecil and Walsingham flanking the Queen. Whenever she wanted to throw her weight around, she preferred to have those two dancing in attendance. They both bolstered her power and needed to be reminded that she was the one making the final decisions—in my life, as well as her own.

I swept into a low curtsy, preparing for the long count.

The Queen didn't disappoint. She allowed me to stay in obeisance while she began her tirade.

"Who do you think you are?" she asked into the air above my head. "You, with your petty sense of what is right and what is suitable, with your infantile quest for justice to your wounded sensibilities. You chose the grandest stage of all to unmask Cavanaugh's indiscretion, leaving me no recourse at all but to chastise him. Do you have any idea of the damage you have caused to your own fortunes, let alone mine own?"

Whatever I had expected the Queen to say, this was not it. I was staring at the rushes, scrambling for thoughts, when Elizabeth suddenly realized that my brain was probably working. "Rise!" she commanded. "Face me!"

I stood up promptly, settling my legs beneath my skirts in a vain attempt to speed the blood returning to my feet, lest she ask me to walk anytime soon. I knew better than to directly oppose her words, but she still was seeking validation of her suspicions. She did not have me yet.

"Your Grace," I said deferentially. "While I cannot deny a certain . . . satisfaction in seeing Cavanaugh so publicly set down, I assure you my hands were not involved in his unmasking, verily I swear." And this was true enough. Only one of my hands had been involved in that merry trick. Not both.

"That's not possible," she snapped back at me. "It was too neatly done. You cannot deceive me, Beatrice. I've known you too long. Always, always you want more." The Queen punctuated her words by rapping a folded fan against the edge of her throne. "You could not be satisfied with just any man at court. You set your cap for one of the oldest and richest families in the realm. You could not wait for a seemly time to push for a betrothal. You choose *August*, when I had to find something to take the court's minds off the disruptions of the castle. And when your marriage had been rightly delayed to keep those same minds on me, where they should be, you somehow found out about Cavanaugh's mistress and reacted like a petulant child."

I couldn't help my eyes from widening. "You—" I swallowed. "You knew?"

"Of course I knew, you imbecile!" Elizabeth leaned forward in her throne, her eyes shooting daggers. "I know everything that takes place in this castle that might impact my plans, and quite a fair amount more than that, as well you should know." That little line was meant more for her advisors, but I took the blow as if it had been intended for me. "Lord Cavanaugh had decided to buy my graces with his coin, and I had decided to let him, which was the only reason why this marriage was going forward. That, and he promised to rid me of your presence the moment I decided I no longer needed you."

Anger and outrage welled up within me, and it was all I could do not to spit fire. Instead I curtsied. Meg was clearly onto something with this. "Your Grace," I murmured as I did so.

The move seemed to mollify her, and as I rose back up, her face had lost some of its mottled fury. "But now you've made a mess of it, as you are wont to do. I have had to cancel your betrothal altogether."

I allowed myself a small shiver of relief at that. I'd worried that she would still tie me to Cavanaugh, but it appeared that—for the moment—I had some reprieve. Sadly, my respite did not last long. "I shall have to create an entirely new focus for the court, however, so the furor of Cavanaugh's disgrace can diminish and he can reinsert himself into my favor."

She mulled over that, tapping the fan against her chin, her eyes as flat and lifeless as a snake's. "Hmmm," she muttered. "I may have just the thing."

That . . . didn't sound good.

But I had no way of knowing what the Queen's plans were. She dismissed me summarily, and I had hardly made it back to the maids' chambers when another summons came round, announcing a court-wide audience in the Presence Chamber at ten o'clock yet that morning.

"What could this be now?" Jane grumbled. "I canna bear another dance, I will tell you plain."

"It seems unlikely that she'd schedule another frolic," Anna said. "The castle staff are all but dead on their feet." Still she frowned too, looking up from the three opened manuscripts she was perusing, no doubt trying to catch out the translations in some fatal flaw. "What happened with her, Beatrice?"

"She said that she had to create a distraction," I said dully. I was suddenly tired. So, so tired. I could no longer care about queens and their distress. I frowned, however, to see my fellow maids staring at me. "What did you expect?" I asked irritably. "She holds me to blame for the court *learning* of Cavanaugh's indiscretion, not him for actually *being* indiscreet. If anything, I'm an infant for even assuming I could have attracted the attentions of a man who would love me for me alone." I put my hands to my face, willing the world away for just one precious moment. "She's probably right."

I felt the wave of surprise slide through the room—not at the bitterness of my words but at the fact that I would share my feelings so openly. Bare honesty wasn't my usual practice or inclination. Not even among them. This truly had been a night and a day for revelations.

"Well," Anna broke in firmly, as ever at my side, though I did nothing to deserve her loyalty. "She is right in thinking this will distract the court, as long as the announcement does not have anything to do with Cavanaugh directly. I heard he was quite unwilling to leave his apartments after his shaming last night."

"Tell me you're not serious." I raised my head, then rolled my eyes at her serious expression. "Oh, leave off!" I scoffed. "It's not like the man was stoned at the stocks. He was interrupted in the midst of kissing someone other than his betrothed at a ball. He will survive it."

"He's still a man," Sophia said, her gaze shifted to the right, as if she could see something in the walls that was hidden from the rest of us. "If this weren't all for the best, I would be far more concerned for you, Beatrice. Lord Cavanaugh is more dangerous in his disgrace than he ever was in his pride. You should have a care around him."

I frowned at her, a tremor of unease resettling itself in my bones. Alasdair had said much the same thing when he'd thought Cavanaugh still had some contractual hold over me. "Sophia, I never know if you're speaking from knowledge gained in this world or out of it."

She blushed, looking impossibly beautiful, even in her simple brown frock. "Then you know exactly how I feel. But I do believe I speak the truth, Beatrice, no matter how I know it to be true. Cavanaugh does not wish you well."

"Well, I cannot say I wish him well either, so we are matched in that."

"But he has the power still," Meg mused. Her opinions on marriage were already well known in our small group—the further away she could get from that vaunted state, the happier she would be. "If he wanted to maintain your betrothal, and was thwarted in that, he is dangerous. If he is glad to have the betrothal severed, but is nevertheless affronted by the turn of events, he is still dangerous. And if he seeks to regain you as his bride, he is perhaps the most dangerous of all."

"And since when have you become an expert on men?" I asked archly, but there was far less sting in my words than there used to be. If I was losing my taste for sparring with Meg, then perhaps there *was* reason to worry.

Meg, for her part, shook her head. "Men, not much at all. But the roles men played in the Golden Rose, I know well. There seemed to be no end to the outrage they would express over quite the most minor of slights—and if it was the woman whom they'd set upon to claim as their own who was doing the slighting, well. Heaven and earth could not stand in their way until they'd meted out punishment."

That pronouncement caught us all up a little short. It was Jane who broke the silence. "I can, ah, see why you might not be interested in marriage, Meg," she observed dryly.

Sophia's laugh was a tinkle of amusement, but it jarred us anew just the same. "Meg, she will marry, and she'll have us all to apologize to." Then she blinked, the color rising swiftly in her cheeks. "Oh!" she said. "That thought just came to me, Meg. I've no way of knowing, truly—"

"Be at peace, be at peace," Meg said, raising her hands to forestall Sophia's continued apologies. "I cannot marry while I'm serving the Queen, and I have easily another year of that before Cecil or Walsingham will set me loose. Whole lives can change in that time. We can talk of marriage another day."

The clock struck nine bells then, and we hastened to get into our court finery. Though an assembly was nowhere near as stiff as a formal event, there still were protocols to be followed and laces to be drawn. It seemed we spent most of our days tying up our gowns or unlacing them, and our sleeves and collars and skirts besides. Ordinarily I found the process relaxing, but not this day. I doubt I'd felt a moment's peace since I'd stepped foot inside Saint George's Chapel mere days before, prepared to become a bride.

Within the hour we were at our appointed places in the Queen's retinue, looking on with fervent interest at anything Her Royal Drama felt inclined to do. The Queen was circulating among her cherished nobles, being fawned over and flattered, and thanked ever and anon for her gracious feasting of the three nights past. The whole of the court swelled the Presence Chamber, it seemed, though I knew better. Lord Cavanaugh had not made an appearance.

I'd received my share of idle looks and not so idle speculation as well. Still, I remained fairly certain that my unmasking of Cavanaugh and his skirt had not been judged to be mine own doing. I too had spies throughout the castle, and they'd reported to me that I was mostly pitied and occasionally the recipient of someone's knowing nod about how brazen girls never got their man. But both of these reactions were preferable to having the court know the truth.

A steward rang a bell, and the Queen turned, her eyes alight with mischief. For just a moment they rested upon me before sliding away, and I felt every muscle in my body tense, every nerve go as taut as a bowstring. That look had spoken volumes in its brief touch. *I told you I was stronger than you*, it seemed to say. *And now you will pay for your impertinence.*

Elizabeth mounted the few short steps that led to her dais, and then caused a brief flurry of laughter when she spun around, glistening in her gown of sunshine yellow, which was shot through with amber embroidery and ribbons the color of cinnamon. "What, ho, but we have had a merry time of it, have we not these past few weeks?" she declared, her voice overloud in the crowded space, as if anyone dared whisper in her presence.

A smattering of cheers broke out, and she put her fists into her skirts, playfully tilting her head beneath her diamond-studded crown. "I say, but have we not?" she challenged again. This time the crowd responded far better, giving out lusty "huzzah"s and applauding Elizabeth wildly.

"But!" she cried, and raised her hand to further command the attention of the room. "I am here to tell you that our delight is not at an end. We have yet another surprise for your delectation, which I am exceedingly happy to share."

Beside me Jane's groan was so heartfelt that I could practically hear it vibrating the rushes, but the Queen was not yet finished.

"We—the whole of the court, whoever can ride or be carried, shall depart the confines of Windsor for a very special progress! Now, what do you think of that!"

The cheers came again, but some were more forced now, though the applause was loud and long. I could understand the hesitation of some of the savvier members of court. The Queen went on progress several times a year to allow her castles' armies of servants to turn her royal residences upside down, ridding their halls of fouled rushes, the scraps of feasts, stained tapestries, and every manner of garbage that was constantly piling up in corners and cabinets and undercrofts. But while her castle was getting cleaned, some poor soul of a nobleman was forced to feed and entertain Her Royal Exactitude in the manner to which she had quickly become accustomed.

I immediately began making lists in my head. She doubtless expected her Maids of Honor to go with her, which meant traveling clothes and lesser gowns that could be worn in various ways to cut down on the packing. Meg and Jane were barely civilized as it was, so I'd need to offer them additional castoffs in time for them to try them on and resew as needed. Travel always was a bother, but at least it wasn't wintertide. We could still get by with only a few trunks of clothing for the lot of us.

"Where? Where, do you say?" The Queen trilled in

triumph, laughing at the palpable excitement of her court. I wonder if she had any idea how devastating her progresses could be upon the households on whom she descended. The great cloud of dust that accompanied a Queen's progress was as fell as the harbinger of doom. I glanced idly up then, my mind still working, and was transfixed to see the Queen's gaze upon me once more.

No! I thought, but a scream was already starting within me, dancing along my blood, battering my bones. *No, no, no, no, NO!*

"We shall go to the home of my dearest of maids, Lady Beatrice Knowles!" the Queen shouted out in counterpoint to my unspoken wail, as all of the blood in my body rushed to my ears. *She can't do this. She won't do this!* She had to know that my homestead was a falling-down relic of a castle, and a heavy day's ride—or more likely two, all the way to Northampton. She had to know that we had barely enough coin to fill our own tables with food, both for ourselves and our retainers. She had to know that the harvest was just now upon us and the servants would need to be working the fields and orchards, not playing host to a brawl of overstuffed courtiers and spoon-pinching ladies. She had to know!

But the Queen only stared at me, her smile broad and damning.

Oh, she knew, all right.

"Make ready, one and all of you," she cried. "We depart in two days' time for Marion Hall!"

CHAPTER TWELVE

And it would have been only one long, hard, miserable day of travel too, once we'd finally gotten on the road. Except for the rain. Which made it two.

After a truly remarkable run of sunshine and warm breezes at summer's end in Windsor, we seemed to race toward the chill grey censure of winter the closer to Marion Hall we rode.

The two days Elizabeth had originally predicted it would take the court to assemble its collective self for the great lurch north had mercifully turned into five. And as I had sent both my father and a brace of riders galloping off within three hours of her pronouncement, I had relatively high hopes that my ancestral home would at least be swept out by the time the Queen arrived.

Father, for his part, had seemed blithely unconcerned about the progress, until I'd shown him the household accounts that I'd received just two weeks past from our manager. Then he'd understood. The Queen would be bringing fully fifty people with her, including servants, ladies, courtiers, and guards. All fifty had to be fed. All fifty had to be housed. All fifty had to be given free run of our stores of ale and spirits. Father had blustered, then ranted, then eventually had come round to the same realization that I'd had there in the Presence Chamber, as Elizabeth had sung out her gloating command: There was nothing we could do but open our coffers for the Queen.

After that, he'd left without another word.

Now we five Maids of Honor plodded on in the pouring rain atop steaming, bedraggled steeds, having gained Elizabeth's permission to range ahead of the court proper to ensure the hall was presentable for her. At first she'd seemed against this idea, but after several hours of steady rain she'd seen the right of it. Better to be certain that there would be a warm fire and a full table of food at the end of your journey than to needle your fellow travelers. Elizabeth herself would have preferred to race ahead with us, I was certain. For all her legions of flaws, the woman did love fast horses.

I lifted my head, peering out from beneath the rim of my cloak. "Anna, except for the smell"—*which was deadly*—"these cloaks are a work of genius."

"The smell almost makes them not worth it." Anna's laugh was rueful. "But it is good to be dry, and to have a chance to test them on horseback." A month ago and more, now, she'd coated plain woolen cloaks with a thick salve of lanolin, reasoning that if it kept the sheep dry, it should keep us dry as well. She'd been right, but there was a price for such success. Dry, the cloaks looked like any other woolen covering. But once they got well and truly soaked, they not only kept us protected from the rain. They also smelled like wet sheep.

Fortunately, we'd been far away from the court before we'd discovered this.

"Dry trumps everything," Jane said from her post at the back of our small group. She alone of us was dressed as a man, offering up the very fair reasoning that one of us needed to be astride and give the appearance of being a guard. But in truth Jane just hated the sidesaddle; she'd learned to ride with the boys in her village, and she refused to give up control of her steed no matter how indecent it looked. "One last rise, Beatrice, and we'll have lost the farthest outriders."

We'd been told to stay within view of the Queen's guard, but their loyalty was to the Queen, not her women. So gradually we'd moved faster and faster along the roads, trotting and cantering. I needed all the time I could at Marion Hall before Elizabeth descended.

"Good," I said, surveying the forest as it stretched before us. "We're almost to the break—"

"What ho! What's this?" Meg danced her pony around, peering hard into the driving rain. "Beatrice, is that—"

"Of course it is." I frowned and rode to the fore of our group, but I'd recognized the rider immediately, resting exactly where the trees parted and the path into the forest could be found. "How in God's name did Alasdair MacLeod gain permission to join the Queen's progress? What could he possibly be doing here?"

And why did my heart give a little leap to see him? He'd been at every turn and corner in the castle in the days following my public reveal of Lord Cavanaugh's indiscretion. Not approaching me, exactly, but not staying away either. He'd lurked in the shadows like a dark-eyed god, watching me and those around me. I hadn't known whether to be flattered or annoyed, but annoyed had seemed smarter.

Seeing him here, however, so close to my home, inspired a whole raft of different emotions. Had he seen where I lived? Surely he had to have done so. And what had he thought? Was he planning to heap yet more humiliation upon me? Was that why he'd ridden so far into the woods, away from Marion Hall to greet us?

"Well, be glad we've the company, no matter who it is." Jane's words cut into my increasingly darker thoughts. "We could use the protection. I'm not a fan of woodlands. There is too much that can be hidden."

"In this forest in particular," Sophia said, and I glanced at her, startled to hear her voice. She'd ridden silently for much of our travels, her gaze intent and her expression rapt. I always forgot how constrained her life must have been, as niece to the Queen's astrologer. Even though he was only a few years older than the Queen, John Dee already seemed to be an old man, buried in his books and muttering over his charts. He was not often at court—and he never asked after Sophia, at least not since her betrothal to Lord Brighton. I thought on that now. Was John Dee complicit in the apparent plot that had been perpetrated to separate Sophia from her father? Was it because of this rumored Sight that she had? But surely he couldn't have known about that. Sophia had been a little girl when her mother had died and she'd been kidnapped, according to the papers Jane and Meg had found in Lord Brighton's study. How could she have demonstrated any powers at all, when she could barely speak?

In any event, now Sophia was looking around with solemn eyes. "Who lives here, in these woods?" she asked as we headed into the hidden swale.

"It's the southernmost tip of Salcey Forest," I said. "No one lives in it." Not exactly true, but I was in no mood to slice the point more finely. "We'll go quite a ways through it before we reach our holding. But the main road would take an age." I paused, scowling ahead at Alasdair. At least he would make the girl feel more comfortable. "Do you not feel safe, Sophia?"

"Oh no, that isn't it. . . ." Sophia's words petered out as she peered into the forest, but she didn't turn her horse into the wood, at least. I had no time for an enchanted woodland experience.

"Well, I for one will be glad to get under cover," Anna huffed, shaking out her cloak and sending water flying. "I'm not sure how much longer our cloaks will last."

Then we were trotting into the break of trees, with Alasdair riding toward us on his magnificent horse. It certainly hadn't come from the Marion Hall stables, I could see at a glance. Too big.

"Well met!" he boomed, then touched his hand to the reins, turning his horse just slightly. "God's bones, but you smell like a herd of—"

"Enough!" I raised my hand sharply. "What are you doing here? I did not realize you were part of the Queen's progress." It was not unheard of for Elizabeth to bring foreign courtiers on her jaunts, but really? Scotsmen?

Alasdair grinned at me through the rain. "As lovely as ever, my lady, and scented like a rose."

"You're not answering my question."

"Because it's not a necessary one." Alasdair lifted the edge of my cloak. "So that's why," he mused, turning the flap of cloth over and inspecting both sides. "Ingenious, and if that's why the smell is so strong, I'm thinking an herb concoction of vinegar and heather—"

"What's this? What's this?" Anna nosed her horse forward as I yanked my cloak out of Alasdair's hands.

"We do not have time for this discussion!" I protested. "We need to get—"

"Aye, aye, to Marion Hall," Alasdair said over my words. He turned his horse in earnest and faced north once more. "And so get there we will. Your father mentioned ye might try to break away from the group, and he sent me to escort you."

"My father?" I asked, my eyes going narrow even as we moved into the wood. "Pray tell, what occasion had you to speak with my father?"

"I helped him saddle his nag to make haste for his home, and one thing led to another, as oft it does. He invited me and a few of my men to help with the rabble about to descend on Marion Hall, and here we are." We were moving at a reasonable clip through the woods now, and Anna had been right. The thickly wooded Salcey Forest provided just enough space for two horses to move abreast, once you got out away from the main road, but the canopy of trees allowed a swift and welcome respite from the rain.

Jane was already out of her cloak, and for just a moment I envied her breeches and jacket. "I've got the bigger horse," she said. "I'll carry the cloaks. The smell doesn't bother me."

What does? I wondered uncharitably, but I allowed Alasdair to help me out of my cloak, trying to mask my irritation as he and Anna fell into an immediate discussion on Scottish cures for foul-smelling sheep. Instead I forged ahead. I knew this woodland well. For all of our financial straits, Marion Hall had been blessed with a thriving stable of horses, and gentry from all over the county would trade with us for foals and mares. We'd staged races and festivals when times were better, and as a result I'd ridden more than my share through the overarching canopies of Salcey Forest.

Now I peered through the wood, forcing myself to glance only once at Sophia. She was sitting straight and prettily, her skin flushed and her eyes shining, as if she were a princess herself on procession. But she no longer looked about with worry, and I allowed myself to relax the tiniest bit. If she couldn't sense that others roamed this wood, then perhaps it was currently empty. Lord knew that Alasdair tromping along on his great warhorse would have been loud enough to scare even the hardiest of souls away.

We traveled on for a few hours more, not so fast to lather the horses but at a clip that suffered no delay. Anna chatted with Alasdair and even drew Sophia out in conversation, while Meg and Jane seemed caught in a thorny discussion of what truly rested under the Round Tower of Windsor.

For myself, I just wanted to press on, press on. A thousand and one catastrophes awaited me in the tottering wreck of my home, and I'd need a dozen lifetimes to fix them. Instead I had but three hours.

Finally the trees began to dwindle, and I urged my mount faster, coming up the small rise just as the clouds finally parted and the sun peaked out to brighten the last scatter of rain.

There, nestled in the valley, lay Marion Hall.

Built to withstand both weather and woe, the folly of a mule-brained twelfth-century baron who'd fancied a castle when merely a house would have done, the imposing stone edifice of turreted rose granite sprawled out in ungainly fashion across the lawn. The estate encompassed dozens of rooms, courtyards, and sheds, all of them now bustling with activity, with servants and children and grooms and cooks racing about in panicked flight. And as the wind picked up its measure and skated toward us up the hillside, swirling and whirling with playful abandon, I could hear the unmistakable sounds . . . of screaming.

"Welcome to my home," I sighed.

CHAPTER THIRTEEN

I didn't wait to discuss the chaos I saw before us, but rode toward it in a madcap fury equal to what was already taking place at Marion Hall. I feared the worst, especially when we raced up to the stables to find them completely empty of man or beast.

Alasdair had swung down from his horse almost before it had stopped, and helped me out of my sidesaddle. "Don't look so distressed, Beatrice. Jeremy is a good lad. He had the idea to send all the horses out to line the great road up to Marion Hall, a horse and rider at every quarter mile. Gathered up many of the horsemen in the village too, to make a proper welcome."

"Jeremy?" I stared at Alasdair. "But who is watching him?" I imagined the twelve-year-old imp I'd left behind at Marion Hall late the previous year. I'd returned to my home after Queen Mary's death, deep in mourning, as had been the rest of the court. But we had barely begun preparations for the coming Christmas when the summons to return to court had arrived. The new young Queen had need of me, I'd been told. I must return to London at once to serve her.

My father had been in alt; my mother had not grasped the significance. And neither of them—nor I—had realized exactly what service I would be asked to perform.

But Jeremy at Christmastime had not only been the oldest of the fostered children at Marion Hall; he'd also been one of the wildest. "Surely you have not left him alone?"

"He seems used to it." Alasdair shrugged. "And from all indications is doing a fine job."

The other maids had dismounted now and were seeing to their own horses. Jane took my mare's long reins. "Off with you now. You'll want to see to whatever the shouting is in the house." She grinned. "I plan to remain in the stables as long as humanly possible."

"Beatrice, this place is a wonder!" Anna burbled, standing up on a mounting stool the better to see across the courtyard to the main house. "It's a veritable medieval castle!"

"And every bit as damp," I warned. But I was already bustling out of the stables, Alasdair at my heels. "You don't need to escort me in my own home," I assured him, but he merely laughed and kept beside me.

"I'll escort you to the end of my days, my lady. And I confess I'm also curious as to the screaming."

I entered the wide-flung doors, servants carrying sloshing buckets and armfuls of fresh-cut rushes. "Lady Beatrice!" the first one who recognized me cried, bobbing. The poor girl skidded to a stop and almost fell. "Begging your pardon, m'lady, but I'm afraid yer mum has taken a turn. She'd thought she could entertain the children in the west drawing room, but—"

"My mother!" Well, that explained it. "Here." I took the girl's rushes out of her arms and thrust them at Alasdair. "Help her do whatever she's doing, please." I eyed the girl, her name finally coming to me in a flash of recognition. "You're Sarah, no?" I asked, and was faintly peeved to see Alasdair's surprise that I knew a servant's name, even if it had taken me a moment. The girl's eyes widened, and she blushed.

"Yes, ma'am," she said, bobbing another nervous curtsy.

"Sarah, put Alasdair to work, and any other visitor who is already here. There are four maids in the stables who would be happy to lend a hand. How close are we to being ready?"

Sarah rubbed her forehead, leaving a streak of dust and sweat across it. I felt a renewed surge of irritation at the Queen. Really, could she not have picked another household to torment for a fortnight? It had to be mine? "With the rain finally ended, we have everything in place for guests, though they will be fair to bursting out of every window, beggin' your pardon."

I waved off her apologies. The servants did not stand on ceremony at Marion Hall unless there was a formal event—which was about to start, admittedly, but hadn't yet. "Well, that's their own fault. The Queen knows what the hall will hold. That she brought a retinue of fifty courtiers and ladies, servants and hangers-on, is her own poor luck. Where are we putting her, the bridal suite?"

"Aye, 'tis the prettiest room by far, with a view to the rising sun." Sarah bit her lip again. "Your mum has not slept in it in an age."

As if on cue another wail went up from the west of the

hall, and I stiffened, catching up my skirts. "Dinner this night—we're prepared? They'll be hungry but tired, praise God. The formal welcome will be put off a day at least."

"We've had—help . . . of a sort," Sarah said, her gaze skittering from me to Alasdair and back. "We're as ready as we can be."

Panic danced along my nerves. I knew the help Sarah meant, and help like that could get the Knowles family stripped of our estate, should anyone become the wiser. And here I was bringing the nosiest people in England to our threshold. But there was nothing for it. "Then that's all we can do," I said. I fled out of the room and down the long corridors, barely noticing the empty walls and austere, outdated furnishings. We'd sold most of the contents of Marion Hall during the lean years, and though we were finally back on our feet again—no thanks at all to my father but to the hall's stern chamberlain, who'd finally stepped in to save us—no one would say we were living in luxury.

The wild laughter and outcries of children assaulted me, the closer I got to the western drawing room. The name itself was a misnomer—the room was more a broad covered balcony, open to the wind and sky but protected from the harsher elements of snow and rain. Even today's torrent would not have disturbed its occupants. The room was a favorite of guests and residents alike, and seemed to draw children like moths to a flame.

And as I wheeled around the corner into a burst of sound, I was greeted by the one treasure Marion Hall still could boast proudly—fully a score of fostered children, who now appeared poised to engage in a battle to the death with wooden swords and thick cloth-wrapped staves.

I searched in vain for my mother, but from what I could see there was no one in the room more than four feet tall.

"Lady Beatrice!" A third of the contingent seemed to scream my name at once, and I was beset with an attack of my own, children pushing and shoving their way toward me, grabbing at my skirts, pulling at my arms, a dozen voices shouting at once even as the shyer or smaller children scampered out of the way.

"Enough," I cried. "Enough!" What had my mother been doing with these children, and where was she now? I had not expected her to keep up ably with the rabble, but she should at least have had a servant with her to manage them . . . or a well-armed guard.

The one benefit of the onslaught of children—all of them clean, I saw, which at least was one boon—was that it cleared the rest of the room of their fury. And then I saw my mother.

She half-sat, half-reclined on a long chaise that had clearly been carried to the room for this purpose. Although the rain had ended and the sun was now warming the open sitting area, she still had a heavy blanket drawn up all around her. A thick glass carafe sat next to her on a tiny table, with God-only-knew-what inside it. For her part, my mother drowsed in blissful repose, oblivious to the chaos around her.

"Mother—ow!" I contorted my body backward as one of the scrabbling children latched on to my hair to gain a leg up onto my person, but no sooner had I divested myself of that climbing monkey than another two had grabbed my hands, a third at my elbow, urging me to join the fray. I looked into their faces and saw the eagerness of children too long ignored. My heart twisted, as it always did around happily romping children. I saw in them all that I had lost and could never get back, and I normally went to any lengths to preserve their precious childhood, away from the prying demands of life.

These children at this moment, however, had gone outside of too far. Their manners were deplorable, and whatever they had done to my mother was not to be borne.

"I said '*Enough!*'" I cried, using my loudest voice. I shoved the closest of the children away into their sprawling fellows, creating a space for me to breathe. I knew the respite would hold for only a moment, so I pounced on it.

"What manner of play is this? Have you exhausted Lady Anne so completely that she has collapsed on her chaise with none of you the wiser? Who started this?"

There was stunned silence for a long moment, and then one of the taller boys stepped forward, Matthias Smith, whose mother had died five years past. "I did, Lady Beatrice. We were only going to show 'er what we'd learned from the guards. They've been teaching us to fight! . . ." His words trailed off as he turned to my mother, who shifted in her sleep but didn't waken. "But she was . . . tired. She told us to carry on."

I tightened my lips. "And 'carry on' means a full-scale war in an open drawing room? On a day when we're expecting the Queen herself to arrive?"

Matthias opened his mouth, then shut it. He knew he was in the wrong. The other children, taking his cue, had the grace to look abashed. Jeremy had been their hero when I'd been here last December, but it now looked like it was Matthias whom I would need to manage.

"So what are we to do?" I asked him seriously, clasping my hands over my skirts. "Are we to hide you all from the Queen, or put you on display?"

I surveyed the wreck of children. Yes, they were clean, after a fashion. But their clothing was scuffed and torn, their hair was awry, their eyes still bright with energy. Queen Elizabeth was fond of many things, but children were generally not among them.

"I shouldn't think we should all meet the Queen this day," Matthias said. He'd turned as well to survey the gang of children, stepping into his role as spokesman and leader more fully. "She will doubtless be—" He glanced at my mother, the only example of a noblewoman he'd ever known. "Tired."

"She will," I said quite seriously, not bothering to correct his misunderstanding. "But perhaps you can decide on how you would like to see her—a formal presentation to the court? A musical event?" I had to work to keep myself from laughing at the looks of shock and dismay on their faces. "A demonstration of your fighting prowess, as her junior guard?"

Matthias straightened, even as the children gasped with delight. "D'ye think we could, Beatrice?" he asked, forgetting the "lady." "D'ye think we—"

"The Queen would be honored to see the fervor of her youngest subjects," I said, and it was true enough. The Queen was honored to see the fervor of any of her subjects, at any time. But children who adored her gave her a certain measure of additional joy, their unfettered enthusiasm heaped upon her without an agenda.

"Lord Bart!"

I glanced up, startled, to see my father and Alasdair standing in the doorway. My first thought was that I needed to fix my face, my hair—as it surely was standing on end from my tussle with the children. Then I remembered: This was Alasdair. I didn't care what he thought.

The children did, it seemed. They stood for a moment, stock-still, transfixed by the brawny Scot.

My father jumped into the fray, immediately pressing his advantage. "Allow me to introduce another warrior who can put you through your paces: Sir Alasdair MacLeod." Father waggled his brows. "He's from *Scotland*."

That got him several appreciative "oooos," and Father grinned at one of the youngest as she toddled up, reaching out. Ever the charmer, Father swooped the little girl up into his arms, as she gave a delighted giggle. "But now, I'm afraid Lady Beatrice is quite correct. We can't have you imps interrupting the arrival of the Queen of England. She has traveled through deplorable conditions to reach us, and the last thing she needs is a houseful of screaming children to greet her."

Then again, maybe that would curtail her visit.

I was about to suggest as much, when Father clapped his hands sharply, no mean feat, as he still had the toddler girl—a new one to our fold; I didn't know her—in his arms. "For now, back to your rooms, and if you are found out of them, expect to be put to work. We've got a whole house to prepare for the Queen, and precious little time to do it. Go!"

The children scampered off, one of the older girls obligingly peeling the little girl out of my father's arms. But I was already turned and striding toward my mother, who'd seemed to waken at my father's voice, as she was ever wont to do. Not for the first time, my heart twisted at the suffering he had brought her.

Father reached her first, however, and was already dropping to his knees. "Anne, Anne," he murmured, pushing back her hair. "How are you feeling, my sweet?"

"Oh, B-Bartholomew," she hiccuped. Her eyes were pale and glassy. I marveled at how far she'd slid, now that she was back in her own home. How had she been able to manage the trip to Windsor and even my wedding without anyone being the wiser to her ailments? "I'm so glad you've come home."

"We cannot have her see the Queen like this," I said, and my mother turned her head, like some woodland bird hearing a familiar trill. My father grunted assent.

"No, we cannot. We'll say that she is abed with some ague or another. It has worked well enough in the past." He made to lift her, but Alasdair beat him to it, picking up my mother in his strong arms as if he were asked to perform such a shocking service every day.

"Oh!" my mother breathed, a bit of life coming back to her cheeks. Her gaze wandered up to Alasdair's face. "Do I know you?"

"I'll lead the way," my father said. He glanced to me as I picked up the wine carafe and gave it a surreptitious sniff. I winced.

"What is it?" he asked tiredly, as if he weren't the reason

why my mother had chosen to loosen her grip on reality.

I shot him a black look. Nine months ago, before I'd gone into service as the Queen's spy, I hadn't known precisely what was contained in the pungent mixture that now swirled inside my mother's drink. Nine months ago I hadn't yet begun my studies of poisons and potions. My mother was drinking a stiff concoction of sherry mixed with opium—or laudanum, as the drug was called in this watered-down state. No matter how sweet the sherry, it still was a pungent, bitter brew. "Where would she get opium?" I challenged him. "And how long has this been going on?"

A look of pained resignation flitted across his face, and he nodded to a steady-eyed Alasdair to precede us out the door. "Since long before you were born, sweet Beatrice. Since long before you were born."

CHAPTER FOURTEEN

Things did not much improve after that.

The Queen arrived wet and bedraggled, and was immediately swept into the great banquet chamber of Marion Hall. With the ale and wine flowing and a roaring fire in the grate, and dozens of courses of "simple country fare" to weigh her down, Elizabeth stayed in a modestly good mood for the balance of the day. Then my father brought the Queen and her retinue into the bridal suite, with me in deferential attendance, as my mother was still abed in her own rooms. He made a coy art of explaining to the Queen how a secret panel opened into a tiny room between the bride's and the groom's suite, a "relic of a bygone age."

No one would be housed in the groom's suite, my father assured the instantly intrigued Queen; she would have complete privacy. This of course struck her as the silliest of plans, given the size of the house, and the two of them agreed that several of her guard should have that suite, including her Master of the Horse, who'd come along for this unofficial sojourn in the north. These stalwart men would not only protect her, she reasoned, but their shared quarters would give the household some relief. Marion Hall was already filled to bursting. My father would just need to keep the secret of the panel to himself; neither her guards nor any of the other guests needed to be aware of it.

I stepped away from their conversation to allow my father the opportunity to respond with earnest-eyed gratitude and assurances that the Queen would always be safe in Marion Hall. Of course, I knew the whole truth, and I had to acknowledge mastery when I saw it. The duplicity of my father had never seemed so neatly done.

Robert Dudley was the Queen's Master of the Horse, and now he would be but a short passage away from the Queen herself. Of course, the Queen would be with her ladies, and Robert with a brace of guards, but when two people had a mind to meet, they would. And my father had just given the Queen the perfect opportunity to meet the man upon whom it was whispered she bestowed her highest favors.

I wondered if my father planned to use this information to his benefit somehow. Opportunity did not equal action, and Elizabeth was shrewd. But still . . . it bore watching.

After the first night's rest and an admirable break of the fast that must have completely exhausted our cooks, still reeling from the night before, our stablemen prepared to take the Queen out on a tour of the grounds. Even though she'd traveled two long days this week already, not all of that had been on horseback, due to the rain. She'd been stuck in a creaking carriage over rutted roads for far too long; the Queen was more than ready to gain some exercise in the open air.

And so the next days ran one into the other. We spent a season's fortune on feeding Elizabeth's court and slaking their thirst, and I prayed nightly for some crisis of state to recall her back to Windsor or London. But nothing came of that—even Cecil and Walsingham seemed at their ease to roam Marion Hall and sequester themselves in corner rooms for hours on end, while the Queen took her amusement at the hunt or on horseback or in long, bracing walks through the more cultivated sections of our domain. She'd even found our overgrown hedgerow labyrinth, and it was only with the greatest of pressures that she was convinced it was too dangerous to venture within; we'd not trimmed that monstrosity in a generation, and there was no telling what creatures made their home within its borders. She'd met the villagers and even a finally sober version of my mother, and declared herself entranced by the forest that hemmed in the "quaint" Marion Hall.

The Maids of Honor equally took their rest, though they were far less of a drain on our larder and alehouse than was the rest of the Queen's retinue. And even I fell into an easy pattern. My days were filled with management of the estate, and my evenings . . . with Alasdair. He accompanied me on my rounds, he found me after every meal for a stroll and conversation, he helped me with the children—all without being asked.

I could not even say what we talked about on those walks. Nothing of importance, surely. The garrulous Scot seemed insistent to keep the conversation light—on the caretaking of the gardens, the husbandry of the fields, and endless rounds of discussions on horses and stabling and bloodlines. When we came onto my father's collection of manuscripts in the library, however, I was surprised again. Alasdair immediately homed in on one of our prized holdings, a folio from the Lindisfarne Gospels that Father had been given for safekeeping during old King Henry's reign. Whether the good King realized my father had spirited the manuscript off to Northampton was anyone's guess. But even as I thought on it, I locked the precious script away. It had already been pillaged once by an English monarch, during the Dissolution of the Monasteries. I had no interest in it being lifted a second time.

Still, Alasdair's excitement about the gospel pages knew no bounds. He'd come alight with fervor at its clean lines, its rich colors. He'd seemed transported by its beauty, and as I'd watched him in his zeal, I'd found myself thinking less and less of him as a Scotsman here in England to garner funds and support for his people . . . and more and more as a young man, barely two years older than myself.

Not that I cared for him, mind you, or had begun growing fond of him. Not even in the slightest. At all.

But he was . . . easy to talk to, I'd give him that. And attractive, in his rough, masculine way. His hands were strong, his back broad. His smile easy. And sometimes, when he thought I wasn't looking, he would gaze at me with eyes so hot and intent, I should think he was trying to imprint me on his very soul—

Which did not matter at all. Truly.

Unfortunately, respites are never meant to last. Marion was not Windsor, and a fortnight was too long to keep Elizabeth the Self-Indulgent in good spirits.

Now the Queen was growing restless, some hidden peevishness breaking to the fore, and she'd demanded to be entertained this night "in a manner that outshines all others," when we were all about to drop dead on our feet as it was.

It was the tenth day of her visit. Although every preceding evening we'd had music and dancing and even the children's guard demonstration—which Alasdair and his guards had helped carry off thoroughly and well—Elizabeth declared that she was bored.

Bored.

I'd long since cared about reviewing the accounts. Our chamberlain grew more ashen-faced with every passing day, and the servants, while cheerful enough in demeanor, roamed around the Hall like the desperately ill waiting for a surcease that only death would bring them. We dared not run out of provisions. It would be a shame to our household, which mattered little to the Queen. And to the Queen herself, which mattered a great deal. Our positions at court depended upon our abilities to entertain our monarch, even if we barely had two loaves of bread to rub together.

And so tonight, at the Queen's demand, we were to have another feast. My father and I stared across the table where we'd met to plan it. He looked as wan in the thin morning light as I'm sure I felt.

"She's trying to bankrupt us," he said, with the grace to still sound faintly shocked. He refocused on me, and his lips twisted into a tired little grin. "I really didn't think she hated you so much, my sweet, but it appears I've underestimated you once again."

"You did what you could." I shrugged, too tired even to fight anymore. "We must have a dance—it's the easiest plan. And we must bring up the village ale."

Father scowled. "Far too strong." He shook his head. "Courtiers and ladies do not drink the way we do deep in the forest, Beatrice. They'll not be able to handle it."

"I know, Father. But we've no other options. Our own stores are fully depleted, and we've still got at least a few more days of this lot. Don't even get me started on the state of our larders. Were it not for our ability to barter, we'd have no food left at all to grace Her Majesty's table."

"And I've no interest in betraying the true wealth of our holding," Father mused grimly. "Thank God only the stones of Marion Hall know its secrets."

I felt irritation flash within me. This little mantra of Marion Hall used to be a favorite of his, back when I was just a child and before Mother's dark days outnumbered the lighter ones. "Now is not the time for reminiscing, Father," I snapped.

He sighed, shaking his head. "You have the right of it, Beatrice, but promise me one thing."

I sniffed, glancing back over the list of requirements for the night's revel. "Now's not the time for promises, either." I should have known by my father's long pause that I would not like his next words. I looked at him when he did not speak. "What?"

Father's face was set in implacable lines. "Allow Alasdair to court you in earnest tonight; if just for tonight."

"I *beg* your pardon?" I reared back, completely flustered. "What do you mean, 'court' me? I have spent my every waking moment with the Scotsman, and well you know it!"

"You have held him at arm's length," my father snipped back. "Talking, talking, talking, fie. You'd talk a man to death to keep him from leaning too close or touching you."

"How dare you!" I gasped. "I have comported myself with honor and chastity, and—"

"And the Queen wants you to swoon over the damn boy, so you should swoon!" Father crashed his fist onto the broad table, stunning me into silence. "We are here at this impasse because of your little stunt with Lord Cavanaugh. I cannot say I blame you for it, and it was neatly done. But Elizabeth clearly pays attention whenever you are with the young Scot. You do not need to tell me that she's ordered you to squire him around; I know you well enough to know you would not tip your cap for a man without money or name. So the Queen takes pleasure in seeing you consort with someone you despise, what of it? Is it so *impossibly* onerous for you to do what you are commanded, to ensure that the Queen sees you in the young man's arms, doing whatever it is she has asked of you? If you won't do it for yourself, do it for the family—we need her favor, and we need her gone."

It was quite the longest and most earnest speech I'd heard my father give in years, and it extinguished my outrage like a pinched-off candle. I couldn't even berate my father for his betrayal of his only legitimate child. He was a creature of the court, and he saw the truth plain enough: We had to placate the Queen if we ever wanted to get rid of her. She was my direst enemy, and she had all the power. It was like choosing the open sea as your foe.

Worst of all, Father didn't even know how close his words had struck. The Queen *did* want information out of Alasdair, along with watching me simper and pout, and here I'd spent the last several days immersed in conversations that had had nothing to do with anything. I was not doing my job, and sooner or later there would be an accounting.

"Very well," I said, bringing my father's gaze back to mine. "Tonight we shall go a-courting."

We'd gathered up all of our papers when a clattering at the door to the chamber alerted us. A moment later Sophia and Meg burst into the room, their eyes wide with dismay.

"We have a problem," Meg said, noticing my father a second too late.

Then she curtsied.

CHAPTER FIFTEEN

I managed to get my father out of the room on the pretext that the problem was no more than a girlish foible over a dress or a handkerchief. Whether he was truly stupid or he just didn't have the energy to question, he left—though not without a parting shot.

"You'll remember to do your part?" he asked, ignoring Meg's perplexed frown. Sophia was staring resolutely at the wall.

"As if you'd ever let me forget." My smile was forced, but he saw in it whatever he wanted to see, and he was off.

"Now," I said, rounding on Meg. "What is it? Did somebody die? Did a servant insult some lady-in-waiting?"

"Don't look at me," she said, nodding to Sophia. "She's the one who sounded the alarm. She should be the one who tells the tale."

"All right, then, *what* tale?" I asked, endeavoring to keep the sharpness out of my tone. Sophia no longer looked like she would blow away in a stiff breeze, but there was still a . . . an etherealness about her, a fey quality that seemed to grow more pronounced even as she began to find her voice. "Sophia, did you, ah . . . see something?"

"This place, this place," she breathed, lifting long fingers to her brow for a second before recalling herself. "I am sorry, Beatrice, but yes. I can't be sure it will come to pass—you know how my visions aren't always quite accurate."

It is a testament to my supreme training as a spy that I did not throttle Sophia myself, just to get the words out of her throat and into the open air. Instead I waited her out as if I were in the midst of a curtsy long count, knowing that my misery would perforce be short-lived. Even Meg began to fidget, though, and Sophia blinked, once more back with us.

"But this vision keeps returning, swift and sure," she said. "It involves one of your maidservants, though she is not to blame. She has caught the eye of Robert Dudley."

I flashed a startled glance at Meg, who looked bleakly resolute. "I knew you would see the import of this," Meg said, and Sophia began wringing her hands.

"He finds her in the stable and steals a kiss from her, and that is all well and good. She is modest and maidenly, in the first blush of her womanhood, and her response to Dudley's kiss is chaste enough. But the Queen has seen and she realizes—she realizes all that she cannot have, even in the midst of her grand luxuries and power. She sees her own weakness and her own vulnerability to a love she can neither fight nor forget. She sees, and—she does not react well."

"The maid, the maid," I whispered, trying to imagine which of the serving girls would have found herself in the stables, at the mercy of a Queen's man. "Does the Queen see her face? Could she identify her?"

"No—no, it is not that. The Queen can see only that she is a young woman being kissed by Dudley and then reacting with shock and dismay. The girl backs up, her hands to her cheeks, and shakes her head quite clearly. She does not invite Dudley's advances, even though he is quite dashing in his riding attire, only just returned from his exercise with the Queen."

"Does the man have no sense?" Meg muttered, and I had to agree. If he'd only just arrived back, then so too had the Queen. For him to corner a maiden with his monarch so close by showed a marked lack of concern for his own head.

But Sophia was continuing. "But the Queen also sees Dudley stepping forward, as if determined to have another kiss from the girl. The girl stumbles back, the Queen calls out as if she is newcome to the stable, and the scene clears."

I gave a low groan. "He forced Elizabeth's hand. He forced her to break up a tryst else see for her own eyes his perfidy." I gathered up my skirts. "Has this already happened? Is it a vision of the future or the past?"

"I—I don't know," Sophia said as we rushed into the hallway and down the long corridors to the side entrance to Marion Hall. The stables were just a short dash away from that doorway, and if we could catch Robert Dudley before he followed his flirtatious whims, we could perhaps forestall the Queen's mighty fury before it landed on all our heads.

But it was not to be. We'd no sooner reached the doorway than we saw the Queen striding forth from the stable doors, a grinning and strangely smug Robert Dudley trotting along in her wake, his eyes drinking in the sight of his jealous Queen.

"He knew! He is doing this merely to bait her!" I breathed.

Meg swore beside me. "I have to think you're right," she said, and Sophia gave a soft mew of distress.

"Oh, Beatrice, your lovely hall," Sophia whispered. She raised her stricken eyes to me. "There will be a rout."

I grimaced, thinking of the casks of too strong ale that even now were being stacked along the walls of Marion's Great Hall, and knew Sophia wasn't relying on any second sight to make this prediction. The first sight would serve well enough.

"Drink well this night, both of you," I said, and sighed. "It looks like we'll need it."

It was even worse than I'd imagined.

The Queen crackled with anger all through dinner, her wit shrewd and cutting. She abused my father, myself, and the whole of our staff. She raised her brows in disparaging disapproval at the renewed absence of my mother. She turned back dish after dish of exquisitely prepared meats and breads, contenting herself only with sugared pastries and sweets that she washed down with our heavy ale. Even that she took exception to, but only until the sheer volume of its potent brew hit her squarely.

Then came the dancing.

Robert Dudley, for his part, claimed the first dance with the Queen, but she rebuffed him in a brilliant rebuke that merely had him grinning back at her even as he bowed and stepped aside. He was delighting in egging her on, and the Queen demanded that fresh ale be served all around.

"A dance, my lady?"

I jolted to hear Alasdair's voice at my side, but I turned to him with a practiced smile. "Of course, good sir," I said, and he raised a brow as he escorted me into the line of dancers. It was a Volta, and the Queen had chosen one of the most well-built earls for her dance partner over Dudley. This was a wise move—first it showed her off to good effect during what was undoubtedly her favorite dance, and second, it gave Dudley the opportunity to see another man squiring Elizabeth.

However, that wasn't much help to me. Alasdair and I joined the group of dancers who ringed the main attraction, the Queen and her partner—Henry, the Earl of Rutland, a favorite of hers said to be on track to become lord president of the north. The Volta was an only barely civilized dance, and the Queen, now well in her cups, preferred it played violently fast, with the pipe and tabor, cittern and shawm, clanging together in an almost frenzied urgency.

Alasdair noted the change in tempo immediately. "It appears your Queen has a mind for exercise," he noted, grinning as we circled each other, drawing close together, then stepping apart in sharp, rapid steps. He bowed to me flamboyantly, and I sank into a curtsy, nervously eyeing the neckline of my gown to make sure his now hungry eyes did not see too much. I was unaccountably panicked in the circle of his attention, and I sought an easy retreat.

"If you cannot keep the pace, good sir, you've but to say

the word." My words came out more flirtatiously than they should have, but there was danger here. Alasdair had lost the softer edges of the young man who'd attended my wedding all shaven and smooth. His beard was coming in more fully now, and even his clothing seemed less kempt, rougher and earthier. His hands on my face and against my arms were firm and strong, and would not be denied.

"Beatrice, you ever know what words might fire my blood the most," Alasdair said, his jaw as tight as his tone. "And never cease but to speak them."

He stared at me as the music picked up another pulse of energy. By dictates of the dance I was then required to leap up into his arms, and I did so with my face set in its haughtiest lines, feeling a jolt of awareness as his hands clamped over the thick folds of my dress at my hips and he lifted me high. He lowered me back to my feet with a bit less speed than necessary, his eyes smoldering as a wicked smile curved his lips. "I think this is my favorite English dance," he said, then swung me out again.

I bristled, but there was nothing for it. The next steps of the dance pressed his chest up against my back, and I arched my arms gracefully in the air, swallowing as he drew his hands firmly past my elbows to the outer curve of my arms and shoulders, then farther down the line of my torso, his fingers just barely grazing the fullness of my breasts. It was perfectly chaste, and exactly in line with what the dance required, but I was still startled when he then swept me up in his arms, turning me round and round in time to the ever-quickening music.

"But surely you did not come all the way to England just for the chance to dance?" I managed, not needing to force the breathlessness into my voice.

He pulled me closer to him still. "I came to England to secure the treasure of my homeland," he said, turning me ever faster. "But, aye, I just may stay to complete the dance."

Alasdair set me back to my feet but grudgingly then, eyeing me possessively while I flitted away from him and gave a flourish. His grin turned even more wolfish as I followed the next prescribed steps of the dance, running back to him and jumping into his arms. I gasped as he clasped his arms around me, staring at me as we twirled around the floor to the climactic crashing music. He set me down and lifted my hand high—so high I had to arch up against him on the tips of my slippers, until he allowed me to sink into the final curtsy of the dance.

Alasdair brought me up again as everyone wildly applauded the Queen, the two of us lost on the edges of her triumph with her ginger-haired courtier, as Robert Dudley, finally chastened, seethed and looked on.

But I could not tear my gaze away from Alasdair's. He still held me, tight and close, the heat from his fingers searing mine, his heart pounding loudly enough for me to hear through his crimson doublet. In his gaze I felt something I had never experienced before, a suitor who stared at me not as if I were his servant or his toy, or even the altar on which he would sacrifice all. I felt—real. Empowered. Safe.

"My lady," Alasdair rumbled in a voice thick with emotion and something else, something I could not quite identify but desperately wanted in that moment to understand. Then he seemed to catch himself, his next words almost strangled. "I canna stay with you at this revel tonight," he said. "Promise me you'll stay safe?"

I arched a brow. "Since when have I had sway over your schedule, my lord?" Though in truth, Alasdair had barely left me alone for a moment since we'd arrived at Marion Hall. What had changed? What was happening? With a deceptively casual toss of my head, I rushed to learn more, taking the easiest gambit first. "Pray, tell me no one else has caught your eye?"

Heat seared me as his gaze raked over my face. "No, my lady. You of anyone canna think that—"

"Lady Beatrice!" squeaked someone at my side, and the moment was lost almost before it had begun. "Lady Beatrice, the ale has all been tapped!"

"What?" I whirled away from Alasdair, and then I saw it. The Queen at the close of the Volta had ordered every last keg opened, demanding that her court not leave the room until the last of the ale flowed. The rich scent of barley and hops almost fouled the air with its thickness, and the Queen herself stumbled to the side, only to be caught up again by Dudley, laughing and cheering, urging her on.

And that was when I noticed something else.

I wasn't the only one who made this realization either. Across the room four other young women caught the sudden sense of wrongness in the air, looking up from their cups and conversations to take note of the one thing that was clearly lacking in this room.

Not the Queen and her rabble of courtiers. That was a constant. Not my father and my servants. They were desperately scrabbling to keep up the flow of food and drink to the ever-rowdier crowd. Not even one Alasdair MacLeod, who'd caught my sudden shift of mood but did not remark upon it, hovering only at my side should I need protection. None of those worthy souls were missing.

But Sir William Cecil and Sir Francis Walsingham, the Queen's staunchest and most trusted advisors, who were normally no more than three steps away from Elizabeth wherever she should be?

Tonight they had vanished.

I turned back to Alasdair, and stopped, startled by the suddenly empty space.

Now he had vanished too.

CHAPTER SIXTEEN

Unfortunately, I had no time to search for the Queen's advisors—or Alasdair, for that matter. Just as I realized that all of these worthies were missing, the Queen declared another dance and demanded that all her maids attend her. We were caught in the roiling snake of lords and ladies for another two long hours.

I sent most of the servants to bed for a bit after Her Drunkenness finally took her leave, and the five of us maids then got to work trying to keep Marion Hall from being set on fire by ale-soaked courtiers. Not even my father remained in the end, spiriting away to some corner or another for whatever respite he could find. I couldn't blame him, this one time. The situation was challenging enough for me to face in the grim light of dawn.

The morning after the revel dawned bright and clear, and anyone looking at Marion Hall from the outside would have thought it to be the most idyllic of medieval castles, pristine and newly awakened in the fresh morning light.

Inside it was a ruin.

Now I stood gape-mouthed at the destruction of the Great Hall, shoulder to shoulder with my fellow maids, clearly the only people not related to me by blood or fealty who'd stayed sober the night before. But the servants were up again and bending to their task, so I set to work as well, beginning by salvaging any unbroken flagon or trencher. I first dispatched the servants to remove the tapped casks and fling wide any window we had access to in the manor house. All of the lovely sweet rushes that had been carried into Marion Hall naught but a few days before were now being hauled out by servants struggling not to gag on the reek of them.

Elizabeth had already sent down word that she would be dining in her rooms for at least part of the day, along with her ladies. I sent up some of my mother's laudanum-soaked sherry to her, with strict instructions that she should not overdo it. With any luck the accursed woman would ignore me as usual and sleep the day away.

A buzz of excited voices broke out on the far side of the room, and I straightened, my apron full of reclaimed utensils, to see Alasdair arrive on the scene. He strode in like he hadn't abandoned me the night before, and was now commandeering the children to assist the servants with the easier tasks of clearing away the rubble. I frowned at him across the space, and he winked at me broadly. Irritation spiked my already exhausted nerves. I didn't know what I thought of him, precisely, but the thoughts I did have were decidedly not charitable.

"He's an interesting young man, isn't he?" It was Anna who spoke beside me, and I turned to her, glad of any distraction to pull my attention away from Alasdair's hearty laughter. She was stacking scraped plates according to their size and type and sorting recovered spoons, and I tumbled my own collection beside her. "Come all this way from the Isle of Skye with a brace of his men, without any real purpose? Seems a bit odd."

"What do you mean?" I frowned down at her, then lifted a plate to set it on her growing pile. "He wants the Queen's money, and her promise of arms. Just like all the Scots do."

"Mmm," Anna said, signaling for a servant to come and take the tallest of the stacks away. "But the timing of his arrival is of interest, is it not?"

"The timing?" I tried to recall when Alasdair and the Scots had made their presence known to the Queen. "It was late summer, yes? They were part of the grand presentation of delegations. We had foreigners falling out of windows that week."

"It was directly after the Queen had returned from London, a trip that certainly swayed our participation in the Scottish rebellion, since it marked our delivery of the Earl of Arran safely back into his father's arms. Then, poof, a swale of Scots arrives at our door, Alasdair at their head and at your heels. And here we are, just weeks later, that much closer to Scotland ourselves, and Alasdair here with us once again. We seem to be awash in all things Scottish."

I groaned, rubbing my back as I bent over to retrieve a slightly bent silver fork from among a scatter of overturned benches. "Anna, if you're trying to suggest that there's more to Alasdair than it seems, you'd best come out and say it. I'm too tired for subtlety today."

Anna laughed grimly. "I'm trying to suggest that there's

more to Alasdair than it seems," she said. "Meg and Jane think that there was a secret meeting last night in the middle of all of this." She waved vaguely around. "And you said he vanished last eve just as Elizabeth made her final run at your ale stores. Do you know where he was off to?"

"I don't," I said ruefully. I wanted to ask Alasdair about it straight out, but direct communication wasn't my stock in trade. And I wasn't certain I had it in me to dissemble this morning.

"Nor do any of us. But consider this: No sooner did the Lords of the Congregation arrive at Windsor than we upped and headed north. Curious timing, don't you think?"

"But not all the way to Scotland," I protested. "That is another several days' hard ride. And the Lords of the Congregation didn't travel with us."

"Didn't they?" Anna returned. "How closely did any of us watch who came and who stayed behind? And why leave the good Lords in Windsor, while the Queen makes an example of you by bankrupting your estate? Smarter by far to bring the Lords along with the Queen's retinue and finalize their negotiations under your roof."

Anna's voice was uncharacteristically firm, and I frowned at her self-assurance. "Don't you, too, get smart with me, Anna Burgher," I groused. "I've enough on my hands with Sophia coming into her own."

Anna shook her head. "Still, I think we should have an accounting of your complete guest list. It would not be all that difficult to see if certain of the Lords are here, whether they're hiding or no."

"They aren't," I said firmly. I would know by now, even if I hadn't at first. "They may have left Windsor with the Queen's progress, but they could have easily departed our company along the way. And you know yourself that we ranged ahead."

"Ah, I suppose that is true enough." Anna blew out a breath, considering, then turned to our second topic at hand. "It is interesting to watch Sophia, isn't it? I swear we needed only to get her out from under Windsor's shadow for her to really blossom. Her headaches are concerning, but I rather think it must be like using a muscle that's not been tested before. It's rather fascinating, all in. I have been researching every book I can spirit out of John Dee's library at Mortlake, but there's nothing in any of them quite like what we're seeing with her. Surely Dee knows what he has in Sophia, don't you think? Given that he quite clearly came by the girl by less than savory methods?"

I gaped at the girl, momentarily taken away from my own worries, which may well have been why she shared this little bit of news. "How exactly have you 'spirited out' John Dee's books?" I demanded. "Tell me you have not gone all the way to Mortlake and broken into his library!"

Anna's eyes fairly sparkled, and she possessed the air of a woman well contented that someone finally knew her secret. "Mortlake is only twenty-odd miles away from Windsor, and I know how to ride a horse, Beatrice. Getting in and out was simple once I convinced Dee's staff that I was there on the man's behalf."

"And you did that—how?"

"Forgery." Anna grinned. "You get to the point where you recognize someone's handwriting so well, 'tis only a matter of time before you can replicate it."

I shook my head. "Help me understand. You wouldn't so much as smile back to a boy who was eyeing you at court, but you'll risk arrest and imprisonment to read a few books?"

"Well, talking to boys isn't what I'm good at," Anna said, shrugging. "Solving mysteries is. It only makes sense that I'd focus on where my talents lie."

We talked on then about what Anna had learned in John Dee's books, and I saw her come alive with excitement as she spoke, fairly crackling with knowledge and passion for what she'd read in books so old, their very pages had begun to crumble. Most of all, however, I saw her staunch support for the strange sprite we found in our midst, Miss Sophia Dee.

We returned with zeal to our cleaning, and only then I realized it was full noon and the manor finally resembled the home of my birth. After a simple lunch of bread and soup, I wandered out onto the open lawns of Marion Hall, eager for a respite from the smell of sour ale.

I shouldn't have been surprised to find Alasdair waiting for me.

I wiped my hands on my apron before removing the garment, nervously reaching up to smooth my hair. Alasdair took the apron away from me and set it aside, then batted my hands back down. He tucked my right hand into the crook of his left arm. "Your hair looks lovely, my lady, as it always does," he said. "You also look like a maiden in need of a walk. Where shall we off to?"

"Wherever," I said, glad for any distraction to keep my mind off everything changing all around me so quickly. Both Sophia and Anna were transforming into people I wasn't quite ready for them to be. Why couldn't I change so quickly and so well?

"On an estate this large, 'wherever' could mean half-way back to Windsor." Alasdair laughed, breaking into my thoughts. "But let's make it an unofficial survey of your holding. The Hall itself you know too well of late, but I think she'll make a full recovery."

"No thanks to the Queen," I grumbled, and Alasdair tightened his arm on mine. "And where did you disappear to, before even the last of the ale was tapped?"

He shrugged. "We both saw the ale, and what comes of ale being tapped is invariably theft and disruption. I knew I had to notify your guards—and mine—to redouble their watch."

I arched a brow, regarding him sidelong. "That surely was not your responsibility."

"And yet it was my pleasure nonetheless," he said mildly. "Your father asked me to have a care should the revel grow too overloud or long, and it was quickly becoming both."

"Then I should thank you, I daresay," I said stiffly, though something still rankled in his words.

He chuckled and patted my arm. "Never that, my lady. Never that."

We walked in silence then to the stables, where the children were helping the groomsmen care for the dozens of mounts our guests had ridden to Marion Hall. Alasdair lifted a finger to his lips, and even in my annoyance I could not forestall a smile. It had not taken the Scot long to realize that the adulation of the children was exhausting. We slipped past the stables and down the lane, coming around to the back of the castle. I thought about the Queen's irritation at the poorly kept back lawns of Marion Hall, and my humor dwindled again. "Elizabeth seems honor bound to make my life miserable," I muttered.

"You do have a knack for upsetting her," he said. "Though Sophia told me what set the woman off in truth."

I raised my brows at that. "Sophia talked to you?"

"Aye. She's a tiny slip of a girl, isn't she—but she sought me out at last night's debauch, lest I think your distraction was the result of any ill will toward me."

That did have me turning around. "She did what?" *Why on earth?*

"She seemed quite adamant, so I let her tell her tale." He waggled his brows at me. "And indeed, when I did have the chance to dance with you, I did not find you distracted at all."

"Indeed." I turned and faced forward again, ruing my fair complexion for the flush that now stained my cheeks. I moved ahead, and Alasdair grasped my hand lightly, letting me set the pace. We no sooner rounded the last bend of the mansion, however, than his steps slowed, and I glanced back at him, irritated anew as he planted himself and stared in wonder at what now lay before us. I tugged on him again. "Oh, come on. You cannot be serious."

"Can't I, now?" Before us stood circle upon circle of the Marion Hall labyrinth, its ragged hedges a legacy from the same batty baron who'd also erected the hulk of stone behind us. Like everything else about my ancestral home, the labyrinth was a wreck and a ruin.

Alasdair, however, would not look away. "What fell secrets shall we find here, I wonder?" he asked, and tightened his hand on mine.

CHAPTER SEVENTEEN

"I say, leave off," I protested. "The only secrets that place holds are rotting branches and dead creatures."

I tried to tug him back to our walk, but Alasdair was steadfast.

"You mean to tell me no one ventures back here?" he asked, rooted in place and staring at the labyrinth as if it held the secret entrance to the fairy realm. "Not even the children? It would be the first place I would go, were I still a child." He chuckled ruefully. "I've been sorely pressed not to enter it myself, and I've been here but a few days."

"If you were a foster child here, you would not enter it, no. Not if you wanted to stay at Marion Hall," I said levelly. "We've made the rules quite clear. No one but the servants are allowed back here, on pain of being removed from the house entirely. If there were a few additional stories planted about children being spirited away in the night from ghosts awakened in the labyrinth, well—there's naught I can do about that." I grimaced, thinking of the same stories that my father had told to frighten me. "That's not to say that a few of the hardier children haven't breached the outermost rows of the labyrinth, but in truth they honor my father's wishes for the most part. He has no interest in seeing them hurt, and the servants keep a sharp eye as well." I shook my head, staring at unruly hedges. "It always gives newcomers a bit of a turn when they first see it, I will tell you that."

"It is an impressive bit of gardening," Alasdair said dryly. "You have never kept it flourishing? It does not look so abandoned as that."

"You're seeing only the outside," I said. "We make an attempt to keep that trimmed. And when I was little, my father staged a campaign to improve the entire maze, inviting the whole of the countryside to take part in opening up its pathways and clearing it of brush and leaves. They found a perfect open space in the center, clear but for a small, marble-lined hole in the ground. A spring burbled up from below that, and it fairly glistened in the sunlight. He would delight me with its tales, but then he said it was cursed."

"Cursed!" Alasdair's eyes flared wide. "You canna be serious. I wouldn't think your father given over to such imagination—or you."

"Yes, well . . ." I looked away. "I was a child. I believed a lot of things back then."

Alasdair had the grace to stop staring at me—though it took him several long seconds to find that grace. When he did, he returned his gaze to the monstrosity of the labyrinth. "Well, it couldn't have been that cursed. Your father didn't tear it down, now, did he?"

"No, he did not," I said bitterly. "But he also did not

dispute the story that the center of the labyrinth was a place to be avoided at all costs. He and the villagers have talked over the years of returning the grounds to open lawns, but really, the cost would be extraordinary. And with a house the size of Marion Hall, you learn to conserve your pennies."

"Aye," Alasdair said, turning back to take in the Hall's rose granite walls, glowing like a promise in the bright sun. "She is a beauty."

"A beauty!" I scoffed, surveying the hulk with a more critical eye. "You must live in a frightening place indeed, then."

He grinned. "In a manner of speaking, aye. My family has worked to make our castle a fortress, in any event. It has been home to a long line of chieftains before me, including my own father—and, God willing, a long line of chieftains after. And before you ask, no. I am not the firstborn. I would hardly be allowed to take men to England and dance pretty dances with foreign ladies if I were supposed to carry on the great banner of the MacLeods."

"Mm," I said, wondering at his words. So not only a son of a barbarian but a second or third son at that. Not that it should bother me, of course. I was not going to be this man's bride, but still. I found myself unaccountably depressed. "How many do you have in your family?"

"Not so many as you," he teased. "Just a half dozen of us, three of them lasses. But already my sisters have graced us with bairns of their own, and of the laddies I am the only unwed." He waggled his brows at me, and I felt another hard jolt in my stomach. Surely he didn't think he had a chance with me? I *had* to make a fortunate marriage to assure my position in court! That was all I'd ever worked for, and what my family—and I—desperately needed.

Focus! I was the one supposed to find information out about the blasted Scot—and he was in a talkative mood about something of substance finally. If that something was the curse of the dilapidated hedgerow, I would take it and to spare. "So, tell me about your family, good sir. What hulking fortress do you call home, that you think Marion Hall is an English jewel?"

Alasdair chuckled. "My home is Dunvegan Castle, and it stretches up from the rock of Scotland in defiance against the very heavens. It's surrounded all round by the sea, easily one of the best protected castles on Skye."

"By the sea!" I stared at him. "So how do you get in and out? By boat?"

"An' up through the sea gate, aye." Alasdair's brogue was thicker now, his eyes lifting up and to the northwest, as if he could recall his castle to him by words alone. "'Tis a wondrous place, though not entirely a kind one. 'Twas built for defense and defiance, and not for pretty things." His hand tightened again on my arm. "Still, it has a beauty all its own. I would bring you there one day, my lady, for you to see its wonders, both inside and out."

"Indeed," I said, by rote, not knowing what else to say. Well, that wasn't entirely true. I knew precisely what to say: the flirtatious comment, the quickly forgotten promise.

But I had no intention of going anywhere with Alasdair MacLeod after my work with him for the Queen was done. He was a captivating diversion, but a diversion nonetheless. I had a family of foundlings to care for, not the least of which was my mother, and a falling-down Hall to shore up. I would not be setting off on an adventure to the middle of nowhere.

"So, what beauty lies within such a sturdy rock?" I finally asked, thinking it safe. Immediately I regretted my decision. The faintest surge of excitement in Alasdair's mien was enough to make me want to run away. *I would never follow you to a land of barbarians and warriors, you fool,* I wanted to cry. *You are mad to even suggest it.* But I could at least show interest in his ancestral home. That didn't seem too much to ask of myself, even if manners appeared to have deserted me. "Do, ah . . . do you mean just the austere beauty of its strength?"

"Not only that." Alasdair turned me to him and tilted my chin up. "My family holds treasures like none other in Scotland," he said, his manner suddenly too intent. "We consider it our duty and our right to hold such beauty close, and protect it from all who would take it away. Not least of which is the Fairy Flag."

I frowned at him. "The Fairy Flag?"

He seemed to recall himself, blinking at me in surprise for just a moment. Then he grinned and shrugged, the thrall apparently broken. He returned his gaze to the hedgerows as he spoke. "'Tis magic, my lady, pure and simple."

Once more he tucked my arm into his, and we turned to continue our walk, edging ever closer to the labyrinth. "The Fairy Flag is a furl of silk gifted to the MacLeods a thousand years ago, it is said, by the fairy folk themselves. It holds great power, and never have we unfurled it in the midst of battle but we haven't won the day."

I lifted my brows at that. "It assures success in war?"

"Aye, it does. Since time unremembered."

I smiled, getting caught up in the image of an ancient flag held high for all enemies to see. "From the fairy folk themselves, you say? Then it must be a wonder. Does it fly at Dunvegan Castle?"

"Och, no." Alasdair shook his head. "The thing is already tattered, as my ancestors pieced off sections of it to press into good luck charms before they realized the full of its magic. Now it is kept in its own treasure box, for use whenever the clan needs."

"And you've seen it?"

"'Tis my own family's treasure, Beatrice." Alasdair looked down at me. "Of course I've seen it."

"Well, where did it come from in truth, then?" I asked. "Your country was not exactly known for its silk production—especially not a thousand years ago. It had to come from somewhere."

"Legends abound." Alasdair shrugged. "But the most likely is that it truly did come from the fairy folk. They've got every reason to ensure Scotland stands strong, do they not?"

I looked up at him, but his face was set and certain. "You can't be serious."

"Oh, but I can. The legends run too long, and the truth of the flag's power canna be disputed. Even pieced off and worn as it is, there is something about the cloth that you just simply sense." He squeezed my arm. "You'll see what I mean, I have no doubt."

My heart gave another lurch, real worry beginning to thread along my nerves with something else, something I couldn't quite name. I struggled to keep the conversation on track. "So whyever did you choose to leave such a vaunted place, then?" I asked archly. "Magic, beauty, and the wild North Sea—why would you consent to be your clan's delegate to the English court?"

Even as I asked the question, something about it struck me as particularly apt. Alasdair was a Scot from the Highlands—and by his own admission, a member of a particularly self-sufficient clan. He had as much need of an English Queen's money as he did a third foot.

Alasdair hesitated a long moment, not answering, but before I could press my point, a burst of movement from the back entrance to Marion Hall caught our attention.

Sophia ran pell-mell toward us, her skirts hitched high in both hands. She was wearing a frock of pale lavender, and her hair hung free, making her look exactly like the sort of fairy sprite that might have gifted Alasdair and his family with their precious flag.

"Sophia!" I called out, and only then did the girl seem to recognize that there were others in this place. "Sophia, what is wrong?"

"My head—my head!" she gasped, and the moment she stopped before us, I could see she was as pale as a ghost. Her large violet eyes appeared as stains of deep color against the faded tapestry of her face. Even her usually bright lips and cheeks were now a wan, soft pink. She dropped her skirts and brought her hands against either temple, closing her eyes as if to shut out noise. "I cannot stop what I'm seeing! I must get it, I must go!"

I exchanged a look with Alasdair, and he nodded, edging to my side to prepare to catch Sophia before she bolted away. "Go where, sweetling?" I asked carefully, leaning down to lift the girl's chin with the softest touch of my fingers. She was shaking violently, but she held herself still, a fawn being examined by a hunter, unsure of when the blade might fall. "What do you need to get?"

"Now!" she said, as if I'd asked her when, not where. "I must away now!" She whirled away from us both, her eyes going as wild as her hair. She danced a few steps of a reel I did not recognize, her arms spinning, her feet moving fast. "I cannot stand it another moment. I must know—I must understand!"

Alasdair lurched forward, but he was too late. Sophia was off again with almost unnerving speed, dashing away into the one place on the estate where even he could not catch her for certain: the Great Ruined Labyrinth of Marion Hall.

CHAPTER EIGHTEEN

As one, Alasdair and I raced into the barely cut away opening of the hedgerow, and then stopped almost immediately at a snarl of brambles as soon as we turned left. A piece of lavender-dyed fabric hung from one of the branches, and Alasdair plucked it off as he pushed the brambles out of the way for me. "Hopefully she'll still be clothed when we find her," he muttered. I hurried forward.

"I—it's been so long, but I remember there was a mathematical construct of sorts to the choices," I said. "There's only one way through the hedgerow, and that's through the center. She has to be going through the center—though, how she would know how to get to the center, I cannot guess."

"From the look on her face, she didn't need to know an equation to get through the maze," Alasdair said. "She barely looked when she ran toward the thing, but her steps were sure. Here, let me get that."

Lifting away the worst of a sagging hedgerow, Alasdair helped me duck under the greenery while I stepped over a large tree branch that had somehow found its way into the maze. We turned right at the next opening, then left again, and I slowed my urgent stride as we made our way deeper into the labyrinth. "Should we call out?" I asked him, eyeing the tops of the hedgerows. They were half again as tall as I was, and though we were catching bits and pieces from Sophia's gown and the ribbons in her hair, the girl herself was nowhere in sight.

"She probably wouldn't answer, but you would alert any servants to your presence here," Alasdair said, swearing as he ducked under another cruel sprawl of nettles. "What in blazes possessed you people to plant thorns in this hedgerow?" he complained. "It's like something out of a children's tale."

"We didn't . . . plant them." I frowned, my eyes going to the hedges even as we scurried past. The brambles seemed to burst out at regular intervals, sprawling out in ungainly style in the way of weeds grown wild, but a curious uniformity seemed to be developing as to when we could expect them to sprawl out of the hedge and leaf-strewn path. "At least, *I* didn't plant them, and I can't imagine who would. Once begun, removing them from the hedges would take an entire army of gardeners."

"And a generation of time," Alasdair said wryly, and I contented myself with thanking him every fifth step as he lifted away some obstacle or pushed me through it. The sun was climbing in the heavens, and the heat had to be building, but the hedges seemed strangely cool and fey as we worked our way along.

"Another . . . right, I think," I muttered as we came into

a tighter spiral of passageways. There were no brambles here, and the absence of them was a palpable relief.

"Right?" Alasdair jogged forward a few steps, and then paused to examine another thick fallen branch. He reached out for my hand. "Just as with the Volta, my lady. I don't want you to step on this one. It seems like it's been here awhile."

He swung me into his arms, and I felt the heat of him intensely as he hopped over the offending branch and then moved forward with me still in his grasp. I wriggled to free myself, and his hold grew tighter. "I see another log in the way up ahead," he said. The touch of his lips on my hair made me go still and taut in his embrace. "This is for the best."

I closed my eyes for just a moment, savoring his hold on me, perhaps more so because we were hidden away from the prying eyes of Queen and court. But as we rounded the next bend and came upon a perfect open space, I didn't need to ask for Alasdair's arms to loosen. His hold went slack around me as we both stared, and he set me lightly to my feet.

"What in the name of heaven—" he breathed, as I turned around in the space, staring at the perfectly trimmed hedges, the leaf-free grass, the pristine pool bubbling with water that gleamed almost golden in the full light of day.

"I don't know— I don't see how this is possible," I stammered, unconsciously reaching for him. He gripped my hand, and we moved forward, toward the small stone bench that stood beside the burbling fountain. "There are no brambles here, and surely the maze should be shot through with leaves and nettles and fallen branches here most of all, with the open space and access to sun and rain."

"It's an uncanny place," Alasdair allowed. "And this spring . . ." He knelt down without loosening his light hold on me, and dipped his hand into the water. "This cannot be—"

"Get away from there!" Sounding like a frightened five-year-old girl, I hauled him back from the spring, my father's words ringing in my ears. "Don't do that, please," I said, trying to sound reasonable as Alasdair's startled gaze met mine. "That water—that water is poisoned!"

"Well, it's hardly—" He broke off as I put my hands to my cheeks, all of the warnings and half-joking gibes and dolorous predictions clanging around in my head. "Beatrice, what's wrong?"

I wheeled away from him, pressing back against the hedge. "Nothing—it's nothing."

"It seems like it may be more than that."

"It's none of your concern!" I snapped, and immediately he stiffened.

"I have troubled you. My apologies, my lady," he said gruffly, then stepped away from me, attempting to find the opposite hedge fascinating. For my own part, I could have slapped myself. The entire point was to *charm* the rough Scotsman, not rebuff him. But every word that came to my mind was flippant and stupid and false, and after his candor about his family, I owed him more than that. I owed myself more than that.

"My mother," I said at last, my words hollow and chilled.

"She . . . she was here. They were both here. I was so very small, but I remember that. They were here and they were happy—truly, genuinely happy. The dark spells had not begun then, the times when she was away but not away. But, then—then she was happy. They laughed and shouted and danced around, and she . . . she—"

"Beatrice?" I heard the word, but could not track it. Could not see anything beyond my own memories.

"She drank the water of that well and then she got so much worse, so much terribly worse. She never wanted to see me and she never wanted to talk and she crept around her darkened room and whispered to the servants and she barely ate and—"

"Beatrice!" Alasdair was in front of me now. I could see him as if I were outside myself, watching him take my shoulders, watching him shake me, hard. But the images in my head blocked out what I was seeing in this moment, my mother's quiet surrender and my father's bleak scowls, the laughter of the children around us like a shielding cloak to the poison that was held within our tiny family, with no boys to carry on my father's name and a mother who was but a shell and—

"Beatrice!" came the shout. "Beatrice, my love, come back to me!"

I heard Alasdair's pleading voice, but I couldn't fight my way back. It was as if the shroud of the past decade and more of my life had been stripped away, baring for me the truths that I had never allowed myself to see. I felt myself dropping into darkness when Alasdair's hands suddenly seemed to spasm on my shoulders, and he hauled me up close, pulling me onto my tiptoes as his head bent and his mouth branded itself onto mine.

Heat exploded within me. I gave a little cry. Then my arms were around him and I felt his hands at my back and head, cradling me into him even as he pressed me so closely against his body that it seemed that the two of us had become one. This was not the courtly kiss I had allowed to keep the English nobles at my beck and call. This was not even the stolen embrace at the close of a dance or in the tapestry-lined antechambers of a darkened Queen's castle. And this certainly wasn't the lecherous advances I'd endured from men of every stripe who'd thought to transgress a step too far in their wooing of me, before I could break away and put them in their place.

These kisses were nothing like that. They were primal and real, made of fire and soul and spirit, and I found my every horrible memory burned away with the flames now stoked within me, a surge of heat seeming to fuse my bones together with a strength I had never known. Alasdair's hands held my face now as if he were afraid to break me but even more afraid to let me go. And yet he kissed me still, raining soft touches upon me in benediction—my forehead, my eyes, my cheeks, and then my mouth. Then drawing his lips down farther still with a ragged groan, along my jaw and into the sensitive hollow of my neck, my own desperate gasps seeming to drive the breath from his very body. He trembled violently against me, and when he raised his gaze to mine, I was seared anew by the emotion burning within his eyes. "Beatrice," he said brokenly. "Don't ever leave me like that again."

I swallowed, then finally pulled away from him, even as both of us realized the extreme impertinence of his words. He blushed crimson, and my heart did another wrong lurch, beating sideways somehow. "My lady, I do—"

"Shh," I said, not trusting myself to put my finger to his lips, though it was a move I'd practiced coyly on courtiers since I was barely twelve years old. "I apologize for frightening you. It was my fault— I allowed myself to fall into dreams and memories from when I was very small." I forced myself to smile, to wave an airy hand. "This is not a place to haunt one's dreams, good sir, and yet it seemed like that to me, so young was I."

My little speech allowed Alasdair time to straighten, to smooth his doublet down with a distracted air, as if he'd just emerged from a dream of his own. He looked around the space. "What happened here?" he asked gently.

"Nothing whatsoever." I shrugged. "It was only that I had it so fixed in my mind that this was the last place my parents had truly seemed happy together, my father and mother laughing—even dancing—by this burbling pool. Her scooping up the water and letting it play in her hands, taking a draught of it."

I felt my body stiffen but forced myself to hasten on. "Taking a draught of it, then another, so pure and golden she declared it."

An odd look chased over Alasdair's face. "Well, Beatrice, I think you misunder—"

His words were cut off by an unearthly scream.

"Sophia!" I gasped. We sprang farther apart, spinning round, but the scream was not close—and it was not back toward the house.

"Is there another way out of this maze?" Alasdair asked, but I was already giving chase.

"Yes!" I cried as we wheeled out of the open space and back into the labyrinth, going left this time instead of the way we'd entered. "But it deposits you directly into the forest. Father always intended to clear more of the land, but he never—he never—"

I gave up speaking as Alasdair pushed past me, running fast. We leaped over logs and branches and dashed under yet more brambles, but the way out took longer than the way in. I growled with frustration at every step, but Alasdair pulled me forward and kept the pace. Still, my memory failed with the terror that gripped me. I'd journeyed so few times the latter half of the maze, and even that had been so many years ago. We finally burst out onto the forest grounds, and though it was full day, it seemed that we were caught in a fairy wood, so thick and green and still was the darkness.

We bounded into the trees as far as we dared, shouting and calling out into the green velvet wood. "Sophia!" I called, my voice urgent with fear. "Sophia! Where are you?"

No one returned my cry.

CHAPTER NINETEEN

Rather than fight our way back through the brambles and logs and branches and the strange hidden space at the center of the labyrinth, Alasdair and I forged our way back to Marion Hall through the heavy wood of Salcey Forest. My feet were about to fall off my body by the time we returned, and it was now well past midday, with the Hall appearing more or less put back together and a few bleary-eyed courtiers stumbling about, still looking a bit worse for the wear from their late-night debauch.

I held my head high and sailed past servants and guests alike, not even drawing a frown at my disheveled appearance. It was always thus, I'd found. People saw what they expected to see. In me, they expected to see a prim and perfect English rose, haughty and cold and always in control. The idea that my heart was pounding and dread coiled in my stomach would never occur to them, and the speculation that the tall, broad, hot-blooded young Scot by my side was the cause of more than a little of my disquiet wouldn't either.

Alasdair, for his part, was blessedly silent while he guided me through the corridors of my ancestral home. He bowed to me as I curtsied at the chamber where I'd housed my fellow maids, an unassuming room at first glance that got larger the deeper it went, ending in a lovely view of the back lawn of Marion Hall.

"I will see if she has returned by much the same route as we did," he said quietly as we both rose again. "Though, I canna think we would have missed her."

"Do that." I nodded. "Anything you learn—anything at all, please let me know." I frowned, thinking furiously. "And locate Thomas Clark, the head gardener. He may be able to offer ideas of where we might find Sophia."

Alasdair nodded and was off.

"Beatrice, well met!" Anna looked up as I entered the room, surrounded by books from Marion's library, such as it was. Her manner instantly tensed. "Whatever is the matter?"

"Some help, please?" I asked, not stopping. Anna uncurled herself, and Meg and Jane got to their feet in an instant.

"What happened?" Meg asked. They followed me as I went at once to the tall windows of our chamber, and they helped me open the casement wide to give us a full view. "What is it we're looking for?"

There was no hint of lavender in the midst of all that green, of course, and I sagged back.

"You've been in the wood," observed Jane, reaching out her hand to not quite touch me, as if she could scent the coolness of that green mystery on my skin, and feel the heat still roiling off me. "And you're deeply troubled as well." She glanced around the room and came to the same conclusion as the rest of the small group.

"Sophia!" Meg's eyes bulged, and she put her hand to her mouth, turning again to the spectacular view of Marion Hall's labyrinth. "Say she did not go into that thing alone."

"Well, not quite alone," I said grimly. "Alasdair and I gave chase, but she seemed to know where she was going—which is impossible, frankly." I looked over to Anna. "She complained of a headache. I thought you had found something that could help those."

"I ran out of my tonic!" Anna fluttered a hand. "It's not like I have my herb garden here. I had to use what was close at hand."

I gaped at her. "'Close at hand'? You gave her something you created here?"

"Of course!" Anna frowned at me. "But it was nothing exotic, in truth. I was chatting with your cook and told her about Sophia's discomfort. She gave me a steeping bag and a cup of mulled wine. Sophia said she felt better just by inhaling the fumes, and it did smell potent—though neither Cook nor I could puzzle out just what was in the concoction. She said she'd found the bags in the cupboard when she'd first arrived, and couldn't tell me what was in them. They were marked only with the letters *D* and *T*, and the other servants had thought them a remedy for all sorts of maladies. I couldn't identify any of the herbs in it except motherwort, they were all crushed and dry. But I tried it first."

"You didn't!" Meg's eyes flew wide. "Anna, that could have been poison!"

Anna shrugged. "Cook has been doling it out to the children and servants for the past five years that she's been here, so it seemed safe enough. She swore she'd never seen better for easing the mind." Here Anna blushed a little. "I didn't ask her about it, but she said your mother refused to try the bags, not knowing their provenance. I can't say as I blame her, but—"

"At least it would be better than laudanum," I said, finishing her thoughts for her. "I think I might agree with you there, Anna. But did Sophia drink this potion? And it had no effect on you?"

"She merely inhaled it while I was with her." Anna made a face. "I actually didn't drink much of the stuff. The taste had some mint to it, but overall it was far too bitter, even in the sweet wine. Sophia claimed she would lie down for a bit to sleep the headache off, and when I returned here, she was gone, and so was the mug."

"She wasn't carrying it out on the lawn," I mused. "She said she'd had visions—dreams—and that she had to get into the labyrinth."

"And she's not there anymore," Jane finished for me.

"She's not, and I don't know how she got out without assistance." I bit my lip, thinking of the precious time Alasdair and I had wasted in the center of the labyrinth. What a debacle!

"Well, the wood is large and well stocked with game, or so your servants say," Jane said, her flat words drawing me back. "We'll need to find her soon."

"Yes," I said, thinking again of the other inhabitants who

still roamed unchecked through the Salcey Forest. I resolutely put those thoughts out of my mind. I'd been at court for a decade with no one breathing a word to me of any indiscretion about Marion Hall, and my father was not a fool. Even if he had found ways to trade with all and sundry to feed the Queen and her court these several days past, he would have kept his forest free of any vagabonds and scoundrels.

"Very well." Jane's gaze searched the forested land beyond the labyrinth as if it were territory she was well used to exploring. "We'll need any able servant who can be spared without causing notice and who can sit a horse. Sophia weighs but nothing, so she can easily be carted out of that wood, as long as she's found without injury."

"Oh, don't even say it," Anna said, her face beginning to look a little white. "You don't think that potion—that draught I gave her—you don't think it caused her harm!"

"We think no such thing," Meg said firmly. "Sophia is Sophia. She doesn't need potions or draughts to do unexplainable things. Her visions have been growing more intense; we all know that. Just this morning Cecil also had her cornered in the dining room, Beatrice, demanding of her this question and that, as if she were a court fool who could spout prognostications at his demand."

I frowned at that. "Cecil! That is rich, given his own disappearing act last night. Maybe Sophia could scry where he and Walsingham were spirited off to." *And Alasdair too, for that matter.* "What was he asking?" It couldn't have been an interrogation of anything that might have put Sophia at risk—that would have triggered the rules of the "Queen's

Grace," as symbolized by the plain gold band on the middle fingers of our right hands.

"Oh, he was trying to be coy," Meg said. "I drifted close enough to hear them, but Cecil knows me too well. He switched to asking her about her wedding plans the moment he thought I could eavesdrop. Before that, however, he was asking her to reveal threats to the Crown."

"Threats," I said. "That seems a little vague, wouldn't you say?" I shifted uncomfortably. Given what I'd had to suffer at the Queen's hands, *I* could verily be considered a threat to the Crown of late.

Meg nodded. "Sophia thought so too. She parried his request with a sweet smile, then told Cecil that his wife would have another child in but a few years, who would grow up to make him even prouder than those children who had come before. Cecil was so puzzled by this news that he quite didn't know what to say, and then he noticed me standing there and couldn't say more in any event. But his face was alight with planning when he strode out of the room, and I think Sophia must have known that her time as the quietest of our group was coming to an end."

"How difficult for her," said Anna, her fingers tightening on the book she'd carried with her from the bed. "There could literally be no end to the questions she might be asked, yet she cannot govern what she sees."

"Not as far as we know, anyway. But we do not even know the full extent of her abilities, which is perhaps the greater danger," Jane said grimly. At my questioning look, she shrugged. "Think on it. The girl sees visions, which is impressive enough, if she can control them. But what if she can do other things of equal value to the Crown? What if she can determine the future worth of a man, or his character, or decide whether he is guilty or innocent of some past or future crime? What if she can puzzle out his secrets without his saying a word, no need for torture or threats?" She nodded into our stunned silence. "Aye. Her skill would be worth a king's ransom then, and I wouldn't trade places with her for any amount of gold."

"Do you think she knows all of that?" Meg asked, her gaze returning to the labyrinth. "Do you think she fled?"

"No," I said resolutely. "I think she is quite out of her mind with delirium, chasing after ghosts that only she can see. But that doesn't mean she's not in danger, just not from anyone but herself at this exact moment."

A knock on the door startled us, the world conspiring once more against me.

One of the servants stood there, hesitant, a young boy I did not recognize. He must have been added to the staff since the last time I'd been at Marion Hall.

"Yes?" I prompted when he would not speak.

"Lady Beatrice!" he cried, his thin voice too loud for the room. "I have been asked to summon one of your company to the Queen's presence. A lady—I mean a maid—I mean Sophia Dee!"

CHAPTER TWENTY

Well.

Royal command or no, we certainly couldn't produce Sophia Dee anytime soon. Still, we were forced to spend precious time organizing the most trusted of the servants to search for Sophia—quietly. Then we worked out our own plan on the walk to Elizabeth's suite of rooms.

With the Queen already in high dudgeon, we needed to lie carefully and well to keep her from storming through Marion Hall, determined to find a missing spy. I would do the lying. It was, after all, my greatest skill, and it was also my house. Jane and Anna would bolster my account of Sophia falling ill and being quite unable to speak to anyone for any length of time, without quite possibly causing them to contract a horrible ague. Meg would feign a coughing spell at that moment, and with any luck we'd be banished from the Queen's presence.

As a backup distraction Meg would also pocket one of the Queen's jeweled cuffs or pins or brooches—something she had worn the night before at the revel, large enough to be immediately missed. Of course my own staff of servants would be blamed, and the house would be in an uproar for hours over the questioning and the outrage of it all. Then the piece would be found in some little cubby where it would have been perfectly reasonable for the Queen to dally. The Queen would not be able to say with certainty that she had not lost it there, and there would be ample forgiveness all around. The whole folly would take up a half dozen hours if executed well, and then it would be nightfall and hopefully Sophia would have been recovered.

It was indeed a sensible plan. Pity it all went to ruin almost immediately.

We knew that something was amiss the moment we reached the upper landing. Cecil was standing there alongside Walsingham, looking as fell as a winter's storm.

"Where is Sophia?" he demanded, and I rolled my eyes.

"Sick again, my lord. Wherever else did you expect her to be? I swear I had to spend most of the day apologizing to Lord Farley of Hampton Mews for her spewing her dinner on him in such a violent manner."

He blinked at me. "Who?"

"Lord Farley," I said, continuing to walk resolutely toward the Queen's chambers. "You don't know him. He's of the local gentry, but the man has a mouth on him like a braying mule. It would be best for him to not noise about that the Queen's company is infected with a virulent ague, I should think. Meg herself developed a cough and I've done nothing but ply her with spirits since she awoke this morning." Beside me Meg grinned toothily at Cecil, then sniffled, and I could see him flinch back in revulsion. God love the man, he did truly hate to be sick. I patted him on the arm. "If we can't beat this thing, we'll simply have to drown it out, don't you think?"

"This is *nonsense*," Cecil blustered, but he hastened ahead of Meg, Jane, and Anna into the Queen's quarters, and I heard them all acknowledge her royal presence. I had picked up my skirts to join them, when Walsingham laid a hand on my arm. It was all I could do not to jump out of my skin.

"A moment, if you would, Lady Beatrice?" Walsingham's words were silken with intensity. I paused, and looked up at him, not bothering to hide my surprise.

"But the Queen?"

"The Queen can make do with the rest of her maids. She wanted Sophia, but any of you would have done, as long as all of you came trotting along." He sniffed. "She has become obsessed with the idea that Cecil and I are not being fully forthcoming with her about the activities surrounding the Scottish rebellion. We have already given her our report, of course, but she insists that somehow you might be able to add to our findings, whether by skill or, in Sophia's case, by Sight. It's quite—charming, in its way, how much she's come to depend on you in such a short time." He tilted his head. "Or at least upon the idea of you."

Staring at him, I was caught by the strange subtlety of the man. Here was the Queen's most trusted spymaster, but what did we know of Walsingham, truly? Did his loyalty remain with the Queen, or with England? Surely those were one and the same, were they not?

"Exactly as you say, Sir Francis," I said demurely, though

my heart had begun to beat again in a strange, erratic rhythm. "How may I serve you?"

He gestured for me to walk with him. "You did not appear to be overly distraught at the destruction of your carefully laid plans for your wedding to Lord Cavanaugh," he said, slanting a glance at me. But if he was going to talk of court, then this was ground I knew well. I'd been trained from the cradle in the art of dissembling, and the rapid change of subject merited no more than a half lift of my brows. He would have to do better than that to trip me up.

"I was certain that the Queen acted for the good of the Crown, Sir Francis, when she postponed my wedding. When I later observed that Lord Cavanaugh's affections lay elsewhere, I was grateful that I'd learned of it in time. He is a good man, and will make someone a good husband, even if it is not my fortune to be wedded to him."

"It could still be, you know," Walsingham said idly. Our long strides were taking us to where the eastern and western wings joined in a narrow gallery, but he showed no sign of stopping. "The Queen could yet decide to marry you off to Lord Cavanaugh, or really any other man of her choosing."

"That is true enough, Sir Francis," I said, smiling easily. "My fate has always been in her hands; and verily if it would serve her needs, I would not argue to being affianced anew to Lord Cavanaugh." This of course was a patent lie. I would argue through every means possible, and call in every marker I'd ever granted throughout the whole of the court, to avoid such a marriage. I suspected Walsingham knew this as well, and as we approached the western wing, I felt him gathering himself round to the true meat of this conversation.

"You know she does not like you," he observed, and I granted him a quick grin.

"I do so know it, yes."

"And yet, of all her well-placed noble ladies, she chose you to be her spy. Do you not find that odd?"

Walsingham did not know what I had done to earn the Queen's grudging patronage. He knew only that she hated me, yet still kept me close. He may have suspected where our unholy alliance had begun, of course. But I alone knew what had transpired between the fourteen-year-old Elizabeth and the doomed Thomas Seymour, all those years ago at Sudeley Castle. Something more than what she'd admitted, certainly—and something less than what her detractors had suspected. But I had not spilled my secrets in the face of questioning, even as a frightened seven-year-old girl. I certainly was not going to spill them now.

"The Queen, though she has no reason to do so, considers me a sort of lesser rival." I shrugged. "She thinks to keeps her friends close, and her enemies closer."

He nodded, but his eyes glittered in the half-light. "That is part of it, true enough. She also, however, seeks full dominion over you as a woman, not just as your Queen. Or have you not noticed how sharp her tone has turned when she addresses you, and how pointed her stare?"

Uneasiness threaded through me. Walsingham could not question me without the Queen's presence, but that did not mean he could not fill my ears with lies. Or, perhaps worse, truths.

“I am afraid I do not understand your meaning, Sir Francis,” I said as we turned the final corner on the western corridor. “The Queen has ever treated me with grace.”

“Oh, come now. Now that the Cavanaugh alliance has been broken, she means to stick you in some hole in the middle of nowhere, Lady Beatrice. You know it as well as I do,” Walsingham said. “She merely has not yet found one sufficiently deep.”

I did not know how to respond to this, so I opted for light indifference, though I was chilled to my bones at how right and true his words struck me. “Think you so?”

“I do indeed.” He slanted me a glance. “You have been spending much time in the company of Alasdair MacLeod,” he observed, and I instantly tensed. I had to keep up the game of our coy repartee, but it felt wrong to me. The words I had to speak felt like chalk in my mouth.

“If you are here to tell me my need to entertain Alasdair MacLeod is at an end, then I well thank you for it,” I said with a shrug. “The Queen’s request that I shadow him has been educational but not terribly informative. He and his family side with Scotland against any who trample against it—especially if they’re French. The question of religion is not as strong a call to arms as is the question of their independence from French rule. They will defend their island rock against any who would take their freedom away.”

“The MacLeods do not hold sway only in Skye,” Walsingham said. “They’ve cousins to the south throughout England, staunch Catholics, I am told. And yet they would fight for the Protestant cause?”

I fluttered a hand. "And what family does not have divisions as such, particularly across borders?" I smiled a little wryly. "Though, I cannot imagine that their English cousins' faith remains as strong during Elizabeth's reign as perhaps it was before; or at least as public."

"True enough," Walsingham agreed. "But MacLeod and his extended family are well positioned to aid in a *Catholic* plot, not a Protestant one; and we must be ever vigilant that any dissenters to the Queen's rule do not gain a foothold, no matter how slight." He stepped into the western drawing room, with its great area open to the sky. Thankfully, there was neither child nor intoxicated mother in sight. Praise heaven for small favors. Walsingham glanced around the room, then turned back to me, satisfied that we were alone. "We need more from you, Beatrice, and I think you know it," he said, his words deceptively mild.

I looked at him now, even more tense. Unaccountably, I felt the need to protect Alasdair from this schemer. To reduce his importance as a potential pawn. There was one sure way to do that, and I sighed deeply, affecting a weariness like to drag down my bones. "You want me to keep making eyes at the Scot, don't you," I groaned, not bothering to match my low tones to his. "Say you are not serious."

"I heard reports of the Volta from last night's revel," Walsingham said levelly. "You do not find his presence a comfort?"

"I find his presence a chore, Sir Francis," I snapped. Perhaps the only thing worse than the Queen's meddling in my affairs was Walsingham lending his clumsy hand to the stew. "I will entertain him for the sake of the Queen, but make no mistake, I take no joy in it."

"There are those who saw you walking with him again, earlier today. You did not seem affronted by his company then, either, though the Queen herself was still abed."

"The Queen's command knows no slumber," I retorted archly. Even in this I could not speak plainly, but I could at least set Walsingham's mind at ease regarding my feelings for Alasdair MacLeod.

He was a distraction to me. A diversion. Nothing more.

Truly.

And so I sallied forth. "MacLeod is a Scotsman, Sir Francis, and as such he shall not capture my heart, my mind, nor even my interest except as it pleases my Queen. I am willing to lend him my wide eyes and batted lashes to keep him enjoying his stay in her court." *And to strip him of every ounce of knowledge he has, to feed your voracious appetites.* "But make no mistake, I will be the happiest of girls to see him depart for his rock of a fortress to the north."

Walsingham stared at me, hard, then seemed to come to some decision. "Your devotion to your Queen knows no bounds, it would seem," he said, but his words were not entirely flattering.

I chose to respond to them as if they were, however, and sank into a curtsy. "I do what I can for England," I said.

Disconcertingly, he was still staring at me as I rose. And it was not a good stare, but one born of plots and secrets that I could only guess at. *What is his game?* I wondered. *What is his real intent here?*

"You'll do it for longer than most, I wager." Walsingham bowed prettily back to me. "But, enough. I daresay the others' audience with the Queen is already at an end. I will make your excuses, if you do not wish to share her company."

I didn't bother to point out that he was the one who'd swept me from the Queen's company in the first place, but I merely thanked him. Something seemed suddenly wrong in the air around me, some tension I'd not noticed before. Walsingham left me, and I stood for a moment longer in the reflected daylight of the western drawing room.

And then I heard it.

A long, lusty sigh—as if a slumbering bear had just roused itself from its winter nap—sounded from one of the great broad-backed chairs not ten feet away from me in this room I had thought empty. I knew that sigh. Just as I knew the young man who'd uttered it, who even now unfolded his tall, magnificent body from the chair and stood up to stretch his arms toward the ceiling, his back to me for just a moment more.

Alasdair MacLeod.

Walsingham, you insufferable ass! He had brought me here for his questioning, and then, once finished, had deliberately tried to undo all the work I had done with Alasdair. But why? It made no sense. But maybe—maybe Alasdair had not heard everything. Maybe everything was not lost, maybe—maybe—

"That," Alasdair MacLeod said into the silence, as if he were addressing the very sky and forest beyond the open balcony, and not me at all, "was certainly diverting."

The blood drained from my face, my hands, my heart. It would have pooled in a widening stain on the stone at my feet if it had had any way to do so. With only the greatest of efforts, I kept my face an arch mask of feminine defiance as Alasdair turned and favored me with a hard smile. He took three long steps toward me, still staying carefully away, and made a courtly bow. The air between us shimmered with intensity.

A thousand apologies sprang to my lips, but I could not force myself to utter them, all the coquetry of my past long years at court failing me when I needed it most. "Al—" I finally managed, but he lifted a lazy hand.

"You will find, for our many flaws, we Scots are a proud and discerning lot," he drawled, his hard gaze raking over my face with a heat that belied his calm words. "A proud man would leave you to your lies, my lady, you and your entire court of deceivers."

Then he leaned closer to me, his breath warm and sweet as it feathered against my ear. "But a discerning man would not give up until he'd discovered just what rests beneath all of those layers of lies you've been telling for all these many years . . . and especially these last few weeks." He paused a moment more as if he could not help himself, then bent forward to press his lips against my ear. "And perhaps most of all, these last few moments."

I could barely hear his next words, so hard was my heart pounding, so heavy was my blood rushing in my veins.

"I look forward to that, my lady," he said.

Then he was gone.

CHAPTER TWENTY-ONE

I made it through the rest of the day without collapsing from mortification—either from Alasdair's reproach or the fact of the still-missing Sophia—but it was a close thing. My reactions to every word or gesture in my direction seemed completely disproportionate, and I had to school myself to remember who Beatrice Knowles was, and what she stood for, at least thirty times.

Alasdair was mercifully absent but for occasional reports to one of the maids or another about the fact that Sophia had not been found. Our covering story had been spread throughout the castle, and with half the court still abed with headache and upset stomach brought on by eating me out of hearth and home the night before, no one missed Sophia much. Cecil and Walsingham closeted themselves in their rooms as well, which was all the same to me.

The conversation the maids had shared with the Queen had been fruitless, with Cecil giving a dull accounting of the progress of the Lords of the Congregation in their battle against the French—and the Queen demanding if Anna, Meg, and Jane knew anything different from Cecil's accounting. Of course, they did not.

Currently the Protestants were marauding their way through every Catholic church they could find in Scotland, Cecil had advised, destroying priceless artwork and statuary. The violence of the rebellion was beginning to sway the common folk into believing that such force was necessary to turn away the French, and now dozens of pamphlets decrying French rule were being circulated to aid the cause. The Reverend John Knox was still beating the drum against the French as well, but no mention was made of his desperate letter to the English court, where he tried to masquerade as the good Protestant John Sinclair.

Why did the Queen keep her knowledge of John Knox's duplicity to herself? we wondered. Was she trying to trip up her advisors? Or did she not believe what we had told her?

Now the sun was setting quickly in the western sky, and we had gathered in our rooms after a blessedly subdued evening meal that had not included Her Peevishness. The Queen was still overset and holding court in her apartments. Meg's convincing sniffles had cleared us all of entertaining her for this night, and for that I could have wept with relief.

A sharp knock roused us from our stupor, and we turned to see Alasdair standing at the open doorway. "My lady Beatrice, ladies." He swept me a short bow, then nodded to the other maids, the perfect gentleman.

"You've found her?" I asked quickly, allowing myself a few short steps in his direction.

Alasdair's hand forestalled me. "We have not. But I

wish to share with you that Marion Hall has apparently received additional guests this evening, under the cover of darkening sky."

I frowned. "Additional guests?" Had the Queen sent for reinforcements? "Who? From where?"

"That I have not ascertained." Alasdair gave a wry grimace. "A few of your foundlings were hiding in the hayloft when the men came in on horseback, heavily cloaked. The newcomers enjoined your guards to keep their peace about their arrival—to not share the information with anyone. No threats were made, but it was clear they expected their orders to be obeyed."

I frowned. "And our guards went along with it?"

Alasdair shifted slightly. "Your father was escorting the men, it appears," he said. "He took everyone into the house as well, still cloaked and silent. The children couldn't see where they went after that."

I stared at him. *My father?*

Jane had ambled up to us, taking an extra step toward Alasdair where I could not. "How many men? Did they say?"

"Eight—two of them dressed as guards," Alasdair said, and Jane nodded.

"So the Lords of the Congregation have arrived at last," she said.

"But why here, and why now?" Meg mused, her voice startling me. I had not heard her draw close. "And what does your father have to do with them?"

Alasdair shrugged, but I beat him to the most likely explanation. "'Twould have been nothing for Cecil to ask my father to ensure the Lords' safe passage," I said. "He or Walsingham could have made the request without sharing who the men were. And with the Queen's seal of approval, my father would let in the devil himself."

"I think you have the right of it," Alasdair agreed. "They must be making their exodus back north."

"Beatrice? Could you, ah, come here?" Anna alone had not joined us at the doorway for Alasdair's news, and was instead peering through an odd contraption of glass and metal that she'd also apparently lifted from John Dee's study at Mortlake. She'd discovered that she could look through the crude device and see far things as if they were nearer, but the blurriness of the images gave me a headache. Now she looked up from the hunk of glass and squinted into the gathering night.

"Well," she humphed as we drew close. "This thing is completely useless if my own eyes can see more clearly." Even Alasdair chose to accompany us to the window, though he stood well away from me. I tried to convince myself not to care about that. "Do you see that there?" Anna pointed. "In the heart of the forest? What on earth could they be? They almost look like lanterns."

I peered out over the darkened patch of forest, and there, far deep in the thicket, I could see what Anna had picked out. My heart dropped to my feet.

"I see them," I said with a sigh. "And they are lanterns. Made of strips of fabric draped over a frame of wire."

Meg turned to eye me with surprise. Of all of the maids, she was the most well traveled, her Golden Rose acting troupe having tromped their way across most of England. She knew who'd made those lanterns, and she knew why I hesitated to explain.

I felt Alasdair's glance upon me as well as I struggled to continue. Why had my father not watched for the return of these accursed people? Why did they choose now to squat upon our lands? "They are the Traveling People," I said.

Anna put her hand to her mouth, though Jane, Meg, and Alasdair did not seem to value the weight of this statement as much. Anna may not have been born of a top-tier family, but even those in the lower gentry knew the rules regarding Traveling People. They were to be turned out of your lands the moment they were discovered, and given no safe harbor.

"Oh, Beatrice," she moaned. "Not this. Not when you have already suffered so much from this progress."

"Well, what of it?" Jane asked, slanting us both a confused glance. "So there are Travelers in your forest. They aren't troubling anyone out there. What harm could they be?"

"They're Egyptians; that's harm enough." I shook my head. "If this lot is the same one that has traveled our land in years past, they are fortune-tellers and rogues, but not a bad sort. They help with the harvest, and with trade. You could often find herbs in their caravans that no one else could procure, and they doled out potions along with their portents that actually cured many an ill. We have never had any trouble with them, but they are still strangers to this land, and as such they are the first to be blamed for aught that is wrong."

"That's where the kitchen got those possets," Anna guessed. "I knew those herbs were not culled from any back garden. And Lord knows that the reaction Sophia had to them couldn't have been normal. Cook thought she'd just sleep and clear her head." Anna's gaze went back to the dancing lights in the wood. "But there is nothing for it, no matter what benefits they bring. There isn't enough work for the regular folk, 'tis said, so the Travelers must be expelled. Elizabeth's not the first of her family to do the expelling, either," Anna said. "Her father deported them, and the Queen's sister, Mary, as well."

"Mary was far worse," I said. "In this as in all things. After the Egyptians Act, everything was turned upside down."

"Egyptians Act?" Alasdair asked. "We have no such thing in Scotland."

"Well, you are barbarians," Anna said reasonably. "Of course you don't. And you've Travelers of your own kind, just not from Egypt. Those people out there, though"—she nodded to the deep forest—"they might be killed just for being Egyptians, no other crime than that. And your family, Beatrice." She said the last words as a whisper. "If you are found in the fellowship or company of Travelers, or even having benefited through trade with them, which surely you did to pull off feeding so many people . . . you could be killed as well."

"Killed!" Alasdair's shock was plain. "And we're the barbarians?"

"I . . ." I swallowed, but the words had to be spoken. "I understand if you cannot keep this secret for me. It is a crime, as Anna says."

"Oh, pish."

"Oh, hush yourself!"

"Oh, Beatrice, you cannot be serious—" The words tumbled over one another, each of the girls lining up beside me to assure me of her solidarity, even as Alasdair frowned at me. I didn't know my fellow spies all that well, for all that we'd lived several months in one another's company. I certainly didn't trust them. But what was done was done. I had implored my father to urge the Travelers on their way, to suggest they depart for Scotland, since Alasdair's words were true enough. Egyptians might still be shunned in the northern climes, and even deported back to the Continent. But they would not be killed there. We civilized Englishers reserved that right.

"In any event," Anna said staunchly, recovering first, "we cannot think on that now. I would be willing to bet that's a celebration going on in the deep wood. And what better cause would the Travelers have for celebration, with their myths and mystery and magic, than finding a seer in their midst?"

Jane cursed under her breath. "She's safer with a band of rogues than in the clutches of wild animals, or broken somewhere in a ditch . . . but not by much."

"We have to go get her," I said resolutely, even as Alasdair started to protest.

"Aye," Jane said. "That we do."

Our plan was made in haste, and executed under the same dark cloak of night that had brought the Lords of the Congregation to Marion Hall. Though Alasdair seemed completely put out at our insistence to handle this search ourselves, he refused to let us travel alone. He finally relented with adding just two outriders to our company—himself and one of the older grooms. All of Marion Hall's staff knew of the Travelers in our midst, of course, the whole of them now at risk of the Queen's displeasure should the forest celebration come to light.

For once I did hope Cecil and Walsingham were still closeted away with their precious Scottish Lords, ideally somewhere without windows.

We set off due north and entered the forest just past the edge of the labyrinth, its hulking hedgerows hiding secrets of their own. I felt Alasdair's gaze upon me as we passed it, but I kept my face carefully forward, glad that the moonless night hid the blush that climbed my cheeks at the memory of his completely inappropriate and troubling kiss.

It didn't take us long to hear the Travelers.

And they were not just celebrating, we quickly realized; they were bringing the very forest to its knees.

The music reached us first, simple drums and bells on chains that were struck in sharp, percussive rounds, the tune running fast and sure, keeping time to some unseen dance. Then the lights, strung up in the trees and over tents and wagons, drew us ever closer. At length we dismounted, and led our horses close enough for easy reach, and instructed the groom to stay with the small herd. He did so reluctantly, clearly thinking that Alasdair alone was not sufficient protection for four hapless young women setting off to find one of their own in the heart of a Traveler celebration.

We finally reached the last stand of trees and brush that separated us from the revel. This was one of the Travelers' traditional encampments, cleared out in a broad circle in the center of the forest, a burbling brook providing an ideal resting spot. And Anna had been correct about the reason for all the music and laughter.

A ring of men and women, laughing and calling out encouragement, were clapping and stomping as a couple spun in the circle of the others' protection, their movements lithe and beautiful as the music soared, their energy as sure and true as the roaring fire that provided the backdrop to their wild, frenzied dance.

We had found Sophia.

CHAPTER TWENTY-TWO

We could do nothing until the music stopped, but in truth we didn't have to make the first move. I saw the wave of recognition move through the Travelers even as we hesitated at the edge of their circle. With a sharp nod to the musicians, a man who must have been the leader of this troupe held up a hand.

The frenzied music stopped with a last, percussive burst.

Sophia and her young man collapsed against each other, laughing so hard, they were crying, and the crowd around them gave a throaty cheer. Then the ring opened toward us, and Sophia chose that moment to look up.

Seeing her, my heart caught in my throat. This was not the pallid girl of Windsor Castle, with pained eyes and thin, pinched lips. No, this Sophia was utterly changed—her hair wild and free, her face bright with heat and excitement, her torn lavender gown draping off her shoulder to bare an expanse of flushed porcelain skin.

"Beatrice!" she cried, and peeled away from her young man to fling herself through the open space toward me. I caught her easily as she flew into my arms, and immediately smelled the sharp, sweet spice of mulled wine.

I raised my eyes heavenward even as I grappled with Sophia, her body slewing around in my grasp.

She was drunk.

"Who thought it was a good idea to give this girl wine?" I demanded, not bothering to introduce myself. With Sophia calling me by name, this troupe would know I was the daughter of the lord who owned this land. I might not have remembered them, but chances were good that they'd remember me.

"It's really good!" Sophia gasped, then hiccuped. Two men stepped forward—well, a father and son, I could see at a glance. The older man looked to be in his fifties, and his hair was a perfect mane the color of steel. He wore peasant garb, a loose-fitting jacket and breeches. But a bright-colored silk scarf fluttered at his neck, and his manner proclaimed him Egyptian royalty. This would be the leader of their group, but I didn't recognize him. Of course, I'd been perhaps nine years old the last time I'd seen a Traveler this close.

"Lady Beatrice Knowles," the leader spoke, and though I didn't recognize his face, the voice caught me up short. That I remembered. This man had sung to me when I was a child, and his voice had been a thing of beauty. "I am—"

"Stefan Behari," I said, the name surfacing from the depths of memory I had thought long since covered over and forgotten. I looked then to his son. "And you must be Nicolai?"

The young man scowled at me, his eyes fixed on Sophia,

but the older man grinned broadly and clapped his hands together. "She remembers! The proper lady all grown up remembers a poor tinker, who knew naught but to sing for his supper all those years ago."

"Your supper and food for your entire troupe, if I remember now," I said, jostling Sophia to one side. "What did you give her?" I asked again.

"Not much at all, in truth." It was Nicolai who spoke, and his voice carried the same resonant timbre as his father's. The idea that these two might sing together thrilled me to the bone, despite the fact that I was still manhandling Sophia to keep her from falling flat on her face. "She took the merest sip of wine, and spilled some on her gown, but she came to us already in a state, like a wild fawn out of the woods."

"No mere fawn." The father took up the tale, and the two of them now regarded Sophia as if she were a woodland goddess. "She is a creature of Sight and magic, whose vision far exceeds her understanding." His gaze shifted to me. "She is of your company?"

"She is," I said. "And she has been missing for nearly a full day. I have to get her back to the Hall—and you should have a care, Master Stefan. You know better than to call such attention to yourselves. You will be caught out, and there are many who would suffer for it."

"Not the least the grand Knowleses of Northampton?" Stefan said, his words the slightest sneer.

"Well, yes. We might be beheaded. But what would happen after is of more account," I said coolly. I didn't much like Stefan Behari, for all his lovely voice and roguish manner.

"Without my father, my mother would die; if she herself escaped the axe. Without my parents, our household would scatter. The children returned to their holdings, the servants forced to seek work elsewhere in some grand house already filled with a staff of its own. Without the oversight of the Hall, the village would suffer, the land would founder, the animals would wander. You and yours with any luck would be on your way, traveling to a new location to take up residence and trade or tinker. But you would leave behind a land much worse for the time you spent here."

"And so, what? You would ask us to flee?" Stefan bristled. "You would ask us to be deported and uproot our families and our way of life, maligned and mistreated wherever we roam?"

I'd heard this argument a thousand times. I hoisted Sophia higher in my arms. "No, Stefan Behari. I would merely ask you to be sensible. To not light a hundred lanterns and dance a merry jig in the middle of a silent forest when a household full of the Queen's men lies sleeping not two miles away."

He shrugged. "The movements of your royalty are of no concern to us. We live our lives but freely, harming none. And without our aid you would never have been able to board and bed your precious Queen."

"Well I know it," I said grimly. My father had doubtless come tearing back to Marion Hall from Windsor Castle to find what had to have been an un-provisioned household and a poorly prepared staff. "Were you compensated for your time, your services, and your goods? Did my father deal with you fairly?"

"He was as fair as ever," Stefan said easily. "His need was

great, but he knew it. That makes for easy bargaining, and his gold is ever fine."

I frowned at his mention of gold. "Well, then, you have no reason to risk that bounty, do you?" Looking around at the ruddy faces, the ready grins despite our intrusion on their celebration, I suspected several casks of village ale had traded hands as well as any coin or clothing needed by the clan; Father certainly had precious few trinkets to trade. "You could at least help the man keep his head."

"We cannot live but that we dance; we cannot move but to the music." This wasn't Stefan who spoke now but Nicolai, who strode forward to me boldly and reached for Sophia. I could feel Alasdair bristling behind me, but the Scot held his peace as the young Traveler gathered Sophia up in his arms. "Sophia came into our midst as a gift, and as a gift she must be returned. But her protection by the Rom only begins this day, Lady Beatrice, it does not end. She too easily slipped through your fingers; you must have a greater care for her."

I watched Sophia snuggle into Nicolai's arms, and I wondered how much of this day the girl would remember—and how much of this boy. He was a tall and striking young man, perhaps the handsomest of their lot I had ever seen. His black hair was worn long and cascaded to his shoulders in a thick, silken mane, and his skin was lighter than his father's, almost olive-toned. He wore a brilliant blue tunic over his black breeches, and a red scarf at his neck. Now his piercing blue eyes challenged me.

"Did she speak to you of what she saw?" I asked.

"She spoke of many things," Stefan interrupted Nicolai's

half-formed response, his words repressive. Their eyes met, and the tension in the air was palpable. "But she was out of her head with the spirits that clamor to communicate through her, as she is coming into her own. We helped give her ways to read what was truth and what were her own fears and anxieties. Her relief was great, as you see." The older man's eyes softened as his gaze shifted back to Sophia. "She is almost too rare to let go."

Beside me Jane's hand stole to her belt, Meg tensed, and even Anna tilted her head, no doubt calculating our odds of taking on this group ourselves. We were outnumbered, though not necessarily outmatched, but Nicolai shifted. "I will carry Sophia to where you've kept your horses," he said. "And give you safe harbor out of the forest."

I managed to keep myself from reminding him that it was my forest, not his. Instead, I merely nodded. "I thank you for it," I said, and I turned, startled to find that Alasdair had moved from the back of our group to stand just behind me, his sturdy solidity a welcome change from the fluid grace of the Travelers.

"A gift! She must have a gift!'

A tiny, white-haired woman burst into the circle, wrapped up in a vivid yellow dress that fluttered out behind her in a swath of heavy silk. In her hands she held a small package wrapped up with paper and string, but as she approached us, she saw immediately that Sophia had fallen fast asleep. "Her light, it burns so brightly," she chirped, and her lined face creased into a toothless smile that quite unnerved me. "Would that it never go out."

Then she turned to me, and that smile instantly hardened, as if she had judged me and I'd been found wanting. "You shall give this to her when she wakes," she said, and it was not a question. "Do not unwrap it. It is for the girl alone, not for the likes of you."

Irritation flashed up and over me, but I just wanted to be gone from this place.

"Of course," I murmured. The woman bustled up and shoved the gift at me. I took it, marveling at its weight for such a small package, and felt the rough surface of the woman's palms as she pressed her hands against mine.

"Ah!" she cried out, cackling, her beady eyes seeming to stare straight through me. "You too shall know great loss and misery, such pain as you had never thought. On your knees in darkness, no one to save you then." She stood back, gloating at me, and her words seem to brand themselves on my very bones. "You'll get what you deserve."

I reared back from her, too startled to even gasp.

"We must away." Jane's stern voice sounded in my ear, too loud, and I felt her hands upon me, turning me, urging me out of the circle of light and music and horror, as the sound of the old woman's laughter followed us into the wood.

CHAPTER TWENTY-THREE

Getting Sophia onto a horse was more problematic than it should have been.

The short walk back to the horses went smoothly enough. Nicolai stalked through the woods without missing a step, despite the fact that Sophia alternated between dozing against his chest and murmuring strange half sentences about dreams and death and danger.

Anna and Meg walked closely behind them, and I knew that Meg was doing her level best to memorize everything the girl said, with Anna beside her to serve as a second, more discerning, pair of ears. This was Meg's gift, after all—her perfect recall of any conversation, in any language, whether she understood it or not. Though some of what Sophia was muttering bordered on madness, between Anna and Meg, they'd puzzle out Sophia's words once we'd gotten her safely home.

Jane ranged ahead, and Alasdair brought up the back of our troupe. He and I didn't speak, but I was glad for his presence. The words of the old woman rocked me in a way I knew they shouldn't have. She was an ancient crone, a soothsayer, and I had irritated her by interrupting the music and dance she'd no doubt enjoyed very much. I was her enemy, English and titled, and she had every right to dislike me on sight. Her curse was nothing so much as a jumble of words sewn together to frighten me.

And, well, it had worked.

I worried Sophia's gift nervously in my hands as I moved through the brush, close enough behind Meg and Anna that I did not have to watch so carefully where I stepped.

What did the woman say, exactly? I would have to get Meg to repeat it for me. Something about knowing misery and fear, about being on my knees, alone and unwanted. It was nigh unto my worst nightmare, so I had to give the old witch that. She'd known exactly what to say to cause me the greatest amount of misery.

A branch cracked behind me, and I jumped, recovering only slightly when I felt Alasdair's firm hand upon my shoulder. "Keep the pace, my lady," he said, removing his hand as soon as I had regained my footing. I found I missed the warm solidity of his grasp immediately. "We're almost there."

"I know we're almost there," I groused. "Stop crowding me."

Obligingly Alasdair slowed his steps, and I trudged along through the wood with my temper steadily worsening. All around me people did exactly what I asked of them, even if—especially if—it took them away from me. Now even Alasdair was doing it. He didn't try to override me, ask what was wrong, or give me comfort. No. He dropped back as if he were glad to be rid of my company. As if staying for another second so close to me would have been too tiresome to endure. As if I were a chore.

My own words came back to haunt me during those last few minutes before we gained the horses. I had expressed my derision about Alasdair to Walsingham, and Alasdair had heard me. But rather than confront me, allow me to explain, or even publicly denounce me, he contented himself with following me at a distance through the underbrush, staring holes into the back of my gown.

Then we were in the clearing with the elder groom and one of the Traveler men, a dark-eyed worthy who looked half-inclined to steal the horses rather than ensure their safe passage. The groom seemed at his ease; my family and our servants had worked alongside the Travelers for far too long to rest on ceremony in the middle of the wood.

Still, it quickly became clear that Sophia would not be able to ride in her condition. She lolled in Nicolai's arms as he came to a halt before the horses and eyed the groom. "You will carry her back?" he asked.

"No." Alasdair stepped forward now. "I am stronger. Sophia may awaken and spook the horses. I will carry her."

Nicolai had swung around when Alasdair had begun speaking, and now the two glared at each other in the darkness. "Step lively, then," Jane said, and I heard her take her mount. "We've all been missing too long. Well and good that we've found Sophia, but if we don't get her back quickly, there will be too much to explain by half."

I strode forth and positioned myself between Alasdair and Nicolai, who still clutched Sophia as if he were afraid to let her go. As soon as I drew near, Alasdair stepped away, turning to tighten the cinches on the saddle of his warhorse, before stepping up into the stirrups and swinging himself over the beast's back. He circled his horse around toward us, but still the young Traveler did not move.

"Nicolai Behari," I said gently, reaching out to place my left hand on his arm. My right hand still held the gypsy's gift, and it was all I could do not to hurl it into the shadows. Instead I patted the young Egyptian awkwardly. "You have my word. Sophia will be as safe as I can make her."

Nicolai's full upper lip curled. "What is the word of an Englisher to me, when you do not even understand the treasure you have in your own midst?" he said, his tone low and almost petulant. "You would just as soon my people leave your land, never to return."

He had a point, but now was not the time to honor it. "You may remain in Salcey Forest as long as you are able, Nicolai, but tonight we must away. Let Alasdair carry Sophia back for us, that we might keep a fast pace," I said. "I assure you we will get her safely home."

"She will never be safely home in the middle of your English court," muttered Nicolai, but he turned to Alasdair, offering up Sophia like a benediction. Alasdair leaned over and took the girl with equal deference, his hold on her protective and solicitous, and I felt a curious tightness in my chest.

I held my place, however, until Nicolai finally released Sophia's trailing hand and turned back to me. "She is very special," he said, his words so soft that only I could hear them. "Try to make sure no one realizes it, or she will never be free."

We shared a long moment of silence. Then I nodded.

"I will," I said.

Nicolai helped me up onto my own horse, waiting for me to settle into the sidesaddle before he stepped away. By the time I glanced back as we rode out of the clearing, he had already melted into the forest.

We arrived back at Marion Hall without anyone raising the alarm. Anna and Jane took a still-sleeping Sophia out of Alasdair's arms, but when repeated attempts to rouse the girl were not met with success, it was quickly agreed that he should carry her into the house. If any of us were stopped, we'd have to make something up and quickly, but with any luck only the servants were still awake.

Alasdair seemed strangely disquieted by this last leg of our journey, his words now clipped and short, his manner rushed. This was just as well, however. We needed speed now most of all, and I was glad for him to hasten our steps.

I regarded my childhood home with a practiced eye, every winking flicker of light from the windows betraying a still-lit sconce or nighttime candle. The first glance caused only the slightest unease, but the second one stopped me cold, making Meg run flat into me.

"Oof!" She gasped out a short laugh, and was making to speak when I caught her arm and shushed her with a finger upon her lips. Her eyes went wide with curiosity, but I merely turned to the others.

"We'd best split up," I said imperiously. "Our company is too large to go skulking through the house." Alasdair turned on me quickly.

"No," he said. "You all should—"

"Go—go!" I cut him off. "Meg and I will stroll around to the front entrance. If we're seen, I can explain away a late-night walk with another maid in my own home easily enough. I can't explain all six of us gamboling about."

He clearly wasn't pleased with this arrangement, but there was naught that any could offer to gainsay my logic, and with his last grumble of disapproval we parted company. I held Meg still until I saw our fellow skulkers disappear into a side entrance of Marion Hall, only the murmur of conversation between Alasdair and the servants disrupting the night.

"What are we doing?" Meg asked, peering at me through the gloom.

"Shh," I said, pulling her along toward the far end of the house, below the western drawing room. "I thought I saw something back here, where there should be no one at all."

"And we're going to seek it out?" she asked. "Without weapons or a brawny guard or two?" Her teeth flashed in the moonlight. "Excellent."

"I said be still," I hissed, pausing as we came around another corner. My steps had slowed now, my eyes straining to see into the gloom to where I swore I saw . . .

And there it was.

A light flickered in the tiny window at the very base of the hall, above what I knew to be the old wine cellar. Old, as in empty, as in a chamber nobody ever used anymore. Not even for storage, though once upon a time it had provided an excellent cool, dry location to ensure that wine aged to its fullest taste.

"What is that?" Meg asked, following the direction of my gaze.

"I don't know," I said, "but where there are lights, there are generally people."

"In your cellar?" She frowned.

"In my cellar." I slanted her a look. "And we did gain several new guests this evening. Perhaps they were guests in need of a quiet place for a conversation."

Meg grinned in the gloom. "Well, that seems promising, but how can we get in there? Not through that tiny window, certainly."

"Not quite, but—come with me." I took her by the arm, and we hastened through the darkness, moving past the row of windows and into a shadowed lee of Marion Hall. A cellar door there lay hidden in the tall grass, and I fished on my belt for the right key. It was the same key as opened every cellar lock in the hall, and it didn't fail me here. The door gave way with a dry, crumbly *woof* of air, and I thanked the craftsman for his choice of timber and fastenings. The wall was not at all the worse for its age or the several bad winters I'd heard tell of in the servants' quarters. Instead a spiraling staircase curved down into the darkness, hewn from the rock itself.

Without hesitating, Meg started down the steps, and it was all I could do to follow her into that pitch-dark space. She clucked with pleasure as she scampered ahead of me, waiting with barely concealed excitement as the low hum of men's voices swam toward us. "They are talking plainly, so sure they are that they will not be discovered," she whispered happily as I descended the stairs and landed next to her. "My favorite kind of mark."

"Shh," I warned, and she sobered. "There are spy holes built into the cellar room. My father had no sooner taken out all the wine than he realized he now had the greatest room possible for visitors to speak with absolute certainty that they would not be overheard. So of course he wanted to make well sure he could hear them."

I reached for Meg's hand, and we walked through the darkness, toward the raised voices. We positioned ourselves in a tight corner, one of the many fissures that had been cut into the walls to allow someone to peer into the space. Some of these fissures had already existed, cut by the same baron who'd built Marion Hall. Though their purpose was not certain, both my father and I had always speculated that either the good baron had thought his servants were stealing his wine or the room had once been used for something other than simple libations. We'd crafted many a tale of secret negotiations in these hidden rooms, with King and country depending on a loyal patriot pledged in aid of the Crown.

And here we were this night, about to embark on a fell plot not too far removed from those childhood imaginings.

Meg and I fit our eyes to the tiny holes, both of us as still as mice. The room beyond was lit up like full day, and though all of the men were cloaked except for Cecil and Walsingham, their speech branded them as Scots, bristling with the thick inflections of their homeland. I gave Meg a quizzical look at their heavy accents, but she just grinned and nodded. She could understand these men, or at least memorize their words. Still, to hear more effectively she adjusted her stance and placed her ear to her spy hole, while I leaned close and refit my right eye to mine.

And that's when it happened.

The door at the far end of the room opened, allowing one last man to enter the chamber, cloaked as all the rest, his shoulders broad, his walk assured. The others turned his way but did not acknowledge him, and he took his place by the door, clearly a guard of some sort who had just assured that their secrecy was absolute. He was dressed in the same dun-colored garb I'd seen the Lords' guards wear throughout their stay in Windsor. If I hadn't seen the man move, I wouldn't even have noticed him, most likely.

But I *had* seen him move. And I knew that walk.

For reasons I could not begin to fathom, Alasdair MacLeod had just joined the secret meeting of Scots and English advisors. And he'd breathed to me not a word about it.

I struggled to make sense of his presence in the cellar room. He was the one who'd told me in the first place about the arrival of the additional guests to Marion Hall. Why? Did he know that I would hear about it anyway, and seek to twist the information for his own benefit? But why agree to travel with us to find Sophia, when he knew such an important meeting was to take place this night?

And, again, what was he *doing* here? And how dare he get angry with me for *anything*, as he had in the western drawing room, since he was perpetrating a lie under my nose as a part of the very Lords of the Congregation upon whom I was supposed to spy!

How could I have missed this connection!

The words of the Scotsmen washed over us like water then for several minutes, and one thing was certain. These were definitely the Lords of the Congregation. There was even the young Earl of Arran, whom I identified only because he eventually dropped his cowl, complaining of heat. The earl was the man whom Cecil had helped bring safely back home from France. He wandered near Alasdair, and I stiffened, pressing my eye so closely to the wall, I was surprised no one sensed the very rafters watching them. But the two men did not speak, and the Lords themselves argued much and decided little, most of it focusing on how much aid the Queen would send in arms and men.

Gradually, however, despite my focus on Alasdair, I became aware of another sound in the distance, a scrape and a shuffle—not constant, but just often enough to seem like someone was repositioning himself or herself much the same as Meg and I were.

Perplexed, I peered off down the corridor. Meg pulled back from the wall and frowned at me, but I motioned for her to return to her task while I stood away from the spy hole, smoothing my dress down resolutely.

Only one person knew the Hall so well as I did. And only one person would also know where to stash a half dozen foreigners who'd come to speak with the Queen's most trusted advisors, in such a way that he could spy on their entire conversation, breath by bloody breath.

My father.

CHAPTER TWENTY-FOUR

I slipped off my boots and moved down the corridor. Questions crowded in upon me. What had Father learned so far by spying on the Queen's men and the foreign diplomats that Meg and I had missed? And what would he do with the information he was gaining?

And perhaps most important, *did he realize that Alasdair was also in that room*?

If it had been any person other than my father, I would have suspected that his interest in the Lords of the Congregation lay solely in the idea of learning something that was clearly intended to be secret. Such was the way of a courtier—knowledge was power in our enclosed society. And the grander the secret the more powerful it was. But power was profitable only if you chose to wield it. And, given that the holder of this information was my father, I had no doubt but that he planned to sell it to the highest bidder.

A dozen possibilities assaulted me as I crept along the corridor, virtually soundless in my stocking feet. Was my father also a spy for the Queen?

This option I discarded immediately; it was simply ludicrous, and my father was too often out of royal favor for him to be considered a favorite of Elizabeth's.

So, failing that, was my father hoping to improve his position in society by learning something of import? Would he slip this information to the Queen at some informal meal over the next few days, or wait until we had all returned to Windsor?

Or indeed did he have in mind some other group entirely—perhaps one loyal to France, or perhaps one sympathetic to the Catholic cause? Would my father help defend or support a cause that would get him labeled a traitor?

He already was in a tangle up to his ears with Travelers on his property. If anyone learned that he knowingly allowed a group of "filthy Egyptians" to squat on his land, his life already was forfeit. But would he go yet a step further and engage in deliberate treason?

How well did I know my father, anyway?

So intent was my thinking that I almost plowed right into the man as he knelt awkwardly on the packed dirt floor, his head canted at an odd angle to gain a better view into the room beyond. When he realized he was no longer alone, I saw him take a deep breath, hold it, and then let it out with the air of a soldier willing to face his destiny.

Then he turned and saw me. His eyes widened, and he grinned.

"Bea—" he began, but I held up a sharp hand, unwilling to speak until I drew near to him. I tiptoed up and hissed into his ear, for once not bothering to hide my fury:

"What in God's name are you doing here?"

Father jolted back, surprise and amusement still evident on his face. "I could ask the same of you," he whispered back, "but I doubt I'd like the answer. Now hush and take the next position." He indicated another set of spy holes. The Lords of the Congregation would be ill-amused to learn their hidden cupboard had walls that were more like windows.

He fitted his head to the wall again, and I did the same. I had to admit, this vantage point was better than Meg's for viewing, but I had no doubt that she would hear and retain more than either my father or myself. Accordingly I focused on what I was seeing.

It wasn't much. Other than Cecil and Walsingham, most of the other men gathered round were almost shapeless beneath their heavy woolen coverings. A few more heads had been bared, and I thought I recognized the Duke of Châtellerault, who was the father of the Earl of Arran. That young earl was now looking almost feral with intensity. I'd heard his temperament was somewhat unstable, and I wondered at his inclusion here in this close group. Still, if he was not to be counted upon, at least this way he could be watched. Also in the group were a baggy-eyed man in a full red beard, and a heavy-jowled frowner with eyes so small, they were almost lost in his face. Everyone still seemed focused on men at arms and ships from the English fleet, and how quickly they could be dispatched to Leith, the port town where the Scottish rebellion against the French was coming to a head.

Walsingham and Cecil, to their credit, gave no solid assurances, though they were open and encouraging and gave every indication that yes, of course, they could bring the Queen around; no, she would not put any undue strictures on the Protestant Scots in return for her aid; and yes, her faith was utterly important to her, and they would ensure she lived up to the sanctity of her position.

This last assertion brought me up short. There was no indication in my father that he thought this statement was odd, but I knew if any of my fellow maids had been standing next to me, we would have been eyeing each other in quizzical concern.

Did Cecil and Walsingham presume that they could guide the actions of the Queen beyond simple advisement? Did they think they could direct her, like puppeteers with a prized doll, to merely do what they thought was right? Up to and including how she worshipped God?

I wasn't a child; I knew the kind of guidance that advisors had given to Edward VI, King Henry's son. They'd bullied and coddled and outright lied to the boy, when needed, to get him to sign required documents or give approval on directives of state. But Edward had been a mere nine years old when he'd taken the throne, and he'd died when he was barely fifteen. He'd needed that type of guidance.

Queen Mary, Elizabeth's older half sister, certainly had not. She had been crowned in her midthirties after successfully deposing the unfortunate Lady Jane Grey, who'd stupidly tried to take the throne, instead of seeing the folly of standing in Mary's way. Jane had seemed savvy enough, from what I had seen at court. More learned than even Elizabeth, or so I had thought. But she had been manipulated by the Duke of Northumberland and been led into the madness of her reign like a sheep to slaughter. And slaughtered she had been.

Of course, Queen Mary had not been ruled by advisors, but then again, there had been her husband to contend with. So the ruling had still been there, just in finer robes.

I realized that the Lords' conversation was drawing to an end, and I leaned back from the wall to see my father doing the same. He stood, dusting himself off, and grinned at me in the weak light streaming from the chamber. "Nice trick that, eh?" he whispered. "I always thought that wine cellar might be put to good use. Never expected it to have such high company, though."

"Why are you spying at all?" I asked, and was rewarded with a cavalier wink.

"Why not?" he said. "If there's information to be had, I might as well have it." He waggled a finger at me. "I find it more interesting, though, that you are here, sweet Beatrice. Why isn't the Queen in this underground hall with her advisors gathered round, instead of sleeping prettily in her own bed—whether alone or with her dashing neighbor?"

"Father!" I hissed, knowing the damning accusation in his words. He just shrugged.

"That's of no account to me, in truth. Being a monarch is a lonely business. But surely she has more of a care for England than to rely upon the accounts of her men, when she might hear with her own ears, eh?"

I had no answer to that, and his expression turned a bit grim. "It is never an easy thing to be a woman, Beatrice," he said. "And a woman in power is more at risk than any other. She invites attention. She is strong when the whole world thinks she should be weak, and there are those who don't like that fact. Remember that."

"And you should remember that we are not talking about some milkmaid but of your Queen," I said, surprising even myself at my defense of the woman I despised. "She deserves better than what her advisors are giving her, if she doesn't know of this conversation." My gaze hardened as I saw his quick smirk. "And if you're thinking of betraying her, Father, by selling the information you've gathered here to the highest bidder, then you should take great care. She would not hesitate to kill you, for even the smallest slight." That was only the truth, and it didn't pain me much to say it. My father was a charlatan and a fool, but he at a minimum valued his own skin. Or at least I'd thought so up until now.

Father put a finger to his lips as the men exited the secret chamber beyond, to enter the short corridor that would lead them through the hidden doorway to the gardens of Marion Hall. When the last of the men had gone, he leaned forward to me once again, his glance uncharacteristically somber.

"You may not realize this, Beatrice, but I've worked your whole life to help ensure your safety and position in a court that grows more dangerous with each new monarch at its head. Though it does my sense of pride good to see you here this night, it pains my heart."

I stiffened, drawing away from him. "I have no need of your *help*, Father."

He nodded, his mask of affability slipping back over his face. "Then just be sure that when heads begin to roll, my sweet, you have the sense to duck."

CHAPTER TWENTY-FIVE

We gathered back in our suite of rooms and divided our knowledge like victors sharing spoils. Sophia was still sleeping off the effects of both the day and night, and Anna watched her with an odd intensity, even as she gave her attention to us as well. Jane stood at the window as if she might jump out of it, and I wondered at how hard it must be to have freedom all around her, without the ability to flee.

But Meg was the principal player in this drama, and she handled the role with her customary mastery. She shared everything she'd heard within the room, but breathed not a word about my father's presence, although she must have guessed that he also had been spying on the "secret" conference. I thanked the heavens above that Alasdair had remained quiet in the room. I still did not know how to manage my knowledge of his presence, let alone share it with the other maids. Because surely I would have to tell the Queen about it. . . .

Surely.

Anna finally roused from the other side of the room.

"Knox was not among the group, was he?" she asked as Meg finished her tale.

Meg glanced at me, but I shook my head. "No. Even he would not be so bold as to tarry in the same location as a Queen who thoroughly hates him."

Anna frowned and shook her head. "Then at last he is thinking sensibly. I confess that the more I hear about the desecration going on in the Catholic churches and abbeys, the less charitable I feel toward the Scottish rebellion. They are killing innocent clergymen, destroying priceless works of art, and shattering treasures, burning manuscripts, and ruining sacred buildings. Destruction like this makes no sense to me—not when King Henry ordered it, not when Mary ordered it, and not when Elizabeth now sits by and allows it to happen."

"It's war," Jane said from the window, though she did not turn to look at us. "It is the great equalizer among all men." We didn't answer for a moment, hoping she would speak on. Jane didn't talk much about how she viewed the world of courts and kings. But her insights were uncanny, and cleaner perhaps because she wielded a blade more easily than words. "We crave order, but order is tedious. Nobles who call themselves honorable cannot pillage and burn, cannot rape and kill, cannot loot and destroy; at least not openly. But give them a cause that hides their true nature, give them a reason to restoke those fires that are never fully banked—well. It is worse than setting wolves upon a flock of innocent sheep. Wolves at least kill for a purpose. Men destroy because it pleases them to do so."

It was quite possibly the longest speech we'd ever heard out of Jane, and I saw Meg's lips moving ever so slightly, committing it to memory.

"Well, whatever it is, it's not efficient," said Anna when we were quite sure that Jane wasn't going to say anything more. "It is a waste of priceless materials if nothing else, materials the Queen could use to shore up her own coffers, if she knew what was happening."

I gazed off into the middle distance, something in Anna's words striking a chord. "Perhaps that's why she doesn't," I said, and I felt rather than saw the others turn toward me. "Think on it. There has to be a reason why Cecil and Walsingham are keeping her closeted away from the discussion. Whyever would they bother, when it's a cause she would support?"

"Because they are obnoxious old goats?" Meg offered cheerfully. Jane snorted, and I smiled despite the weight that was growing in my chest.

Anna pursed her lips. "That is part of it, I have no doubt," she said, tilting her head. "But I think I see where you are going with this, Beatrice."

"The Queen, for all of her bluster," I continued, "does not care one whit for religious beliefs except as they affect her political position. She is her father's daughter in that. She will turn a blind eye to any faith or creed, natural or—otherwise." I glanced quickly over to Sophia, glad she was still asleep. "At least if it shores up her position to do so."

"Well, I wouldn't paint her with so black a brush as that, Beatrice." Meg's tone was earnest, but I waved her off.

I couldn't fathom what the Queen had done to merit the girl's undying loyalty, but I knew Elizabeth far better than a scrap-rattle thief who'd come to Windsor bare months before.

"It's no disservice," I said. "Would that Queen Mary Tudor had had the stability of character and the foresight to have taken a more moderate course in the treatment of her people. Her Catholic fervor has served more to show Elizabeth in the gilded light of moderation than anything our Queen has done on her own. If you're being compared to a monster, you cannot help but seem a saint." I tapped a finger against my lip, then continued as the words formed in my mind.

"But Elizabeth's religious leniency isn't just to ease the fears of an abused populace," I said. "It's also financially wise. Destruction and desecration, as Anna rightly points out, are expensive. And even if the Lords are pocketing at least some of the bounty they are destroying, more ends up melting in the fire or skewered on the end of a blade, ruined for all time. Do you really think Elizabeth would suffer so much beauty to be consigned to the rubbish heap if she had aught to say about it? She could make double the value of the items just by secretly selling them to the French abbeys—and be claimed a hero for adding to England's wealth."

Jane had finally turned to regard us with interest. "She would turn a profit if she could, and use the money to line her own palaces with gold."

"Yes, she would," I said.

"But a measured approach to a rebellion isn't as effective," Anna mused. "Far better to incite the people to become a riotous mob than to carefully and studiously enter abbeys and churches to strip them of their artifacts in a steady and righteous manner. Not when calling for everything to burn sounds so much more exciting."

Jane snorted a laugh, then turned back to the window and gazed out over the broad forest. "So keep the Queen out of the equation, do not trouble her mind with the details of the rebellion, and everyone is happy. She learns the key points, the Scots get her support, and the rebellion can move on however the men in charge believe is most expedient."

Meg folded her arms over her chest. "It still doesn't sit right, though. She's the Queen. She should be involved to the fullest extent that she prefers—not limited in her information. What right do Cecil and Walsingham have to crib their accounts to her as they see fit?"

"The right she gave them, I suppose," I said, but as much as I disliked the woman, something didn't sit right with me, either. Cecil and Walsingham were her chosen advisors, it was true enough. But they clearly had their own agenda when it came to the Queen—currently regarding how she ran her monarchy, but also, all too recently, regarding whom she favored among the men of the court.

Elizabeth had been making cow eyes at Robert Dudley since the moment she'd ascended to the throne. It didn't matter that the two of them had once been cell-mates in the Tower. It didn't matter that he was a well-turned man with courtly grace and refined manners. And it certainly didn't matter that the Queen appeared to genuinely like the man. He was married. And that made their courtship impossible.

All the more curious, then, that Cecil and Walsingham had not objected when Dudley had accompanied the Queen on this progress. Did they want the young Elizabeth distracted?

"Well, I'm not sure if she was fully aware of exactly what rights she was giving away," grumbled Meg. "It seems to me that she—"

A clatter of feet sounded down the corridor then, the flapping stride lengthening in a haphazard style that proclaimed the runner barely more than a child. I looked up as a wild-eyed boy burst into the room without even knocking at the door. "Lady Beatrice!" he wheezed, and I was on my feet at once.

"What is it, William?" My urgent tone brought the boy's color back into his cheeks. Even Sophia finally stirred, lifting her head from her pallet. "Is it my mother? Is she all right?"

"Oh, yes—oh, yes!" William said hurriedly. "Your father sent me to give you word that the Queen is—is on a tear. 'E said the words like that. *'On a tear.'*"

I raised my eyes heavenward. We had barely escaped a full twenty-four hours without having to entertain the woman. Did she never cease with her needs and expectations? "She's on a tear," I repeated, allowing William a few more seconds to compose himself. "And—what? She wants another banquet? She wants a dance this coming night?" I glanced at the window, to see the thin thread of dawn breaking over the horizon. At this point, we had all gotten but a few hours' sleep between us in the past few days, and I was losing my patience. "She wants me to conjure up a medieval joust out of thin air?"

"No, Lady Beatrice!" William protested, his eyes going saucer wide. "She wants to leave!"

That stopped us, I'll give him that.

"To leave!" exclaimed Anna, jumping up with a whoosh of skirts. "Leave as in now? As in going back to Windsor?"

"Yes!" William nodded fiercely. "She wishes to be packed and on her way by noon!"

"She's mad!" I protested, and then a dark thought streaked across my mind, as pervasive as the plague. "She's doing it on purpose. She is trying to ruin my family with the disgrace of a hasty departure on top of eating us out of house and home."

"That cannot be right," Meg put in, even as Sophia nodded, her eyes eerily bright. "We have been well entertained by your father and all of your staff, Beatrice. She has had no reason to complain."

I shook my head, trying to imagine what had set the Queen off, and coming up with nothing. "It doesn't matter," I said, disgusted. "She's Elizabeth. She sets her own rules."

From the corner of the room, Sophia sighed and folded her hands over her skirts. "And she will forever anon," she said, her voice sounding oddly changed.

Jane looked at Sophia from her perch at the window. "Feeling better, are we?"

Sophia swiveled her head to look at Jane. Then her face lost a bit of color. She tried to smile, but all of us noticed her sudden return to fragility. Anna was the first to recover. "Sophia, perhaps you should—"

"Oh, leave off." It was Jane who spoke again, and she

moved off the sill and stalked over to Sophia, then dropped down into a crouch so she could look her in the eye. "Sophia," Jane said. She reached for the girl's hands and caught them up before Sophia could pull them away. "I know what you see when you look at me. You see death. A great deal of death. Perhaps even my own."

"No!" Sophia said, but her voice had lost its fear at least, and her eyes were less haunted. "I do not see your death, Jane. I pray I never will."

This was progress, but Jane wasn't about to let it go. "Then what can you see, girl? You do not need to mince words anymore. If your gift has manifested, there is no going back."

"I know," Sophia said, her words quiet but resolute. "But it is all still so confusing to me. The voices have always been there, but now—now they refuse to leave me alone." She glanced away for just a moment, then looked back to Jane. "I do see death around you, Jane, but I see loneliness, too. A loneliness of your own making perhaps, but one you're not willing to let go." She turned to me, and I steeled myself to not step back, suddenly uneasy in my own home. "I see things about all of you, but they are mere impressions, nothing certain, nothing solid. I cannot see so clearly as that. And in truth I would not want to—not about you. Not about my friends."

I thought about Lord Cavanaugh, and Sophia's prediction that we would have no babies. Well, that certainly had been proven out, given the cancellation of our betrothal. What else could she see about me?

But as Sophia pressed her fingers together, another

thought suddenly sprang to life. "Your gift!" I said, remembering the cackling woman in the forest. "That old . . . woman, she gave me a gift for you!"

Sophia looked up, but I was already across the room, shifting aside gloves and ruffs where I'd stowed the small wrapped package.

"Here," I said, turning around. I walked over and pressed the package into Sophia's hands. "She said to give it to you when you woke up."

"Oh. Thank you," she said softly.

"Well, open it!" Anna said, her hands clasped together and her eyes bright. Anna was never one who wished to leave a package unopened or a mystery unsolved. "Do you think it is jewelry?"

"Possibly," I said, and shrugged as Sophia turned the package over in her hands. "It's heavy and round—perhaps a ring, or some bauble, surely?"

Sophia untied the string and gave a soft exclamation of surprise. She showed us the black ball of obsidian. "It's a crystal!" she exclaimed.

"It's a rock." Jane quirked a brow, clearly unimpressed. "That's useful."

"A crystal! How curious," breathed Anna, and Meg leaned forward too. "What is its significance?"

I tightened my lips, my conclusions already made. No one, perhaps, knew Travelers better than I did. I was familiar with their arcane ways.

The old woman had given our resident seer a scrying stone—the kind of crystal meant for gazing into, the better to see the future or the past. And Sophia may not have had any idea how to use the thing, but she still knew its importance.

Sophia lifted her head then, sharply, and her gaze met mine. In that glance we understood each other. I with my Scotsman and her with her stone, we had secrets we dared not share with anyone else, secrets that we alone must keep for the moment. And for the first time I felt Sophia hand her trust to me, like a quivering bird only just out of its nest.

"Well, it's a beautiful stone anyway," I said. "You can set it into a necklace perhaps, to remind you of your adventure at Marion Hall."

"A necklace." Sophia nodded slowly and looked down at the stone again. "That must be why she gave it to me."

"I cannot think of a smarter use for it," I said emphatically. Not quite the truth—but something less than a lie, at that.

CHAPTER TWENTY-SIX

We talked on, making plans. The maids had agreed by common consent that I would be the one to bring to Elizabeth the tale of Cecil's and Walsingham's potential duplicity. First, I was the one who'd overheard the discussion of the Lords of the Congregation—and reasonably enough, since it was my house that had been used for the meeting. Second, I'd been charged to follow around the Scots like a simpering milkmaid, so it was most appropriate for me to have been the one to have "stumbled" across the secret consultation.

Never mind that Alasdair was now in the thick of things, and I'd breathed not a word of his involvement with the Lords of the Congregation to the other maids. I still wasn't quite sure how to broach that topic with the Queen—or even if I should.

For one, I didn't know what role Alasdair really played with the Lords, if any.

For the second, well . . . I no longer knew what role he played with *me*. If any.

Still, I had to present my information in such a way as to

not goad the Queen to anger. Her advisors had not been candid with her—or I suspected they had not been. If I were to put this fact to her too baldly, she would fly into a rage. If I were to put it too subtly, she would not see the importance of acting prudently to regain her power with Cecil and Walsingham. There was a game in this, and it was a game Elizabeth had to win, which meant I had to act with particular grace.

I tried to meet with the Queen that morning while we were still confined to Marion Hall. I wanted to tell her everything (or nearly everything) we had seen and heard of the Lords of the Congregation. I tried at full daybreak, and then again at noon. And then again at nightfall, as dinner was drawing to a close.

She denied me at every turn.

The Queen, it appeared, did not want to hear about *anything* except how quickly we could get her back to Windsor. It was maddening, and yet quintessentially Elizabeth. She knew I had information for her, and she had decided it would keep. She would govern in her own way, on her schedule. And the world could very well wait for her pleasure.

True to the Queen's command, we'd packed her up as quickly as possible, but it had still required another night at Marion Hall before we'd been able to get Her Obnoxiousness safely on her way. We'd served a light repast, claiming that it would help her travel, and plied the woman with the heady ale that had so pleased her court at the Grand Revel. That was what the servants were calling it now, the party that had completely emptied the larders of Marion Hall and drained its casks: the Grand Revel.

I had a few other words for it, but at least it was behind us.

And the Queen still refused to speak with me.

The Lords of the Congregation, for their part, did not travel with the Queen's retinue back to Windsor. After some additional spying of our own, with Jane following around the guards of the Lords until they'd let slip their discussion as to what to buy with some newly received gold, I decided that Alasdair had *not* originally been invited to join that midnight meeting of the Lords. Instead he had paid the guards to let him pose as one of them. That they'd done so readily was interesting enough—clearly the young MacLeod had posed no concern to them.

But why had Alasdair cared enough to join the conversation in the first place? What had he hoped to gain?

In any event, Alasdair did not join the rest of the Lords and their guards as they left under cover of darkness the night before the Queen's departure. From our outlook in the western drawing room, we five maids watched that worthy company depart. They moved without torchlight under the midnight sky, but we were gratified to see that they chose to take the main road after a bare quarter mile through the trees. They would not run afoul of the Travelers on the main road. And if they did, there would be precious little incentive for them to turn back to serve notice about it, particularly since they were Scotsmen, not Englishers. They had no concern for our laws.

Father had saddled his horse almost immediately after hearing of the Queen's intention to leave, and had returned to Windsor like a shot. We'd not seen him since, but it was all the same to me. As long as Father kept his mouth shut about what we'd seen at Marion Hall, I didn't care where he spent his days.

Now, however, as we neared the enormous ramparts of Windsor Castle after a day and night of travel, I watched the approaching fortress with equal parts relief and trepidation. Our time at Marion Hall had been no respite from the politics of court—far from it. Yet I knew there had been during that fortnight an endless round of gossip circulating among the courtiers and ladies who'd been left behind. I'd need to get caught up as quickly as possible, and reestablish my primacy of place. Unfortunately, in the world of information you were only as good as your latest revelation. And there simply was not a great deal that had happened at Marion Hall that I could actually discuss.

Worse, there was far too much that I *still* had to tell the Queen.

Our return to Windsor had been an easy trip, with the court spending the night at a noble house south of Chepping Wycombe. We arrived at the castle midmorning, and I spent the better part of the day cozening information out of my informants—primarily about the good Lady Ariane and Lord Brighton, reaping the bounty of the questions I'd seeded about the couple prior to our departure for the north. Everything I learned made me glad of heart.

Unlike Lord Cavanaugh's mistress, Lady Ariane was a beloved member of the court, widowed most properly and with a huge estate to run. It had been rumored she'd be on the marriage block as soon as her mourning ended, and I had no doubt that she'd originally found Lord Brighton a worthy enough escort. He was betrothed, after all. He was safe.

But according to my watchers, Lady Ariane now gazed upon Lord Brighton with far more interest than was considered seemly for a woman in mourning . . . particularly if the object of her attention was all but wed. The two were in each other's company quite often—not enough for impropriety, but enough to raise a discerning brow once attention was brought to the matter. Excellent.

The news I learned about my lord Cavanaugh was less pleasant.

He'd been sullen and furious by turns, when he'd been at Windsor at all. His maid merry had not been seen within the castle, and speculation was rampant that he'd either disposed of the poor woman or was continuing his affair with her away from prying eyes.

This information struck me with naught but a hollow blow, and I realized I did not care as much as I should about Lord Cavanaugh's philandering. In fact, I found it very difficult to think on the good lord at all without his visage being replaced by the laughing, swarthy countenance of one Alasdair MacLeod. I told myself that of course I could not stop thinking of Alasdair—he was my quarry.

But he was perhaps something else too.

That evening I finally had my chance to speak with the Queen. Cecil and Walsingham had taken to enjoying long evening walks after the last meal, as if they didn't spend most of each day glued to each other's sides. More often than not they traversed the interior quadrangles of the castle on their nocturnal journeys—first the Upper Ward, then the Middle, then the Lower, where the commoners congregated. By the end of her long days, the Queen was usually well sick of them at eventide and preferred to listen to music or watch her ladies dance, or even be entertained by any of the usual round of courtiers and flatterers who gathered in her Privy Chamber by royal invitation.

I had no interest in watching a flock of fools flutter about the Queen, but it was customary for at least one of her spies to be there. So, for the first time ever, we sent Sophia.

We did this for several reasons. First, especially since her visions were now arriving more frequently, Sophia needed to be accepted by the court. Being in the Queen's company would help assure that. Second, by virtue of the fact that she did not circulate much, Sophia was a curiosity, and as such she flattered the Queen by being novel in her presence. Third, if Sophia was with the Queen, she couldn't be isolated by Cecil or Walsingham. Not that the Queen's advisors could interrogate the girl—but even being in their company was dangerous for Sophia, given her penchant for spouting off visions of pending mayhem. We didn't need them to know how advanced her skills had become.

So, off Sophia went to the Queen with her new obsidian bauble tucked carefully into her dress by Meg, who definitely had a knack for hiding valuables in clothes.

While Sophia laughed and applauded whatever entertainment was being enacted before the Queen, I strode into the Lower Ward, surprised to see it still teeming with people. The early October air was as crisp as a ripe apple this fine evening, and an unplanned celebration of the Queen's return served as good an excuse as any to let the ale flow.

"And if it isn't the perfect spring rose to come and grace us on a lovely autumn's eve."

I startled to the side, reacting too quickly for an ordinary lady, my hands up and ready to defend. I quickly corrected my positioning when I saw that it was none other than Meg Fellowes's former troupe master, James McDonald. "Master James," I said cheerfully, trying not to betray my irritation at this delay. "What brings you all the way to Windsor Castle? Meg said you had returned to Londontown after your presentation to the Queen."

"And yet I found that I could not tarry there, where Gloriana was not present." James grinned in return, then sketched a short bow. "I had to return. Imagine my dismay to learn she was not here at all but on a progress." He glanced toward the Upper Ward, as if he could see the Queen behind her high walls. "I trust she is safely back, none the worse for her travels?"

"She is indeed." I nodded. "Perhaps you should put on another play for her, before this month is out. She craves the distraction of fine acting." *And fine* men, I thought, not uncharitably. James McDonald was exactly the kind of man Elizabeth preferred—dashing and roguish, with smooth good looks and piercing eyes. He looked just as the troupe master of the Golden Rose acting company should—almost aristocratic, for all that he was a commoner, and his countenance was always so poised, so perfect. It made you want to know what he was thinking.

The faintest niggle at the back of my mind struck me again, as it had when I'd first met the troupe master. James McDonald had come to our aid to save Meg, who'd lived with the Golden Rose for all of her young life before finding herself in service to the Queen. Meg's first few months as a spy had not always been easy, and when Cecil and Walsingham had decided to throw her into the dungeon in order to loosen her tongue about certain secrets she'd learned about our Elizabeth, we'd had to be . . . resourceful. James McDonald was definitely resourceful.

In fact, there was always something so—familiar about James McDonald. Then the young troupe master laughed again, and the thought was chased away.

"I should like above all things to distract the Queen," he said. A movement caught my eye, and he turned to follow my gaze. Cecil and Walsingham stood at an odd angle to the crowd, clearly arguing. "But I see you have more pressing conversations to pursue," James continued gallantly, and he gave me another bow. "Still, might you carry a gift for me?"

I looked at him, startled. "But of course, James," I said. "For Meg?"

His slight smile was as filled with guile as any I'd seen in the great rounds of court. "For Jane Morgan, actually. I know she seeks to appear more the lady, and I would help her in the role." And with that, he pressed a small cluster of gold into my hand, and was gone.

I stood there for a moment, marveling at the fine chain and tiny gold locket—a simple oval with a delicate clasp. The locket was empty (of *course* I checked), but still. Master James was giving a gift of gold to Jane? Even though I was certain the piece was stolen, it was a telling act. How delightful it would be to taunt Jane with this! The possibilities were endless!

Then, suddenly, I recalled what I was about. I dropped the necklace into a pouch at my waist and turned toward Cecil and Walsingham. By now they had noticed me, and they waited with ill-disguised curiosity as I made my way across the Lower Ward to them.

"Sir William, Sir Francis," I said, sinking into a curtsy, as their roles and my position dictated. They made their bows in kind but had barely straightened before they were turning me away from the crowd.

"You have news of interest to us?" Walsingham began conversationally, though Cecil's aspect remained frosty.

"Oh, I have news," I said. "But you already know it." I waited just a beat, until I felt the weight of their combined gazes upon me. "In fact, with such news as this, I am honor bound to inform Elizabeth. I just wanted you to know before I did so, in case it—well . . ." I hesitated, not wanting to insinuate that the advisors would openly lie to the Queen. "In case you need to amend any of your accounts of your own activities while at Marion Hall to fit more seamlessly with what I must report."

Cecil looked at me with equal parts annoyance and confusion. "What are you talking about?" he demanded. "Leave off your subtlety, Beatrice, and speak plainly."

Walsingham, I could tell, already suspected what I was about to say. I shrugged, and folded my hands over my skirts. "My family's servants, Sir William, know every crease and crevice of Marion Hall. Not even my father could have warned them all away, not when lords insist upon lighting candles to brighten their midnight meetings, candles that could be seen by those who'd notice even the tiniest of lights in the tiniest of windows."

The realization of what I was saying caught Cecil up short. "Explain yourself."

"You met with a group of Scotsmen in my very cellar, Sir William, and discussed the terms of war. Your conversation was relayed to me in fragments, but I understood its import far better than a house guard could." This was, of course, patently untrue. Meg had forced me to learn the speech almost word for word. It had taken half the ride to Windsor to do it.

"And you think the Queen does not already know of this conversation?"

I turned fully to them, beaming with joy. "Ah, so you've told her! Well, that is great news. When I implied there was a conversation a servant had overheard among the Scotsmen at Marion Hall, the Queen seemed so surprised. I confess I stalled for time to ensure that I could speak with you first. But how reassuring to know you've already shared it with her. My words, then, will simply serve to validate your own."

"Or perplex her needlessly," Walsingham observed. "You cannot think your *servant* could understand the nuances of a discussion among lords, Beatrice. Your half revelations will but disturb the Queen."

"That is a possibility." I pursed my lips, as if weighing a great question. "And yet I do feel so obligated. Perhaps I should tell you what was heard, and you can tell me if it is in keeping with your recollection of the evening. Would that serve as a beginning?"

Walsingham and Cecil seemed to heave a collective sigh. They no doubt believed I'd garnered my information from an illiterate dunce, and not a spy with the greatest recall in all of Christendom. "Yes," Cecil said heavily. "That will serve—"

And I was off. I nuanced Meg's recollections with slight variations—not so large as to disrupt the pattern of the weave, but enough to keep the advisors from knowing she was my source. I added visual cues as well, from the vantage point I'd had at my spy holes, though I mentioned Alasdair not at all. Did they realize he'd been with them in the cellar room? Or had they been tricked as well? I spoke rapidly, being careful not to betray my immense satisfaction as both of them gradually lost their color.

They could deny the words, most assuredly. They could say my servant had made them up. But the mere fact that the accounting was so precise, the words so measured, the language so very much unlike something a peasant could imagine, Cecil and Walsingham knew they were caught out.

And if my story did not tail with what they had told the Queen, her first thought would be that she'd been misinformed. By her closest and most trusted advisors.

Cecil was scowling at me. "Your accounting is quite . . . thorough, Lady Beatrice. You are certain you came by this information from a servant?"

"Yes, Sir William," I demurred. "I know it may not be an

entirely factual accounting, but it is all that I have to offer, and I think valuable even if it is flawed."

"And you go to speak with the Queen now?"

I nodded. "Yes, Sir William. She is expecting me."

It was Walsingham who spoke next. His words caught me up short; the man was as quick and feral as a weasel. "Then you must go, Beatrice," he said, his tone attempting beneficence but striking me as more of a challenge. "Do not tarry another moment. You will see that the Queen already knows all she needs to know, but I'm sure she will not fault you for trying to undermine her advisors."

"Say you do not think so!" I protested. I met his gaze, and refused to let mine falter. "In fact I wish very much for you both to be present for my accounting, to correct any . . . inconsistencies in her mind."

Walsingham's smile showed that he appreciated that I was trying to ensure my trap was tightly sprung. He knew that the presence of her conniving advisors while I gave my accounting would actually do more to prove to the Queen their duplicity, not soothe her fears. But his smile also told me that it would not matter, in the end. He had not become the Queen's spymaster to be undone by a mere girl.

"Pray, it is never the Queen's *mind* that we must worry about," said Walsingham easily. "But rest assured, we will be right along."

CHAPTER TWENTY-SEVEN

I curtsied my thanks and all but ran back to the Queen's chambers. I did not trust Cecil and Walsingham to not try to block my way, but I was gratified to see no evidence of them, and to hear only the Queen's delighted laughter carrying loudly over her crowd of gathered fools. I paused a moment in the doorway, smoothing out my gown, then stepped into the Privy Chamber.

The Queen glanced up at the noise, then dismissed me with a roll of her eyes. She wasn't about to be brought down from her current enjoyment, and I was an unwanted distraction. Sophia, watching, slid her gaze to me and offered a small, apologetic shrug, but I didn't mind so terribly much. I was here, after all. The Queen would eventually have to speak with me.

I moved over to the edge of the crowd and seated myself on one of the open benches as another quartet of volunteer musicians was handed the precious instruments of the court orchestra. I gritted my teeth as I watched the horrified expressions of the rightful owners of the pieces. Ostensibly, if their instruments were destroyed, the Crown would repay them. But Elizabeth had a habit of forgetting small details like that, so I could well understand the musicians' dismay.

Laughing and rambling about, Lord Oxley tried to push an exquisite violin under his fat chin. I held my breath and winced as he noisily raked the bow across the instrument. The delicate piece had made its debut at the Queen's birthday, having only just been brought to England from Italy. Its owner was now as white as a sheet.

The crowd shifted as the musicians changed places, and I took my chance to ease closer to the Queen. This happened three more times in the space of ten minutes, and I was close enough for her to hear me, if Her Haughtiness would ever deign to look my way.

Finally I saw my chance. The music at an end, a few of the courtiers were at last bidding her a good evening, and I edged myself closer to her side. "Your Majesty," I said, with just the appropriate level of deference laced with urgency. "I have the news you requested."

"Later, later." The Queen waved airily. "You can await my pleasure like a proper maid of honor. As you can see, I am quite busy."

"Of course, Your Grace," I murmured, lowering my head as I curtsied so she would not see my eyes. It was good that I did. When I lifted them again, it was to see her staring at me with sudden, sparking anger. *Oh, wonderful.* Would I never learn to temper my tone to three shades humbler to avoid her censure?

"On second thought, you may tell me now, Beatrice," the

Queen declared, her words overloud in the small space. "Since you seem to feel your news is so urgent, pray tell enlighten us all!"

"Your Grace?" I barely managed as hot blood rushed to my cheeks at her unexpected attack. She well knew that my words were for her ears alone, but now the whole of her inner circle was eyeing me with malicious amusement and no small amount of curiosity, wondering what I would say next.

"Speak, girl, speak!" the Queen demanded. She leaned back in her chair, the symbol of the intolerant despot. "What is it you have learned that is of such interest to the Crown?"

My mind was scrambling for purchase, but every idea I came up with I rejected just as quickly. The Queen was wholly aware that I was going to share with her privileged information, even if she did not suspect my sources. She knew this was information I could not report to all and sundry.

Yet still she was mocking me, daring me to come up with some credible tidbit to feed the voracious vultures that now pressed close around her. She was asking me to tell them something new. She understood my role within this court, and how much I set store by secrets. She wanted me to reveal one of them now, just to get myself out of a scrape.

But I had nothing. Anything I'd learned at Marion Hall was either too sensitive to share or not interesting enough. None of it would do.

I was being made to look the fool, on a stage made excruciatingly more public by the fact that it was so small. This was a tidbit of gossip that the courtiers would relish spreading. This was a moment to laugh about behind opened fans as

I was tracked with amusement through the halls of Windsor Castle. Instantly I saw the web of whispers cast out over the court, and the sheer panic at the disaster that would follow jolted me into action.

I straightened, looking at the Queen with resigned disappointment. "Very well, Your Grace. I had hoped to keep it a secret from the court for a bit longer, but I have learned that a highly secretive and astounding new play is being written in your honor, by the players of the Golden Rose. They so enjoyed honoring you at your birthday that they began at once on a play to be staged as part of the Samhain festival at October's end."

The Queen narrowed her eyes at me. If she found Master James and interrogated him, I hoped he would have the good sense to play along. "And why was this play so important that you must interrupt my leisure and inform me tonight?"

"Well, I . . ." I slid my gaze out to the court. "I sincerely beg of you not to share this—"

"What? What is it?" The Queen straightened in her throne, the first indication that even she was beginning to believe my deception.

I clasped my hands together beseechingly. "For this production to work I must enjoin you all to absolute secrecy."

The entire crowd was leaning into the space surrounding the Queen now, curiosity lacing their breaths like sour ale.

"The play is being quite cunningly written to reveal a particular secret of each of its players. And the actors in this entertainment—if you dare!—shall be chosen from the Queen's court itself!"

I was now being completely preposterous, and for a moment you could have heard a scuttling mouse in the room, so silent and shocked were the courtiers. Then at once there was a great cry and clamor as each member of the group sought to support or dispute or seek enlightenment, depending without question on how intent they were on keeping their secrets . . . well, secret.

Elizabeth, not being a fool, watched their reactions with unmasked interest, and then her eyes found mine. She knew I'd tricked them all—even she had faltered at the end. And she approved. But that didn't mean she wasn't going to make my life a living—

"I heartily approve!" she cried out, and that drove the courtiers' reactions to an even higher pitch. "Let the play be enacted at the festival of Samhain!"

A cheer rang out then, punctuated only by Cecil and Walsingham striding into the room, their faces a comical mask of confusion and forced jollity.

"Your Grace!" Walsingham intoned, and the man so rarely spoke that everyone quieted immediately and turned, their eyes bright with what this new entertainment might provide. "We present you a final . . . distraction for your evening." He gave a flourished bow, then gestured to the Great Hall. "Your people await you in the Presence Chamber."

"What now is this?" Elizabeth asked. She stood, and her hands went to her hair as her closest ladies-in-waiting fluttered around her, smoothing her from gown to crown. But her expression betrayed her delight. "What have you planned, Walsingham?"

Cecil had commandeered the musicians and was already ushering them out of the room, while Walsingham smiled indulgently as the Queen made her way through the parting, whispering crowd. "Your people have missed you, my Queen, with your recent progress. They wish only to see you again."

With that, a lyrical cascade of music sounded from the Presence Chamber, and Walsingham produced a taper from his doublet and lit it in the nearest sconce. "Pray that you bring light to them all?" he asked, and he handed her the taper.

She frowned at him, but I could tell she was intrigued. My heart was finally getting back to normal after my own series of lies, and the information about the Lords of the Congregation still burned inside me. But the Queen sailed away from me into the Presence Chamber, and four courtiers immediately greeted her, their tapers raised high. Obligingly she lit each of their candles with her own, and they turned in a rustle of capes. The Queen gasped at what happened next, and from my vantage point still atop her dais in the Privy Chamber, I marveled at it too.

Walsingham and Cecil were geniuses.

Within a few short minutes the entire Presence Chamber was filled with winking, blinking lights, each held by a courtier or lady that the advisors seemed to have produced out of thin air, in clothing fine enough to pass for ballroom attire. The music struck up, and a tall, well-dressed man—had to be Dudley, which just showed you how desperate they were to distract the Queen, that they'd enlist the help of a man they detested—escorted Elizabeth to the center of the floor. They began to dance, looking for all the world like a fairy Queen and her suitor. Even I was enchanted, and I had the least reason to be.

I moved into the Presence Chamber as servants began to fan out through the crowd, replacing tapers with cups of ale or wine. The sconces around the hall were all lit, and the great fireplace was ablaze at the corner of the room, but without the large candelabra lit high above us, the room retained a romantic, warm glow.

I caught sight of Meg, who gestured to me urgently. With one last furious glance at Walsingham, who returned my scowl with a smug smile of his own, I moved over to Meg, unsurprised to see her standing with Jane, Sophia, and Anna.

"What is it?" I asked.

"It's another blasted dance, not a full day after we've arrived back in this godforsaken hulk of rock," muttered Jane as she stood atop a short bench, giving her already impressive height the added advantage to see over the crowd. "That's what it is."

"Cecil and Walsingham must have known you wanted a private audience with the Queen, and came up with this to distract her for a few more hours, at least." Anna arched her brows. "But with a dance come dancers. And in the rush of rousting attendees to join in this 'special surprise' for the Queen, our favorite advisors gathered up both Brighton and Lady Ariane. If we have any luck at all—"

"We do," Jane said from her perch. "They are standing quite close together at the west wall, looking like they know they should separate but are not quite able to do so."

"Indeed." I tilted my head and surveyed the gathered assembly. If I couldn't get to the Queen immediately, at least I could do this while I waited. "I rather think it's time for the dancing to begin, then, wouldn't you say? Perhaps a Branle leading into a Gavotte?"

"A Gavotte!" Anna's eyes were bright. "But not everyone might know that dance as yet. It's only just come up from France, and there's the—there's the— Oh." Even in the warm light of candles, I could see her blush. She'd just remembered the precise dance step required at the end of the Gavotte—one that would serve our needs ably, as it happened.

Meg frowned at Anna, then at me. "The Gavotte?" she asked, deadpan. "Please tell me I do not need to learn another dance."

"You would like it, Meg. It would allow you to divest your partner of every piece of coin he carries."

"What is this of Meg and dancing?" The rich Spanish baritone of Rafe Luis Medina flowed over us, and Meg turned a bit too quickly for propriety, but not so much for sin. Rafe bowed to her elegantly. "I should be honored to escort you, sweet Meg."

"And I shall be honored to step on your feet," Meg answered, but she beamed nevertheless, and I felt an odd pang in my chest as the music shifted and flowed around us. Had I ever looked like that with Lord Cavanaugh? Open, and happy, and brimming with love?

I put that thought right out of my head as Meg put her hands out to Rafe. "Do you know the Branle and the Gavotte?"

Rafe quirked a brow as he bowed over Meg's fingers. "I do indeed, but I suspect not all of the worthy courtiers here this night will fare so well."

"It's dark," I replied. "They'll manage. Jane, can you let the musicians know? They never turn you down."

Jane's smile was inscrutable as she stepped off her bench. "They learned quickly."

"Meg, Anna, and yes, even you, Sophia—you need to get dancers. Make it seem natural, like you're just pairing off lords and ladies standing near each other—"

"Oh!" Sophia nodded. "Yes, that should do nicely." We all turned to go, but I held out a staying hand to Jane, keeping her a moment more.

"Ah, Jane . . . ," I began, ruing the speed with which I had to do this. There was still something of great import for us to discuss, and I had not the time to do it justice!

She frowned at me, suddenly tense. "What is it, Beatrice? What's wrong?"

I fished in the pouch at my skirt and drew out the thin chain of gold with its lovely locket. "Nothing's wrong," I said. "Here—this is for you."

She frowned, taking the delicate strand from me as if it might bite her. "You're giving me a necklace?"

"Not I," I said, watching her closely. "James McDonald bade me give it to you. As a gift to make you more comfortable in your home of courts and kings."

Jane blinked at me, stunned, and in that moment I was glad I hadn't found a way to taunt the girl. I don't think I could have surprised her more if I'd gifted her with an elephant. Closing her hand over the slender necklace, I gave her fingers a light squeeze. "It's true," I said. "It's yours."

Another several seconds passed. Then suddenly, as if realizing anew where she was, Jane straightened, scowling as she thrust the necklace into her bodice without taking the time to clasp it around her neck. "James McDonald is ridiculous," she said, but there was no denying her heightened color, no mistaking the brightness of her eyes. "And we have no time for this. I'm going to go badger the musicians now."

Just that quickly we were off. True to her word, Jane pounced on the musicians, but I had no concerns there. They of all people would know the latest music, and would be desperate to try it. Out of the first few dozen couples I approached, more than half expressed delight that they knew the dance—and the rest, frustration that they didn't. This would be a small court coup for those who could take part in it.

And then I was on Lord Brighton, who appeared to be trying very hard not to stand so close to Lady Ariane but was failing miserably. "Lord Brighton, Lady Ariane," I said, curtsying before them, although I did not by rights need to do so. "We are assembling a dance to please the Queen. Do say you know the Branle?"

This was a coy beginning, but I could not afford a no. Everyone knew the Branle.

"Oh, yes—I mean—I—" Lady Ariane blushed furiously, her gaze fluttering to Lord Brighton and then away, as if she were a girl of sixteen and not a woman aged thirty years. I found I liked her immediately. Her first husband, I had learned, had been a boor and a drunk, and had left her widowed after an especially unfortunate combination of wine and horse-riding. He'd also left her rich, but too old for many of the men of court to consider as a bride.

Lord Brighton was of sterner stuff, and he eyed me with concern. "I should mayhap dance with my betrothed, Lady Beatrice," he said quietly, his words low enough to evade Lady Ariane's ears.

"Oh, pish," I protested. "'Tis a dance, nothing more. Please do say you'll join it? Both of you?"

Lord Brighton looked over at Lady Ariane then, and I felt the tremor of their attraction shudder through me like fire. So he did love her as well. Then this was even more to the good.

"I daresay one dance would not be seen as amiss," he ventured.

"Oh, Lord Brighton, I would not want you to do anything that makes you—" Lady Ariane began.

"It's decided, then," I said crisply. "The music will start shortly, into a traditional round of Branles. I must gather additional dancers." Boldly I reached out, took their hands, and joined them together. I wished I had Sophia's gift for secreting out truths, but even I could feel the heat of their joined hands, the quickening of their pulses. "Thank you ever so—" I pulled away then, tossing my last words over my shoulder. "And oh, yes—it ends in a Gavotte."

"A what?" Lady Ariane called out, but I was already into the crowd, whisking away. The music started a bare few moments later, and I saw Anna's bent head next to the

Queen's, sharing with her this newest excitement for her pleasure. Anna also adroitly moved Elizabeth and Dudley into the circle now occupied by Lord Brighton and Lady Ariane. The Queen seemed well-pleased, and I hid myself against a column. A quick search of the room revealed that apparently the Scots had not been included in the roistering of nobles that had filled the Presence Chamber; Alasdair was not among us. To my everlasting relief Lord Cavanaugh had also chosen to ignore the advisors' summons; he was nowhere in evidence. Thus freed from distractions both enjoyable and loathsome, I could pay careful attention to the action unfolding before me.

The measures of the Branle started easily enough, the dancers moving in long circles. First they stepped a few light hops to the right, and then they moved back to the left, all the while holding hands. When the music changed to announce the Branle Charlotte, the dancers easily adapted to include the short pointed-toe kicks along with their steps. Then the Branle des Lavandières was signaled, and there was great laughing and cheers as partners broke apart and acted like washerwomen scolding each other, then clapped and hopped in a circle, all in time to the music. Every time the couples returned their hands to a clasp, I noted the slight change in both Lord Brighton and Lady Ariane. They glanced at each other, they smiled, and there seemed to be a quickening in the air around them.

Then the music changed to a Gavotte. Great laughter rose up from the assembled crowd as the dancers quickly tried to move their feet to the hopping, skipping, twirling steps of the new dance. I wasn't so much concerned with their skill as with their enjoyment, and the Queen, who loved nothing more than a challenge, was of course the most extraordinary dancer of all. She fairly sparkled as the music wound toward its inexorable close, the point at which the dancers broke line again and returned to their partners, leaning in for the most chaste of kisses.

Except for Lord Brighton and Lady Ariane.

In that precious, perfect moment the Queen broke away from Robert Dudley and swept her gaze right. *She* saw Sophia's betrothed lift his lips from Lady Ariane's, saw the flash of ardor between the them, the pure, spontaneous desire. I marked Elizabeth's immediate understanding of the unplanned intimacy of that kiss, and the calculation in her eyes.

As a single, moneyed, and lovely female of the court, Lady Ariane was a greater problem than Sophia. Elizabeth needed her married off. And Sophia, well—she was a spy coming into a very intriguing and potentially valuable skill. At first her betrothal had probably seemed like a good idea to the Queen, as a means to secure Lord Brighton's money and take a potentially troublesome girl off her hands, should Sophia's gifts not manifest. Now, however, with the benefit of time and consideration, I suspected that perhaps such a betrothal was no longer as desirable.

And I had just given Elizabeth the ability to solve two problems at once, with her none the wiser to the real reasons behind my scheme.

Or so I hoped.

CHAPTER TWENTY-EIGHT

The music moved on to another dance, and the moment passed with only the most discerning members of the court understanding what had just transpired. Fortunately, Lord Brighton and Lady Ariane didn't realize they had been discovered, both of them removing themselves from the dance floor and returning to stand at the edge of the crowd, now slightly farther apart than before. I narrowed my eyes in the shadows. It would do them no good.

"A dance, my lady? Since that seems aught you Englishers are capable of doing to spend your time?"

I forced myself to stay still for just a moment more before turning to smile up at Alasdair MacLeod. He seemed . . . larger, somehow. More real than the men of the court whom I'd just so skillfully arranged on the dance floor like pawns upon a chessboard. And he stared down at me as if daring me to say no.

I found I did not want to say no. I gazed at him with equal challenge. "You are dismayed by the fact that we are far more civilized than you?"

Alasdair rolled his eyes. "Your country would be better served by having its men on the battleground, not walking around in circles."

"Ah, but don't you realize?" I said as I crossed in front of him. "More political decisions are made on the dancing floor than could ever be reached in battle." *Like the decision I just orchestrated, in fact.* I took his proffered arm. "See? Even you deign to engage me here, while on the battleground we would be direst enemies."

"Never that, my lady," he said gruffly as he led me to the floor. The music settled into a sedate Pavane, and I welcomed the slow pace that allowed for conversation but not too much intimacy. Even having Alasdair's hands hold me at arm's length was disconcerting, but this was the man who'd lied about his actions in my own home. I had no qualms about presenting him a face that betrayed not one of my emotions. His next words, however, caught me off guard.

"So what game was this that you just enacted, showing Sophia's betrothed in such a poor light?"

"Pray, what?" I arched a brow at him as we turned. "I surely don't—"

"You cannot hide from me, my lady Beatrice," Alasdair murmured, his quiet words effectively cutting me off. We were walking forward now, the measured steps taking us slowly around the floor. "I saw you huddled with your fellow maids, then the five of you spinning out like a scatter of birds. I tracked you through the crowd as you turned heads and hands to the floor, and then I saw you pause overlong with a most unusual couple."

"Unusual?" I asked. "I should say they are well matched."

"Well matched, aye, but for the fact that one of them is betrothed. And not to the other."

I shrugged. "It was but a dance."

"It was not 'but a dance.'" We circled forward then. "You directed them like a general commanding troops into battle. They listened to you, even though you're a mere wisp of a girl."

"I beg your pardon—"

"And then you whisked away to watch the drama unfold, safe in the shadows. I knew exactly when you had achieved your goal."

"I think you go too far," I said, sharpness honing my words. How much did Alasdair know about me? There was clearly more to him than I had suspected if he had a hand in the secret meetings of the Lords of the Congregation. But how deep did his duplicity go? Was he merely being a flirtatious cad, or was he some cutthroat spy for Scotland? *I had to be more careful!*

"And I think you are running out of lies, my lady," Alasdair said lightly. The music stopped, but he did not loose my hand. "Pray walk with me awhile," he said.

"I would rather dance."

"And I would rather you walk, especially as, if I am not mistaken, your Queen is watching you with interest. She seems well pleased that you are following her directives to play up to the roguish emissary from the north, and she is wondering what you are learning from him. Do you not wish to curry her favor?"

I'd held my body quite still as he'd spoken, my feet moving only with the force of his stride. I would not look over to see if the Queen was staring at me, as he'd implied. She likely was. The Queen considered me first and foremost a tool to do her bidding, and she knew well how much I'd originally despised Alasdair MacLeod. Had that really been only a few short weeks ago, on the day I'd walked down the aisle of Saint George's Chapel?

"Very well, then," I said rigidly. "I could use some fresh air."

"I believe it. This court reeks of English sweat and stale beer."

"How pretty your phrasing," I said through my teeth.

"And how honest," Alasdair gibed back. But he was guiding me out of the Presence Chamber and down the long corridors, holding me close on his arm as if he were afraid I would bolt away like a startled deer. He didn't slow until we'd crossed out onto the North Terrace, and the sudden icy breeze that sprang up to greet us took my breath away.

"Oh!" I exclaimed, instinctively drawing back. In response Alasdair released me only long enough to pull off his short cape and wrap it around me, before pulling me forward once more.

"The wind is not so strong in the lee of the walls," he said. "And it does us both good to breathe freely once more."

"I—thank you for your cape," I managed. I was surrounded by the very essence of Alasdair MacLeod, the thick woolen cape far softer than I would have given him credit for, with its edges lined in a rich, silken fur. I had not noticed how luxurious his cape was until now, or how much it smelled like him, leather and earth and open sky. I even caught the faintest hint of heather, and I drew it round me close.

"It is not all that I would give you, my lady," Alasdair said. "And well I think you know it." Then his lips twisted, his tone going hard. "Though of course, I overstep, knowing your disdain for me as you are 'forced' into enduring my 'attentions' so steadfastly against your will."

Oh, go hang yourself. "And yet here you are with me again."

He chuckled then, soft and sure. "And yet here I am."

I glanced up at him, knowing I should launch into my own interrogation, to learn what deceits the Scot was weaving in our very midst.

But all I seemed to notice was that Alasdair's body was strong and sturdy against the chilling breeze, his broad shoulders silhouetted against the starlight of the northern sky. That, and I seemed a little dizzy, all of a sudden, my breath coming a bit too fast. This was not good. This was not sensible. And yet I did not want to leave the shelter of Alasdair's presence, didn't want to break the spell, didn't want to lose this moment quite yet.

He was watching me, and so I gave him my best smile. "Well. You speak of giving gifts, good sir, and yet I've only your cape for a short while. What else would you grant me, while you yet tarry here, before you are called back to hearth and home?" I'd tried to make my words arch and sophisticated, but instead I sounded breathless, and more than a little bereft.

If Alasdair noticed, he was unmoved. In fact, he was practically like a statue, as still and stoic as the walls that rose up around us. I waited for him to say something, and I pulled his cape around me more tightly as a chill stole over me that had naught to do with the crisp night air. And still he stood, silent.

So I waited.

And waited.

It should be noted, waiting is not my strong suit.

"Are you just going to stand there and say nothing?" I finally demanded, and Alasdair turned toward me then, crowding me into the stone corner, but still seeming impossibly far away.

"Aye," he muttered. Then he cupped my face with his hands and brought his lips down to mine.

This was not the same kiss as what we'd shared in the center of the Marion Hall labyrinth, nor even the courtly kisses or impassioned embraces I'd experienced with far too many courtiers to count. This was the kiss of command, of power, and of being claimed. I felt the warning rise up within me even as my body seemed to go a little slewy in the knees, my heart pounding fiercely and my brain suddenly mute, giving me no idea of how to extricate myself from this madman's arms.

And I found I didn't want to know.

I sighed against him then, and felt Alasdair's immediate response, his arms dropping to my shoulders to hug me fiercely close as his lips pressed more deeply against mine, his breath ragged and raw. I allowed this to go on a few moments more, only because of the Queen's command that I chat up the Scotsman. Only for that reason alone.

The fact that my hands had found his arms and clung to them as his muscles bunched beneath the heavy embroidered sleeves was of no import whatsoever. The fact that my own legs had suddenly become so unbalanced that they required me to lean heavily against Alasdair just to remain standing, meant nothing either. And as for my breathing; well. I would have been a poor spy indeed were I not able to convince a man that I was entranced by his very person, completely swept away by the power of his kiss.

It was all tremendous practice for my courtly spying skills.

So of course I reached up and drew his head down so that he might kiss me more thoroughly.

Sometime later Alasdair lifted away from me. I found myself completely encircled by his strong arms, his cape pushed off my shoulders, still providing warmth but not as much as that which seemed to shimmer between us. He rested his forehead against mine, as if willing himself to pull more fully away, then breathed a tortured sigh. "What am I to do with you, my lady Beatrice?"

The answer that first sprang to mind was scandalous to the extreme, so I gave a slight shrug. "Well, you've kept me company through this dark night, so I suppose that is a beginning."

"But not an end." He reached out and touched his finger to my chin, lifted it until my gaze met his. His eyes were dark and intense in the shadows, and I felt my nerves go tight with a sudden worry I could not name.

This was no longer a boy playing a game of flirtation but a young man who looked at me in a way Cavanaugh never had—nor ever could. But was he also a traitor in our midst?

"What thoughts plague you now, sly one?" he asked, his eyes searching mine. "You are shaking."

"I am cold," I lied, pulling away roughly to resettle his cape. "I think we should return."

"Of course," Alasdair said. He turned me, his strong arm curling around me and sending another cascade of heat through my body. But before we'd crossed the threshold, I'd already slipped off his cape to hand it back to him, effectively changing from one persona—that which existed outside the strictures of the court—to another, the Beatrice who'd survived long years under the constant scrutiny of others, mindful that but a single false step would be her last.

Alasdair caught the shifting of my mood, but rather than turning petulant, he merely grinned at me. "You would not last long outside this world of dalliance and deception, would you, my lady?" he asked.

I frowned at him, stung by the barb not so carefully hidden in his words. "And you would not last long within it, I should think."

He chuckled, all of his intensity from the North Terrace gone, as if he too were one person outside these walls and another within. "Perhaps and perhaps not," he said. "As this is all we have together, however, I will take it."

I found my pride stung far more to the quick than it should have been at his easy dismissal. "Well, then take it and be gone with you," I said. "If we mean so little to each other, there is naught to keep us together this night."

My retort was met with Alasdair's soft laughter in the

darkness. He caught up my hand even as I prepared to take my leave of him, and spun me back around. He stared at me long enough to make me feel uncomfortable, then lifted my hand to his lips for a brief but fiery caress. "Perhaps there is more than you think, my lady," he murmured.

Then he stepped back into the shadows and slipped away from me.

CHAPTER TWENTY-NINE

It was nearing midnight when I reached the Presence Chamber again, and I was pleased to see the room was finally emptying of courtiers and kin. Bone weariness stole upon me as I surveyed the crowd. The Queen had departed, and her advisors, too. I suspected my absence had given all of them reason to celebrate—there would be no more conversation tonight. And though the hall still sported revelers ever happy to partake of royal wine, there would be no good intelligence-gathering here. The players were too low level.

I had just decided to drag myself off to bed, when a page presented himself at my elbow. "Lady Beatrice?" he squeaked, and I fought to forestall a laugh. He reminded me of little Jeremy from Marion Hall a few short years earlier, all pomp and puffery, thrilled to be moving in the world of adults at last, though he was still just a boy.

"Hullo." I nodded. "Were you called up to duty because the other pages are fast abed?"

"Yes, my lady." He grinned back at me. "Everyone is

exhausted having prepared for her return, but Her Majesty seems never to tire!"

"Well, you are doing a fine job." I fished in my pouch for a shilling and pressed it into his palm. "For the next market day," I said as his eyes went round. I waited a moment, and then another. "Ah . . . did you have a message for me?"

"Oh!" the boy gasped. "Oh, yes. The Queen sent me here special for you!"

All of the joy of the moment fled with his words. "The Queen?" I asked. "She wishes to see me?"

"She does indeed, my lady." The boy nodded forcefully. "If you will come this way?"

He turned and gestured to me, as if I didn't know the way to the Queen's private chambers. But I let him lead me along, my mind churning with possibilities. It was the dead of night, for the love of heaven! Could the bat want me to run some foolish errand? Did she wish to interrogate me for the unveiling of Sophia's father and Lady Ariane—or worse, to punish me? Or did she merely want the report I'd promised her earlier? Or—good heavens—more information on the completely fictitious Samhain festival play to be acted out by James McDonald and the Golden Rose?

The problem with running so many lies at once was that they could all become a tangled skein—with very little notice. Mine was not a skill for the faint of heart, I tell you plain.

We arrived at the Queen's chambers far too quickly, and the boy bowed his way into the room just far enough for the guard to catch him up by the ear. "The Queen!" the lad exclaimed. "She sent me for Lady Beatrice!"

"It's true," I said, laying my hand upon the guard's arm. The man was so startled that he dropped the boy nearly three inches back to the floor, his face growing bright red.

"You may approach," the Queen commanded, and the guard stepped away as the boy scampered off.

I entered the Queen's chambers with more than a little trepidation, noting that her ladies had all moved to the farthest corner of the room to give us the illusion of privacy for this audience. I was tired and my nerves were unaccountably frazzled. I felt out of sorts. But all of that changed the moment I came face-to-face with the Queen.

She was still in full regalia, which surprised me. She stared at me with unmasked malevolence, which did not. She did not speak a word until I came close enough for her to spit upon.

I was prepared for that.

Instead she clasped her hands at her waist, as if she were a tutor about to scold a child, and not a woman a mere seven years older than I. "Well," she huffed. "You've made another mess of it, now, haven't you?"

"Your Grace?" I asked, truly not trying to sound stupid or full of guile. But I had not one idea to what specific mess she was referring. So I went for the safest option. "If you mean my leaving the Presence Chamber in the company of Alasdair MacLeod, I assure you—"

"Not that, you stupid twit. You know very well that isn't my meaning." She scowled at me. "Tell me at least that the boy has told you something interesting, though, while we are on it? What of his family in Skye? Why does he tarry so overlong in our midst—where do his loyalties lie?"

"His loyalties lie with Scotland," I said primly. "And, perforce, with England, now that the French are threatening to rule." My mind was racing. How could I convince Elizabeth of Alasdair's dedication to the cause without betraying that he was far more involved with the Scottish rebellion than she could ever guess? And that I suspected his reasons for remaining in Windsor had a great deal more to do with the Lords of the Congregation than with his interest in me? I decided to distract her with nonsense. "His home in Skye, however, has served as the subject for an intriguing legend straight out of the Highland mists. He claims he possesses a veritable Fairy Flag that can help his clan win any battle it undertakes." I rolled my eyes. "So we have that to look forward to, an' we ever call upon his aid."

The Queen looked at me sharply. "A Fairy Flag? What is this?"

"Just a trifle, really." I waved a hand. "A family relic said to be a gift of the fairy folk themselves that assures the bearer a victory in battle if the flag is displayed at the battle's outset. They set great store by its bits and pieces, though I am sure it is for naught."

"Indeed." The Queen considered that for a moment, then lifted her hand to her face and rubbed her brow, suddenly seeming much older than her years. "Still that is of no account in our present impasse. I mean, of course, the revelation of Lord Brighton's affections for Lady Ariane. You've served them up quite neatly to me, I'll give you that. And yet I cannot help but wonder why you should trouble yourself."

She fixed me with a baleful stare. "You and the witch are not exactly fast friends."

I drew myself up short at that. "Sophia is not a witch!" I breathed, almost afraid to say the words out loud. "Pray tell me you do not believe that she is!"

"Mmf." My defense seemed to mollify the Queen, and I realized she'd been testing me, to throw out such a shocking word. *But why a test? Sophia is one of her own!* "I guess we'll see the true nature of Sophia's abilities soon enough," she said wearily. "But either way, you've quite undone the girl's betrothal. I suppose it is a good thing. At least for Brighton." She said these last words with dark menace. "You've made Sophia's life far worse, though you do not know it."

I shrugged, artfully looking away. "I confess I wanted you to know about Lord Brighton's attraction to Lady Ariane," I said, my words a gamble. But sometimes, with the Queen, a little confession of personal failings could go a long way. "I am still too stung from my lord Cavanaugh's actions to see the same thing happen to Sophia without doing, well"—I waved my hand helplessly—"something."

I couldn't and wouldn't say more—about Brighton's full subterfuge. I wouldn't tell Elizabeth that this man had risked his very life to lie to his monarch, in the pursuit of keeping his daughter safe. That revelation would open up more questions than answers—who'd stolen Sophia in the first place, and why?—and doubtless Brighton would hang for treason. That wouldn't be a very good end for the newly reunited father and daughter.

My thoughts roiled as Elizabeth sighed again and fixed

her gaze on the far wall, as if doing mental calculations. "With Brighton's riches there will be no dowry needed. And Ariane is doubtlessly barren, after the beatings she suffered at her dear husband's hands." She glanced back to me as I stiffened, her next words sharp as she answered my unasked question. "Of course I knew, you child. But the woman was penniless and of good, sturdy stock. And I was not the one who sanctioned her marriage. My dear departed sister did. So if anyone is to blame, she is. But I'd have done the same, wagering Ariane could outlast any meat-fisted oaf. She did, and she has the coin to show for it. Unlike you, I might add." Her eyes narrowed. "I did not fail to notice how poorly Marion Hall is showing these days. I would have thought you would have held on to Cavanaugh with both hands."

A dozen sharp retorts boiled up at this, but none of them would serve. "You are correct, of course, Your Grace," I said instead, as demurely as I could. *You obnoxious spiteful vicious shrew.* "My response to his . . . indiscretion was not fully thought out."

"Responses to men rarely are," the Queen said, but for once her words were not laced with vitriol. "Very well, girl. Get on with what you have to say. We do not have much time before the next interruption will descend upon us. What is it you learned at Marion Hall that was so important you could not wait to tell me until a more civilized hour?"

I refrained from reminding her that it had been her choice to have me discuss this now. I couldn't risk Cecil and Walsingham showing up again, having suddenly suspected that their plans at last had been thwarted. Still, I needed to choose my words carefully.

"Your Grace, I had occasion to learn of a conversation between your advisors and the Lords of the Congregation whilst you were at rest at Marion Hall," I said. "I am certain that Cecil and Walsingham told you of it, but—I simply wish you to be fully apprised."

The Queen had grown more icy as my speech had progressed, and by its end she was positively frostbitten. "When did this happen?" she asked quietly.

"Three nights past. You were asleep."

"Asleep," she repeated the word, as if she could not quite make sense of it. "And what . . . was this meeting about?" Now her words were almost a whisper. A whisper of a woman who did not know whom to trust.

Something shifted in me then, as profound and powerful as anything I'd ever experienced with courts and kings. I hated Elizabeth, make no mistake. She was mean and vindictive and petty and small. But she was also my Queen, the future of England. And it was at her feet our fortunes were laid. History would not look back on her with understanding and commiseration if she allowed herself to sit upon a puppet throne. History would not consider Cecil and Walsingham heroes if they ran her kingdom for her. It would merely think of Elizabeth as weak. That anyone would consider this proud, defiant, fiercely independent woman as *weak* was something that could not be borne.

She was my Queen. She was my country.

I knew what I had to do.

Save for the fact of Alasdair's involvement, I told her everything, and without stinting. She did not interrupt, but I could see her anger ebb and flow as she noted Cecil's and Walsingham's interpretations of her directives. I had no way of knowing whether or not those directives were in keeping with what she truly wished, but by the end of my recitation, one thing was plain: the Queen had aged.

Another tiny sliver of her girlhood had been shaved away on the anvil of her monarchy, revealing the steely and inviolable ruler beneath. I wondered what would be left of Elizabeth at the end of her days. But I suddenly got the impression that such an end wouldn't be anytime soon.

"Thank you, Beatrice," the Queen said, and though the words were stated with some grudging surprise, they were plainly spoken. "It goes without saying that you need not inform my advisors of this conversation." Her gaze slid to the door as a guard appeared, and she appeared to draw within herself. "You shall accompany me now, as witness."

I blinked and hesitated just a moment before curtsying in acquiescence, staying my questions until I rose again.

"Witness to what, Your Grace?" I asked.

She gave me a withering glance that warned me I'd do better to keep my mouth closed henceforth. "To the first Inquisition regarding Sophia Dee."

CHAPTER THIRTY

I had all of ten minutes to compose myself as we stalked through the halls of Windsor Castle in the dead of night, heading God-only-knew-where. Meg and Jane might have whiled away countless hours wandering the castle, mapping its every inch, but I'd never taken the time to learn much of what they'd discovered. I'd been too busy dancing and flirting and ferreting out secrets held within the *rooms* of Windsor Castle to pay much attention to the actual *walls* of the place.

Now I felt the dry clutch of panic seize my throat, and for once it was for someone other than myself or my own family. I found I didn't much like it. With my own family there was a sense that no matter what, we could get ourselves out of a scrape—be it financial, legal, royal, or otherwise. The lot of us had always been fast talkers, and we knew the power of a well-timed compromise. We'd suffered with poor grace, perhaps, but we'd suffered with a purpose: because we believed that eventually we would be back on top.

With someone like Sophia Dee there was no such assurance. She was alone, save for the wardship of John Dee and her betrothal to Lord Brighton. Dee had not shown his face at Windsor for an age, and with my actions of this evening, Sophia was quite effectively un-betrothed. This was what the Queen had meant by saying I had harmed Sophia's prospects, certainly. But how could I have known the girl was in actual danger?

My mind skipped over all the possibilities even as we paused at a doorway I'd never really noticed before, a door that really seemed much more wall than passageway. Two guards now stood on either side of it, but I couldn't recall ever seeing anyone quite positioned in that exact spot. In any event, the door stood wide now and revealed a curving stone staircase that led down and away from civilization.

The Queen lifted up her skirts and glided through the doorway, leaving me no choice but to follow.

What is it she wants me to say? I wondered as we twisted our way down into the bowels of the castle. It smelled curiously wetter the farther we descended, as if we would come out into some ancient cavern dripping with dew. Instead the stairs opened into a reasonably sized stone chamber—mercifully dry—with rushes on the floor that looked like they'd lain there for at least half a century. There were a few wooden chairs scattered around the room and a long table pushed up against one side, but the main attraction of the chamber was not its furniture but the six men in hoods who stood at attention as we entered. They bowed to the Queen, murmuring their greetings and—shockingly—she curtsied back.

This was bad.

The Queen could use a curtsy to coy and flirtatious

effect, it is true, but a curtsy was also an acknowledgment of power, one to another. You did not curtsy to underlings. And to a Queen, anyone other than another monarch was an underling.

I somehow doubted that we had lined up six kings of the Continent before us. So who were these people and what power did they wield, to command such respect?

I lifted my chin under the combined scrutiny of the men beneath their shadowy hoods, moving my gaze from one to the other. I could not identify any of them by height alone, and their peaked hoods looked like the stuff of nightmares. I suspected they were men of the cloth . . . but not priests, exactly. The Queen would never have troubled herself over the censure of the Church.

Her richest lords, however, would be a far different story. But if these were her richest lords, then I should know them. I peered into the gloom, trying to see through both cowls and shadows.

"Thank you for meeting with us, Your Majesty." The first man's voice was slickly insinuating. It slithered out into the space between us and coiled there, like a snake ready to strike. "You do honor to our service to rid the realm of those who would bear false witness against God." He paused, breathing for a moment as we waited. "But who is this you bring with you into our presence, when we seek only to question you?"

"You seek it, and yet you dare *not* question me," the Queen said. Her words were regal but mild, and the more damning because of it. "I am your Queen. Therefore, I can be questioned by no one except Parliament, on punishment of death to my accusers. I daresay you do not represent Parliament, so surely you see the problem here?"

Silence greeted her words, and in that moment even I could have cheered Elizabeth. This was not a woman to be cowed by those who skulked around in cloaks and hoods. These men had believed they would force her to the question? They were learning their mistake.

Of course, if she wasn't going to answer questions, then . . . who would?

"Beatrice Knowles is dedicated in service to me and to the Crown." The Queen supplied my answer for me. "You may ask her any questions in my stead. She has complete knowledge of the subject, having been a part of my retinue since I took the throne."

"She is a worthy witness." This came from the fourth man in line, a fatter man whose girth strained his simple black robe. "I have seen her with the girl."

"Very well," the snake-voiced man oozed. "Then it shall be our pleasure to see her serve God." I felt his gaze upon me intensify. "On your knees, girl."

I stiffened, looking at the Queen in alarm. I saw her mouth tighten, but she nodded, once. *Of all the insufferable, idiotic, ridiculous . . .*

I stifled a sigh as Snake Voice drew in a sharp breath to deliver a reprimand, and I knelt on the floor. The Knowleses had never been a devoutly religious family, although we followed all the forms of whatever faith the Crown preferred. This had gotten a little more challenging over the last several years, but at least all the royal faiths had one thing in common: They loved to make their adherents kneel. I'd gotten quite good at the process, learning how to keep my back straight, my head lifted. And I had the advantage of voluminous skirts, which I deftly folded over so that my knees would not bruise on the dusty floor. I rued the ruination of the silk, but I'd find a way to eke the money out of the Crown another way.

Before I'd fully settled myself, the questions began.

"Where did you meet Sophia Dee?" Snake Voice slithered. "How long have you known her?"

"I met her in early December, my lord," I said, pleased at the sound of my voice as it cascaded off the close walls. "I had not met her before."

"She was not a member of court?"

"No. I served under Queen Mary, and in the court of her brother, King Edward, as well."

"Half brother," rasped another man, I think standing at the far end. I inclined my head.

"Half brother," I agreed. I thought about saying more, but held my tongue. When you are being questioned by curs in hoods, it's best not to betray too much, lest you betray yourself.

"And the girl appeared in early December—how?"

"I had been chosen as a maid of honor to the Queen upon the death of her sis—half sister, Mary. Late last year I came to Whitehall Palace to serve the Queen. While I was there, I was present when Sophia Dee, ward to her uncle, John Dee, came visiting. The Queen chose her as a maid of honor as well." The mention of John Dee was met with thick disapproval, and I fought to keep myself from rolling my eyes. The Queen's astrologer might have been a few bricks shy of a sturdy keep, but he was one of the smartest and most learned men in England. He had tutored Elizabeth on all manner of sciences, and his library at Mortlake housed a collection of books that was quickly on its way to becoming the most celebrated intellectual treasure in all of Christendom. He was *not* a threat.

"Why did the Queen choose her?" came the next sharp question.

I paused for just a moment, as in truth I'd wondered the same thing in the early days. "I—I believe the Queen pitied her," I said, gratified to feel the change in the temperament of the woman beside me. The Queen would not look at me, but she clearly marked my careful words. "Sophia Dee was painfully shy, quiet, and all but forgotten in the care of her uncle. The Queen sought to put her to work, that she might serve worthily in the new royal court."

"Hmmph." Snake Voice mulled that over a bit. "And how does she spend her days?"

"She fetches. She sews. She studies languages and music and dance. She takes her meals with the other maids and ladies. But most of all she serves the Queen." I thought it prudent to avoid mention of our select group's study into poisons, garroting, and thievery. As spies to the Queen, we'd traded embroidery for espionage most of our days, and Sophia had taken these lessons alongside us. She was quick-witted and sly, and could almost disappear into any room she entered. But those were not the attributes of a polite young woman of the court, so I had no intention of sharing them.

Snake Voice must have sensed my hesitation. "Your response here must be utter truth, on penalty that you sin against both God and England," he said, edging forward toward me. I could smell the scent of sweet smoke around him, like incense laced with opium, and I felt my resolve harden. Another addict . . . and a telling weakness that I might be able to use one day. He was breathing heavily, and I recognized the dry sound that I had not been able to place before.

My mother breathed like that.

"Does Sophia Dee worship Satan?" hissed Snake Voice, and the intensity of his question brought my focus sharply back to him. "Does she study his black arts?"

"Sophia Dee worships God and serves the Queen," I said solidly. "No one else."

"You're not answering the full question, girl." This voice was almost melodic after Snake Voice's snarl, and I tilted my head to discern where it originated. The man next to Snake Voice, as thin as a sapling, stood hunched in his robes as if he were constantly apologizing for being a bit too tall for any room he occupied. "Does Sophia Dee partake in any activities that are unnatural—be they scrying, praying to false icons, concocting potions or brews to heal the sick or harm the healthy, or studying the mystical arts? Does she consort with other false prophets, Egyptians, or heretics, even if for the purported purpose of academic study? Her uncle is a great scholar and mathematician, and a professed student of the arcane, though he has proven his devotion to God. There would be no surprise in her working alongside him to expand her own knowledge. What know you of any of this?"

I know that you are the real danger in this group. However, I also knew that the best lies were ones seeded with truth, and that these men had not come idly by their questions. Sophia had been raised by a man considered by many to be a heretic and blasphemer, the stepson of Satan. She'd been in the man's house, she'd studied in his library. And, let's be plain, Sophia was not exactly the most normal of people, even on her best day. I considered my next words carefully but quickly, as too much of a pause was worse than none at all.

"Sophia was John Dee's ward, and as such she was well aware of her uncle's interest in the mystical arts," I said. "She learned to be a very quiet girl, as he studied all the time. She learned to exist without much social interaction, and so now crowds disconcert her and she prefers to work alone on her embroidery above all things. She is an indifferent reader, and shows no inclination to texts on religion or spirituality. She is a devout Protestant, however, and a dutiful servant of God." This last bit jarred against my own ears, and I smiled to smooth it over. "Sophia Dee is very humble and quiet, my lords. If you wanted me to name ten people in the court who might be heretics, I could—but she would not be one of them."

"What is this?" Another of the men, hitherto silent, perked up at the idea of other courtiers to interrogate.

"Who?" chimed in the last man, shuffling forward eagerly.

"We are not here to discuss anyone but Sophia Dee," the Queen retorted, her voice like iron. "You have asked your questions, and been answered. Are you satisfied?"

"We will not be satisfied until the realm is rid of those who are a crime against God," Snake Voice replied. "Be careful that you do not go too far with your policies of tolerance that you allow the derelicts of spirit to gain power in England, Your Majesty. You must remain ever vigilant. We serve as your watchers, but we are also watching you."

"And exactly what do you mean by that?" The Queen's voice had turned as chill as death. "Your threats do you no service here."

"Threats have no place with a daughter of God such as yourself," the tall man interjected smoothly. It was a verbal set-down to Snake Voice, who visibly stiffened as if he might have been swallowing his own forked tongue. "We seek only to ensure that your reign be both long and fruitful, that you might serve as Gloriana for decades to come."

"Mm." Gloriana wasn't fully mollified, but as usual, flattery was the best avenue to her good graces. "Then you would do well to curb your dog." The tall man merely inclined his head. Nobody seemed to notice that I was still kneeling on the stones. I didn't dare look in the direction of Snake Voice, but I could feel his hatred emanating out through the room. Surely the Queen could feel it as well. "Are we finished?" she demanded.

"For now, my Queen," the tall man said. "For now."

CHAPTER THIRTY-ONE

I remained kneeling as the men left the chamber, until it was just the Queen and me, alone. Not even the guard remained inside with us, preferring to wait on the stairs leading back up to the real world. I imagined him leaning against the wall or even standing at his ease on his feet, like a normal person. It was a nice thought.

The Queen seemed to be lost in rapt contemplation of the brick walls of this homely little chamber, but I wasn't an idiot. She liked to see me on my knees. She'd prefer that I spent the whole day there. If she could have figured out a way for me to walk while kneeling, she'd have ordered me do it even when she was not around.

She hummed a little to herself, but at least it wasn't a tune. This was more the "hmmm" indicating that *the monarch* was *deep in thought*. Had there been any musicians still awake in the castle to hear the sound, I suspected the unmelodious noise would have been adapted to a fully orchestrated choral performance before the next trumped-up Fairy Queen of the Goddess Moon festival we'd have to throw in Her Vanity's honor. So at least that was one benefit of being alone with the Queen. I tried to think of other benefits, but failed miserably. In fact, I'd knelt long enough to compose an entire elegy to the woman's death before she finally spoke. "You have served me well this night, Beatrice," she said. "It goes without saying that you cannot speak any of this—to anyone. I would have asked Meg, but she did not know Sophia when the girl first came to court. Anna is too lacking in guile, and Jane would have sooner attacked the men and silenced them for good than take part in such a little play as we just enacted here. Sophia's gift hovers on the verge of revelation, but it is a gift that puts her at terrible risk. I need your discretion." I sensed her glance at me then, the weight of silence between us—not just the silence of this room and its secrets, but the silence of another room, at Sudeley Castle, a room and secrets that had once nearly cost a young princess her future. "I believe I can count on you for that."

"Of course, Your Grace," I said quietly. What was it my father had always said? That the value of secrets held was ever more powerful than secrets shared?

I'd never realized the full truth of his statements until now.

However, if I was going to be stuck kneeling for the foreseeable future, I could at least learn something while I was there. "Who were those men? Priests?"

"Doubtful." The Queen gave a derisive snort. "The Lords of the Congregation are not the only nobles who choose to do their business by skulking around under cover of cloak and darkness. But if you would defeat a scorpion, you must keep it in sight. Now that I have given you as a witness to Sophia's actions, you can expect to be questioned anytime, for any purpose, day or night."

"Without you?" I asked, not even bothering to hide the fear in my voice. Questioning was not always a gentle process in the courts of kings and queens. To my great relief Elizabeth's laugh was short and dismissive.

"Hardly," she said. "You'd be dead before the end of the week."

This . . . did not make me feel better, actually, but the Queen finally glanced at me. "Well, quit simpering, girl. Get up," she said, as if I'd been loafing around on the floor for my own health. I hauled myself upright with as much grace as possible, then stooped to brush my skirts. Which was why I wasn't looking at the Queen when she levied her next attack at me.

"I have decided that you should be married," she said.

I composed my face into a semblance of not-screaming as I rose to face her. "You have, Your Grace?" I asked mildly.

"I have." She eyed me with speculation, like I was a prime hog set out for the butcher. "You are passably attractive and stealthily duplicitous, and richly capable of destroying any who stand in your way, but you are also loyal to me—and, I see, to your fellow spies." She raised her hand as I would speak. "No, do not thank me. It is not wholly a compliment I give you."

I blinked at her, trying to find any compliment in her preceding words. I supposed "attractive" would count, if you didn't include the "passably" before it. But the Queen was continuing on. "But I find that to truly gain your full worth, I must position you in a place of greater intimacy with those about whom I wish to know more."

This suddenly was not sounding very good. "And so you shall betroth me to another man upon whom I should spy?" I asked carefully. I didn't like my options of those men.

"No, no," the Queen said. "I shall betroth you to a man who will be so grateful for the honor that he would gift me scepter and sword, should he have them. Yes." She nodded, still eyeing me. "That would do nicely. It will be a bit of a shock to the court, but they do well to be surprised now and again."

I looked at her with growing concern. "You surely do not mean Lord Brighton?" I asked cautiously.

"Him! Oh no. I only agreed to that betrothal to get his coin for the Crown. That will also be achieved by granting him Lady Ariane's hand in marriage. And as you can see, Sophia has become a bit of a thorny issue for me." Her mind leaped nimbly to the new subject, allowing me a moment's respite from this sudden intractable turn. "She needs to comport herself more normally, Beatrice. Meg can help with that—she's been in court long enough to mimic the ladies. You can as well."

"Of course, Your Grace," I said brightly. "I brought her to your audience today specifically—"

"I know, I know." The Queen waved her hand again. "There is naught you do that doesn't have two or three reasons, a contingency purpose, and as many side benefits as you can extract."

Once again she was speaking almost more to herself than to me, but I frowned at the cutting remark. *That isn't wholly true,* I wanted to protest. Not all of my relationships and actions were built on lies and deception. . . .

I paused, thinking about that, and felt my heart twist a bit. *Was* this true? Did I love no one for who they were? Did I do anything that didn't serve my needs?

The Queen could go no longer than thirty seconds without being entertained by the sound of her own voice, however, so she picked up her narrative again. "But with Sophia in the public eye acting the role of a proper lady, her strange and troubled months here can be more quickly chalked up to nerves and new surroundings. And, freed of her betrothal, she can circulate more easily with the young men of the court. Those she hasn't already frightened witless, that is."

I nodded, as nothing needed to be added here. But the Queen nodded back, her eyes focusing on me once more. "You, however, will serve admirably as the betrothed to Alasdair MacLeod."

Despite my careful preparation against this very announcement, I could not stop my exclamation. "Alasdair!" I said, speaking quickly so she could not hear the betrayal of my own thudding heart. "But, Your Grace, he is not even English—and worse, he is not titled or flush with lands that are positioned for your advantage." *Nor is he rich,* my mind screamed. *Or well-behaved. And he has already lied to me once, and who even knows how many more times?* "While I live to serve my country, in marriage as in all things"—*just not to a man I cannot control*—"I cannot see how he can be of such import to you. Worse, while a casual flirtation has netted me the intelligence I have shared with you"—*and more information than that, truth be told*—"no one in the court would believe you would affiance me to a Highland Scotsman who is more brute than man. There is no value in it to you. And finally, my Queen— Well, I fear we do not suit." This last sounded rather desperate, even to me.

"Quite the contrary, on all counts," the Queen said, apparently also finding my protestations lacking. "Here, walk with me. I tire of these surrounds."

She processed out of the chamber as if it were a drawing room, and we climbed up the long, curving steps once more. My brain was even more a-churn going up than it had been going down. After this night, I doubted I'd be able to see any staircase at all without feeling queasy.

We resurfaced in the long, broad corridor, and the Queen took my arm in hers as if we were bosom friends. The better for her to spin her terrible words into my ears alone.

"You are the perfect match, in all respects," she said. "First, you've tarried enough with him that any betrothal between you will seem to be the result of some girlish foolishness."

I stiffened reflexively, and her grin was quick and malicious. "It cannot be helped," she said. "Second, MacLeod is a Scotsman, and the betrothal of the two of you will serve to send a message that England's and Scotland's interests are perhaps more closely aligned than anyone had previously thought. We'll do well to make the announcement as public as possible, as quickly as possible—though the marriage itself will not be necessary anytime soon." She *hmm*'d a little again, and I wondered if this was a sign that her mind was going soft. It certainly would have explained this new pile of rubbish she was heaping upon me. "Third, the boy may not be flush with funds and land, but I rather doubt he's as poor a prospect as you say. He brought his entire retinue here, on horses finer than much of what we have in our stables, and his retainers' clothes are not coarsely spun. He may be a ruffian and a boor, but he's not as penniless as you."

I thought on this as we rounded the last corner and proceeded down the final hallway toward the Queen's chamber. I . . . supposed it was possible that Alasdair had money. He never talked of it, and most men with money did. He was proud of his people, and his land, and the huge rock of a castle that his clan called home. But rich? It still was difficult to believe that.

"And then, of course, there is the Fairy Flag."

This time I did pull away, and we stopped in a preceding antechamber to the Queen's own rooms, hung with lush tapestries that glistened in the candlelight. "The Fairy Flag?" I repeated. "But that's just a relic—and a myth. You cannot think it a serious advantage."

"I can and I do," the Queen returned, crossing her arms. "Would you deny England anything that will help us gain the upper hand in battle? Would you let soldiers and sailors go needlessly to their deaths because you were too stubborn to open your mind?"

"But it's a *legend*, Your Majesty!" I protested, even in the face of her growing annoyance. Really, she was my Queen, but I could not stand by and allow such lunacy to proceed.

"I'm sure there are enough scraps of that Fairy Flag to make up seventeen new flags of a size equal to the original. It's not like they're the bones of a saint, Your Grace. These are a superstitious people, who hold on to beliefs of fairies and gold and monsters in their lochs."

"Nevertheless." The Queen raised her hand, indicating that this interview was at an end. "You will secure me the relic for England. That is not a request, Beatrice, but an order."

I curtsied, not trusting myself to speak. And the hateful witch kept talking.

"Tomorrow I will announce to Alasdair and your father your betrothal, and secure the terms of the marriage contract. You need not be present."

I whipped my head up, and she saw the anger simmering in my eyes. Saw it and took delight in it. "Then there will be a formal announcement before the evening meal, and music and dancing afterward. We'll send messengers to London and Edinburgh and Paris. As old and formerly grand as your family is, the significance will not be missed."

"Must you announce it so abruptly?" I moaned, not able to stop myself. "My betrothal to Lord Cavanaugh is only just canceled. It would be unseemly."

She shrugged. "Give me a reason not to."

I looked at her, startled. "What do you mean?"

"I mean, you stupid girl, that Alasdair and your father will know at once. The contract will begin to be negotiated, and your future is in their hands. I care not a whit for that. But if you want me to leave off from announcing it to the world quite yet, I can give you a few more days to accustom yourself to the idea. And my price is a simple one. If you crave my silence for yet a little while, then you know what it is I want."

I did, but she could not let this moment pass. She leaned into me, her dark eyes sparking with intensity in the flickering light of a dozen flames.

"Get me the Fairy Flag."

CHAPTER THIRTY-TWO

I left the Queen's presence still reeling, stumbling back to the maids' quarters on feet that thankfully knew the way themselves. By the time I reached my own pallet, I was so exhausted that I could barely stand. I slumped, puzzled by the sight of my bed, knowing that I needed to strip off my ornate ball gown but not having the faintest idea how.

With a rustle of plain cotton, Jane was at my right. A second later Meg was on the other side, and Anna at my back. They were untying laces and unclasping hooks, and Sophia was in front of me on her knees, easing my feet out of slippers still marred with the rock dust of the spiral stone staircase. Within seconds I stood in only my shift. I opened my mouth to speak, to share with them the worst of what had happened, as there was no good in this night, only darkness.

Instead they eased me down onto my bed and drew the covers up close. "Hush now," Anna said, laying a cool hand to my brow. "Morning will be here soon enough, and you are too tired to think. We will protect you this night, Beatrice, so set your thoughts away."

I stared at her another moment, the urge to laugh bubbling up in the back of my throat. They couldn't protect me—nobody could protect me. Not from the Queen, not from myself. And not from what I had to do.

No one could protect me anymore.

A moment later I was asleep.

I woke the next morning with the kind of start that had me sitting upright in my pallet before I was fully aware of my surroundings, gasping and whirling, ready to do battle. A thin, reedy light streamed in from our high windows, announcing that dawn, at least, had awakened before I had.

Well, not only dawn.

Four sets of eyes now regarded me in varying states of repose. Jane, as ever, sat up on her pallet, her back against the wall. On our first day at Windsor, she'd dragged her bed over to the wall facing the door of our room, and I doubted she ever truly slept for longer than a few hours at a time. Meg and Anna were still curled up in their covers, awake but trying to convince themselves that they could still take their rest with their eyes open. And Sophia sat fully dressed, her hands in her lap. I darted a glance down at those small white fingers, worrying her obsidian jewel, and then up again to her eyes.

Swallowing, I nodded to her. "Good morning, Sophia," I said. "I have so much to share with you."

She stilled then, and in her hand the ball of obsidian rolled and spun. "I—" She hesitated. "I know, Beatrice," she said in her quiet voice. "I felt so nervous, when you didn't return. We all of us were frightened, and I—I could not bear the not knowing anymore." She gave a little shrug, and the ball in her fingers rolled and rolled. "I am so glad that you are safe."

"I am safe," I said. But I found myself staring at the gorgeous black orb glinting against Sophia's white fingertips. *What does she mean, she could not bear the not knowing? How could she—*

And then it hit me.

Sophia had turned the obsidian stone into a showstone. Somehow, some way, she had figured out how to use the large black crystal for scrying, as the old Traveler woman had doubtlessly intended.

In doing this, however, Sophia had committed a crime against the church—and I knew suddenly that this crime would not be her only transgression, and that this path might well be her undoing in the coming months and years. She had decided to use her gifts.

"Well, what is it, then?" Anna asked, yawning broadly. "There is so much that went on last night, I suspect you scarce know where to begin."

"First and perhaps most important . . . ," I began, and hid my own wince. My second sentence of the day, and already I was lying. Not an auspicious start. "I expect the Queen will later today quietly and firmly advise Lord Brighton that he will not remain betrothed to our Sophia."

Sophia smiled beatifically, as Meg clapped her hands. "Bravo!" Meg said. "It was a masterful play, Beatrice, and I doubt that few took note of your part in it." Her expression turned a little coy. "Other than Alasdair, of course."

"He did more than take note," scoffed Jane. "He took

Beatrice right on out to the North Terrace." She glanced at me, an unusual curiosity in her eyes. "It was a bit chilly out on that terrace, I should think."

"It was at that," was all I allowed, trained well enough to stay the blushes that would have climbed up an ordinary maiden's cheeks. "Unfortunately—and I may as well let you know this, since you'll hear it soon enough—the Queen has decided that there's more I might get out of Alasdair as his betrothed than simply as his conquest. She plans to announce our intention to wed as soon as it is politically expedient to do so."

That stone landed with a thud in the middle of our small group, so shocking that silence ringed the room for one long second. . . .

Then two.

Then everyone started speaking at once. "Your intention to wed!" Anna exclaimed, catching up her hands to her breast. "You cannot be serious!" Her eyes were both shocked and intrigued, in that curious way of Anna's that allowed any twist of fortune to be better endured as long as romance played a part in it. "He's nowhere near the man of political standing that Lord Cavanaugh is."

"But he's several times more the actual man," Jane put in, leaning forward to rest her elbows on her knees.

"Is this some sort of new political ploy the Queen is testing?" Meg asked, tilting her head as her agile mind jumped through the drama Elizabeth was about to unravel for her court. "She seems to be making a game of it with all the men she's been setting up in betrothals, only to knock them down again. I cannot think Alasdair will take kindly to her machinations—unless he first approached her to ask for your hand?"

"Hardly," I said, snorting. "Alasdair MacLeod is many things, but a man willing to prostrate himself before the Queen to ask for an Englisher's hand is not one of them. And to your question about political plotting, Meg, I have to think it's exactly that." Well, I knew it was exactly that. The Queen wanted me close enough to pry off a scrap of cloth from the Scot that was probably no more sacred than his torn trunk hose. Still, that was the only political merit to this betrothal. A marriage between one beggared noblewoman and an unmanageable Scot would not prove anything to anyone about the predisposition of England toward its neighbor to the north, and the Queen had to know that. So that left me with a balder truth: As far as Elizabeth was concerned, I was sure, the true value of this betrothal was that it might merely serve to ruin my life.

Bankrupt my family.

Shame my name.

No wonder she liked the idea.

But, though I could never share this, there were other issues with a marriage to Alasdair. It put me in the path of the one man who could cause my heart to beat like a clatter of stones, my hands to sweat, my eyes to fill with tears, and my breath to come fitfully between my lips, like he was both poison and cure in one heady form. I could not predict Alasdair—I could not guess his movements or prepare for his words, and I could no longer trust myself around him without sharing too much. It made the idea of spying on him absolutely ludicrous.

I still had a chance to set things right, however. I could get her the Fairy Flag, but since I didn't believe the thing actually existed, that was a problem. I explained the flag to the other maids, and they promised to keep a sharp eye for the relic, but I did not hold much hope for that. However, if I could find out what Alasdair's role was within the Scottish delegation and the Lords of the Congregation, then perhaps the Queen would lose interest in this insane betrothal and allow me to find some other man who could protect my family and preserve my name. Someone who could never touch my heart, let alone break it. Yes, surely that was the wiser course.

Surely.

We discussed the rest of the evening's events—my conversation with the Queen about the Lords of the Congregation, her orders for us not to share our confidences with her advisors. This development did not sit well with any of us. We took our orders from the Queen, of course, but Cecil and Walsingham were around us constantly. If they knew we were holding back, they could make—and had made—our lives extremely uncomfortable. And yes, of course, we were all trained liars, but so were they. And they'd been perfecting the art longer than we had.

I did not tell my fellow maids about the questioning. I would eventually, I was fairly certain. They needed to be aware of everything that took place within Windsor's walls. We never knew who would be targeted next. But I owed it to Sophia to let her know first the full extent of the danger she faced. She'd gathered some of it, I thought. At least that was what I'd assumed when I'd seen the shock in her eyes as she'd worried her obsidian stone. But she couldn't know the details, and she needed to. She needed to understand her accusers, even if I could give her no accounting of what they actually looked like.

The day began in earnest then, and we maids dispersed to our daily chores and requirements.

Anna and Meg were off to our old schoolroom, where they'd been poring over the books Anna had stolen from John Dee's library. Anna had quickly learned that Meg's unique ability for memory made her a valuable ally in the study of ancient texts. Anna had but to make a notation aloud, and Meg not only remembered it but was able to recite it back to her at the close of the session.

Jane retreated to the guards' quarters, where she was learning the arts of fighting with her feet as well as her hands.

Sophia, like myself, was due in the Queen's chambers. But I had no interest in hastening my immersion in the plots of the court this morning. Especially since I was likely to be the primary topic of conversation. And I did still need to speak with Sophia.

"Walk with me?" I suggested, even as we bid our good-byes to the other girls. Sophia nodded quickly, her morning ensemble a quiet gown of dove-grey silk. I would miss seeing her being outfitted in the latest style from her father/betrothed, Lord Brighton, but of course she could not go on accepting gifts from him if they were no longer to be wed.

We set out, keeping far away from the common area. Once again I wished that Jane and Meg had prevailed upon me to learn more of the secret passages through the castle. I knew the one to the Queen's chamber, of course, and the one that led to the exterior of the castle walls. But neither of those appealed—they were too close to everywhere we did not want to be.

So we ducked into the Blue Room, and I made quick work of checking the tapestries. Sophia went to the windows that looked out onto the North Terrace, and opened them wide. A playful breeze skittered in, with just the tiniest bite to it. Winter would be drawing down all too soon, I knew. But at least we could breathe in the fresh air in this room, preserved from the elements.

Sophia paused a moment there, her eyes far to the north. "What troubles you, Beatrice?"

I hesitated. The Queen had forbidden me to speak of what had transpired between myself and the six hooded Questioners, but if Sophia herself had seen aught of it, well . . . that was another thing entirely, was it not? "Why don't you tell me my troubles?" I asked gently.

Sophia bit her lip. "Six men in hoods?" I nodded, and she swallowed. "They questioned you. A-about me."

I nodded again, and she put her hands to her ears. "It is coming to pass—it is coming to pass," she hissed. "Oh, Beatrice, there is danger all around!"

"The Queen has no interest in your being singled out by these men, Sophia," I said firmly, wanting to ease her however I could. "She will not allow them access to you." *Only to me,*

I thought. "But you must have a care. You have spent your entire life in the house of John Dee, and he has enemies."

"I have not spent my entire life with him." Sophia's eyes were fixed on the wide forest, and I paused to consider her words. She had been taken from a loving father and mother—by whom? And given to Dee—why? The story at court was that Sophia was Dee's niece, but what was the truth of the matter?

Then Sophia disrupted my thoughts by turning to me in a rush. "Can you teach me, Beatrice?" she asked. "Can you teach me to stand like you, to walk like you, as if no one can reach you and no one should try? Can you show me how to be a lady in this court with cool assurance, and how to not act"—her voice broke on her final word—"fey?"

"Of course," I said immediately, though in truth I was shocked by the question. Shocked and . . . more than a little intrigued. Anna could delight in romance, Jane in death. I'd take court politics anyday. "And Anna can teach you how to respond to your questioners—be they official or otherwise, while Meg can teach you how to read the crowd, to know their actions before they even know them themselves." I smiled a little, thinking on it. "And if all else fails, I think Jane now knows how to kill someone with her toes."

"Oh, thank you." Sophia sighed, then seemed to gather strength. She looked at me in the way I had come to associate with one of her trances, but before I could bring her back to reality, words began spilling out of her. "You are far more gracious to me than you have any idea. A light will follow you where'r you roam. I don't care what I see around you; I refuse to believe it. There is no way so much fear and crushing sadness will surround someone so strong as you." With that, she bounced back and hugged herself, then turned and fled the room—though, where she was going, I could not fathom. I suspected not even she could say. Hopefully she'd end up in the Queen's chambers, however. Eventually.

Still, I stared after the girl, stupefied, until I finally found the voice to speak into the now empty space.

"Fear and crushing sadness?"

CHAPTER THIRTY-THREE

I was making my way to the Queen's chambers when Walsingham intercepted me in the hallway.

"Lady Beatrice," he said formally, bowing to me in full view of the guards. "Walk with me?"

"But of course, Sir Francis." I took his proffered arm and fell into step with him, not at all surprised when he angled me away from the Queen's apartments, though more than a little chagrined. I was not quite up to an interrogation this early in the morning, especially by someone so skilled at the art. As if sensing my discomfort, Walsingham patted my hand with almost fatherly commiseration.

"I understand congratulations are in order," he began smoothly. "The Queen informed us of her decision to wed you to the favorite son of the clan MacLeod. Your father was not quite as taken aback as I expected him to be."

The comment cleared away my malaise, and I grimaced with wry amusement. "My father is rarely taken aback, unless he must visit 'aback' to find his stash of ale." Still, I could not keep myself from asking the next logical question.

"How did he receive the news of my betrothal?" I asked.

In response Walsingham just clucked his tongue. "Your father, if nothing else, is a practical man. He never once betrayed concern, and through his intercession, I am sure, the Scotsman managed to keep up a level of decorum as well."

I closed my eyes briefly just thinking on it. As much as I would have wanted to see Alasdair's face when he was informed of the Queen's "generous" offer, I would not have handled it well if he'd laughed. Or fainted. Or argued with her. "Was Alasdair . . . surprised?" I asked.

"No, interestingly enough," Walsingham said. "Though he has been among us but a short while, I get the impression that the lad has taken his measure of our Queen and her court, and simply resolved to survive the experience."

"Well, that is good," I said faintly. I'd never considered myself an "experience" that someone must "survive," but I supposed there could be worse things. "So he accepted the Queen's decision?"

"After a fashion," Walsingham said. Then we turned down a less peopled corridor, and the very air around us seemed to close in. "But I do not interrupt you this day to talk about your wedding, Beatrice, as charmed as you might be by the Queen's manipulation of your life."

It took all my training not to stiffen. "I do not know how to take your meaning, Sir Francis."

"Oh, I do not doubt for a moment that you know how to take it. I understand you walked with the Queen late last night. Where is it you were heading?"

"Is this some sort of test, Sir Francis?" I asked, leaning

away from him so I could face him more directly. "If you know that we were together, would you not also know where we arrived?"

"I would, except—and this is curious—the Queen had her own guards roaming along behind her, sweeping up onlookers like old rushes and tarrying with them until she was well out of sight. One might almost expect that the Queen had puzzled out that she was being watched, even in her own castle."

"Oh, my. She would have to be a suspicious soul to believe that," I said, my tone as lightly mocking as his. Walsingham had also grown up in the courts of kings. He very well knew that you could not trust even your own shadow, for fear that it would tell your secrets if the price was high enough.

"And yet I find that no one was able to track Her Grace until you were both seen returning to her royal chambers. At that point you left quickly enough, but I would know what you had shared with the Queen, Beatrice. Your spying activities are of no use to England if they are not bent to the proper service."

"Indeed, Sir Francis." My brain should have been scrambling, but the fatigue from the previous evening was still preying hard upon my focus. I decided that the best lie, in this case, was the most outrageous one. "Oh, very well," I sighed. "The Queen wished to pay a visit to the Viscount Grimley."

"She *what?*" Walsingham rewarded my duplicity with an impressive amount of shock. "The Viscount Grim—"

"Pray, Sir Francis, have a care." I held up a hand to silence him. "This is not information I would have noised about. The

Queen was very particular about being discreet."

"Well, I should say," huffed Walsingham. "Viscount *Grimley*?" he asked again, as if he couldn't quite believe it. "Of the *Cotswold* Grimleys?"

"'Tis what she said." Viscount Grimley was fifty years old if he was a day, and so racked with perennial illness that even his bones coughed when he walked. He was a sharp-witted man, which is why the Queen suffered him in her court, but he made everyone uncomfortable just by entering a room. "She bade me wait outside his chambers while she entered, but in truth she did not remain there overlong." I could perhaps have chosen a more attractive pigeon to draw Sir Francis's attention, but Grimley would serve. Still, it would be smart to color the insinuation with just enough smoke that if the Queen had to defend it, she could. She would not thank me for it, but I could always point out that I chose such an unappealing suitor for her precisely to give her protestations of innocence that much more weight.

"And what was her . . . demeanor upon leaving the viscount's chambers?" Walsingham asked, his voice faintly strangled.

"Satisfied," I said. I could not deny the faint curl of pleasure in my stomach at the images I was evoking. It served the Queen's spymaster right for trying to follow his own Queen. And it was not the first time I'd spun one lie about the Queen to protect her from a more damning truth. "But I cannot think this conversation interests you truly, Sir Francis. What more word have you from the north—that you can share with me?" I gazed at him guilelessly. "I know now you will not tell me any tales you have not already told the Queen, but I would know what intrigues I'm marrying into, as it were." *Does he know that Alasdair was in the cellar room of Marion Hall with the Lords of the Congregation? And if so, will he tell me?*

Walsingham tightened his lips, but seemed to come to a conclusion to tell me something rather than nothing at all. "If we are sharing confidences, Beatrice, understand this: We would know the Queen's moods," he said. "She appears to trust you once more, and you have gained her ear."

Ah. So this would be how it would go between us. Whether he liked it or not, Walsingham knew I now had somehow earned the Queen's friendship anew. He would tell me his tales of almost-truths in exchange for any secrets I learned about the Queen.

Tedious, but not surprising.

I nodded to him gravely. "I want only what is best for England," I said, and that response seemed to please him.

"The Lords of the Congregation have returned north," he said. "The Queen has pledged her aid to them, as it serves England to keep the French away from our Scottish neighbors."

"Do you know the timing for such an intercession?" I asked, my tone low and careful.

He eyed me. Perhaps I'd been a bit too careful. "As early as Twelfth Night, and as late as Easter."

"That seems wise timing indeed." I slanted him a look. "And now it is my turn to share a confidence, just as soon as I have one to share."

Walsingham released me then, and I stepped away from

him, noting that he had returned me to the Queen's Privy Chamber, that I might take up my mantle as dutiful maid and tricked spy. "I appreciate your time, Sir Francis," I said. "I will watch the Queen."

He sketched me a short bow, his smile bland even as his eyes were mirror bright. "And I will watch you, Beatrice," he said.

Not closely enough, as it turned out.

CHAPTER THIRTY-FOUR

Alasdair was waiting for me in the Queen's chambers. I wasn't entirely surprised. If I were the Queen, I would have also wanted to see my enemy's face when she first encountered her downfall. I managed to gaze serenely and without particular interest in Alasdair's general direction, before presenting myself to the Queen.

Elizabeth, true to her word, was not going to formally announce my betrothal to the court quite yet. But the whispers about it would still have all of Windsor in thrall, which was bad enough. She gazed at me smugly as I lifted out of my curtsy; her glance going from me to Alasdair to my father, whom I now realized was also skulking in the shadows at the back of the room, then back to me.

It was all I could do not to sigh aloud. Her Royal Tediousness could be very good at subtlety when she wanted to be. This, clearly, was not one of those times.

"'Tis a fine day, is it not, Lady Beatrice?" the Queen asked now, putting a slight emphasis on "fine" in case anyone had missed the significance of her pointed looks.

"It is, Your Grace," I said sweetly. I could do sweet. It was the first mannerism I'd learned at court. "And I'm so pleased you are in good spirits."

"I truly am." She lolled back in her throne, her face settling into lines of beatific generosity, and instantly I was on my guard. The Queen was many things, but beatific and generous were not among them.

This was bad. For all of us.

Her next words confirmed it. "In fact, I am inclined to indulge my romantic nature today. Let us all adjourn to the Upper Ward and have a lunch *en plein air*." She nodded to her servants, who looked faintly aghast, but they melted away immediately, no doubt to alert the cook staff about the Queen's capricious decision. "Alasdair MacLeod, surely you can assemble your men to join us? The Scots above all people must appreciate a fine autumn day such as this."

"Of course, Your Majesty," Alasdair agreed, his rich full baritone drawing the curious eyes of the ladies only just beginning to hear the rumors of our pending wedding. I kept a smile on my face, but it was a close thing.

"Excellent." Elizabeth nodded. "Perhaps we can have some style of friendly competition. Are your men any good at archery?"

"Among the best in Scotland, is all." Alasdair shrugged. A delighted rumble sprang up from the spoiled courtiers, and Elizabeth laughed in that annoyingly false way of hers.

"Then we shall have to put them to the test. We do not have time to set up a joust, but archery—well. That shall work nicely. But go—go! Enjoy your morning. Perhaps there is a lady you might escort out into the open air for all to see?"

Oh, God's bones. I felt my anger mount as the Queen continued her prattle. Alasdair, playing along, chose me as a partner. I curtsied to him with all the grace I could muster, grateful that he hadn't tried to spare me the humiliation. If he'd chosen another woman, that would have just spurred Elizabeth on to greater ploys to get him to come round to choosing me. And then, inevitably, she'd tease me as being the lesser choice.

This way the bandage was ripped off my pride roughly and quickly, and then it was done. I beamed up at Alasdair as he took my arm, trying to remember how I'd looked at Cavanaugh just a bare month earlier, all wide-eyed and full of hope and expectation. It seemed like I had been much younger then.

"You look like you've eaten a small bird," Alasdair noted as we made our escape into the Upper Ward.

"You could have said no to the betrothal, you know," I said, suddenly angry at everyone—the Queen, for her meddling. My father, for his weakness. And Alasdair, for acting like becoming my betrothed was just another item ticked off a long list of things to do on his holiday to England, with him still not knowing that I had uncovered him as a liar and quite likely a spy for Scotland. I had no idea what had transpired in his conversation with the Queen, and the not knowing was driving me mad.

"That would not have served my interests," Alasdair said, his words infuriatingly bland. He angled us around the gathering crowds. A host of servants were already running about, setting up pavilions on the lawn for the Queen and her retinue, and arguing about where to put the long tables for food so as not to get in the way of any errant arrows.

The Queen's guard had also gathered to discuss how long to make the archery rows to demonstrate the true mastery of their skills. With the blithe indifference of someone clearly not used to court intrigue, Alasdair continued to walk us right out of the Upper Ward and along the curve of the Round Tower. There were more benches here, and even trees, but the Round Tower reminded us that we were still safe within the walls of an impregnable fortress.

Alasdair paused to allow me to sit, then settled down next to me, taking my hands into his.

I just as quickly pulled them back, unable to stop the sudden clatter of my heart at his audacity. "Good sir!" I said, glancing around. There was no one staring at us, but that did not mean we weren't being watched. "The betrothal has not been announced as yet. I pray you honor my virtue by not asking for undue a-affection between us, at least until it is announced, if it is announced, which of course it will be." I was mortified by my little speech. Not because it wasn't the correct thing to say but because I'd stuttered it out like a breathless little girl. *Very impressive, Beatrice.*

Alasdair just grinned at me, and his expression was positively wolfish. "You think your Queen is playing politics with this betrothal," he said. "But as you note, I did not say no."

"Which you easily could have done," I pointed out. "What is your stake in this, that you agreed so readily to marry a foreigner? Are you, too, playing politics?"

"It would be fitting, no?"

This of course was no answer at all, but at that moment one of Alasdair's men approached, his face at once contrite and curious. "Good morning, Niall," Alasdair said, smiling as he stood. "You have news?"

"Aye." Niall ducked a bow to me, like he was still trying to figure out the movement. "If I can borrow ye for a moment?"

"My lady?" Alasdair turned to me, and I nodded, nonplussed. This was exactly the kind of moment that I should have seized to spy upon them both. But I just sat there like a dullard.

Meg could have read their lips and pieced together their conversation. Sophia could have discerned their futures with a glance at her obsidian stone. I, on the other hand, was squatting there uselessly, unable to figure out a single thing to do to get the information the two men were sharing. I scanned the Middle Ward, impatient and bored and furious with myself for being so pointless, and that was when I saw it.

One of the ladies of court was standing off to one side of a nearby tree, her hands clasped together, her manner clearly expectant and waiting. She shot looks over to the brawny Niall with ill-disguised impatience, and I at once realized that she'd taken a fancy to the man. I glanced back at Niall. He was handsome enough, I supposed, though he didn't hold a candle to Alasdair. Still, he was fair and tall and probably no more than a few years older than Alasdair—perhaps twenty-one or twenty-two. And the lady—I couldn't remember her name; she was newcome to court, and I'd been busy of late—seemed completely consumed by him.

I strolled over to her, as guileless as a newborn lamb.

"Well met," I said, and so focused had she been on her man, she fairly squeaked with surprise.

"Oh!" she said, coloring. "Lady Beatrice! I did not see you there."

"I understand." So the woman knew me, but I couldn't place her to save my soul. Where had my training gone? And why had it chosen now to desert me? I followed her surreptitious gaze back to the two Scots, and made my gamble. "I should probably be jealous if you're watching the young MacLeod—but I suspect it's his friend who has captured your interest?"

"MacLeod? Oh!" She colored, and I knew I had her. She'd already heard of my betrothal, though no one was supposed to know. I could use that, though. "I did not realize that was him," she said faintly, and I pushed out a wry chuckle.

"Well, that story will make its rounds soon enough, for all that it is not true." I sighed.

She glanced at me sharply, her attention finally torn from Niall. She knew the power of information at court. "Not true?" she asked, feigning only casual curiosity.

"Well, not exactly," I hedged. "Promise me you'll keep it close? I've been about to burst with this news."

"Oh, of course!" she said, and she put out her hands to mine. "What is it?"

I grasped her hands with girlish glee. "I'm not the only woman of the Queen's court whose betrothal Elizabeth is negotiating," I said, and the woman's eyes flared wide with interest. "The Queen has the desire to demonstrate that the

Auld Alliance between England and Scotland is well and truly firm. To do that she wants a bevy of English misses and lords mated with our Scottish neighbors. Can you even imagine!"

"I cannot," the woman said, her eyes straying again to Niall. "Do you—" She swallowed. "Do you know who the Queen has in mind?"

"She referred to them only by their Christian names, and I don't know everyone at court, I'm afraid, and—"

"Catherine Meredith Anne Marie!" the woman blurted. "Did she include that one? To be betrothed to Niall Garrett?"

"Oh!" *Thank you, Catherine Meredith Anne Marie.* I hesitated, biting my lip. "Well, in truth I should not be saying anything. Alasdair and Niall are friends, and I would hate to betray their confidences."

"But you cannot stop now!" the woman interjected. "And Niall trusts me—we are friends! Why even now I know what he is sharing with his captain—Alasdair. He couldn't stop speaking of it in his sleep last night—" Her eyes flared wide. "I mean—"

"Hush now," I said over her sudden blushes. I squeezed her hands, the soul of understanding. "Your secret is safe with me." My tone turned just the slightest bit more pointed. "What did he speak about?"

"Soldiers rallying to the cause of the Scottish rebellion," breathed Catherine Meredith Anne Marie. "Niall's clan—at Alasdair's request—has just thrown their support into the Scottish rebellion."

I lifted my brow. "He spoke of this?" So there it was. Alasdair was not on hand merely to learn about the talk of the Lords of the Congregation. He had a task as well. To build support for the rebellion, and commit men and arms to its cause.

"Well, not to me, precisely. And I confess, I find it all exceedingly tedious. All this talk of tyranny and battle in the middle of the night, when we have such precious few hours together . . ." She sighed and looked again at Niall, and it was all I could do not to slap her. Here she was being given battle preparations from a foreigner, and she wanted their talk to devolve into whether or not he found her eyes of the deepest blue?

I schooled myself to not sound impatient. "Yes, well, men never do find the right time to confide in us, I guess," I said. "You are kind to give him solace that he might feel so comfortable to talk in his sleep."

"Kindness!" She snorted. "'Twas hardly that. It was a tincture from that herb mistress in town. She said it would help him speak his innermost thoughts. Fat lot of good that did. All he could rattle on about was the men the clan was sending to Fife to join in the battle."

"A . . . tincture?" I asked, keeping my voice as flat as possible. She'd poisoned Niall? With some sort of homemade truth potion? Made by a local herb mistress who was likely one part gardener and three parts witch? And we spies didn't know the recipe? "How frustrating that he didn't speak of you."

"Oh, he did eventually," she said, shooting me a knowing grin. "Once I chased away his words of battle with kisses. But first there were the endless talks about the plans of the French to gain a foothold in his homeland and turn the Scots into their serfs before they moved on to conquer England. All foolishness of course, but he did seem intent. The MacLeods are apparently spearheading an effort to ensure that all the clans to the north and west are ready at arms. Your Alasdair has become quite the leader among the clans—they will follow him into battle and beyond if he asks them to do so." She turned her wide eyes back to me. "So, did the Queen mention my name?"

"She didn't." I squeezed her hands to take the sting out of my words. "But the day is yet short. You may land your Scot before it is through."

"Oh, I do so wish it," Catherine Meredith Anne Marie said. "They are just not like the English."

Well, that was true enough. They were bigger and brawnier and smelled of leather and heather and spice. At least on their better days. I bade my leave of Catherine Meredith Anne Marie as Alasdair and Niall's conversation took a turn for the more heated, and I barely made it back to my seat before Alasdair glanced up at me, assuring himself that I was in my proper place. I smiled at him serenely, and he returned me a worried look.

When he came back to me, however, he seemed at his ease, gathering up my hand to place it on his arm, proud and defiant to squire me around the Middle Ward. With each step his mood seemed to improve, even as mine worsened. Oh, I kept up my general prattle. I laughed and smiled and nodded . . . but I just—my heart wasn't in it.

Being Alasdair, of course, he noticed. "My lady, what worries you so?" he asked, drawing me into the shade of another tree. There was no one near us, and when I made to look away, he tipped up my chin, his piercing eyes cutting me to the quick. My heart did an awkward little flutter . . . and then I quite lost my mind. All my years of training in the art of questioning, both formal and informal, completely deserted me, and I wanted more than anything—needed more than anything—answers.

I couldn't wait any longer.

"Alasdair." I lifted my hands to his hand, drew it away from my face, and clasped it tightly. "I know you were in the cellar room of Marion Hall with the Lords of the Congregation. I don't— I have to— Why were you there? What were you doing? I—"

Now it was Alasdair's turn to lift his other hand to clasp mine. We stood in the lee of the castle wall, an island amidst a teeming throng. "So that is what is troubling you so?" His expression was wry, though his eyes were still serious. "And here I thought I'd managed the switch most neatly."

"You did!" I blurted, then immediately blushed. "You carried off the role well; I don't think anyone else noticed. I just—I know your walk, your stance. I know you."

"Do you, now?" he said, his eyes darkening. Without hesitating, though, he went on. "The answer is not so complicated as you fear, I suspect; I will tell you plain. I was in that room for Scotland for one reason alone: to preserve our greatest treasures."

"Your treasures?" This was *not* what I'd expected.

He nodded. "In addition to fierce independence and victory in battle, my family has had a long history of valuing beauty. Small wonder that I am so drawn to you, my lady." He squeezed my hands, and I felt my heart lurch. "We prefer to stay out of war that does not benefit us, but this battle is one we must take up. But not because of religion, or even power. Nay, our interest in this battle of men on Scottish soil concerns what might be lost. Priceless works of beauty, created by men of God and artists of worth, preserved through centuries. We would not see such beauty cast into the flames, lost for all eternity."

I frowned at him, taken aback. "You are stealing from the Catholic churches? Before they can be plundered?"

"Aye," he said. "Though I am not sure we would call it 'stealing.' The clan MacLeod has been tracking the work of the Lords of the Congregation for some time. Like most men who have never been soldiers themselves, these rich nobles soon enough decided that their loyal guards could be paid less than a fair wage, as they were doing 'God's work.' Well, men who are poorly used soon find little value in God's work. So when we came along, offering the guards coin for their information and aid, they were happy enough to help. I knew that this meeting in Marion Hall, when it happened, would name the churches the Lords would strike next. With the help of the guards, I stood among the Lords of the Congregation for that brief time, learned their plans, and then sent out my men."

I stared at him, astonished. "You sent out your men, just like that? You will be found out—someone will tell!"

Alasdair shook his head. "Men of the cloth often do not care how the treasures of God are preserved from marauders—only that they are preserved. Most of the priests will not leave their abbeys, though we ask them to do so. But they will give us the most precious of their treasures, that we may keep them against harm."

My customary mistrust surfaced, and I narrowed my eyes. "Keep them or sell them?" I asked, recalling the maids' discussion of what Queen Elizabeth would do with "saved" treasures.

In response Alasdair gave a long, low laugh. "My lady, we have enough gold. We will never see a shilling for the treasures that we store. They are ours to protect, not profit from. An' all goes well, no one will ever know we hold the treasures at all."

"Then why do you do it?" I asked, completely puzzled.

He shrugged again. "For love, and for beauty," he said, lifting my two clasped hands so that he could graze the knuckles with his lips. "And that is enough."

We stood there for only a moment more in shadowy isolation, in time out of time, then, as if by common accord, turned back to rejoin the world of men and mayhem.

Though I was reeling with this new information and what to do about it, the rest of the day passed without incident. Still, I did not immediately try to catch the ear of the Queen in the midst of her "outdoor revels." I tarried on Alasdair's arm for several hours, all of us watching the most boring display of archery that ever graced Windsor Castle. (The Scots won.)

The longer I stayed with Alasdair, however, the more resolute I became. I needed to tell the Queen something of this. I wanted her to know that she had been right—that Alasdair was highly positioned in the Scottish rebellion, and he was someone who would be a good ally. Even if she didn't need to know precisely how and why Alasdair was involved, she did need to know he had power among the clans. Among men willing to fight against the French. That information was power, for her, and that was my job as a spy. I had to let her know.

As evening drew down, I slipped away from the makeshift dinner tables and reentered the castle, safe and at home again among the familiar passageways.

I'd almost reached the Queen's apartments when a hand reached out and grabbed me by the shoulder.

I stifled a squeak of alarm, spinning out of the grasp. I was about to execute a return chopping blow to the man's neck, when I halted, my hand poised like a hatchet in the air. "Oh!" I gasped.

"Yes. 'Oh.'"

Lord Cavanaugh stood before me, his eyes as black as murder.

CHAPTER THIRTY-FIVE

Cavanaugh took advantage of my momentary surprise to grasp my arm again and pull me, roughly, into the antechamber. It was the same one I'd tarried in with Rafe when he'd first come to Windsor, but this man's interests were far more sinister, I could immediately tell.

I shrugged off his arm and stood tall. "Good evening, my lord Cavanaugh," I said primly. "I hope you are doing well?"

"I'm doing very well," he said, his voice razor sharp. "You, though, my dear, will not be doing very well shortly, unless we come to some understanding."

I had heard courtly posturing before, from men as well as women. I had heard idle threats cast about. Cavanaugh did not have the air of a man who was playing games. Or rather, he did not have the air of a man whose game was played for sport. I needed to proceed with care.

"Very well," I said, nodding as I allowed a worried frown to crease my brow. Cavanaugh knew me fairly well. He would be more difficult than most to dupe, but not impossible. "What is it that you mean?"

"To start, I mean that you are going to get the Queen to restore me with grace to the court, to recognize my position and grant me her full blessing."

"I'm going to what?" Despite my decision to play this with skill and grace, this request was outside of enough. "Are you *mad*? I cannot sway the Queen in such a way." And I surely wouldn't be troubling myself to aid his cause.

"You have ruined me!" Cavanaugh spit, and his words carried a heavier sheen of hysteria now. "You, and your stupid ploy to reveal me, have made me a laughingstock at court. My family is one of the noblest in all of England, and you dared to bring me low!"

"My lord Cavanaugh, it was not I who chose a very public ball to embrace my ladylove. Where is she now?" I asked archly, casting a glance about. "I do hope you don't have her hiding in the tapestries. They are very dusty this time of year." I beat the nearest one. "Are you in there, dear?"

"She is gone from Windsor," Cavanaugh said darkly. I immediately left off my game, now troubled. What had he done with the woman? She'd appeared capable and sturdy, but she'd been employed by the Queen. Forget about Cavanaugh's hurt feelings. Had I ruined her life in truth by bringing her into the focus of the court?

"Gone from Windsor *where*?" I asked, playing the flounce. "It is not she who wished to be on that dance floor." I opened my eyes wide, part terrified little girl, part chattering court gossip. "Please do not say you killed her!"

"No!" Cavanaugh drew back as if he'd been slapped. "She is the least of your concerns, so do not think you can start more false rumors about her. She is more woman than you will ever be."

That stung more than I cared to admit. "So you are still seeing her," I said.

"And that has *never* been your concern," Cavanaugh snapped dismissively. "But if it soothes your sensibilities, no. I have broken off our liaison and settled her with enough funds and recommendations to find good work in the town. She will not starve."

There was a lie in his words, but I could not quite place it. Cavanaugh was not by nature a generous man, though he knew the sense of buying off a woman's silence—especially a woman as level-seeming as this one. Precisely because she had not been born to court intrigue, she'd take his money and hold her tongue. Far more likely that he'd set her up with money and still expected her to share his bed, just not within the walls of Windsor. Still, there was no way I could discern here which of his words were true and which were false. So I opted for a bridge comment. "Then I am glad to hear it."

"As I'm sure you'll be glad to hear this." Cavanaugh's tone was scornful. "You will convince the Queen to change her mind about me, to reinstate me in the court with full grace . . ."

I waited for the remainder of his request, that he also be reinstated as my betrothed. But as the moment drew out, I felt the tiniest bit of dread creep into my stomach. Cavanaugh, unlike his mistress, *was* a court insider. His plans, perforce, were more diabolical.

Finally I couldn't stand the waiting. "Or—what, Lord

Cavanaugh? Surely there must be a price to my rejecting your request."

"My request is not quite through, my lovely Beatrice." His lips twisted on the words, but he reached into his doublet and pulled out a letter. "But come. You'll want to read this, I'm sure."

I rather doubted that, but I pushed my feet forward. I joined him under one of the few lit sconces in the room. Cavanaugh had a formal piece of parchment—a letter—heavily inked with a slashing script. He showed it to me, then pressed it into my hands. "Go ahead. You can have this copy," he said smugly. "I have had three more made."

That . . . couldn't be good.

I took the pages with a steady hand, then held them up to the light. I read carefully and thoroughly, with my eyebrows arched in indifference. As if I were reading any court letter, from king or countryman. What was on these pages, however, was much more damning than any casual letter.

Cavanaugh could sense my sharpening focus, even if I betrayed no other reaction. "Yes, my lady Beatrice. With the Queen refusing to grant me leave to join her at your rather-more-humble home than I'd realized, I had to take extra measures. I sent three of my associates along with Elizabeth's courtiers, who quite enjoyed eating your food and draining your casks of ale while noting that, it seems, your mother is quite mad."

With what I considered to be extraordinary patience, I forced myself not to tear the man's eyes out. I'd learned how to perform that gruesome act earlier in the summer, and it seemed like a wonderful time to put the lesson to use. "I am grateful for the diagnosis of your friends, Lord Cavanaugh, but—"

"Keep reading," he said, gloating.

And then I saw it.

It appears that the good owners of Marion Hall have not adequately instructed their servants in the proper treatment of foreigners, namely dark Egyptians, who have stained their forest within a quarter hour's ride of the manor house. These Travelers squat upon the land, which is the Knowleses' property, taking food and water and livelihood from the surrounding villages and farms. Worse, the staff of Marion Hall fully admit to stocking the home's larders with potions and trinkets from the traveling troupe currently residing without censure on its land, and were not immediately aware that such interaction between them and the filthy Travelers was a crime against the Crown, punishable by death. They spoke openly of the "care" and "consideration" the household has long shown to unmentionable types, even during "previous persecutions" of same. Clearly a decades-long history of treason is demonstrated, which I leave to your careful handling. Rather than give the alert to the servants, who might then warn the rabble, we departed without further word.

As I read, my heart seemed to shrivel and die within me. Who in the world would have told strangers about the Travelers? Old Mary in the chicken yard? The ancient groom, Tom? We had so many servants and pensioners at Marion Hall that it was impossible to keep track of them all without instituting strict rules and regulations that would have made everyone's life sheer misery. But we clearly had gotten lax on the important topics. And now we were in Cavanaugh's noose.

"I do not think I need to explain to you how dire this information is, Beatrice," he said, his words silky with threat. "It goes beyond your family being ruined, although that will certainly result. Your father and your mother will be held accountable, and they will be executed for their troubles. You yourself might lose your pretty, conniving head. Your servants and staff will almost certainly be turned out by the new lord and lady of your ancestral home, for fear that the servants' friendships with unmentionables might taint the family fortunes. They will likely starve."

I found my breathing was not working correctly, the air coming into my lungs in swift bursts and starts. Cavanaugh was now impossibly close to me, his breath smelling of ale and overcooked meat, his entire body quivering with excitement. For my part, my mind should have been racing through alternatives, contingency plans, fresh perspectives. But all I could see was my mother, as pale as a ghost, surrounded by the group of roistering children who represented the large family she had longed for, before she had been sent down a path to sadness and dark days.

"You cannot prove this," I finally managed. Cavanaugh just laughed.

"Of course I can," he said. "And I should take great delight in doing so. I could likely regain my prestige within the court based on that service alone, without any great effort. But that's not of interest to me, dear Beatrice. Would you like to know what is?"

I swallowed, trying to force my voice to remain haughty, though all the world was spinning around me. "You want me to have the Queen reinstate our betrothal?" I asked. It was a reasonable thought, but even as I gave it voice, I knew how gravely I'd blundered. Cavanaugh leaped upon my words like a cat playing with its dinner, his long rolling chuckle rippling through the room.

"Our betrothal! Rest assured, I have now seen the folly of that course. Though I had thought you could be managed with sufficient forcefulness, I have since come to realize that the cost would be too great—it would take too much time and effort to bring you to heel. Oh no, Beatrice. Do not imagine for a moment I still want to be tied to you in wedded bliss. Your cunning mind would not rest until it tore to shreds any man so sorry to be your husband—just for something to keep you occupied in between dress fittings. Your shrewish mouth was not made for kissing but for harping, and your eyes would find only fault in any man you'd choose. I would no sooner wed you than I would rip out my own throat, now that I have seen you for who you truly are."

"Then—what?" I asked, confused. Cavanaugh had already made a great demonstration of his discovery of my family's financial straits. I could not offer him prestige in court. Only the Queen could do that. There was nothing at all I could offer him, in fact, other than—

Lord Cavanaugh saw my face the moment the realization struck me, and his grin turned harder, more malicious. "Ah, yes, my Beatrice," he purred. "You do have something I want. I want to ruin you, as you clearly tried to ruin me. But unlike your childish reveal of a kiss, there will be no question within the minds of even the lowest servant of the castle exactly how far you've given yourself to me. You will be known as my lover and as my castoff, in lurid, scintillating detail, and there will be no one in all of London who won't know of your disgrace."

He settled back on his heels, his smile broadening as he saw the reality of my position crashing down upon me. "I am not without mercy, of course. I will keep my word, as a man of honor. When you are well and truly ruined, I will keep my pledge to ensure that no one ever hears a word about your family's treasonous activities. They will be protected." He cast an appraising glance over me. "But you will *never* have the noble marriage that you so crave. By the time I'm done with you, not even a farmer would take you to wife."

He paused then, and cocked an aristocratic brow at me. "So what shall it be, Beatrice?"

When I didn't respond right away, he grabbed my chin and forced my head up, chuckling at whatever he saw in my eyes. "No longer the proud bitch, are you?" He grinned. "I would like to reveal our new relationship at tomorrow's performance, I think. That should do nicely. Do we have a pact?"

"Please," I said, forcing myself not to pull away. "Give me a few hours to prepare myself to come to this decision, I beg of you."

Cavanaugh shrugged, lifting his thumb to drag it hard across my lips in an act of conscious brutality. "You cannot escape me now, Beatrice," he sneered. "But do not try my patience. Secrets such as your family's are too good to keep for long."

CHAPTER THIRTY-SIX

I got through the rest of the night and into the next morning with no one suspecting a thing. Or at least not the whole of the thing. My mind refused to focus too long on any one topic. It sheared around Cavanaugh's threats like they were impassable rocks on the shoreline when all I wanted was the safety of the beach beyond.

I dimly realized that people were talking to me, trying to draw me out. Anna first, with her glance taking me in like a puzzle she needed to solve, and then Sophia, her eyes so luminous with pain that it broke my heart to look at her. To their credit, my fellow maids did not try to intrude upon my misery after I delivered them a few sharp words. I let them think that I was despondent over my betrothal, that I was nervous at the thought of marriage. I let them think whatever they wanted.

God knew I was going to be giving the whole of the court plenty to think on soon enough.

I stood now in the Queen's Privy Garden, mercifully alone. The night was drawing down, and we soon would be gathering in the Presence Chamber for a feast and then the choral performance that Cavanaugh was doubtless looking forward to with great relish. I'd seen him, of course, throughout the day. He'd made a point of staying within my eyesight, looking at me far too intently, a secret smile playing about his lips.

If any of the court had been watching, they would have been able to draw their own conclusions after the farce of the evening played out to their delighted eyes and viperous minds. But if something were to happen to me in the meantime, like perhaps I should drown myself in the Thames, then they would think nothing of it. Cavanaugh was playing his cards exactly right.

And now I had to play mine.

Because of course, I could not meet an untimely end. I could not run, I could not escape. If I did, then my troubles might well be over . . . except for those of my immortal soul, of course. But far worse would be the plight of those I left behind. My father would be disgraced by my death or flight, but he would not have time to dwell on that long. Instead he would be thrown instantly into Cavanaugh's snare. The letter would be revealed, the Egyptians found on our property. My parents might be beheaded or simply exiled, but all of Marion Hall would be destroyed by the scandal.

I could not do it.

I stared at the fountain in the center of the space, my hands working over each other as though I were a washerwoman rubbing cloth over stones. I could sense Alasdair behind me, of course. He had not let me far from his view since I'd left him yesterday afternoon, full of information to share with the Queen.

Except I'd still not talked with Elizabeth. Even though all the terrible things that Cavanaugh had said about me were true—I *was* cunning and conniving, I *had* been trained to bring others low—my body now shook with every step, my eyes swam with tears. My mind and heart were choked with the wretched business of my own life. I could not divulge Alasdair's secrets to Elizabeth on the cusp of my own humiliation; if she still wanted the story after I was destroyed, then so be it. She was my Queen and country.

For at least another little while.

But Alasdair did, at the very least, deserve to be set free of me before I shamed him publicly at Cavanaugh's side. And so I straightened my back, sensing his approach. A few moments later I heard his quiet footfalls, and then his calm, sturdy presence was at my side.

"You are very sad, my lady," he observed, as always not wasting time on pretty speech.

I twisted my lips. I'd spent a lifetime finding ways to craft unpleasant news in a manner that would leave my victim feeling strangely comforted by my dismissal of him, but now I found that all my careful training deserted me. As it always seemed to do around Alasdair. "I am, good sir," I said, turning to him and raising my face to his.

He lifted his brows, his gaze searching my face. "'Good sir'?" he asked. "You think you may want to try using my first name, as we are to be wed?"

And here it was. I swallowed again, and forced myself

to keep my hands at my side. "About that," I said. "I—" The words would not come for a moment, and I gritted my teeth, steeling myself to get through this as I had ever gotten through every shaming conversation of my life. "I fear we do not suit, good—Alasdair." I could hear the words, mocking me even as they recalled what I had said to Elizabeth. But I believed them, didn't I? They were the truth, weren't they?

Of course they were.

I could never love Alasdair MacLeod—his strength, his power, his sense of purpose. His loyalty, his grace. He was not for the likes of me.

"I fear we do not suit," I said again. The dam broken, it was as if some other person began to speak for me, her words calm and measured and haughty, though I could feel my body turning hollow, tears melting my bones. "I think you should return to your home without a bride in tow. We are so dissimilar."

"We are not so dissimilar as that, my lady." Alasdair's rebuttal was quick and comforting, and sent a knife into my heart.

"No!" I said harshly, raising my hand to cut him off. "Allow me to finish." My voice sounded ugly now, rough and untutored, and I built all of the reasons—the good, valid, and wholly true reasons—that condemned any relationship between us before we even began. "I love luxury and comfort, and you live on a hulking rock on an island in the middle of a barren and desolate country. I am learned in languages, music, and the arts, and you know only the life of a warrior. I would be no good bride for you, and you would soon learn the dark side of my nature. My mother you have met; I am but her daughter. My father you have met; I am but his daughter as well. The worst of both their natures commingle in me, and I would betray you at a moment's notice to get my way. And my way would be to return here, to the gentle life of the Englisher. I am not meant for the harsh and terrible winters of the north."

Alasdair made to speak again, but I could feel the tears threatening and I placed my hand against his chest, savoring the solidity of him for a precious moment before I pushed him roughly away. "No, I say!" I fairly shouted, lifting my chin to say the most hated part of my carefully prepared little speech. "I am not for you, good sir. I crave to return to Lord Cavanaugh. He is the man that I love, for all his flaws. He is the man I will be with, however he will have me." *He is the only man despicable enough to deserve me, a woman who lies and deceives with every waking breath.*

"Lord Cavanaugh!" Alasdair said, the shock on his face plain, anger and outrage threading through his voice. "You cannot be serious!"

"Pray, did someone say my name?" The drawling voice I had once thought so cultured now crawled like beetles along my skin, and I turned, legitimately surprised to see Cavanaugh strolling toward us. He was outfitted in the highest fashion of the court, his foppish attire immediately labeling him the buffoon beside the powerfully built Alasdair.

"Beatrice," Cavanaugh breathed my name as though it were an intimacy, and he caught up my hand and held it to his face. It took every ounce of strength for me to let him do it and not shiver with revulsion. "How good it is to see you again, and how lovely you look."

I bared my teeth at him with sick sweetness, then turned to Alasdair again, staring at him blindly as I was smote with the extraordinary wave of pain, sorrow, and outrage that seemed to roll out of his body like a crushing tide. I tried to pull my hand from Cavanaugh, but he held fast, and I was left with trying to speak words over the crashing of my own heart. "You see, good sir, I—"

"Yes," Alasdair said curtly. "I do certainly see. Fear not, my lady. I will not stand in your way. And now I bid you a good day." He bowed to me, so shallowly that it was barely a brief nod. Then he turned on his heel, completely ignoring Cavanaugh, and stalked back through the garden until he disappeared into the shadows of the growing evening. I thought I would hear his diminishing footsteps for the rest of my days, around every corner.

A lifetime of Alasdair walking away from me.

But Cavanaugh did not give me long to grieve. "That was well done, Beatrice," he said sarcastically, lye dripping from his words. "I should not have wanted to deal with the indelicacy of that oaf calling me out in front of the Queen."

I turned to Cavanaugh and felt my heart harden into a small knot of stone. For Alasdair, I would sacrifice my pride. For my family, I would sacrifice my position. But this man, who would take so much from me without a second thought, him I would kill one day. It almost made what was about to happen to me worth it.

Almost.

"So let us go over the terms of our contract," Cavanaugh said with relish, drawing me to a bench closer to the edge of the garden. "Sit, sit. I would that you be comfortable while we discuss your disgrace."

I sat, but I found I was no longer numb. A cold sort of certainty was growing inside me, starting from my belly and extending out through my arms and legs and hands and feet. The very last portion of my body that it affected was my mouth, which now curved into a brittle, perfect smile—and my eyes, which turned to my tormenter with a calculating precision that even I recognized from somewhere else, someone else.

I suddenly found myself thinking of Jane, when she had been brought into the castle, not flailing and kicking as Meg had been, nor wide-eyed and wondering as Anna had been. Nor even as mute with confusion and worry as Sophia had been.

When Jane had been brought into the castle, she had been silent, stoic, and brutally hard. Her eyes had been those of granite; her very skin had seemed chipped with ice. And her mouth had formed a hard line of both resignation and fierce intention. She had already killed by then. And she had already died.

Thank you, Jane. With her as my mentor, I could get through this. I would get through it.

"Now," Cavanaugh said, drawing the word out. "Allow me to recap." He pulled out the accursed letter, fluttered it in front of me. "I have here proof of your family's unfortunate transgression with the Egyptians on your land. A transgression I will not hesitate to share with the Queen. To assure my silence, you will agree to consort with me however and whenever I choose, in public or in private, and to deny no one when they ask if I have ruined you. Which I certainly will have done, before this night is through." He glanced over the letters and eyed me keenly. "In case you were wondering."

I stared back at him, plotting his death in horrible ways. I was up to thirty-two when his expression faltered, but only slightly.

"It will be my absolute pleasure to do so, you should know," he said. "And then, when I am through—quite through—and you are sufficiently punished for daring to embarrass me, then I shall deposit you in whatever hovel is still willing to claim you. You will know your family is safe—from your servants to that horde of foundlings who plague your halls, from your deranged mother to your insufferable father."

And then came a movement beside us that sent a chill anew down my back, and my mortification was complete. Was there nowhere in the castle where one could speak and not be heard?

Apparently not this night.

"Insufferable!" came the deceptively mild voice. "I say, my good Lord Cavanaugh, I am wounded."

My father strolled into the garden.

CHAPTER THIRTY-SEVEN

To his credit, Cavanaugh did not even flinch. He'd spent more time at court than even I had, and he was well used to being overheard. A dim part of me wondered if he'd sought me out in this garden exactly so he could be overheard. The plan had a certain malicious merit to it.

But now he stared at my father, and I finally turned as well, forcing myself to lift my gaze to the laughing drunkard, the fawning courtier, the charming secret-gatherer I'd known all my life.

And I blinked.

My father's face was still set in its outwardly cheerful manner, his eyes bright, his grin easy. But something had changed beneath the surface. There was a cold fury that had taken hold of his bones somehow, rendering them thick and unyielding beneath the malleable skin. His body, too, belied an intensity I'd never seen before, even as he sauntered up to Cavanaugh with the affected grace of a lifelong courtier and stood at his leisure, absently drawing his fine lawn gloves off his hands and tucking them into his waistband.

The move looked oddly like that of a man about to do battle with his fists. Cavanaugh must have thought so too, because he immediately began to bluster.

"You have *nothing* to say to me anymore, Knowles," he said. "What goes on between your daughter and myself is our own affair. There is *nothing* she is doing here that she hasn't agreed to fully, and there is *nothing* you can do about it." He caught my hand and pulled me to him, a parody of two young nobles in love. "She'll be the first to tell you."

"My daughter's mind is ever her own, and has been since she was scarcely five years old," Father said, smiling benignly at me even as his eyes flicked down, coldly, to stare at Cavanaugh's hand gripping mine. I was slowly coming out of my fog, realizing that I needed to turn this conversation into safer waters—but to where? I wasn't sure how much my father had overheard, but his crime in this was far greater than what mine was about to be in the eyes of the court. Surely the sacrifice of his daughter was worth saving the family's lives?

"Nonetheless," Father said smoothly. "I should say for shame, Lord Cavanaugh, for feeling that you need to compel any woman, let alone a gently bred girl, to lie with you in your bed."

I felt my eyes go wide even as Cavanaugh stiffened. "How dare you!" he spit out, his face turning a shade of purple. "How dare you insinuate—"

"And how dare *you*," my father returned, cutting him off. "From what I overheard, you are behaving as boorishly and scandalously as the most common of brigands—and trust me, I can repeat it to the word, to the letter."

That stopped me, and I shot a glance to the shadows of the garden. My father could generally be expected to remember no more than what room he'd most immediately left. Was Meg somewhere, lingering in the darkness? Had he brought her here?

"What I heard was a man reduced to creating trumped-up nonsense in order to cajole, coerce, and then downright threaten a woman of proud and noble standing to be his doxy. Really, my lord Cavanaugh. I did not expect much of you, but I did expect more than this."

"'Trumped-up nonsense'!" exploded Cavanaugh. He yanked the copy of the letter out of his doublet and shoved it at Father. "This is hardly 'trumped-up nonsense.' This is an accounting of treasonous and criminal activities taking part on your property with your full knowledge and approval. Do not even think to say that because you are an absent landowner, you are not responsible for what goes on at your estate."

"I would not ever give up the responsibility for my estate," my father drawled in response. "It's not in my nature."

"Then you deny what these papers hold?" Cavanaugh seethed. "Because I am here to tell you, you cannot. The accounts of these men are incontrovertible. They are bonded and sealed. They are telling the truth."

"Ah, the truth!" My father said the word with relish. "The truth." He folded up the papers and handed them back to Cavanaugh, who took them with clipped precision. Then Father reached down and flicked our hands apart as if the very sight of us joined caused him revulsion.

The player in me, the manipulator, wanted to take the floor now. My father was clearly not going to deny the reality of what those letters held. He was caught dead to rights, a traitor to the Crown. Harboring the unclean infidels on our land would cause his downfall and the ruination of our family, and even Cavanaugh began to relax, seeing that Father had no recourse. I knew I should step forward now and smooth things over, assure my father that I, of course, wanted nothing more than to remain with Cavanaugh in any way he would have me.

But something held me up, some niggling suspicion that my cause was best served by keeping quiet. It chafed to appear weak, but how many times had I gotten what I most desired by appearing to be weak and helpless, moments before going in for a verbal strike?

Father glanced at me sharply, almost as if I'd spoken, and I merely beamed at him. *The show is yours, Father. Please don't make this any worse than it already is.*

"Very well, then," Cavanaugh said. "If you are in accord—"

"But the truth is such a tricky thing, is it not?" my father continued, as if Cavanaugh had not spoken during his prolonged reverie. "The truth can serve as a charm or a curse. As with yourself, Lord Cavanaugh. How well you have benefited from a secret closely held."

Cavanaugh narrowed his eyes at Father. "What in the devil are you talking about?"

"Tell me, good fellow. How is your father doing?"

"My father?" Cavanaugh's gaze darted to the entrance to the garden, as if he were afraid that the man, once summoned, would appear from their vast estate to the south. He did well to be afraid. Robert Cavanaugh, current Marquess of Westmoreland, was a fierce man to behold. Angry, brash, and vital, he bashed his way through every social gathering he attended, setting the women atwitter and the men on their heels. It was hard to believe the slender, foppish Cavanaugh came from such stock, except that his mother was as pale and raven-haired as he, shrinking ever away from her earthy husband. The court gossips had consigned their union to the flames the moment Cavanaugh had been born, with Westmoreland taking on one mistress after another.

When Cavanaugh had assured himself that his father would not be pounding his way into the garden, he flicked his gaze back. “My father is well, thank you.”

“A proud man, he is.”

“I fail to see what relevance this has to anything,” snapped Cavanaugh. “My father would scarcely give you the time of day.”

“Oh, I think he’d give me far more than that, Lord Cavanaugh, for what I know about you.”

From another man those words would have been dismissed as mere folly. But my father had been a court insider for longer than Cavanaugh had been alive. I stared at him now, as completely at sea as Cavanaugh was. “What are you talking about?” Cavanaugh asked, gathering his hauteur around him like a cloak. “You know nothing about me.”

“Indeed.” Father’s demeanor had completely changed now from charming jester to cunning politician. “Then allow me to tell you a story. I could produce my own letter on the subject; I think you'll recognize the hand of she who wrote it. But we are far from that necessity, I should think."

"What letter?" Cavanaugh began, but my father held up his hand.

"For once in your life, boy, shut up," Father said. He cut a regretful glance to me. "I truly did not think he was quite this despicable, Beatrice, or I'd never have saddled you with him. I always suspected you'd dispose of him if he got too tedious, but I rather thought you two suited well enough. And he certainly had the money you were so convinced we needed, though I tell you plain, we've all the gold we could ever want."

"Dispose of me?" Cavanaugh protested. "What on earth—"

"Gold?" I managed.

"Allow me to put it to you as plainly as I know how, Lord Cavanaugh," Father said, cutting us both off and returning his attention to Cavanaugh with a curl of his lip. "When I considered to whom I might betroth my only child, I wanted certain . . . assurances in place. It had to be a man she could find happiness with—and you certainly seemed a reasonable choice, though I find your newly discovered reprehensible nature to be quite a disappointment. It had to be a man who was not as smart as Beatrice. Again, you served well." He held up his hand again to stay Cavanaugh's blustering. "But most important, it had to be a man from a family that was more beholden to me than the reverse."

That seemed to dampen some of Cavanaugh's fire. Again, in an ordinary conversation between ordinary men, this exchange would have held precious little weight. But these were men who trucked in secrets. Their idle banter had brought down some of the highest noblemen in the land. "Beholden in what way?" Cavanaugh asked.

"Your mother—lovely woman though she is—is quite barren, Lord Cavanaugh. Always has been." Father allowed these words to sink in as he cast a now apologetic glance my way. "I had the occasion to learn this when your mother and I met in the court of King Henry. A childhood illness rendered her quite incapable of giving birth, and she'd tested that theory often enough to know it to be true before we'd even met."

I widened my eyes at this shameful admission. How could my father know such intimate details about another woman at court? "Though she was newly married to your father, I fear they did not suit in temperament, and she was quick to look further afield for—ah, solace." Again the hasty glance my way, and I stifled a groan. My father appeared to have bedded half of England over the course of the last three decades.

"You lie," said Cavanaugh, though his words lacked conviction. "If she is barren, then how . . ." His voice petered out, then rallied. "I am my father's son! You have no proof."

"Your mother came to me, quite desperate, in the third year of her marriage," my father said. "She had begun to fear that her husband suspected not only her barrenness but that she'd known full well her state prior to their marriage. This, as you know, would be grounds for an annulment, especially in King Henry's time, and your father was a great favorite of the King. Truly, extreme measures were required." Father tilted his head then, skewering Cavanaugh with a steely glare. "Fortunately for everyone concerned—especially you—your father was due for a prolonged tour in the King's command. At my suggestion your mother fulfilled her wifely duties with him with enthusiasm for weeks before he left, then bade him off with words of true love and endless devotion. Quite a happy man, your father, and fully convinced that he'd return home to a baby after his time at the battlefront was at an end. And of course, your mother was not going to disappoint him. Within weeks of his departure, she began to show signs of being with child. As her belly swelled, so did the rounds of congratulations, but there was still one little detail to work out. You."

"But she was with child," Lord Cavanaugh said dumbly. "You said so yourself."

"She was *not* with child," Father scoffed. "She was stuffing her skirts with rags and eating herself silly, trying to put on weight. And then we found you, squalling and dirty, in a back alley of London. Your real mother was desperately poor, but she'd been a fine-looking woman in her day, before the muck of life had dragged her down. Tall, slender, and dark-haired, not unlike Lady Anne. She was strong, but she was starving."

By now all of the color had drained out of Cavanaugh's face. I also felt unsteady. A secret such as this! That father had kept all these years! "What did you do?" Cavanaugh whispered.

"We paid her in silver for you, assured her that you would have a life of luxury beyond her wildest imaginings. That you would be a lord of the land." Father's face had also grown tired in the telling of this tale, and I saw the lines create fissures along his skin. "She didn't want our money, you know. She would have given you up for naught but the hope of your survival," he said. "You shame her this day."

That rallied Cavanaugh. "You have no proof of this!" he blurted, and Father sighed.

"Leave off your unholy contract with my daughter," he said. "And go find Lady Anne. I had her write a letter to me to save my own skin should her husband ever discover our duplicity. I'm not proud of that, but neither am I stupid enough not to use it." He shrugged. "And she wrote it without hesitation. Lady Anne trusted me not to betray her unless she somehow betrayed herself. It was a bargain she was willing to make."

Cavanaugh stood there a moment more, a hundred and one rebuffs, redirects, and restatements forming in his mind in true court form. But even he recognized that this threat was real, and needed to be dealt with, before he could continue his campaign with the Queen . . . and me.

"This isn't over," he said, seething.

My father smiled thinly. "Oh, but it is. Now go, and take solace in the fact that your secrets are safe with me . . . as I know mine are with you."

He turned to me with a broad smile and held out his arm. "Beatrice, my sweet, do you fancy a turn about the garden?"

It was only then that I saw the faint sheen of sweat on his brow.

CHAPTER THIRTY-EIGHT

Dread tightened my gut as my father gracefully swept me away from Cavanaugh's stunned form and up the garden walkway. A thousand questions consumed me, but the first was also the most important.

"Are you sweating because you lied?" I asked quietly. "Is none of that true?"

"Hmph," Father said, though he paused to fish a handkerchief out of his doublet. A quick glance back assured us that Cavanaugh had already taken his leave of the garden.

"I'm sweating because I told the truth," Father said, managing a wry grin as he mopped his brow. "As I've told you before, sometimes information withheld is far more important than information given. But when information is given at the right time, it can change a thing drastically." He chuckled. "I'm not used to so much honesty. It can take a lot out of a man."

He resumed our walk, and I tried to compose myself, but failed miserably. "All of that is true?" I whispered, hoarse with shock. "Lady Anne lied about her own pregnancy while her husband was away serving the King, then tricked him with a foundling from a London sewer?"

"She did," my father said, and his gaze was distant now, as if he could see the woman and her squalling infant once more. "Cavanaugh's real mother was a beautiful woman, Beatrice—or had been, before the ravages of her circumstances had stripped the meat from her body and the youth from her face. She at first thought we were going to steal her babe to sell it into even worse circumstances. As tired as she was, as broken, she could never have allowed that. When we had finally fed her enough that she was sensible, she understood what it was we were offering."

"You say 'we,'" I said, dry-mouthed. "Lady Anne went with you?"

Father hesitated only a moment. "Yes," he said. "She did not want to, but I insisted. I could trust no one else in this, could expand the circle no wider than the two of us. And, further, I wanted her to see the gift she was giving this woman, but also the obligation she was accepting. She who could never have children, taking a child from a woman who had only a child to give. I needed her to understand that responsibility, and to care for the boy with every fiber of her being, for the plan to work." He shook his head. "I knew the mother would not give up the boy for money . . . only for the assurance that his care would be better than she could ever give him."

I bit my lip, wondering at these words from my father, who had never seemed to notice when I was there or not, so busy he'd been with court.

Then I forced myself to think about my father not with disdain and derision but with a wider view.

He cared for the other children at Marion Hall, I had to give him that. The children had started coming to us shortly after the incident in the labyrinth. Father had welcomed the distraction, and in all truth Mother had seemed to delight in caring for the children of others—even taking them in and lodging them, as it had quickly come to pass. He'd allowed that to happen. He'd given that to her.

And he *had* cared for my mother, after a fashion. He'd brought the children to Marion Hall to surround her. He had never shamed her for her dark spells, even though I still felt he could do more.

Had he also cared for me? For so long I had believed I was just a tool for him, a mouthpiece in a royal setting, a gatherer of secrets, a symbol of strength. But had I misread that situation as well?

Rather than think on that too long, I found my mind returning to the woman who'd so bravely given up her child, that he might grow up safe. "What happened to her, the woman in London?" I asked, knowing the answer. A woman in such a desperate condition, even with money in her hand, would not live long. Not in the streets of London, where the weak were preyed upon like sheep.

Once again my father surprised me. "I have not seen her in perhaps five years, but I visited her in the Abbey Saint Charles then, when Cavanaugh reached his majority. I gave her a miniature of the man so she could see he'd turned out rather well." He tightened his lips. "Of course, miniatures do not reveal what lies beneath the surface. That she will never know."

I looked at him, feeling unreasonably close to tears. "You got her to a convent?"

He shrugged and patted my hand, and though he would not look at me, I could see his own eyes were strangely bright. "It is what I would have wanted for my own daughter, were she ever to find herself in such dire circumstances. There are advantages to this life we lead, Beatrice. Kindness is the least we can give back."

Then with one last squeeze of my fingers, he was gone.

I turned as well, to make my way to the Queen's Privy Chamber. As I walked, I thought of the rabble of children that even now were carousing around Marion Hall, tearing tapestries and upending planters. My father had saved them with his gallant gesture, as much as he had saved me. But there was still the Queen herself to see, my report to give.

And somewhere, in the dark reaches of Windsor Castle, Alasdair still hated me.

Part of me wanted to run to him, to explain everything. But the stronger, louder part of me knew that such a path was folly. The mere fact that I'd been willing to consort with another man during my betrothal to him was an unpardonable sin, and he would not deign to know the circumstances.

And, in truth, what sort of bride was I? At this moment I was going to the Queen to share information about Alasdair's battle strategy. Though I did so feeling well assured that I was not putting him into harm's way, how could I know that for certain? What if the Queen took the information that I would give her and planned some sort of false attack on the

MacLeods to stir the Highland Scots to more fervent action? It would be the sort of thing she would find reasonable, a small sacrifice for the greater good.

What of it? Before these past weeks, I had neither known nor cared about any Scottish soldiers on a spit of land thrust up out of the cold sea. I was English, born and bred, and I was a spy for that England. My words would help save English lives. My loyalty would help ensure my family's safety. That was enough. That had to be enough.

My heart grew colder with each step I took toward the Queen. What I found when I reached her, however, was not what I'd expected.

She wasn't alone.

Cecil and Walsingham were at the Queen's side in earnest discussion, and her ladies were milling about, well away from their conversation. Sophia was in the midst of the group, chatting with remarkable ease, and I felt a surge of relief for her, one bright spot in all of this madness.

When I approached the dais and waited to be acknowledged, however, the tone of the room quickly changed. The Queen glanced up at me, then straightened, her spine stiff. With a sharp command she ordered her other ladies-in-waiting to depart. That left only Sophia, who sat with her eyes shining in the dim light, as if she had seen and experienced all of my pain.

"Very well, Beatrice," the Queen commanded. "What have you to report?"

And I told her.

Well, mostly.

"The Scots who visit within our walls carry not just felicitations for you but battle plans," I said. "And Alasdair MacLeod is quite a bit more than we thought he was."

The Queen's eyes widened, even as Walsingham's narrowed. "Battle plans for what, Beatrice?" he asked. "What role do the MacLeods truly play in this?" I gave Walsingham a terse smile, my father's words from just moments ago coming back to me. Sometimes information withheld is far more important than information given. I would not tell him of Alasdair's desire to protect Catholic treasures. It was enough that he would fight on the side of the Protestants. I did not need to share precisely why, or in what manner. That was for Alasdair to do, and I rather suspected he wouldn't.

"The important part is this," I said. "The clan MacLeod is eager to show that even if they hail from the other side of the country, they are not ones to sit idly by and allow the French to set up battlements on the beaches of their homeland. They are willing to pledge men and arms to fight for the Protestant cause, and they will do whatever it takes to ensure its success." I slanted my gaze back to Elizabeth. "They are starting to gather the clans, Your Grace. They will enter into an alliance with you that is to your favor, I should think. The time to make those alliances is now."

Elizabeth snapped her fingers, and a page dashed up to her. She bent, whispering something into the boy's ear, even as Walsingham folded his hands over his chest. "And how came you by this information?" he asked curtly. "I cannot think MacLeod was so forthcoming, or do you have him ensnared in your talons already? Your betrothal is not even fully announced."

"I did not hear it from Alasdair," I said, my words just shy of a retort. "He is more subtle than that."

"But you do not answer the question," Cecil observed, and I shrugged. I cared not a whit for Catherine Meredith Anne Marie and her Scottish laird, Niall. I cared only that I got through this interview without breaking down.

"Alasdair's man Niall was drugged by one of the ladies at court, a woman who found a tincture of truth serum at one of the local huckster stands here in Windsor."

Walsingham's eyes flared. He favored poisoning, whenever possible. Clean and impossible to track back to its source, it was the ideal weapon for spies. "What huckster?" he asked sharply, and I shook my head.

"You'd have to ask Lady Catherine. She's likely to be found trailing after Niall with a moony look on her face and more poison up her sleeve."

"To what end?" the Queen asked, plainly confused. "Why is she spying upon the man?"

"Not to learn his battle secrets, I assure you." I explained the woman's infatuation, and her desire to know Niall's amorous intentions toward her. As I spoke, the Queen looked outraged, then intrigued.

"We need that tincture," she mused, and Cecil finally put in a word, huffing with exasperation.

"What we need is more information. This man Niall says his countrymen are already on the move toward Fife? Or that they are planning the march?"

"Oh, leave off, Cecil!" I gritted out, then immediately caught my words. We stared at each other, but I could not—would not—say the words he was daring me to share. "You should just ask Alasdair straight out." *Since you likely already know the answer, even if you don't know his real motives.*

"And that is what we shall do," the Queen said, standing taller, her bearing regal, even as her advisors exchanged pained glances. "You have delivered your man, Beatrice. You have served the need." Her voice carried loudly throughout the chamber, and even the mice in the walls stood at attention. Her Imperiousness had just issued a royal decree, and had made it sound as though I'd contributed more to her machinations than I had. Walsingham flicked an annoyed glance at me, but I was strangely troubled. Something suddenly did not feel right in the room.

"Your Majesty!" The squeaking page had returned, dashing up out of the gloom. "I present you—I present you—"

He stopped, heaving huge breaths, and only then did I hear new paces, heavy now, where before they must have been feather soft. The paces of a man who surely had heard Elizabeth's practically shouted words, and who could only guess at their meaning, coming on the very verge of his arrival for an unexpected audience with the Queen.

"Alasdair MacLeod, Your Grace," came the voice, as powerful and compelling as the young man who owned it.

Alasdair stepped into the sconce light, and swept the Queen a bow. He rose again and did not so much as glance at me, and I heard Elizabeth's words, echoing again and again.

You have delivered your man, Beatrice. You have served the need.

I could feel the intensity of Alasdair's shock rippling off his body for just a moment, and coldness swept through every inch of me. He thought I'd told tales about him, his most private confidences. He thought the Queen was congratulating me on a job well done. He thought I'd betrayed him—not once but twice. All in the same night.

And he was right.

CHAPTER THIRTY-NINE

The Queen and her advisors left us then, taking Alasdair and withdrawing to Cecil's private chambers. It was up to Alasdair now to determine what I had shared, and hadn't. My childish decision to withhold the details of his family's desire to protect church treasures may have been all for naught. But even if it hadn't been, I was still no prize. I'd still shared every scrap I'd learned from Lady Catherine about the MacLeods' battle plans. What woman does that to her betrothed?

A woman who was also a spy, I supposed.

I could tell that Sophia wanted to leave the room immediately, but I raised my hand to keep her where she was. Sure enough, a guard was quickly positioned at the door. We were not permitted to leave, then. The Queen might still have use for us.

At length I strolled over to where Sophia was sitting and took a seat on the velvet-covered bench just off the Queen's dais. She kept her hands clasped in her lap, and her obsidian bauble was nowhere in sight.

"Did you foresee what would happen with Cavanaugh, Sophia?" I asked. "Do you know?"

"Tell me your father reached you in time." Sophia's words were urgent, even as her gaze remained upon the guard. "I was so worried."

I gave her a sharp glance. "You told him where to go?"

"I had seen you with Cavanaugh in a garden, yes." Sophia grimaced. "It was in the eye of the obsidian stone. I didn't know which garden, of course. Heaven forfend I am given all of the information at once when I most need it. But I knew the nature of your argument, and that it was one you would lose without intercession." She turned kind eyes on me. "You cannot do everything alone, Beatrice."

"Well, I have not had much experience with the generosity of the court." I shrugged. "But I thank you plainly. Without your help I would not be standing guard over the Queen's empty throne but would probably already be well on my way to ruination."

Sophia's next words were gentle. "But that is behind you, and your entire life is before you still." She looked down at her hands again. "I also saw my father and Lady Ariane."

That took me out of my own thoughts. I had heard little of Lord Brighton's reaction to his change of brides. "How are they faring?"

"Very well." Sophia said the words with equal parts happiness and relief. "He sought me out, of course. We had a conversation that was rather fraught, once he knew that I knew why he'd betrothed himself to me in the first place. But I did not tell him about the obsidian stone. I did not tell him that I saw him in a long and happy life. There are some answers that just lead to more questions, I fear."

"You have the right of that." Still, something did not quite sit well with me. It was as if I were missing one crucial piece, without which I could never find solace. I glanced at her again. "Do they know of your abilities? Cecil and Walsingham—and the Queen?"

Sophia's face lost a bit of its color. "Not fully, but they suspect my gift has manifested," she said. "My uncle has met with the Queen. She had . . . questions. He gave her answers."

"And you know of this how?"

She smiled then, the expression wry and wise beyond her years. "I would gladly tell you it was in the obsidian stone, but the truth is more mundane. Meg told me; she and Jane had closeted themselves near the conversation."

"You must be more careful," I said. Still, worrying over Sophia's issues was infinitely more interesting then dipping a toe into the roiling sea of my own. "Do you have any clue as to what happens next?"

"The Questioners will return, I suspect, with Bible and crucifix to bear." At my sharp look she almost giggled, looking for all the world like a girl discussing her first ball instead of her first Inquisition. "Don't worry, though. I can hold both items without issue. I checked."

"You *checked*?"

"I thought it prudent." She smoothed her fingers down her fine gown, one of the last she had received from Lord Brighton. "Anna has been doing research on the kind of tests they put witches to, both in England and abroad."

"Of course she has," I said. "I suspect those being put to the question are not being treated kindly?"

"You would be correct in your suspicion." Sophia gave a delicate shudder. "I tell you this: I am glad that Walsingham will be present, and that the Queen will be besides. This gold ring she gave us will come in more useful than she ever anticipated, unless I miss my guess."

I rather suspected that the rings proclaiming the Queen's Grace could just as easily be taken off our fingers as they had been put on, but I was not about to suggest that to Sophia. We would just have to make certain that she was never caught out alone.

I cast a glance down the hallway that led to Cecil's office. "I wonder what my future will hold," I said grimly. "Or can you still not bear to tell me?"

My blade had been expertly aimed, and it hit its mark. Sophia's gaze flew to mine, then sheared away. She clasped her hands tightly in her lap, her mouth quivering in a despairing grimace. "Not everything I see happens, Beatrice," she said miserably. "You know that."

I couldn't help it—I burst out laughing. Such were my nerves this day that seeing someone so upset about my own pending unhappiness was impossible to fathom. "Sophia, truly. You will not be the first person to predict my downfall. And doubtless you will not be the last." I gestured her to draw near. "But come, do your worst. It is better to be prepared for what might happen than to live in wonder, no?"

She moved toward me, but at that moment the guards stepped smartly to the side and bowed. Sophia and I quickly stood and dropped into our customary curtsies as the Queen strolled into the room, followed by her advisors and Alasdair. But I wasn't looking at them through my lowered lashes. Instead I glanced to the side, noticing as if for the first time that Sophia's neck was long and gracefully arched, her profile perfect. How had I never seen this girl as a rival? Had my opinions of her been so colored by her "differentness" that I'd failed to see such beauty because of the strangeness that surrounded it?

What else did I miss, blinded by the court and its perceptions?

"Arise," the Queen said airily, and I knew immediately that she was well pleased by whatever arrangements had been reached in the privacy of Cecil's office. I lifted my head to gaze serenely into her eyes. They held approval and—something else. Something that set my nerves on edge again.

Calculation.

"Thank you most plainly once more, Alasdair MacLeod. It does England good to have such allies as your family to the north." The Queen nodded to him as he executed a flawless bow. Then she turned to mount the short stairs to her throne. She sat, taking her ease, and left the rest of us to stand. Sitting in the presence of her standing court made clear who the most important member of the group was. It was a favorite move of Elizabeth's. I suspected it was one that would not wear off with age.

I turned and looked at Alasdair's face. His gaze could easily have slid over to meet mine, but it did not. He watched the Queen as if she were the only woman in the world. "We are well met, Your Grace," he said. "I am glad to serve where our interests are mutual and the outcome is so precious to us both. We will be ready."

The Queen beamed magnanimously at him, then drew breath to speak again, when Alasdair raised his hand.

"Another moment of your time, Your Grace." This time he did allow his gaze to shift to me, and I felt its weight like a burn. "I would grant you a treasure of our people, so precious that it is fit only for a Queen."

This arrested Her Avariciousness entirely, and she waved him on with an indulgent hand, sitting forward slightly on her cushioned seat. "A gift?" she asked coquettishly. "Well, this is an unexpected delight."

Alasdair reached into his pocket and pulled out a golden oval half the size of his hand, which hung from a heavy gold chain. He allowed the chain to dangle in the air, catching the sconce light, but it was plain to see that the charm at its base was a reliquary of some kind. I lifted my hand to my mouth, knowing what words would come next.

"You may have heard of the legend of the Fairy Flag," he began, and the Queen stiffened with surprise, her glance flying to me. She'd asked for me to ferret the flag away from Alasdair, not convince him to give it to her openly. She would be wondering what, if aught, I had to do with his sudden burst of generosity, and I was wondering the same. How had he known the Queen wanted the thing, and whyever would he give it to her?

"It came to my people before the turn of the last millennium, and its origins are shrouded in mystery," Alasdair continued. "Some say—and most believe—that it was gifted to my forebears by the Queen of the Fairy herself, in thanks for some aid rendered. This we will never know, but one thing is true enough: When we fly the flag or carry its markers upon us, we are but certain to ride to victory. Each of the sons of the MacLeods is given a token of the flag, to carry forth and keep us from harm, or to give to the woman who captures our spirit."

Alasdair's words were spoken to Elizabeth, but I felt their cuts from the side. I remembered how he'd kissed me in the labyrinth behind Marion Hall. I remembered how he'd held me, if ever so briefly, sheltering me from the harsh winds of the North Terrace. And I remembered his face when he had stared at me in the Privy Garden bare hours before. Had I originally been the woman who had captured his spirit? Had he thought to give the token to me?

I would never know now.

"From the Queen of the Fairy to the Queen of England, I grant you this gift of the clan MacLeod," Alasdair said, stepping forward to mount the first steps of the dais, and then reaching out to deposit the heavy necklace into the Queen's greedily outstretched fingers. "This is our gift to you."

"Oh!" The Queen unlocked the delicate latches of the reliquary, making the contents of the piece available fully to her eyes alone. From where I stood I caught only a glimpse of a satiny white cushion, and then a scrap of faded yellow silk. "It looks so very old!" she exclaimed, holding the golden amulet up to the nearest torch. She lifted her gaze to Alasdair. "It must be priceless."

He shrugged. "We canna say where it is truly from, so there is no way of knowing. But it is yours. May it bring you all the luck in battle and in peace that you could ever wish."

"And I thank you for it." She watched a moment as Alasdair backed down the stairs. Then she abruptly stood.

"As you have claimed a moment of my time, allow me to claim one of yours." He stopped on the steps, looking at her, but it was not him who the Queen's cool eyes were staring at.

It was me.

"I have come to a decision," the Queen said.

CHAPTER FORTY

The Queen was speaking, but for just a few seconds, despite all my long years of training to hang on a monarch's every syllable, I somehow could not quite hear her words. I felt on the edge of a precipice, the crash and rumble of dark waters surging upward to swallow me whole.

The moment could not last, of course. My attention snapped back into focus with the Queen's strident laugh.

"In truth, good MacLeod, I cannot think that marriage was on your mind when you traveled so far from your home to visit us here in England. Am I correct?"

Her tone was light and playful, and Alasdair matched her jollity with a raised brow and a boyish grin. "No, Your Grace, it was not."

This would have been the ideal time for him to glance over to me with longing eyes and speak words of affirmation or continued interest. But Alasdair did neither of these things. He stood there like a marauding conqueror, one foot planted on a lower stair, his knee bent, bantering with the Queen like they were old friends. "I confess, it gave me a bit of a start. I was accustomed to stories of English hospitality, but I canna deny that you did them all one better."

"Hmm, yes. Well, in truth you have served us well in building an alliance *without* the need for matrimonial ties. In our wisdom, we have not aired the possibility of your betrothal to Lady Beatrice much outside these far walls."

Not aired the possibility! I looked at the Queen with a face wiped dead of any emotion, my practiced, poised smile upon my lips. As if she could tell me I was set next for the executioner's block or the latest country dance, and it was all the same to me. But she well knew how much her "decision" would cost me.

First, I'd failed to hold the interest of the scum-dragging Cavanaugh. Now not even a Scotsman would have me. I'd have to spend much of the next year proving my worth to possible suitors young and old, or come up with some new spin upon the age-old story of the jilted bride, before the court's tongues would wag about my possibilities again, instead of my problems.

The rational part of my brain was processing this, even as Alasdair and the Queen chatted and gibed as if I were not even in the room. But the not-so-terribly-rational part of my brain had gone silent and shocked. And my heart . . . well, my heart was another thing entirely.

"And I propose you one better, in truth," the Queen continued, her voice carrying a girlish lilt that was more affected than any other I'd heard. She'd have to take acting lessons from Meg before much longer if she wanted to play the part of the blushing maid. The throne was aging her with every passing day. "You have a man of your company who has quite captured the heart of a lady of the court."

"I do indeed?" asked Alasdair, his grin now broadening. "We Scots do have a way of catching the eye, I'll tell you plain. Who is the man?"

"Niall— Oh, what was his last name?" The Queen turned to me. "Beatrice?"

"Niall Garrett, Your Grace," I said, forcing my voice to sound light and engaged.

"Ah, yes." The Queen clapped her hands. "And the young Lady Catherine is quite in love with him. Do you know if he has a mind to marry?"

Alasdair shrugged and spread his hands. "I can but ask, Your Majesty."

"Do that, then." She nodded firmly. "We may have an alliance yet." The two of them laughed and agreed that yes, this would be a brilliant thing, and I found my mind returning to the churn of my own darkness.

"What say you, Beatrice?" the Queen demanded now, her voice suddenly loud, like she was talking to a simpleton. "Shall we set the good MacLeod free of his marriage contract to you, that he may go and find another bride more suited to his strength?"

If Alasdair was startled by the Queen's direct slap of me, he did not betray it, and I certainly was not going to. Everything I'd done—had tried to do—was turning to ashes around me. But she clearly expected me to speak here, and so speak I would.

"I live ever to serve you, my Queen," I said. "You and

England. If it serves you better to not betroth me to Alasdair MacLeod, then of course I bow to your wisdom."

I refused to look at Alasdair, though once again I felt his gaze upon me as I was giving my pretty little speech. Well, he could look his fill and then be gone to his desolate isle in the middle of nowhere. I'd already told him to find someone who suited him better than I did. Apparently, he'd agreed. So now he could choose a woman of his own country to be his bride. He could choose six, for all I cared. I wouldn't—couldn't—let this little scene break me. For my family, I would be strong and proud. For my family, I'd remain unruffled by the Queen's cruel words. For my family, I would tilt my chin just so, slant my gaze thus, and smile as if my reputation had not just been dragged through the mire.

"Then it is done." Elizabeth clapped her hands again. "I will summon Lord Knowles to discuss the particulars, but we have agreed in principle, and you, my young man, are free of a Queen's desire to meddle in the hearts of her people."

Alasdair's grin didn't slip; his manner didn't shift. He cast me off with no more concern than he would doff his tunic. He bowed first to the Queen, and then to me. I didn't even hear him depart, with the roaring in my ears, but as I made my own curtsy to leave, the Queen's next words drew me up short.

"So, then—you have served me well, Beatrice, and now I have repaid you."

I looked up, startled, and caught the malicious look of triumph in the Queen's eyes. Had she known that in the end, I had done the one thing I'd sworn I would not—could not—do? Had she known I'd fallen for Alasdair? I looked around and saw that Sophia was no longer in the room, nor the Queen's advisors. So I was left alone with the vicious shrew.

"Repaid me?" I managed. Her smile, if anything, grew broader.

"Of course! You made your lack of interest in Alasdair clear, and now he is no longer to be a bother to you."

"Ah! Of course, Your Majesty." In that moment I did not know if the Queen was baiting me or if she truly believed she'd done me a service. Not that it mattered, of course. Alasdair hadn't seen fit to fight for me; nor should he have. I had betrayed him at every turn.

"Even better," she continued on, "Cecil and Walsingham now know better than to keep information from me. I will just learn it anyway," she said. "The question of the Scots has been solved in a way far better than I could have imagined, and we are in a position of power whenever we choose to strike. The Lords of the Congregation will prevail, and the French will be beaten back. All these things are assured this day."

She tilted her head, all satisfaction and guile. "So where should we go from here?" she asked, drawing out the question with a long pause. Idly I wondered if she knew about the MacLeods' interest in treasure collecting. It did not seem so, and the thought was one tiny bit of joy amidst the pain I knew was still to come.

I was not mistaken.

"Indeed, yes," the Queen proclaimed suddenly, having

clearly come to some private resolution. "I need to announce some new husband for you, else all the world will know you have been twice jilted in my care. But I think—I think we should wait a bit. See how the court settles out after our guests depart for their home and we prepare for the move back to London—yes." She tapped her fingers on her lips, as if she were settling a grand question of state. Or the dinner menu. "Yes. London would be a suitable location to get you settled, once and for all."

"Of course, Your Grace," I said, my words clear and light in the tight space between us. She had caught me—briefly—in my grief. But I wouldn't give her that satisfaction again.

"Excellent," the Queen said, then yawned behind her hand. "This has been a most satisfying day, wouldn't you agree? Attend me back to my rooms. I find I am fatigued."

And thus it happened that I spent another two hours preparing the Queen for her bed, bringing her wine, brushing her hair, and listening to her chatter with her ladies of the bedchamber. Not so long ago I would have given much to be in such rarified company. Now I catalogued the gossip with rote disinterest, wishing once again that I was not Beatrice the court insider, but Meg with her fabulous memory and quick hands; Sophia with her powerful gifts; Anna with her intelligence; or Jane with her cruel knives.

I finally was set free well after midnight, the Queen realizing that I was not, in fact, one of her indentured servants, and sending me along to my bed. But I could not return yet to the maids' quarters. There was no room in Windsor that could hold me this night, and I fled to the North Terrace, then stepped out into the chill wind that somehow did not cut through the rising tide of misery that flushed through me, thick and hot.

I moved all the way to the small balcony that overlooked the wide grassy plain leading to the Thames. And quite without expecting it, I found myself on my knees.

I was not a religious person, I tell you plain. I believed in God, of course, though the dictates as to the worship of that God I left to my monarchs to decide. But the tears that rose up within me and spilled out of my eyes were not a lamentation to the heavens. The heavens had no care for me. The tears were not even a cry to my family or my fellow maids, for whom I would sacrifice much and much again, and who had come to my aid when I'd needed them most. I did not cry to these; they would not heed my tears.

I cried to myself. And for myself.

For the little girl who'd stared adoringly at the father destined to leave for court and kings, and who'd stood by in fear and confusion as her mother had withdrawn inch by painful inch into a world hazed with drugs and despair. For the young innocent at court who'd learned too quickly how not to trust. For the bold and hopeful insider whose manipulations had landed her the most coveted role in the land—bride-to-be of the splendid Lord Cavanaugh.

And for the stupid, foolish girl who—whom no one loved at all.

But *I* loved. I loved with a strength and fervor that filled my very bones and blood. I loved so much, I could not breathe. I loved Alasdair MacLeod. And it was too late.

It was wasteful and pointless to cry these tears, I knew that. There was no one to see them. I could not melt the hearts of my admirers or soften the opposition of my foes. I had nothing to gain and much to lose to be seen here in this state, my face a terror, my hair disheveled, my gown getting creased and ruined on the rough surface of the Terrace. And still I cried, and still I rocked. And held my own arms where no one would hold me.

I would be strong in the morning, when the eyes of the world were on me again. Tonight, lost and alone, I cried for the weakness I could never show.

A gift had been given to me, if only I'd had the eyes to see it, the heart to accept it. That day in the Presence Chamber, when Alasdair had walked before the crowd and singled me out with a grin and a wink, I'd been given a gift of connection, of love, of possibility. I had shunned that gift. I'd turned it aside with callous disregard. I could not even accept an honestly offered smile. I was so deeply broken that there would be no fixing me. I had been fashioned as a tool for one use—to survive in court. And survive I did. Survive I would. I was alone and would always be alone. I did not deserve Alasdair. I did not deserve anyone.

Except the one who hated me even as she needed me, desperately. The Queen and I deserved each other.

In that moment I remembered the old woman's face who'd caught me up in her clutches in the heart of Salcey Forest, cackling at my distress but perhaps more at my disdain. She had warned me, and her words flowed back over me like a bitter tonic. *You too shall know great loss and misery, such pain as you had never thought. On your knees in darkness, no one to save you then.*

At the time, I had thought I would be threatened by some great treachery outside myself, someone who wished me harm. I had thought the Queen would betray me, or even one of my fellow maids, innocently or otherwise.

I never could have guessed that, in the end, my greatest enemy would be . . .

Myself.

CHAPTER FORTY-ONE

I vaguely remember the tap on my shoulder, the strong arms lifting me, but the guard who deposited me at the maids' chamber was gone before I could fully will myself back to consciousness.

Unsurprisingly, the maids were all awake, but this time they did not rush to me to remove my clothing and tuck me into bed. We stared at one another across a great chasm of understanding, and I'd never felt so old.

"What happened?" Sophia spoke first, and if she noticed the irony of her words, she gave no indication.

"You didn't explain?" I asked.

She shook her head. "I did not understand the whole of it, only what I saw. And in any event, it was not my tale to tell."

I shrugged and crossed to my pallet, beginning the process of undressing myself—no easy feat, but it occupied my hands and mind while my mouth took on the story. My fellow spies, sensing my need to not be touched, stayed where they were.

"It's all undone," I said, my voice curiously flat. "Cavanaugh will not be bothering me again, to start." I glanced over to Sophia. "Did I thank you for that? I do not know if I did."

"You did," she said, and I nodded. Sophia had been the one to send my father to me, even as Cavanaugh had been landing his coup de grace. All the maids would have known what was happening. "Your father came to see us, after. He assured us that you would be unharmed by Cavanaugh, but enjoined us all to tell him were we ever troubled by him again."

"I don't think we will be." I paused then, wondering what Cavanaugh was thinking this dark night. To have every belief you've ever held about yourself upended and destroyed—that would be a challenging thing. Would it be worse than having every belief about yourself proven true? That I didn't know.

I stripped off my sleeves, and then Meg did move, slipping up behind me to unlace the back of my bodice as if it were yet another costume to pack away. True enough, I supposed.

"Then I managed to get to the Queen and share with her what I knew of the MacLeods' battle plans." I grimaced. "I thought I was being so clever and safe, sharing only part of what I knew, the part that would not, I hoped, bring harm to Alasdair or his men." I spoke his name mechanically, ignoring the hard knock of my heart at its sound. "But it was all for naught. He came but moments later and shared, I am sure, far more with the Queen. They went to Cecil's chambers and apparently executed some sort of agreement between the clans and the English, the Scots pledging support if—or I should say, when—Elizabeth decides to march upon the French."

"And what did the Scots get in exchange for this?" Anna put in, her finger pressed against her lip as she focused fiercely on my words. "Alasdair must have had sought some boon, and it's not as though Elizabeth could repay him in gold or goods. The Queen's coffers are all but bare."

I let my gaze slide past her to the wall, and pushed on. "I couldn't say. But once those agreements were struck, Alasdair presented the Queen with a relic of the Fairy Flag—a relic that has been in his family for centuries. I didn't even realize he'd known of the Queen's interest in the thing!"

If I'd thought that proclamation would surprise them, I'd been sorely mistaken. I narrowed my eyes at their sudden muteness. "I don't suppose any of you had anything to do with that, did you?"

Anna and Meg shared a glance; Sophia looked at her hands. But it was Jane who finally chuckled. "A scrap of cloth is what you're talking about, you know. Barely a stitch. Not good for covering even an inch of skin. If I heard about the treasure from one of the Scottish guards and dropped a word in passing that the Queen would set great store by a gift of such a prized treasure, what was the harm in that?" She pulled out a blade and was eyeing it in the darkness. "Seemed an easy trade for a Queen's favor."

"But it was a relic!" Anna protested.

"Well, yes—if it was even a piece of the real flag," Meg scoffed. "Which I'd wager it wasn't, given Alasdair's easy offering of it."

I frowned. "Well, he seemed quite sincere. . . ."

Now it was Jane's turn to scoff again. "He would."

"But enough of the trinket, Beatrice," interrupted Anna. "What happened then?"

"Elizabeth was well pleased." I returned to my tale, my voice still mild, as if I were recounting the events of a distant cousin's birthday. "And so, to thank Alasdair properly, she canceled my betrothal. That would have been the last of what you saw, I think, Sophia?"

Sophia nodded. "You stood as pure as ice in the wake of her announcement, betraying no emotion. You were magnificent, Beatrice. I do not think I would have been able to stand so strong."

I quirked my lips at her loyalty. "I doubt you'll ever need to do so," I said. "But I confess I was not fully paying attention, after her first words registered. She dismissed you all?"

"Yes. You smiled your acquiescence, and she clapped her hands and dismissed everyone, saying that she wished to speak with you alone."

I raised my brows at this. How had I missed such a command?

"Alasdair went first," Sophia said. "But by the time I reached the corridor, he was gone, and only Cecil and Walsingham were walking away, their heads together, discussing something I could not hear. I rather thought it was the relic, and not the agreement with the MacLeods, but I have no proof of that. I waited, briefly, to see if Alasdair would return, but the guards were eyeing me strangely, and I did not wish to appear to be eavesdropping."

I nodded. "That was wise of you." Sophia had enough issues without drawing the attention of the Queen's guard.

I shook myself, realizing that I now stood in my thin shift, and settled down upon my pallet. "And that's really the whole of it. The Queen proceeded to tell me, once we were alone, that she was well pleased with the day's events, that I had done well, and that she would find a proper match for me after the story had fled the tongues of her courtiers. Probably in Londontown, when we return there for the winter."

Meg snorted, a decidedly unladylike noise. "What is her fascination with seeing you wed?" she asked. "I should think you would be done with men and marriage for at least another few years."

I smiled, but of course Meg did not know the whole of my requirements. Despite my father's assertion to Lord Cavanaugh that our family had more gold than we could ever want, I knew the truth. Marion Hall still needed money more than I needed a respite from the machinations of court. We needed a stable marriage to someone with a title and land of his own, far away from Northampton. With the security of a decent marriage, my family would remain safe, my servants would not starve, and my secrets would be kept.

Even freed from Cavanaugh, I was not free.

"But what of Alasdair?" It was Sophia who spoke now, her voice strange in the darkness, like that of an ephemeral sprite. "Surely I did not imagine his affection for you. It was plain in his eyes from the moment he set foot in the Presence Chamber all those weeks ago!"

I laughed, but not unkindly. Sophia, for all her odd ways, had always been treated as special. She was beautiful, of course, but I suspected that even before her gifts had begun to manifest, there'd been a fantastical nature about her, a sense of a being who was not entirely of this world. The glances cast at her would at times be cruel and at times simply curious, but there was also a wonder to them, and even a hope, that something so lovely and mysterious could be living among us ordinary people.

I held no illusions about the glances I received. "My reputation, if it hadn't proceeded me, was shown off to best effect that day, Sophia," I said. "I had done everything I could to make myself beautiful, and I flirted with every nobleman who walked through the Queen's door." Just as I'd been ordered to do.

"You need not work very hard to make yourself beautiful," Meg said staunchly. "I was there as well, and I know how terrible I looked, no matter how I tried."

"Well, you were stuffed into that monstrous dress, Meg. What choice did you have?" I gazed at her with genuine affection. Meg had endured the gown I had lent her—a gift from an aunt who clearly despised me—with her usual pluck and wit. No wonder Rafe de Martine was so taken with her, even if he was a Spaniard. She acted without overthinking everything, knowing that no matter where her feet landed, she'd be able to run if nothing else.

Whereas I took no step without considering every path that might emerge. It made me tired just thinking on it.

"But it's of no account. Alasdair saw what he wanted to see." *What I was.* "A maiden ripe for flirtation. And his time in the English court has been the more pleasurable for his chase of me. But it was a chase, nothing more."

"But he allowed himself to be betrothed to you," Anna protested. "Surely that is not the action of an idle flatterer!"

I sighed. They were right, and Alasdair had not been to blame here—I was. I owed them the explanation I could never share with him. "I pushed him too far," I said hollowly. I could hear the sorrow in my own voice, but I continued. "I told him we did not suit. I told him I didn't want to be his bride. I told him to go home, and that I—that I loved—" I broke off, the words turning to dust in my throat. I couldn't, wouldn't say it. Not ever again.

Jane filled in the words for me. "Lord Cavanaugh," she said flatly. "You wanted Alasdair to break ties with you, before that filthy dog claimed you as his own."

"Oh, Beatrice!" gasped Anna. "You lied to him!"

"I had to!" I burst out, and I angrily dashed my hands across my face, willing the hot, hated tears to stop falling. "Cavanaugh was going to ruin me, publicly and with great fervor. And Alasdair—" I drew in a ragged breath, my heart pounding in my ears. "Alasdair is a good man. He is strong and sturdy and so, so proud. He would have given me everything without a second thought! I couldn't let— I wouldn't— He did not deserve someone so low as me!"

That startled them all to silence, and I turned abruptly, my shoulders bowed, even as I watched my own tears drop onto my bed in a widening pool. No one spoke for a long moment. But, then, there was nothing to say. With wooden movements I began to take down the coverlets of my pallet, to prepare myself for sleep. I was surprised when I heard Sophia's soft voice in the gloom.

"Would you like . . . Would you like me to see your future, Beatrice?" she asked, the words tentative and shy.

I closed my eyes against a fresh spate of tears. "Sophia, you have already done so much," I said, shaking my head. "I have decided after all that I do not like knowing what's going to happen to me. It's hard enough living through it the one time."

Sophia bit her lip and nodded. "I understand," she said. "Of course I understand."

"Well, I have no such concerns," Anna piped up. "Sophia, if you're looking for someone to try your gift on, I am more than happy to serve!"

And just like that, my pain lightened. I turned, eyes wide, as laughter rolled through the chamber and Anna fairly rushed to Sophia's pallet, bouncing like a girl at her first country dance. But as Sophia picked up the obsidian stone, she gasped out a startled "Oh!" Even in the shadows I could feel the fear wash off her.

"What is it?" Anna asked, her body going rigid.

"Anna, you must have a care," Sophia said, her voice strangely sibilant. "Do not go again to Mortlake and the library of my supposed uncle. You will be discovered—you could be killed for what you know!"

"No!" Anna breathed, then laughed nervously to cover her own shocked response. "Oh, pish, Sophia. Surely a few moldy books can't hold such power as that."

Sophia did not seem convinced. "I mean it, Anna. There is something very dark in that library. I cannot quite see what it is."

"Then I will be very careful, and bring a strong torch," Anna said staunchly. "I'm telling you, the world of letters and science is a civilized one. There certainly is no danger in a library. I've practically lived in them my whole life." She patted Sophia's hands, looking into the younger girl's eyes. "Truly, Sophia," she said. "Nothing and no one will keep me from learning. You must see the right of that."

Sophia finally smiled, though it looked like the effort cost her. "Just be careful, Anna."

"I am never anything but—to Beatrice's everlasting dismay, I daresay." There was laughter then, and more joking, and the spell of the obsidian stone was broken. We all turned back to our beds and made ready for a few hours' rest. I found myself watching Sophia, though, well into the night.

She didn't sleep, and neither did I.

CHAPTER FORTY-TWO

The next few days went quickly enough, filled with the usual round of errands and studies and tasks for the Queen. Walsingham and Cecil caught me just this afternoon and sent me on a task of some interest, bidding me to take Jane and Sophia into the town of Windsor. This was unusual in that Jane's skills did not marry up well with mine. She was polished enough when she had to be, but the farther she found herself outside castle walls, the more she got a wild and distant look in her eye, like an animal who could scent its own freedom in the distance. I had to assume she was there just to make sure we didn't get murdered on our way into town, but I didn't begrudge her the assignment. She needed the escape as much as any of us.

Sophia's role was easier to discern. We were going to the herb mistress that Lady Catherine Meredith Anne Marie had consulted to give her a truth tonic for the unfortunate Niall Garrett. Niall was now hip-deep in marriage contracts with the love-struck Catherine and was quite unsure as to how he'd gotten himself into such a pickle. But the herb mistress was of far more interest to us. Styling herself as "Mistress Maude," she lived somewhere in the countryside but came to town during market day to sell her wares from a gaudy stall. She did not come up to the Lower Ward celebrations; so it was off to Windsor for us.

Sophia was quiet as usual, but Jane strode forward eagerly in her walking gown, exhaling a huge sigh of relief the moment we cleared the walls of the castle. "It's a good day to be out," she said, and I smiled to see her happy. I didn't often see Jane openly enjoying anything that didn't involve her roughing up some unfortunate guard. It made for a nice change.

I looked around the bustle of the small town, which was bristling now with country folk for market day. The houses and buildings were all hunched together over the cobbled streets, and we hadn't had a decent rain in days, so the entire place was dusty rather than muddy—a small favor to us.

We reached the marketplace and paused a moment, taking in the sight. It was three times as large as the collection of stalls in the Lower Ward, and the prices, we could see immediately, were much lower—targeted to the commoner, not the courtier. Jane immediately bought and thrust a meat pie at Sophia, commanding her to eat, and even I tarried at the ribbon stall. On a lark, I purchased a small clutch of the brightly colored strands. Perhaps I would weave them together, as a reminder to take pleasure in the small joys in life.

"What ho! Fine ladies out to take their air? What a surprise is this!" We turned to the familiar voice, but with Sophia's fingers full of meat pie and me with my handful of ribbons, it was left to Jane to greet Troupe Master James

McDonald properly. She bowed slightly, and I saw his gaze go to her collar, saw the glint of gold along the column of her neck. An unexpected rush of pleasure skittered through me at the sight. Though it was tucked away, almost out of sight, Jane was wearing the locket James had gifted her!

As if to put truth to my words, a sharp blush rose along Jane's cheekbones, and I watched in utter fascination. True enough, James had paid undue attention to Jane when they'd met as part of the Golden Rose's last command performance before the Queen. But was there truly to be something between the two of them? And would there be scars before it played out?

"Master James," Jane said, her voice overloud. She made to draw away, then seemed baffled as he caught up her hand and placed a courtly kiss on what had to be fingers roughened by punching and brawling and knife throwing.

"Jane Morgan." He smiled, and his eyes were lit with an intensity of their own. I continued to watch the exchange with keen interest, noting that Sophia appeared unusually focused on her pie.

"Ah! This is great timing," I said brightly, ignoring the sudden unhappy mew of my own heart as their gazes met and held, before James finally turned to me. "You've received my message about the play for the Queen? I apologize for giving you so little notice."

"I have, and it is no trouble at all," he said amiably, letting go of Jane's hand after another squeeze. Jane, for her part, snatched her fingers back as if she'd been burned. "I may have just the thing to serve the Queen's needs," James continued, "and present the Golden Rose to great effect. Still a bit of planning to do, but rest assured, *The Play of Secrets* will be a theatrical event unlike any other Gloriana has ever seen."

The Play of Secrets? Oh, the Queen would like that. "Excellent," I said. "We have much to discuss, then. But today Sophia and I have a purchase to make, and Jane has already expressed her extreme boredom with the proceedings. Could you possibly entertain her for just a few moments? I promise you, we will not be long."

James's sudden grin and Jane's wide eyes pleased me more than they should have. In truth, though, this subterfuge served two purposes. One, it would tie up Jane for long enough to allow Sophia and me to meet the herb mistress, who might take exception to being descended upon by three women of the court. Two, it would tie up James, who appeared to have nothing much else to do and would likely have invited himself along on our journey. Jane's startled, unhappy glance tweaked my conscience, but James made the decision for all of us.

"I would be delighted." He folded Jane's hand into his arm, the movement clearly awkward for her. She looked puzzled, and James patted her hand as if she were a startled colt. "I promise to return her unharmed."

"I canna say the same for him," Jane muttered, but they were already turning away, and Sophia was looking around for a place to discard the rest of her pie. She tossed it to a roaming dog, and we hurried on, eager to complete our mission.

"I don't know that I trust Master James," Sophia said as we turned the corner to the second line of stalls. Mistress Maude's wagon was exactly where Lady Catherine had told us it would be, and the plump woman herself stood in front of it, laughing at some great joke she shared with the stall master to her left.

"We don't need to trust him," I said. "We just need him to occupy Jane for a bit."

"That, we should have no fear of." She sighed, but I didn't have time for her gloomy portents. We approached Mistress Maude and made a great show of looking at her wares. For this playacting, I was to be the love-struck girl, and I wished again that I had Meg's acting skills.

"How can I serve two such sweet young women, eh?" Maude said, sizing us up for paying customers immediately. "You there, I bet it's a love potion what might catch your interest? Or perhaps some pretty perfume?"

"Well, love is all to the good, but I would rather know the truth of my lover's thoughts." I giggled, and Sophia rounded her eyes at me. I don't think the girl had ever seen me attempt to giggle. "Though, in truth, I know you cannot ensure its success."

"What ho, you say?" Maude made a show of looking around as if to verify our secrecy. "I tell you plain, dear. What Maude gives you will work, for the good of all concerned. It's just a bunch of herbs mixed with love, nothing dangerous about it. And truth tonics, well, they are my specialty. Though I am sad to say, I've none of that particular brew here."

"Oh, how disappointing." From what I could see, in fact, Maude's wares included nothing more dastardly than "sweetheart tea" and "headache brew," and I suspected each was as weak as a baby's cry. But this truth tonic seemed promising. "Perhaps you have a shop in town?" I asked, reaching for my money pouch.

"Och, no, dear," Maude said, her eyes never leaving the pouch. "I brew my herbs at home and prepare them for sale, and take care of my husband and his mum besides. 'Tis a full day's work, I will tell you that."

More subterfuge, but a good covering story. Women labeled as witches were generally loners, without family, and certainly without mothers-in-law. Maude was being very careful. I drew out a few coins. "Then I guess the love tea will have to do," I said regretfully.

"I tell you what," Maude said, picking up the bottle and hefting its weight. "Come back to me the morrow after the next new moon, and I will have what you need. The price is steep, but in exchange I will give this to you free. As a promise."

"Free!" I rounded my eyes and took the bottle. "But I couldn't possibly!"

"Free," Maude said. "An' with five shillings when you return, I'll give you a truth tonic like none other. Mark my words, because Maude never lies."

Well, five shillings for any sort of "tonic" was highway robbery, but I nodded anyway and thanked her over and again, and shortly after I was the proud owner of a stoppered bottle of "love tea."

"It smells like wet chickens," I observed of the tea after we'd walked some distance from Maude's cart. "Could you see anything about her while we were there?"

"I could," Sophia said, glancing up to me and smiling in delighted surprise. I noticed that she held her hands tightly closed now around the lovely obsidian stone. "She's a murderess!"

I forestalled my shocked reaction as Jane and James swung into view, the former looking rather desperate. "Beatrice!" she shouted, and hauled James over to us. "Your shopping is complete? You know the Queen is expecting us back."

I gave a labored sigh. "I suppose," I said. "If we must go, we must."

"We must," Jane said emphatically. With as smug as James was looking, I would not have been surprised if he'd stolen a few kisses along their walk. I'd have to ask Jane about it later. From a safe distance.

We had barely cleared the marketplace when Jane cleared her throat. "Did you leave me with him on purpose?"

"On purpose?" I asked innocently. "Well, we could not have allowed James to follow us all the way to Maude's stall, now, could we?"

"Oh, I suppose not," she grumbled. "Still, what did you find there?"

"A potion to render you . . . unappealing to men," I said. "Here, I figured you would like it."

"Beatrice!" Sophia blurted, clearly shocked.

"Good," Jane said. She opened the stopper, wrinkling her nose at the scent. "Are you supposed to drink it or throw it on people? This reeks." But she didn't drop the bottle, and looked at it intently as we strode along.

"Just rub a little on your skin," I said. "But not here. I don't want to cause a riot."

Jane snorted, and stowed the little bottle in one of her own pouches. "So you learned something from Maude?"

"She has a house well outside of town, where she keeps her herbs and bottles, drugs and potions, and all manner of tinctures," Sophia said, her voice clear and low. "She—would be what could be described as a witch, but that's not exactly true. She does not practice any arts but poison, but in that art she is well gifted." She glanced at me. "We have to tell Walsingham."

"Is she a threat?" I asked.

Jane shrugged. "I guess that depends on who she's poisoning."

We digested that as we made our way back to Windsor Castle, and had only just crossed through the King's Gate when I saw a most unusual sight: my father, at a stall.

Buying ribbons.

"I'll, um, catch up with you," I muttered, and left Sophia and Jane staring after me.

Father brightened as soon as I approached. "Beatrice!" he said, beaming down at me. "Just the girl I wanted to most see."

"Who is she, Father?" I asked tiredly. *Does the man have no morals at all?*

At his confused stare, I pointed dourly to the ribbons. "Those. I cannot imagine you're purchasing them for Mother.

And clearly you no longer have to be on your best behavior, since not one but two of my betrothals have been cast aside in the past few weeks. But I should think you would have a care not to sully our name any further."

In response Father tipped back his head and laughed. He gave the bunch of ribbons to me, and I took them with a frown, now possessing two sets. "I cannot think you bought these for me, either, Father," I grumbled.

"I suspect you'll have more of a use for them than I, my dear." He tucked my hand into his arm, and we strolled along the carts for the castle's own market day. It was every bit as boisterous as the one we'd left in town, but the goods were pricier here, and better made. Even the pies smelled richer.

"You've comported yourself well, Beatrice," Father said. "But you are taking too much on. I think you should give yourself permission to live the life of the young lady you so admirably appear to be."

"A young lady?" I looked at him as if he'd lost his mind. "What are you talking about? Have you not been present the last few days—few weeks—the last eighteen years of my life? Everything I've been doing has been to keep up the illusion that I am worthy of my noble blood. And for what? I have been thwarted at every turn, a disappointment to one and all." I frowned, disgusted at myself for even caring. "I couldn't even hold a man's heart when he offered it to me without hesitation, for the love of God. I have failed at every step."

"Have you, now?" Father asked. He gazed up at the sky, which was just now darkening into twilight, and I rolled my eyes. Idly I focused on the second set of ribbons in my hands, weaving them back and forth so they became a sort of wild fairy braid. "You are a young, intelligent, beautiful woman, with all the world before you. Your failures, as you call them, have been merely to bow without ceasing to every whim of the Queen. Do you really want to spend your life as I have, with the yoke of the court around your neck?"

"I need to marry well for the family," I said stiffly, not glancing back to him. "You of all people know this."

"You need to marry well, yes," Father said. "But for yourself, and not for us."

"Oh, Father, leave *off*." I could not forestall the bitterness in my words. "Of course I must marry for us. Who else will refill our coffers? Who else will keep the family from starvation?"

He quirked a brow at me. "The Queen did not do so much damage with her progress as that, Beatrice, for all that I complained."

"Of course she did!" I spluttered. "We are bankrupt now. Don't you see that? We have nothing in the household accounts!"

"Beatrice, sweetheart, I keep the accounts short and our own house ramshackle to discourage our dear monarchs from knowing our true financial position. I thought you knew that." At my blank look, he sighed. "Very well, I will sell more gold. 'Tis all the same to me, though it is quite pretty at that."

"Gold!" I snapped. "What is this about gold? We have no gold at Marion Hall."

Now it was my father's turn to look at me, amazed.

"Beatrice, are you daft? Of course we do. The well is filled to the brim with it!"

"What well?" His shocked countenance merely served to infuriate me, and I racked my brain for ideas. The one that surfaced, however, made no sense. "The well in the labyrinth?"

At his grin, I shook my head, lifting a hand to cut him off. "No. That well *poisoned* Mother, and then you shut down the labyrinth in full. There is nothing in that well but death and sorrow!"

Father's face had dropped during my tirade, and his stare made me uncomfortable now. Uncomfortable and confused. "You saw her dance. Dance and laugh. I remember that," he said, his words coming more slowly now.

"Then everything turned to darkness!" I snapped. "As well you know. She was never the same!"

"And I sent you away." Father's face was ashen now. "That you might find friendship in other houses." He shook his head, glancing away. "You were so sad, Beatrice. So sweet but so sad, and your mother—well, her mind had left us by then." He frowned, then drew in a deep breath before looking at me directly.

"Ah, Beatrice. Your mother's ills did not come from a hole in the ground. They came from a hole inside her. She was given to dark times even as a girl, but I cared for her anyway. Even when she went away in mind and refused to allow me to touch her, I wanted to protect her—and so I did. But the well in the heart of the labyrinth wasn't filled with poison. It was filled with pale gold."

He took my puzzled stare as an excuse to keep talking. "Marion Hall was built on a pathway used by the druids since time immemorial. The Gold Road, they called it, because it was used to transfer uniquely colored gold that had been mined in Ireland, carried to Wales, then transferred through England on its way to the Continent. As it happened, the druids had a lovely habit of giving thanks to their gods by submerging their gold in water along the path of their journey. I knew all of this but never gave it a moment's thought, and there was never any written record of any such a sacred site at Marion Hall. Still, there was that damned enormous labyrinth. There had to be some reason it'd been built." He smiled then, the light back in his eyes. "The Marion Hall labyrinth is centered on one of these devotional wellsprings, but there were no records at all about gold being there—just that the mad baron had been driven to build the thing. When the hedgerows went up, the gold had long been covered over, I suspect, but in the course of our work to clear the labyrinth, we found the old well, and I thought I'd clear out some of the stones that I could see at its base. Rock after rock came out, and—well—"

"You found a well filled with pale gold," I said. *All of those years . . . all of my fears. For nothing.* "And you never told anyone."

Father grinned at me. "Secrets held can be more profitable than secrets shared," he said simply. "And in truth, somewhere along the line I convinced myself you knew. You never had any problem buying a new dress or pair of shoes, after all." He raised a hand to ward off my quick retort. "But what this means is that you need to think about your own future now, not merely the family's. I married to protect your mother, but also for the money, prestige, and position such a marriage brought me. I have well benefited from all of those. But I want more for you, my dear. Security, yes, but more than anything else, love. That is what I wish for you."

I thought of what lay ahead for me, in Londontown, as my father rambled on and we made our way across the Lower Ward and into the Middle Ward. Another betrothal to another lying courtier. "I think perhaps you wish too much."

"Do I?" he asked idly. He stopped. "Ah, here we are."

I looked up. We'd made our way to the Hundred Steps, but that was not what had my heart stopping midbeat.

Alasdair MacLeod stood tall against the northern sky, his face unreadable in the gloom, but his eyes fire bright.

CHAPTER FORTY-THREE

"A walk with you, my lady?"

I stood there, transfixed, as my father seemed to melt away into the background. Then I took Alasdair's arm after hastily transferring my knotted ribbons to my left hand. Alasdair turned and escorted me down the Hundred Steps of Windsor Castle. It was a lovely setting in the full day, dropping down over a wooded hill and ending at the Castle Gate. From there the land flowed out and away from Windsor, until gradually reaching the Thames. But the evening seemed to become too heavy all of a sudden, and I wondered at Alasdair's silence even as we stepped quickly and quietly down. He breathed more easily only after we passed the gate at the base of the steps.

"Did you—wish to speak with me?" I finally managed, and his responding laugh was low and sure.

"It would be a start, I suppose." He stopped me then, in the lee of the castle, where some brave soul had erected a stone bench for visitors to take their leave next to a babbling brook. There was a curious silence to the wood, and I did not want to break it. But Alasdair began to speak anew.

"Our betrothal is broken," he said, and I felt the clamor of darkness rise up once more within me, my father's words chased away. *I cannot be embarrassed over this yet again!* It was not to be borne.

"I am aware of that," I said in a rush, cutting him off. "I do not fault you for it. My actions were inexcusable, and you have responded in a way that was right and just and perfectly understandable. And I wish you great—happiness, back in Scotland, truly I do. I would prefer that you would leave off discussing the whole business, however, and—"

"Beatrice." Alasdair raised a hand in supplication. "I love you deeply, but please be still. For once."

I blinked at him. "I'm sorry?"

"You think so far ahead that you cannot ever remain properly in the moment," he said, touching his finger to my chin. "Whereas, when I am with you, I hope only that this moment will never end."

"But—" I began, and his finger drifted up, to rest upon my lips, effectively silencing me.

"I have loved you since the moment I first laid eyes upon you, Beatrice, that day in the Presence Chamber when you were presented so beautifully to us, an English jewel for all to covet. The light broke over you like it was afraid to share your brightness, and you captured my heart so completely with your practiced smile and laughing eyes, it was all I could do to keep breathing."

"But you were mocking everything—all of us!—and especially the French," I protested. "You barely glanced my way."

"Well, the French provide much reason for mockery,"

Alasdair said. "But don't ever mistake my laughter for disinterest, my lady. I decided immediately that you would be mine, and I have never swerved in that resolve." He smiled at my bewilderment. "It is tough to move a Scotsman who lives upon solid rock."

"Until you saw me with Cavanaugh but a few days past," I said, unable to stop the hurt in my voice, though I was the one who'd done everything I could to push Alasdair from me. "Then you had no problems walking away."

Alasdair shook his head. "Och, my lady. Cavanaugh would have been a dead man before he'd ever gotten a chance to ruin you." He said the words quietly, but that did not dampen their steel. "You pride yourself on your lies, but I have seen the heart of you. I have seen your family, the children of your household. And I have heard their tales. To them you are not merely the fierce lady of the court. To them you are humble and loyal and true. You would do anything for your family, even sacrifice your own life." I made to protest, but the look in his eyes stopped me. "I know every line of you, Beatrice, every glance and whisper, every movement. I have made you my life's work in the short time that I have been a guest of your mighty Queen. You could no more lie to me than you could stop your heart from beating. You must know that."

I pulled away from him, sudden anger pricking the joy that I so wanted to set free within me. "And yet you stood there laughing with the Queen—whom you must know hates me—at the mere possibility of ridding yourself of me? What am I supposed to think about that? Is your love not sufficient for you to remain betrothed to me? If not, then what sort of love is this?"

Alasdair's smile was slow and sure. "It is the love of a Scotsman, who hews to the old ways," he said. "I doona care for your traditions much, but I suppose they are yours. If I could get you by betrothal, that was all the same to me. Jane let drop your Queen's interest in our relic, an' it's an interest I was happy to fan, in my own fashion." He lifted his brows at me and shrugged. "What? If giving your Queen a tinker's forgery of our famed Fairy Flag would free you from such a farce, then I would prefer to make you my own according to a custom that means far more to me."

"That snippet of the flag was—a forgery?" I asked. *Meg was right!* Even though I'd been the first to warn the Queen of the flag's questionable provenance, when I'd watched Alasdair give her the gift, I'd believed in him completely. Clearly, so had Elizabeth. "You tricked the Queen?"

"You should know by now, my lady, I'd never give away something truly precious to me," Alasdair said. "It's not the way of the MacLeods to let beauty slip our grasp." His words were softer now, huskier. "Beatrice. My dear, daft, determined love. When one of my family gives his heart, he gives everything. In accepting this troth to you, I granted you my soul and body and mind as well. None of that has changed. None of that will ever change."

He reached down and pulled the clump of ribbons out of my hand, and the second collection of ribbons from my belt. "We have our own tradition on Skye, that a man may bind himself to a woman for a year and a day. In my country it is to see if the woman still meets with the man's liking after that time."

The wrongness of *that* idea managed to cut through my haze, at least. "Charming," I said dryly.

He grinned at me. "If she does, then they are wed. If she does not, then he may return her to her family, with neither blemish nor stain upon her reputation."

Oh, that is outside of enough. "But that is preposter—"

"A moment, my lady." Alasdair chuckled at my outrage. "That is my country, and this is your own. And as such I think a blending of the traditions is called for." He unlaced the ribbons, smoothing each one out, until they hung in two loose bundles. "I would handfast myself to you, Beatrice, for a year and a day. But the burden of proof that we suit will lie not upon you but on me. If at that time you still wish us to wed, I will come for you. I will take you from your courts and kings, and take you off to the Isle of Skye for a proper Scottish wedding."

"It's so far away," I murmured, held by his touch.

"'Tis. And your father lamented loud and long over this before we came to an agreement I should hope would please you well." He leaned down to brush a kiss over my forehead. "Once the celebrations are past in Skye, we shall return to Marion Hall. That house is too large not to have a family of its own to fill it."

I looked at him, stunned. "Marion Hall? You would live in England?"

Alasdair held my gaze, his eyes dark with emotion.

"For you, my lady, I would live in the shadow of the devil himself."

"But I have lied to you and betrayed you at every turn!"

I protested, hating myself for now finally giving voice to my duplicity, when all I needed to do was agree. But Alasdair had to know. Had to realize what and who he was committing himself to. "We cannot suit, Alasdair," I said. "I was attentive to you only because I was ordered to be. I disliked you from the start."

"Did you, now?" He grinned then, and I stamped my foot in irritation.

"I did!" I said, balling my fists into my hips. "I only spoke with you on orders of the Queen."

"And when we were in the labyrinth of Marion Hall, by the gold-laden spring, and you returned my kiss. Were you under orders then as well?"

"I— Well, I—"

"And on the North Terrace, when I sheltered you from the wind and held you close, were you merely following the directives of your Queen?"

"You don't understand. That was—"

"And naught but three days ago, when you wept yourself to sleep on that same terrace, and I picked you up in my arms and all you could say was my name, over and over again," he said, his words barely audible. "Whose command were you bowing to then?"

I blinked at him, my mouth going dry with surprise. "That was you?" I whispered. "You carried me?"

"I would carry you to the ends of the earth, my lady. One day you'll understand that." He held up the ribbons and called out into the darkness, "A hand with this, indeed?"

And then the woods seemed to give up its secrets, and

four Maids of Honor stepped forth, silent and beaming each of them—the grinning, forthright Jane; the knowing, sly Meg; the completely transported Anna, always in love with love; and finally the ethereal, magical Sophia. They came up to me and took the ribbons from Alasdair. "Wouldn't want these to go to waste," Meg said.

My father emerged from the shadows then, his grin filling his whole face. "A year and a day is not so long, is it, Beatrice? Time enough to serve your Queen, and evade what men she would tie you to?"

At Alasdair's rumble I nodded, surprised to feel my eyes filling with tears. "I've spent most of my life evading the dictates of the monarchy," I said, half-laughing. "I suppose I could spend another year."

"I will return to Skye and prepare my family and men for what we must do to save our land and its treasures," Alasdair said. "And then I shall come back to you." He held out his hands, and showed me how to interlace my fingers with his, as the Maids of Honor carefully tied and knotted two dozen ribbons between us, sealing the contract. "I pledge my fortune to you, my lady. I will bring to you all that you and your family need."

"What I need is you," I whispered.

"Then it appears we are in luck." He stared back at me, fierce and strong and steadfast, his love for me seeming to burst from within even as we stood there, hand in hand, linked together inextricably by two dozen strips of cloth and a fate that seemed unwilling to be denied. "Lady Beatrice Elizabeth Catherine Knowles," he said. "In a year and a day, when I come for you, will you be my wife?"

At that moment, under the starlit sky, there was only one response.

"Yes," I whispered back.

We tarried a few minutes more in the great shadow of Windsor Castle, and in the even broader shadow of my Queen and country. Monarchs had made my family what it was, and monarchs would rule whatever my family would become. And because of that, as had been every generation before me, I was indeed indebted to the Crown.

So for the next year and one day, to Elizabeth Regnant, Gloriana most high, I would give all of those things my noble birth had already claimed for the Queen: my talents and my loyalty, my skills and my unstinting service.

But from this point and ever onward, to Alasdair MacLeod I would give the only thing that had ever been mine own.

My heart.

Reading Group Guide

Continue the latest adventure of the Maids of Honor with these questions.

1. Beatrice's story begins with the event of her wedding to Lord Cavanaugh. Compare the details of an Elizabethan wedding provided in the text with modern wedding celebrations. What is the same? What is different?

2. List the key characters introduced in the first chapter. Who are Beatrice's friends, or those who are sympathetic to her cause? Who does she consider to be her enemies?

3. Drawing examples from the text, what is Beatrice's primary opinion about Queen Elizabeth? How does the Queen treat Beatrice—as a friend, a servant, an ally, or a foe?

4. Describe Alasdair MacLeod. What is his role in the English court? Why does the Queen want Beatrice to learn more about him? Why has Beatrice formed the opinions she has of him? Find one or two quotes that reveal Beatrice's attitude toward Alasdair.

5. Contrast Beatrice's feelings about her father and mother with her feelings for her fellow maids. Who do you think she respects more? Who among the Maids of Honor would you consider to be Beatrice's best friend, and why?

6. Based on the information provided in the text, what is the secret that Beatrice is keeping about Queen Elizabeth? Why do you think the Queen wants to make sure this secret is never revealed? In addition, why is it important for Beatrice to know so many secrets about members of the court?

7. Describe Windsor Castle, the primary setting of the novel. Is it someplace you would like to live? Why or why not? Compare Windsor Castle to Beatrice's home, Marion Hall. How are they different?

8. Lord Cavanaugh, Beatrice's betrothed, upsets her tremendously by kissing another woman. How does Beatrice retaliate? Do you think she was smart to act in the way she did, and what were the repercussions for her actions, both immediate and long-term?

9. Describe the romance between Alasdair and Beatrice. How does the romantic subplot contribute to your understanding of Beatrice as a character? What do you think Alasdair sees in Beatrice that makes him fall in love with her? Cite examples of the reasons he gives in the story.

10. Which of the five Maids of Honor would you most like to be your friend? Which maid do you think would make the best spy, and why? Include examples from the story that support your answer.

11. List the reasons why Beatrice is worried about the Queen and her court visiting Marion Hall. Explain whether or not you think her concerns are well-founded, based on what actually happens during the days that the court resides at Marion Hall and in the weeks that follow.

12. What crime is committed on the Knowleses' family property? What would be the punishment for this crime, if it were to be discovered? Do you think this is a just punishment for the crime committed? Why or why not?

13. Alasdair MacLeod's family has several artifacts that are believed to have special powers. What is the primary artifact that Queen Elizabeth wishes to obtain? Why does she want it? Are there any other examples in the story of the Queen being superstitious?

14. Beatrice is a young woman in a privileged position within the Queen's court, but she also faces challenges in her home life, in her romantic relationship, and in her attempts to maintain an appearance of wealth and high social standing. Describe some of those challenges. Are they similar to issues faced by young women today, or are they very different?

15. Near the end of the book, Beatrice believes she has lost everything and that she is at the mercy of Lord Cavanaugh. But her hope is restored when her father reveals a secret even Beatrice does not know. How does Beatrice's opinion of her father change over the course of the book, and especially after he reveals this secret?

16. At the book's conclusion, Beatrice and Alasdair admit their love for each other. Based on what you have learned about both characters, do you think their relationship will endure and that they will eventually marry? What do you think the Queen will do if she learns of their relationship?

Turn the page for a peek at the next Maids of Honor novel, MAID OF WONDER.

OCTOBER 1559
WINDSOR, ENGLAND

Death always starts as a whisper.

The dark angel hovers just at the edge of the glade, cloaked in shadows. But its voice is clear enough, the undertone so grim, so depressing, the very air around me seems to wilt a little at its passage.

Back on my own plane, amidst Queen Elizabeth's chattering court at Windsor Castle, I would not have heard its dire prediction so well. There, the angels' voices are no more than a puff of wind, the rustle of a playful breeze. Too quiet to be understood but impossible to ignore; an endlessly taunting conversation, just out of reach.

But here in this place that is more their world than mine, here I perceive the angels all too well. Here they shout and clamor; they demand and scoff. Here they insist and wail and rage.

Still, when they speak of death, even the angels are careful to keep their voices low. As if they understood that this is information not made for man to hear.

Man—or in this case, woman.

Death comes to Windsor, the specter murmurs again.

I turn toward it more fully, taking its measure through the gloom of this bleak hollow that serves as our meeting place. For I know this dark angel, and it knows me.

I have dreamed of it since before I could speak, terrifying nightmares that accompanied my loneliest nights and most desolate days. Throughout my childhood I feared it with the whole of my being. But since I have begun entering its realm more boldly these past few weeks, something fundamental has shifted between this grim specter and myself. I have watched it drift closer and closer to where I stand, surrounded by the other angels. As if it cannot stay away from me, despite its clear aversion to the other spirits who grace this quiet space.

For it is not like them.

It does not gown itself in blue-white light, almost too beautiful to behold. Sparkling wings do not flutter around its broad shoulders, displacing the eerie mists of this realm. It does not even style itself as a man or woman, like all the other angels do. Instead, it is a creature of shadow and fire, of pain and loss and despair. Across the hollow it stands, hunched and cowled in its heavy robes, the faintest hint of yellow flame emanating from its hooded head. It bends that hood toward me now, and I feel the blackness of its stare all the way to my physical self. Dread and deep foreboding lance through me, though my physical form remains hidden away, seated on a stone bench in a quiet glade much like this, just inside the edge of Windsor Forest.

But while my body rests safely in that small wooded clearing, my spirit is here, in the angelic realm. And in this place of dreaming, my spirit is strong. Here, I need not mask my oddness, desperate to remain unnoticed. Here I need not cower or shrink.

Here I need only one thing.

Answers.

"*Who* will die at Windsor? Can you give me a name? Or has this shade already crossed over?" I glance into the murk surrounding me, feeling the gaze of some poor departed soul trapped there, who is even now peering at me from the gloom. Its attention seems almost too strong to be one of the dead, too focused and intent, but I have never encountered any creature in this spectral realm that was neither angel nor shade. Perhaps this soul died recently . . . or reluctantly.

A chill slips along my skin. When I was very young, I believed that the angels who whispered to me were people who had passed away, still longing to reach the ones they'd left behind. But I have since come to understand that the dead do not speak in this shadowed realm. The souls of the departed can linger here, true. But they merely wander silently, caught between the world they've left and the world they fear to enter.

I have always pitied those grey shades. Recently, I have come to understand them as well.

For I am Sophia Dee, the much-remarked-upon niece of the most learned man in England. I am the weird girl, with nightmares and headaches and strange visions that assault me at awkward times. The girl who hears whispers when no one is talking, and who sees shadows in the full light of day. But despite all these things, I was also always the girl who knew her place in the world—who at least was certain of her past, if not her future.

No longer.

Because, as I have recently learned, I am not merely Sophia Dee, quiet and strange; the youngest member of the select group of maids chosen to spy for the Queen. I am also Sophia Manchester, the stolen-away child of a wealthy, loving father and a long-dead mother. The girl of pure potential, a symbol and a prize. The soon-to-be mystical warrior, whose power shall lie not in my sword, but in the secrets I will one day snatch from the angels' perfect lips.

And I will show them all.

I will be the seer the Queen believes that I can be. I will earn my title as a Maid of Honor, standing shoulder to shoulder with the other girls who make up our secret company: a thief, an assassin, a genius, and a beguiler. I will see the future so well and so clearly that I will prove to be Elizabeth's most valued asset, worthy of my place in her service. I *will* belong once more within the world of man, even as I learn to walk ever further into the realm of angels. And I will show them all.

Finally.

"Answer my questions, else I will leave!" Most of the angels shrink away from my harsh words, but the grim specter seems to embrace my anger. To revel in it. The wisps of flame, which were at first barely visible at the edge of its cowl, now seem to brighten as my irritation sharpens, and the dark angel's body becomes more solid in its cloak of dun-colored wool.

Emboldened, I take a long step forward, away from the bench that serves as my grounding point within this dreaming plane. The bench is made of pure obsidian, the same material as the small scrying stone I carry around my neck. When I first saw the obsidian bench in this glade, I knew its purpose immediately. It is my touchstone, the way back to my own plane. As long as I can see that bench, touch it, I will always find my way home.

Accordingly, I know I should never lose sight of this bench, though I am sorely tempted. I long to race into the angelic plane without restriction, to learn all its secrets. I dare not, of course . . . and yet I cannot help but wonder what lies beyond this misty glade.

Worse, the specter seems to sense my unspoken yearning. It watches across the open space between us, its silence now a mockery. It recognizes that I am linked to the obsidian bench, as surely as if I were holding on to my mother's hand, a hand I can no longer remember. The dark angel stands there, testing me, and I take another step forward, away from safety. Away from the certainty that I can leave the spectral plane at any moment, the certainty that I am in control.

I am no fool, mind you. But this angel spoke of *death*. And this is information I must have. My eyes never leaving the grim specter, I step forward yet again. I have never been so far into the center of the glade as this.

Then it deigns to speak, and my heart shrivels within me.

Though I see it plainly across the clearing, the dark angel is *also* at my side, bent close to my right ear, its fiery breath hot upon my neck.

Death plays your Queen in a game without end, it whispers. *It circles and crosses, then strikes once again.*

"No! No riddles," I demand, grateful for the spark of anger that drowns out my fear. "Tell me plainly what I must know."

They do this, the beings in this place. They speak in rhymes and twisted verse. I am certain their craftiness is deliberate, to keep me here as I struggle to understand them. But I have no patience for such games this day, not if the Queen is truly in danger. "Elizabeth herself will be attacked?" I ask. "But when? How?"

Across the glade, yellow flames blaze around the angel's hood, licking along the rough wool. Suddenly there is a hiss of words in my left ear, as swift as a murderer's knife. *The death you don't seek is the one you should fear. It aims for the blind, but catches the seer.*

"Stop that!" I jump away, but there is nothing beside me. I look back to where the specter hovers. "I need actual answers!"

It is no use. My dark angel seems done with me, shifting away into the gloom. I know better than to follow it. Instead, I withdraw as well, stepping backward until the obsidian bench grazes the backs of my legs. I sit down firmly, resolutely, and stare out at the specter's retreating form. If its words are worthless, then they are worthless. I will not drive myself to madness chasing it through the shadows.

Not today, anyway.

At the last moment, the dark angel turns to me. Its final words tease at my mind like a faint, mournful cry:

Follow the doves.

And it is gone.

Follow the doves? I groan inwardly. That's like telling me to chase the wind. I close my eyes and allow myself to leave this realm of mists and misdirection.

I feel a familiar terror clawing at me as I resurface in the center of a brightly lit forest clearing, my lungs straining for breath, my hands clenched, my jaw tight—

I open my eyes. Around me, as always, I see naught but my charming glade tucked up against the eastern walls of Windsor Castle. It is a fine October day, and the leaves are ablaze with color. Hastily I tuck my obsidian scrying stone and its chain back into my bodice, smoothing down my simple dress. I draw in several steadying breaths, reminding myself that I am *awake*, I am *alone*. I am, for now anyway, *safe*. Gradually my heart stops its thundering, and I slump on my little stone bench. I prefer this location in the depths of summer, but I cannot deny its beauty even today, with the sun dipping low in the sky, and . . .

I frown, peering upward. How has the sun moved so far, in truth? What time is it?

A distant peal of bells shatters the silence, and I move quickly toward the edge of the clearing. The bells strike one, and I gather up my skirts, preparing to run.

The bells churn on. Two, three. I am running now, realizing that I have been absent for hours. Hours when I was supposed to have been bent to my tasks for the Queen, or for one of her ladies. Hours when I was supposed to have been studying.

Four. Then nothing further. Four then, but not five. I can still make the end of my last class!

I dash through the forest till my breathing is ragged and my lungs ache. *Death plays your Queen,* the dark angel said, *in a game without end.* Does that mean there are multiple threats to Her Grace? If so, from what quarter? And why can't these messages ever make sense?

My lungs almost bursting with the effort, I reach the King's Gate and do not bother slowing down, turning the corner and rushing into the Lower Ward. With the coming of harvest season, it seems the castle has flung open its doors to travelers far and wide—they are all here, and they have money to spend. I dart in and out of the closely packed carts, desperate to get through. Rounding a corner too quickly, I hear a startled shriek but cannot stop. I barrel into a woman whose cage goes flying, setting free—

A small flock of doves.